About the Author

PHILLIPA ASHLEY writes warm, funny romantic fiction for a variety of world-famous international publishers.

After studying English at Oxford, she worked as a copywriter and journalist. Her first novel, *Decent Exposure*, won the RNA New Writers Award and was made into a TV movie called *12 Men of Christmas* starring Kristin Chenoweth and Josh Hopkins. As Pippa Croft, she also wrote the Oxford Blue series – *The First Time We Met*, *The Second Time I Saw You* and *Third Time Lucky*.

Phillipa lives in a Staffordshire village and has an engineer husband and scientist daughter who indulge her arty whims. She runs a holiday-let business in the Lake District, but a big part of her heart belongs to Cornwall. She visits the county several times a year for 'research purposes', an arduous task that involves sampling cream teas, swimming in wild Cornish coves and following actors around film shoots in a camper van. Her hobbies include watching *Poldark*, Earl Grey tea, Prosecco-tasting and falling off surf boards in front of RNLI lifeguards.

🐦 @PhillipaAshley

Spring on the Little Cornish Isles

The Flower Farm

Phillipa Ashley

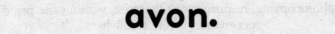

AVON
A division of HarperCollins*Publishers*
1 London Bridge Street
London SE1 9GF

www.harpercollins.co.uk

First published in Great Britain in ebook format by
HarperCollins*Publishers* 2018

This paperback edition published by
HarperCollins*Publishers* 2018

ISBN: 9780008253394

Set in Birka by Palimpsest Book Production Limited,
Falkirk, Stirlingshire

Printed and bound by CPI Group (UK) Ltd, Croydon, CR0 4YY

To my friends Claire and Duncan

Author's Note

Where are the 'Little Cornish Isles'?

The Isles of Scilly are one of my favourite places in the world – not that I've travelled that much of the world, but I've been lucky enough to visit a few locations renowned for their stunning coastlines, including Grenada, St Lucia, Sardinia, Corsica and Southern Australia. There are some beautiful beaches in all of these places, but I think the white sands and jewel-like seas of St Mary's, St Martin's, St Agnes, Tresco and Bryher are equally, if not more breathtaking than any of those exotic hotspots.

From the moment I first glimpsed Scilly from a tiny Skybus aircraft in September 2014, I was smitten. From the air, the isles look like a necklace of emerald gems fringed by sparkling sands, set in a turquoise, jade and sapphire lagoon. (Just remember that we're in the chilly Atlantic, thirty miles west of Cornwall and that it can rain and the fog can roll in. Take your wellies, walking boots and umbrella as well as your bikini!)

Within half an hour of setting foot on the 'Main Island', St Mary's, I knew that one day I had to set a novel there. However, if you go looking for Gull Island, St Piran's, St Saviour's, Petroc or any of the people, pubs or businesses featured in this series, I'm afraid you won't find them. They're all products of my imagination. While I've set some of the scenes on St Mary's, almost all of the organisations mentioned in the series are completely fictional and I've had to change aspects of the 'real' Scilly to suit my stories.

On saying that, I hope you will find stunning landscapes, welcoming pubs and cafés, pretty flower farms and warm, hard-working communities very like the ones you'll read about in these books. I'll leave it to you, the reader, to decide where Scilly ends and the Little Cornish Isles begin.

Phillipa x

Chapter 1

August Bank Holiday Monday

St Mary's Airport, Isles of Scilly

Oh no, surely that wasn't her?

Jess Godrevy's heart sank as she spotted the girl standing guard over a wheelie suitcase in the arrivals hall at St Mary's airport terminal. She was all of five feet tall and looked as if she'd blow away in the first Atlantic gust. Was this *really* Dr Gabriella Carter? Her head-and-shoulders photo had given no indication of how tiny she was – more like a sixth-former than a twenty-seven-year-old with a PhD. Just wait until Will saw her ...

Jess smiled to herself as Gabriella pulled her case even closer, though no one was likely to run off with it on Scilly and they certainly wouldn't get away with the crime if they did. Jess had already nodded or exchanged hellos with most of the staff and locals in the terminal, all of whom she knew by sight. None of them was a criminal mastermind, although some people would say Hugo Scorrier came closest. His unruly black Labrador, Basil, was sniffing around people's luggage while Hugo was deep in conversation with a good-looking, dark-haired man who Jess didn't recognise. Judging by the stranger's sharp suit and laptop bag, he and Hugo were probably discussing some big business deal relating to Hugo's luxury resort on Petroc.

Jess worked her way through the holidaymakers towards Gabriella, hoping the friendly smile on her face would reassure her new recruit.

'Hi there. It's Gabriella, isn't it? I'm Jess Godrevy from the flower farm. Welcome to Scilly.'

'Oh, thank goodness. I'm *so* happy to see you.' Gabriella's voice was beautiful but so quiet Jess had to strain to hear it over the plane engines and boarding announcements. She was very pretty in an English rose sort of way, with creamy cheeks sprinkled with freckles and a mane of strawberry blonde hair tied back in a ponytail. She'd have to be super careful with the sunscreen while she was working outside, thought Jess, ever practical but also aware of her own scruffy jeans, Flower Farm sweatshirt and wild hair. There was never any point in styling it: the wind and the sea spray would dismember any blow-dry in minutes.

'Someone's waiting in the car park to give us a lift down to the quay so we can get the island boat across to St Saviour's,' said Jess cheerfully. 'My brother, Will, is busy at the farm. If he's remembered that you're coming, that is, and hasn't decided to go rowing instead. Brothers, what are they like?'

A brief smile flickered across Gabriella's lips but she still looked like a rabbit caught in the headlights.

'It's this way,' said Jess, regretting her 'joke' about Will, mostly because he might well have forgotten.

'Thank you so much,' said Gabriella as if she'd been invited to tea at Buckingham Palace. She was so sweetly polite, Jess was beginning to think she'd hired a mouse to work as a flower picker and packer at the Godrevys' flower farm. However, during the phone interview a few weeks previously, she'd shown an impressive knowledge of horticulture. The excellent references from the plant nursery she'd worked for during her vacations also proved she must be used to hard work in all weathers.

Jess led the way out of the terminal and through the passengers on the car park. Outside, half a dozen jovial drivers shepherded the new arrivals towards the minibuses that would take them to their accommodation on St Mary's or down to the quay to the smaller 'off islands.'

'How was your flight?' she asked while they walked towards their lift.

Gabriella pulled a face. 'Rather bumpy, I'm afraid.'

'It can be interesting, but at least you got here. It's not unusual for flights to be cancelled.'

Gabriella's eyes widened. 'Really?'

'In the winter, mostly,' said Jess, glossing over the fact that the isles could be completely cut off by fog and storms at any time of year.

'Oh well, I survived on this occasion at least.' Gabriella's smile reappeared, this time for slightly longer, lighting up green eyes, flecked with gold. Jess detected a keenness behind them. She'd already noticed that Gabriella took in everything that was going on around her, as if she was storing away a mental snapshot for future reference.

Jess decided to give her the benefit of the doubt. It was no use judging someone on a few minutes' acquaintance, but if she'd been a betting woman, she'd have staked fifty quid on the flower farm's newest employee not lasting the week.

Personally, she really hoped Gabriella would stay the course. The farm needed extra seasonal workers for the harvest of early narcissi that bloomed in the mild climate at the start of September, long before any varieties on the mainland. Over the summer, the Godrevys also let out a few holiday chalets and there were also goats and a small beef herd that needed tending to. Thankfully, the farm animals were the domain of Jess's mother, Anna, who left Jess and Will in charge of the flower growing and holiday business.

'There's our taxi and chauffeur.' Jess pointed towards a very tall, well-built man in his mid-thirties who was leaning against a golf buggy, chatting to two elderly, but sprightly, sisters. They were all laughing and one of the ladies gave the man a hug.

'Are they friends of yours?' Gabriella asked, pulling her sunglasses over her eyes and peering at the group.

'You could say that. That's Una and Phyllis Barton who run a B&B on Gull Island. The driver's Adam, my ... um ... boyfriend.'

Her toes curled at the description, because it sounded so teenage and she was way past that at thirty-five, but what else could she call Adam? They had been dating – and sleeping together – for six months now, although they'd known each other for almost two years. They weren't living together yet, although Jess was pretty sure that the next step was imminent, given the heavy hints that Adam had been dropping about her moving in to his place.

Phyllis and Una roared with laughter at something Adam had said, and Una batted him coquettishly on the arm. Jess had often teased him that the Bartons were his personal fan club, but now she and Adam were a couple, he'd joked that only Jess would have him.

It wasn't true. It was *so* not true. Adam had plenty of offers from both sexes, locals and tourists. No wonder. At six feet four, he stood out from the crowd in every way. His collar-length curly hair refused all attempts to be tamed into submission so he left it to the mercy of the elements. He was a year older than Jess and his lifestyle kept him in great shape. When he wasn't lugging parcels around as postman or volunteering with the island's part-time fire service, he was playing sport; rugby in the winter and rowing over the summer. Appearances could definitely be deceptive, thought Jess, sliding a glance at Gabriella again. Take Adam. No one wanted to face him in a scrum, but he was a big softy underneath.

'I'll pop round and give you a hand with the gate after fire training on Tuesday!' Adam called after the Barton sisters. 'Don't miss your flights and have a good time on the mainland.'

'Thanks, Adam!'

With a wave to Jess and curious glances at Gabriella, the Bartons scuttled off into the terminal, clutching identical tapestry bags. They'd doubtless be speculating about who the new arrival was all the way to Cornwall and back, thought

7

Jess, but her attention was all for Adam. His tawny eyes lit up when he spotted her and her stomach did a little flip when he walked over and kissed her on the cheek.

He smiled at Gabriella. 'You found her among the crowds trying to escape then?' he said to Jess.

'Of course. Gabriella Carter, meet Adam Pengelly.'

Adam held out a large hand. 'Welcome to Scilly. There's no getting away from us now.'

Jess laughed. 'Not without digging a tunnel to Land's End.'

'Or Canada if you want to head in the other direction,' said Adam as Gabriella took his hand gingerly.

'But I'm sure you won't want to do that,' Jess added hastily, not entirely sure it was true, judging by the doubt in her new recruit's eyes. She had a feeling that if you'd given Gabriella a spade she'd have started digging right there, but then again, if she couldn't get used to a bit of banter and teasing, she wouldn't last five minutes in the close-knit farm team.

Gabriella peered up into Adam's face. He was at least a foot taller than her and built like the semi-professional rugby player he used to be before he'd moved to Scilly from his native Cumbria. Jess bit her lip, trying not to laugh at the apprehension in Gabriella's eyes. That imposing physique and height must have been quite intimidating to strangers.

'Off we go then. Can I help with your bags, Gabriella?' Adam offered.

'Thanks ... and please, just "Gaby" is absolutely fine. Only my granny ever calls me Gabriella. It's such a mouthful, isn't it?' She smiled again, which lit up her expressive eyes, but there was a touch of steel in her voice that took Jess by surprise. Maybe she might last a month rather than a week.

'Gaby, it is then,' said Adam. 'Your carriage awaits.'

Gaby stared at the golf buggy as if it were a toy car. Maybe she'd been expecting a Rolls-Royce.

Adam grinned. 'It's safe ... Ish.'

Jess batted Adam on the arm and he mimed an 'ow'.

'Ignore him. It's *totally* safe. We don't keep a van on the main island because we've no use for it and we use a local firm to collect the flowers from the quay to bring them to the airport. We borrow this buggy off a friend to get around St Mary's when we need to. You'll see lots of them about. Lots of tourists use them if they can't or don't want to do too much walking.'

'Jump in,' said Adam. He picked up Gaby's case as if it were a handbag and slotted it next to her in the rear of the buggy.

Jess climbed into the front next to him.

'Hold on tight. The roads are busy,' said Adam as they drove the buggy down the hill towards the quay. There were about two cars in sight.

'Will it take long to get to the harbour?' Gaby asked.

'Five minutes tops, unless there's a traffic jam at the quay,' Adam replied.

'He's joking, but it could be busy as the Islander ferry has just docked,' said Jess. 'How are the Bartons?' she asked Adam as he steered the buggy around a large pothole.

'The ladies are fine, but their guesthouse is in a bit of a state. I just offered to lend them a hand repairing the garden

9

gate. The sheep keep getting into the allotment patch and scoffing the produce. I can fit it in after fire training on Tuesday.'

This was typical of Adam. He'd help anyone and put himself out in the process. He had no ego and although he was sociable with his mates and customers, he was also shy around women. Jess liked him all the more for that even if it meant that it had been over a year after they'd first met before they'd finally got together on a 'date'.

Adam had asked her to go with him to a folk night at the Gannet pub on St Saviour's at the start of the summer and, since then, Jess didn't think she'd ever been happier. She helped to run a thriving business and lived in one of the most beautiful places on earth. Of course, she didn't need a man to make her life complete, but meeting Adam had unveiled a new layer of joy. It wasn't easy meeting people in a small, isolated community, and finding someone who she'd clicked with so perfectly was wonderful.

'This is the Oxford Street of Scilly,' Jess joked to Gaby when the buggy entered the top of Hugh Street, which was lined with shops, cafés, pubs and the isles' only supermarket.

Gaby checked out the granite cottages and quaint shopfronts. 'Oh. I see. Is this where I'll find all the bars and clubs or are they on St Saviour's?'

Jess exchanged a quick glance with Adam. He was stunned into silence. Jess cleared her throat, wondering how to reply. She turned around, trying to sound calm and positive, while thinking it might be kinder to turn the buggy back now and put Gaby straight on a plane home.

'Um. There are a couple of pubs here and it can get quite lively during the gig rowing championships or if we have stag parties from Penzance over for the weekend. As for St Saviour's, that has a pub and a smart hotel and we sometimes have nights out on the other islands, but there aren't any actual clubs.'

'Oh. I see ...' Gaby pulled a face. Then suddenly she let out a giggle. 'Oh, I'm sorry. That was naughty of me. I'm joking. I came here for a quiet life.'

Relief flooded through Jess, combined with surprise at being taken in. Yes, there was definitely a steely side to Gaby Carter.

'Oh, you'll get that ... after work, anyway. We'll keep you occupied during the day.' *Very occupied*, thought Jess. Late summer through to Christmas and beyond to Easter was by far the busiest time of the year at the flower farm. While frosts and festive mayhem took hold on the mainland, the farm's packing shed would be also manic as they picked, sorted and sent millions of narcissi to bring golden light into the dark nights of people throughout the rest of Britain.

The buggy rattled over the cobbles onto the quayside, which was packed with tourists piling onto the 'tripper' boats that were moored two and three abreast. As usual, there was organised chaos as visitors clambered down the steps, asking if they'd got the right boat and climbing over vessels to get to the one they needed.

At the end of the stone quay, more passengers collected luggage and kayaks from the Islander ferry that made its daily round trip from Penzance between March and November. It dwarfed the open tripper boats, jet boats and yachts bobbing about in the harbour on the high tide.

'We're down here,' said Jess, heading for the steps that led to the pontoons where the Godrevys' motorboat, *Kerensa*, was moored alongside the floating rafts.

'I'll park the buggy while you get aboard. I'll bring the bags,' said Adam.

Jess took Gaby down the steps and along the pontoon. Gaby didn't seem very happy with the wobbly surface.

'You'll soon get used to all of this,' Jess said reassuringly. 'We live and breathe boats here.'

Gaby nodded, but she didn't seem too sure at all. '*Kerensa*. That's a lovely name.'

'It's Cornish for love,' said Jess, jumping deftly onto the boat.

She held out a hand to help Gaby, who climbed aboard more gingerly.

Adam was soon back, handing over Gaby's case and some shopping from the Co-op. He untied the boat and Jess manoeuvred it away from the pontoon and between the smaller craft.

As they skirted the hull of the Islander, Gaby stared up at its crew who were unloading freight and getting it ready for its return journey to Penzance. Even as they passed it, she gazed at the ferry as if she was saying goodbye to an old friend.

'Does the ferry come every day?' she asked.

'Every day throughout the summer except Sundays,' said Jess. 'But when winter comes, we only get the supply boat a few times a week.'

'If we're lucky,' said Adam cheerfully.

Gaby gave a weak smile. 'Oh.'

The little boat puttered out of the harbour and into the lagoon that separated St Saviour's and the other isles from St Mary's. Jess had been brought up around boats since before she could walk but she still had to concentrate on keeping *Kerensa* within the channel markers. The water was so shallow between the isles, there were even rare occasions when you could wade between St Mary's and St Saviour's, though Gaby was unlikely to be on Scilly long enough to witness one of those. She sat in the stern, her strawberry blonde ponytail streaming behind her in the breeze and her dark glasses hiding her eyes. Jess noted the way she gripped the edge of the seat with one hand, and kept the other firmly on the rail of the boat.

Jess had a sneaking admiration for her or anyone who was willing to give up a comfortable life in a lively city like Cambridge for a remote place like Scilly. But she wasn't convinced that a desire for 'a quiet life' and a love of flowers was the whole reason for Gaby's decision to abandon Cambridge and head all the way out here.

Twenty minutes later, Adam threw the rope around the bollard on the small quay at St Saviour's and secured it to the cleat. Jess helped Gaby off the boat and up the steps with her bag. The quay rose out of a small rocky outcrop at the bottom of the island road. Deeper water lapped one side, while the other looked out over creamy sand, currently covered in a foot or so of translucent peppermint sea.

13

Gaby looked around her and shook her head in wonder. 'Wow. It's so beautiful. I've seen pictures on your website of course, but I hadn't imagined the real thing would be anything like this. It's still England, but as if England were set in the Greek islands.'

Jess followed Gaby's gaze towards the long sweep of white sand that ran half the length of the island and the myriad rocky skerries dozing in the lagoon between the main isles. St Saviour's, like Gull Island and its neighbour Petroc, were all clustered around the shallow 'pool' with only lonely St Piran's lying to the west across a deep-water channel.

'It is lovely on a day like this,' she said, quietly proud of her home.

'Not so lovely when you're trying to get the mail delivered in a howling gale or when the fog drops down,' said Adam.

Gaby turned to him in surprise. 'Oh, you're a postman, then?'

'Yes. I deliver the smaller islands' mail.'

'You must have the best post round in Britain.'

He grinned. 'You can say that again.'

Jess squeezed his hand behind Gaby's back. 'Better get going. Will's going to be … um … eager to welcome you too.' She mentally crossed her fingers that her brother was in. 'We can walk to the farm from here.'

Despite Gaby's protests, Adam carried her case and the shopping. Jess had given up trying to stop him long ago. She took the chance to chat to Gaby as they trudged up the slope from the quay and onto the road that ran along the spine of the island.

With Adam a few feet ahead, Jess slowed her pace to allow Gaby to take in her surroundings. She stared out over the Atlantic and spoke softly, almost reverently.

'I must go down to the sea again, to the lonely seas and the sky

And all I ask is a tall ship and a star to steer her by.'

Jess waited, a little taken aback.

Gaby turned towards her with a smile. 'Sorry, couldn't resist. That's from *Sea Fever* by John Masefield. Do you know it?'

'I think I might have heard of it but I'm not that great on poetry to be honest,' Jess replied, quietly amused and also, if she was honest, thinking the lines were very apt for the way she often felt about the spectacular spot she lived in: drawn to the sea.

'The view *is* incredible,' said Gaby, echoing Jess's own thoughts.

'Yes, you practically see most of Scilly from up here and Land's End too on a clear day. Look, there it is.' Jess pointed out a shadowy but unmistakable hunk of land on the horizon to the east.

'Wow,' said Gaby. 'Exactly how far is it?'

'Twenty-eight miles, though it may as well be Canada on some days. The fog can roll in and you can't see the sea at all, let alone the mainland,' said Adam, waiting for them.

'Wow. That must feel like being cast adrift in the middle of the ocean.'

Jess felt a quiet sense of pride in Gaby's awe. 'It can be but on days like this, it's gorgeous. And actually, we're here.'

Chapter 2

'Wow.' Jess hid a smile as Gaby gazed at the five-bar gate set in a high hedgerow. A wooden sign was fixed on the front of the bars.

St Saviour's Flower Farm

A, J & W Godrevy

The sign had been replaced once already since Jess's father, Roger, had left the family home to live with a younger woman, fifteen years previously. Their mother, Anna, had insisted on having his initials erased and a fresh plaque put up showing her children as joint owners. However, the 'new' one needed repainting again, as the names were fading under the onslaught of wind, rain and salt. Olive lichen had started to crawl slowly over the ragged edges of the wood, but it was so familiar that Jess didn't even see it these days. It was only because Gaby paused to examine it that Jess noticed it at all. One more job to add to the maintenance list, though being non-urgent, it probably wouldn't get done at all until it dropped off.

'Come on,' said Jess, smiling inwardly at the impact her home and business was having on Gaby.

She pushed open the gate, letting Gaby go ahead of her. Adam closed it behind them and followed them both in while Gaby scanned the house, outbuildings and fields with sharp-eyed wonder.

The rambling farmhouse where Jess and Will lived with Anna was set back from the road behind a large concrete yard. Jess and Will had no choice but to take over the running of the place while they were still barely out of their teens. Their father had left the farm's finances in a perilous state, but gradually Jess and Will had pulled it back from the brink and developed it into the thriving business that Gaby was now taking in.

'The high hedges are there to protect the flowers, aren't they?' she asked Jess.

'Yes, they spare the crops from the worst of the winds we get in the winter. The office is over here. You never know, Will might even be in there.'

'While you introduce Gaby to Will, do you mind if I check out the *Athene*?' said Adam. 'I want to see how the renovation's coming along. I reckon it'll be ready for some trials after Christmas if we all pull our fingers out.'

Jess rolled her eyes. 'That's optimistic. It still needs a lot of work.'

He smiled. 'We'll get there. I won't be long.'

'OK,' said Jess, amused at his enthusiasm for a half-built boat.

After Adam had left, she led the way to the office, chatting to Gaby along the way. 'The *Athene*'s a vintage rowing boat – though we actually call them gigs. Will and Adam are hoping to restore it to its full glory,' she explained.

'Sounds exciting. Do you row?'

'I've no choice,' Jess laughed. 'Most of us do. I'm in the St Saviour's Women's crew, but we don't take it as seriously as some. What about you?' She eyed the diminutive figure of Gaby.

'No way. I did try out for cox once and crashed the Third Eight into the bank. Did a lot of damage. They haven't asked me back again.' She grinned. 'Worked a treat.'

Jess laughed.

As she guided Gaby towards the office, Jess's thoughts were on her new employee but also partly on the sign at the gate. Even fifteen years on, Jess had mixed feelings about their father: she still loved him, as did Will, even though they hadn't seen him for several years and their brief phone conversations with him were usually tense.

She and Will were twins, and having grown up so closely, they had a strong bond even if they didn't always see eye to eye about the farm. Jess was the steady hand on the tiller: calm, practical and ready to pour oil on troubled waters. She oversaw the business side of things, dealing with suppliers and the bigger customer accounts that required tact and diplomacy.

Will worked every bit as hard as her but his forte lay with the horticultural side of the business. He knew everything about coaxing the different varieties into bloom at exactly the right moment. Storms, fog and even the occasional frost didn't faze him, but he could be impatient and prone to gloomy moods.

One thing they both agreed on, and would have sealed in blood, was their loyalty to their mother and the farm. They'd sided firmly with Anna as the innocent party, but that hadn't stopped them missing their dad in private. They'd felt hurt at being abandoned and angry at having to set aside any of their other hopes and dreams to stay and run the farm. Jess had settled down more quickly to her life as boss, but Will had wanted to go to university and for a long time resented being thrown in at the deep end.

However, this was all now in the past and everyone had moved on: they'd had no choice or the farm would have gone under faster than the *Titanic*.

One sign of the twins' success after fifteen years of hard work was that the business had long outgrown the original small office attached to the farmhouse. Jess opened the door of the new admin block, a large timber-clad building off the centre of the yard. The room was filled with workstations, each with phones and computer screens. The silence hit Jess as she showed Gaby inside.

'This is our admin area and sales office,' she said to Gaby. 'It seems funny to see it empty like this. Normally it's mayhem in here.'

Gaby walked into the middle of the room and took in the blank screens.

'We process the bulk orders from supermarkets and the wholesale market here and take orders from individual customers,' Jess explained. 'I keep an eye on the admin and sales, though Lawrence, our general manager, is in charge of operations. Will's more likely to be found out in the fields or the packing shed. Or the gig sheds,' she added after a pause. 'He's also a stalwart of the St Saviour's rowing club, but he won't be there today. He'll be around here somewhere. He knows you were coming and he's looking forward to meeting you,' she added, hoping that Will would turn out to be more enthusiastic about their new recruit than she feared.

Jess moved on from the office to the packing sheds, which would also normally have been buzzing with workers.

'This is where we grade and arrange the flowers into bunches or ship them out in bulk to wholesalers. You'll be alternating between here and the fields, depending on demand. We all muck in together wherever we're needed.'

Gaby's gaze swept the building, which was open to the rafters. Jess saw her eyes flick from the carpet-topped arranging tables to the floor, where rejected narcissi lay scattered on the concrete. Jess knew that if it wasn't a bank holiday, the place would have Radio Scilly blaring out and be full of people hurrying into the chiller with huge plastic boxes of flowers from the fields or to the quay, or carrying cardboard boxes and tissue paper to and from the arranging tables. It was eerily quiet – and there was still no sign of her brother.

'Will's probably outside,' she said with a tight smile that hid her growing disquiet over Will's absence. They walked back out into the sunlight. Jess wondered whether to try his phone, not that he'd always answer. 'Let's try the bottom field. This way, across the yard.'

The goats spared them a fleeting glance as she and Gaby walked past their pen, before going back to their dinner. Jess also pointed out the beef cattle who were grazing on the heathland next to the farm. She saw Gaby taking in the small rectangular fields where the flowers were grown. Each one was protected from the wind by thick hedges and the green shoots of the first narcissi were just showing, even though it wasn't quite September.

'How long have the Godrevys been farming here?' Gaby asked as Jess pulled her phone from her pocket.

Adam had sent her a text: 'Any sign of the Man yet? Any chance of getting away If You Know What I Mean? Got a surprise for you ...'

Jess felt her cheeks heat up and pushed her phone back into her jeans.

'Three generations now,' she replied, trying to refocus and not think too much about the shivery feeling that Adam's text had given her. 'Apparently when my grandparents started the farm in the 1950s, there were ninety flower farms on St Mary's alone. Now that people buy so many imported flowers from abroad, there are only a handful.'

'St Saviour's survived though,' said Gaby. 'And this set-up is very impressive.'

'Thanks. We try to have as many varieties and markets as we can. We also sometimes work with other farms at busy periods. They supply us with flowers to supplement what we can't grow, or sell ours when we have a glut. It's a fine art, trying not to have too few or too many flowers – that's the tricky part. Too much warmth or too much cold can spell

21

disaster or not being able to get the flowers to market. It's taken years to get the balance right and we're still experimenting and keeping our fingers crossed.'

Jess looked around her at the green shoots starting to appear in the brown earth of the outdoor fields, ready for the new season's harvest. Hard to believe that the first tight buds of the earliest types would be ready to pick in a few weeks' time. These days, sixteen types of narcissi were produced through autumn and winter, far more than in her father's time. It had been Jess's idea to expand their range shortly after he'd left.

Gaby crouched low to touch one of the emerging shoots. She had a dreamy look on her face. 'Do you think the legend is true?' she asked.

'Which legend would that be? Scilly has quite a few,' said Jess, amused.

'The one about how the narcissi first came to Scilly on a Dutch ship.'

'Ah. The onion story.' Jess had heard the tale many times. Supposedly, the first bulbs were given to the Governor of Scilly's wife by the captain of a Dutch merchant ship. She mistook them for onions but threw them out of the window of her castle because they tasted so horrible. The bulbs bloomed in the moat and that's how the islands' flower industry began. 'It's a great story and there may be some truth in it, but we're not so concerned with the past,' said Jess wryly. 'It's the present and the future we want to secure, which is why you'll find plenty to keep you occupied,' she added with a smile.

Gaby nodded enthusiastically. 'Oh. Absolutely. I came here to help you do just that.'

'Glad to hear it. I'm sure my brother will be too. Hold on. There's Len,' said Jess, spotting a middle-aged man striding over the yard through the open door. 'He might have seen Will. Do you want to wait here?'

Leaving Gaby looking at the farm set-up, Jess caught up with Len as he headed into the packing sheds.

'Hi Len. Have you seen Will? I want him to meet Gaby, our new worker.'

Len Scarrock's forehead, already as lined as a contour map of the Himalayas, wrinkled even further. 'That kid over there?'

'She's not a kid. She's twenty-seven and she's had plenty of experience.'

Len snorted. 'As what? A pixie in fairyland?'

Jess clung onto her patience. Len had worked as field supervisor with the Godrevys for years and what he didn't know about flower farming on the isles wasn't worth knowing. But he was as spiky as a whole field of thistles. 'Have you seen Will?' she repeated.

He sucked on his teeth and shrugged. 'Might be in the fields. It's been a good hour since I saw him.'

Jess's heart sank; she was beginning to think Will really had forgotten Gaby was coming and gone to visit his rowing mates. 'OK. Thanks.'

Just then, Adam walked across the yard and joined Jess on the edge of the top field. 'The gig's coming along. Where's Will?'

Jess rolled her eyes. 'This is turning into a game. I should produce a book: *Where's Will?*'

'Hold on, that sounds like him,' said Adam, pointing towards a figure marching from the rear of the equipment storage shed. A familiar voice carried on the air to them.

'No, bloody hell. Next week? That's all I need. You have to come sooner than that?'

Adam grinned. 'I think we've found him.'

Will's voice grew louder, clearly giving some unfortunate supplier the hairdryer treatment down the phone. He'd stopped outside the door of an outbuilding used by the flower picking staff for breaks. *'I can't wait for an engineer until then. It'll be disastrous for my crop. You have to come out. Charter a plane if you have to …'*

'Yes, but where's Gaby got to?' Jess crossed back into the yard but Gaby had vanished. 'Oh God, I hope she hasn't decided to go home already.'

Adam joined her. 'She won't. She's tougher than she looks. Look, there she is.'

Gaby emerged from behind a hedge just as Will strode across the yard, his phone clamped to one ear, the other hand gesticulating wildly.

'Len!' he bellowed, holding the phone down by his side. 'We need to get that damn pump fixed. That's the whole water supply to the farm!'

'The bloody water pump? When did that happen?' said Len.

'About half an hour ago. Haven't you noticed?'

'I've only just come up here from my place. Have you tried fixing it?'

Will threw up his hands. 'What do you think I've been doing for the past half an hour? Bloody hell, why does this always happen on a sodding bank holiday?'

Ouch. Jess cringed.

And oh no ... At the same time as ranting to the supplier and Len, Gaby had clearly come onto Will's radar. He suddenly veered from being on course for Len to making a beeline for her. Jess quickened her pace to try and intercept them.

'Hey! You!' Will bellowed.

Gaby stopped, frozen like a hedgehog about to be run over by a juggernaut. Will shoved the phone in his jeans pocket and homed in on Gaby.

'Oh no. I'd better make the introductions or she really will leg it.' Leaving Adam behind, Jess jogged over but it was too late. Her twin was giving Gaby the full benefit of his customer-facing charm and skills.

She reached him to find him talking to Gaby, with his hands on his hips. 'Can I help you? Are you a customer?' he asked impatiently. 'If you are, I'm sorry, but you shouldn't be wandering around like this.'

'I was just admiring your Innisidgens,' said Gaby.

'My *what*?'

'The Innisidgens. They're just coming into bud, aren't they?'

'Yeah, they are but ...' Will peered at her. 'Look, this is a staff-only area and you should call in at the office if you want to buy some flowers.'

Jess darted between them. '*Will*. This is Dr Gabriella Carter. She's one of our new field workers.'

Will stared at Gaby and his jaw dropped, anyone would think the queen of the fairies had landed on his farm and zapped him with her wand.

'She's a *field* worker?'

'Yes, Gaby is a field worker. I told you she was coming. I've just been to pick her up from the airport. You can't have forgotten,' she added as if Will was a toddler to whom she had to explain everything, which was partly true. She turned to Gaby. 'I'm sorry, I think you took Will by surprise, didn't she, Will?'

'You could say that.' Will glared at Gaby.

She smiled back sweetly. 'I'm sorry for wandering off, but I was fascinated by the Innisidgens. They're the very first variety to come out, aren't they? I know some people loathe the scent and say it's like cat's pee, but to me, they always give me that "back to school" feeling. So lovely to think of them popping up while people are still basking on the beaches.'

Will shoved his fingers through messy brown hair, lightened at the tips by a summer spent outdoors. His eyes narrowed in puzzlement and he peered at Gaby again. 'Actually, I don't mind the scent ... Mum hates it, but I've always thought the Innisidgens mark the start of the season too. A fresh start and all that stuff.'

'Oh, absolutely and my apologies, Mr Godrevy, I hadn't meant to cross any boundaries.' Gaby extended her slender fingers. 'I look forward to working with you.'

Will stared at her dainty hand in surprise.

He must think she's waiting for him to kiss it, thought Jess with a mix of delight and dismay.

'Um, hi,' he said before turning to Jess and snapping out of his temporary trance. 'All hell's broken loose. The water pump's packed in and you know what that means. We've no water for irrigation for the farmhouse or the staff house ...' He glanced back at Gaby. 'So, you have my apologies if I haven't put up the bunting and made some iced buns today, Miss Carter, I've been a tad busy.'

'Oh, no apology needed. Bunting and buns won't be necessary, however appealing they sound. A nice cup of Earl Grey and a slice of sponge cake would be a perfectly acceptable alternative. Gluten-free of course.'

Will's jaw dropped again and he stared at Gaby.

Adam had joined them. He'd obviously heard most of the recent exchanges, judging by the gleeful squeeze Jess felt on her hand. She distinctly felt his body shake as he tried not to laugh. Jess stifled a snigger too.

'Would you like me to make some cucumber sandwiches as well?' Will said smoothly.

Gaby licked her lips. 'Yum. That sounds delicious. Where's the staff tea room?'

Will couldn't take his eyes off Gaby. She smiled innocently back, but Jess could tell Gaby was teasing and could actually feel the crackle of tension between the two of them. It was like pitting a bear and a viper against each other. How would they ever survive the next six months together?

Jess let out a strained laugh. 'Gaby is joking. She knows we all muck in here.'

'Of course I do. So, shall we start again?' She held out her hand once more and this time, to Jess's amazement, Will took it, shaking it firmly but carefully with his grimy paw.

'Welcome to the flower farm, Gaby,' he said, still unable to tear his eyes from her face.

'Thank you, Mr Godrevy. You seem to have a very professional operation here.'

'Thanks. And er ... please call me Will. We don't stand on ceremony here.'

'Thank you, Will. I look forward to working with you and possibly tasting your buns.'

Will opened his mouth but seemed to choke on his reply.

'Have you tried the trip switch on the pump?' Jess cut in, trying to divert Will. 'That was the problem last time.'

His attention snapped back to Jess. 'Of course I've tried the trip switch, but you can have a look if you like. Anything's better than leaving the farm without water until the technician can come out.'

'Where is the pump?' Gaby asked.

'In the shed over there above the well.' Will flipped a thumb in the direction of the other side of the yard. 'It supplies all the water for the farm and business.'

'You're getting a tour of the farm anyway, so you may as well see everything now, not that you'll ever need to go in the pump house,' said Jess. She could feel Adam beside her, saying nothing but obviously enjoying every word of the exchange. He'd be bound to take the piss out of Will about 'his buns' as soon as he got the chance but Jess was only concerned with keeping the peace.

With Will forging ahead, Adam, Jess and Gaby followed him over to a small wooden shed on the far side of the yard. The goats stopped chewing long enough to watch them trudge past, as if to wonder what the fuss was all about.

The door was open and Jess joined Will, who was staring at the control panel above the blue pump, while Adam and Gaby waited outside the cramped shed. Jess flicked the trip switch up and down, and the pump stopped, then shuddered and rattled in an alarming way.

'I do hope you don't think I'm interfering, but could it possibly be an airlock in the pipework?'

They all turned at the small voice from behind them. Gaby gazed at them both with innocent eyes.

'We used to have a similar problem at the nursery where I worked out in the Fens. It's a long shot, but you never know.'

Will scratched his head and pushed out his bottom lip. 'It's making a lot of noise, but there's no actual water coming through.'

'As Gaby said, it could be an airlock,' said Jess.

'It's never had one before,' Will muttered.

'But it *could* be,' said Jess.

Gaby stepped forward and opened the hinged wooden cover concealing the blue pipework. 'It looks very similar to the pump we had at the nursery. Is it worth letting the air out of this vent on the back of the pipework?'

Jess stood by as Will peered at the pipework. 'Yeah. S'pose it could be that. Like I say, we've never had an issue with it before ...'

He turned the vent and after a few rattles and clangs, the pump tone speeded up to its normal smooth hum.

'Certainly sounds healthier,' said Jess.

Gaby pointed to the control panel. 'The current's running through it again. I think that's a good sign.'

Len poked his head round the door. 'Hey! The water's on again. I don't know what you did, but it's worked.'

Len vanished as fast as he'd appeared and Will closed the cover on the pipework.

'Thanks,' he muttered.

'A pleasure. Now if you'll show me to my accommodation, I can settle in and leave you to get on with your work.' She threw a smile at Will. 'I can see you're obviously terribly busy ...'

*

Half an hour later, Jess had completed the tour of the farm and showed Gaby into the staff accommodation. The farm was very fortunate to have a staff house, the glorified name for the converted farm building used by the seasonal workers. The house was divided into individual bedrooms served by communal bathroom and kitchen facilities. While most of the workers were local, some came from mainland Cornwall to work the winter narcissi season, and a handful hailed from Europe.

Jess had introduced Gaby to Anna, who had looked her up and down as if she was a pest that had landed on the narcissi, before grudgingly shaking hands and saying, 'Welcome to St Saviour's.'

Jess and Will loved their mother, but even they had to admit that she wasn't the easiest woman to live with. When their dad had finally left after all attempts to patch up their marriage had failed, she'd been landed with the responsibility of an ailing business and two young adults who'd had to step up and help her run it at an age when they might have been going out with friends or travelling further afield before settling down. The farm had been a poisoned chalice to start with. The shock of her husband's affair combined with the long hours and financial worries had aged her not only physically but given her a hard shell that could look like callousness to strangers.

Jess knew that Gaby should get a warmer reception from the rest of the team. Even crusty old Len had a sense of humour sometimes and the rest of the field, packing and office workers were a friendly bunch who worked hard and played harder.

She took Gaby through to the rear of the staff house where a handful of workers were sitting in a small garden area, enjoying a beer and sunbathing. Normally at this time of year there were around a dozen field and packing shed staff around, while a separate small team worked in the office who Gaby would get to meet soon enough. The sunbathers greeted Gaby with smiles and set about the banter straight away, telling her horror stories about the weather and Len cracking the whip.

Jess watched Gaby carefully, but was pretty sure she was taking everything with a large pinch of salt. Anyway, judging by the way she'd handled Will, she could give at least as good as she got.

Jess heaved a sigh of relief as she walked past the pump house and heard it chugging away. They had running water, a new staff member, and she could finally enjoy the rest of the day with Adam and find out in detail the surprise he had in store for her. She had a feeling it was going to be a memorable one.

Chapter 3

With a sigh, Gaby dumped her bag on the floor of her new quarters. OK ... so it wasn't the Ritz. Not even the BudgetLodge, actually. After eight years of student life, she didn't expect comfort, let alone luxury, but the staff house still came as something of a shock.

Her bedroom was spotlessly clean but tiny compared to the relatively spacious rooms she'd had in her college at university. It had a single bed, a chair, the kind of cupboard her granny liked to call a 'tallboy' and a curtained-off alcove that Gaby assumed was the wardrobe. Not that she'd brought much to hang in it. A small table with spindly legs, one of which was propped up with a pile of beer mats, served as a desk, complete with a candlestick lamp with the kind of tasselled shade that even her granny would have rejected as old-fashioned these days. Still, she knew she was incredibly lucky to have a place to stay at all. Jess had explained that staff houses were as rare as hen's teeth and not everyone who worked at the farm got to live there. Some of the temporary workers had to rent out-of-season holiday lets or get rooms in guesthouses, while the younger permanent staff still lived with their families.

Like most people her age, she couldn't envisage ever being able to afford a place of her own and definitely not on a poetry expert and flower picker's wage. But she wasn't here for the money: she was here to enjoy the view, smell the sea and the scents – and have some solitude.

Not that there would be much of that. The sound of people arguing about a football match was clear and the thick partition walls shook when a door slammed. Jess had shown her the shared shower rooms and the communal staffroom/kitchen area with a large TV where most people congregated after work.

The communal room had been furnished with cast-offs too, probably from the Godrevy farmhouse. The stuffing was escaping from a mismatched sofa. The dining table was surrounded by an eclectic mix of chairs ranging from an oak carver to a deckchair. It was a far cry from the MCR at her college, but actually, Gaby thought with a smile, it wasn't *that* different to home: her parents' place, a ramshackle thatched cottage in a village on the unfashionable side of the city. Hardly anything got thrown out there either.

She unpacked the one small case that she'd been allowed to take on the tiny plane here. If she wanted any more of her stuff, it would have to be shipped over on the ferry. For now, her clothes took all of five minutes to put away and she'd miraculously managed to compress a whole cupboard's worth of make-up and toiletries into one bag. Judging by the state of Len's fingernails, she thought the varnish was going to be superfluous, but even if there were no clubs, there had to be some opportunity for glamming up, even if it was only to watch an episode of *Countryfile*.

At the bottom of the case, wrapped inside a jumper, she found her two most precious treasures. She set one on the table: it was a photo of her with her parents, her older sister Carly and Steven – Stevie – her younger brother. The three siblings had all squeezed onto an old garden swing behind the cottage, with their parents piled in behind. A friend of Gaby's had taken the photo on Stevie's twenty-first birthday not long after he'd taken delivery of his motorbike. He'd always been a daredevil, spending all his spare time climbing, or mountain biking, surfing and trying out extreme sports. He was working as a courier while he saved enough to travel the world, and unlike Gaby had no desire to go to uni or to join the rat race like Carly. He lived for the moment ...

Since his death, every photo with the bike in had been deleted or destroyed, but the memory of his special birthday would be treasured forever. Besides, everyone had been smiling in the photo, no one had their eyes closed or 'looked fat', so it had been deemed a suitable memento of the occasion, printed off multiple times and framed before being given as gifts to numerous members of the Carter clan.

Shortly after that photo took place, Stevie had taken a corner too fast, been thrown off the bike and struck an oak tree at the entrance to the village. He'd survived, technically, but the brain damage had been so extensive that he hadn't been able to breathe on his own. Even worse, all the tests had shown no brain activity at all and they had been told there was no prospect of recovery. A month after the accident, the

Carters had made the most heartbreaking decision any family could ever face and in March, Stevie was taken off life support.

Gaby stared at the photo. That dreadful moment had been almost half a year ago now. How could that be? How fast time flew, even though recently, some days had felt as if she was walking uphill in the darkness against a wind so strong and merciless she thought she might be blown off her feet and never get up again.

The late afternoon sun streamed through her window. Gaby pushed it open and let the cool breeze air the room. Could she smell the sea on it? Possibly not but she could imagine it. She'd made it here and Stevie would be proud of her. He'd be cheering now, just as he would have at her PhD graduation in June.

Gaby had managed to fund her doctorate with the help of several jobs, and scrimping and saving, plus being fed by her parents from time to time. She'd completed her thesis even during the darkest hours. She'd written up the last few pages, sitting by Stevie's hospital bed.

Shortly after he'd died a minor miracle had happened – her college had offered her a junior fellowship that enabled her to teach the undergraduates and would have covered some of her accommodation and living expenses. The opportunity was as rare as rocking horse poo, and there were very few jobs that required a PhD in poetry, but it wasn't the miracle Gaby had really wished for. She wasn't going to get her brother back. And so, with him in mind, she had turned down the offer to pursue a job that combined the two passions in her life – poetry and flowers – and decided she would work on a flower farm.

She'd been in academia – at school, at university – for almost all of her twenty-seven years. She couldn't see herself in another twenty-seven, a crusty academic, rarely having been outside Cambridge. She'd thought long and hard about her future as she sat by her brother's side. He'd never be able to pursue all the things he wanted to do: travel the world, work abroad, enjoy life to the full but *she* could.

When she'd told Carly her plans to work at the farm she'd gasped in exasperation. 'But a *flower farm*? On the Scillies? You may as well lock yourself away in Cambridge!'

'It's Scilly or the Isles of Scilly. Never the Scillies,' Gaby had corrected, trying not to rise to the bait. Carly genuinely meant well, but for her, achieving a dream meant getting a flat in a smart postcode with a car and salary to match.

'I don't care if it's Timbuc-bloody-tu. You're out of your mind.'

'I rather fancy it. I love flowers.'

'OK. I can just about get that, but why there? Can't you go somewhere ... oh I don't know. Exciting? Exotic? Like the Caribbean. They have lots of flowers there.'

Gaby had suppressed a sigh. 'But I love narcissi and Tresco Abbey Gardens is on Scilly – that's one of the most famous gardens in the world.'

'Really? Oh Gaby, I despair.'

That made two of them, thought Gaby, knowing her sister would never understand her obsession with flowers and poetry. She didn't even bother explaining why she'd chosen Scilly specifically because Carly would have been incredulous and disapproving to hear that Gaby had fed her addiction to gardening and countryside programmes during the long hours at the hospital. The TV had been on in Stevie's room for some company and normality mainly, and she'd sat through endless episodes of *Gardener's World*, *Countryfile*, *Countrywise* and their lookalikes.

One programme had stuck in her mind. Ironically it had been at her lowest ebb, after a moment when she'd thought she'd seen Stevie show the flicker of an eyelid, the twitch of a finger. She'd imagined the movement of course, but luckily, she'd never told her parents about it. The consultant had come and done thorough tests and said there was absolutely no brain reaction recorded at all, they were incredibly sorry ... she must have dreamed it ... maybe she might want to go home for some rest?

A few hours later, after Gaby had finished crying, she was half-dozing in her chair and woke to find the TV on. She saw a smiley presenter in a wax jacket tell the audience about the tiny islands where the Gulf Stream ensured the climate was so mild in the winter that subtropical plants thrived all year round and daffodils bloomed in September. The sea had been azure, the flowers and plants dazzlingly bright and the people cheerful and resilient. It felt so removed from the dim hospital room, even though it actually was on her doorstep in global terms. It was beautiful, soothing and peaceful and exactly what she wanted to do.

'*Flowers seem intended for the solace of ordinary humanity.*' John Ruskin's words had slid into her mind after the feature had finished.

She would go to Scilly, she resolved. She would see the

flowers, visit the gardens, live, breathe and work with the narcissi when this was all over ...

Looking back, Gaby realised that was the moment when she accepted that it *was* all over for Stevie. But not for her and that he would never want her to give up or give in. Stevie had escaped the shell of his body the day he crashed the bike. She didn't know where he was now, but her life had to go on, for her sake, for his, for her family's ...

Unlike Carly, Stevie had understood what Gaby's idea of 'adventure' was. She sat on the bed and unwrapped her other treasure: her last birthday present from him: a book called *100 Gardens to See Before You Die*. Since he'd gone, she hadn't been able to open it and re-read his message inside; it was just too heartbreaking. Besides she had committed it to memory long ago.

> *To Gaby,*
>
> *I dare you to visit them all!*
>
> *Don't dream your life, live your dreams – whatever they may be.*
>
> *Love, Stevie xx*

Visiting one hundred gardens might not count as a wild adventure to some people and Gaby doubted if she'd see more than a fraction but after she'd finished her contract at the farm she could make a start, helped by the money she'd earn as a picker. She'd already seen some of the UK gardens and made a list of her favourites – Versailles, Giverny, the Majorelle in Marrakech, Kenroku-en in Japan, the Desert Garden in Phoenix and Adelaide Botanical Gardens.

OK. Her first day hadn't been that exotic so far judging by her encounter with the scowling Will Godrevy and his muddy wellies. However, it was only the first step on the journey and she had at least made it. She turned away from the window and back to her room. She heard swearing from the next room and a thud as the partition wall shook. The bedside table trembled on its beer mat prop. Then there was giggling and shortly afterwards the rhythmic bumping of headboard against wall, accompanied by grunts and groans like someone was trying to finish a marathon.

Hmm. She rolled her eyes. It wasn't much different from her college after all, only the walls were thinner here.

She'd call her parents shortly to let them know she was here and *absolutely fine*. She might even call Carly, if she could track her down between her high-powered job in the City, and her personal training appointments, yoga and mindfulness classes.

Gaby shouldn't be too harsh. Throwing herself even more crazily into her job had been Carly's way of coping with Stevie's accident and the agonising decision that the Carter family had been faced with four weeks later. Carly had decided to leave no space or time for grieving, and Gaby had decided to run away from it.

She didn't just have her own grief to deal with. She was worried how her parents would be able to cope with the loss of a son at only twenty-one. She phoned and Skyped them regularly and intended to go home over Christmas. In the midst of their grief, the one thing they'd been adamant about was that Carly and Gaby should get on with their lives. After Stevie had passed away, her mother and father had virtually pushed them out of the door insisting that their daughters should 'make the most of every minute'.

Had they *really* meant it, thought Gaby, gazing around this strange little room on a tiny island where at least two of the inhabitants – Frosty Will and Scary Len – were hardly delighted to see her. Was flying out here to work on a flower farm 'making the most of every minute' or just a way to hide from pain that would resurface again at any moment? She wished she could fix her grief and sorrow as easily – and miraculously – as the water pump. She was sure things wouldn't run so smoothly in the weeks to come, from any point of view.

Gaby's gaze lingered on the photo of Stevie again. The only personal touch in that bare little room so far from home. It lingered that bit too long and she had to squeeze her eyes hard as the tears stung the back of them.

She mustn't get homesick or maudlin when she'd only been here ten minutes. She wasn't a snivelling postgraduate any more: she'd chosen to come here. Stevie would be rolling his eyes and telling her to grow a pair.

'Everything up to scratch?'

Gaby swung round at the sound of a gruff voice.

'Mr Godrevy. Sorry – Will. Yes, I'm just trying to find room for all my stuff.'

Was that a flicker of amusement as he took in the few possessions?

'It's not Buckingham Palace, but we're planning to do up the entire staff house next season, so I hope you can manage for now,' he said, returning to saturnine mode. 'Not that it's any help, since you're only here for a short while.'

'It's better than a lot of places I've stayed in. I know I'm fortunate to get somewhere to stay on site,' she said, surprised that he felt the need to apologise for the standard of decor. 'And besides, I approve of recycling.'

'Good job.' Will took a sudden interest in the rickety bedside table with its short leg. 'Anyway, I was passing by and I wanted to say thanks for the tip about the pump and I er ... thought I'd mention if there's anything you need, let us know and we'll do our best. The basics we can probably do, the Earl Grey and the gluten-free sponge might take a little longer.'

Oh my God, thought Gaby, was that an actual smile making his eyes crinkle at the corners? His actually rather gorgeous eyes ... His dirt-streaked jeans were still tucked into the muddy indigo Hunters and it was hard not to giggle because Gaby thought she was one of the few people who could find a man in wellies sexy. He looked a few years older than her, his hair was tousled and his eyebrows could do with a bit of a trim, but she had a feeling he might scrub up pretty well. *Very* well – she could imagine him in black tie at a college ball ... though he'd probably rather wear a clown outfit and stick a feather up his bottom, she thought and had to suppress an actual snort.

In fact, if he wasn't such a sarcastic git with no charm or people skills, Will Godrevy would do nicely as a younger hot presenter of *Countryfile* or *Gardening Today*, two programmes she still secretly caught up with on iPlayer. Come to think of it, this place had better have decent wi-fi or she really would go mad. Dare she ask Will?

He glared at her.

OK. Perhaps not *right* now.

He gave a sort of humph that could have meant anything from 'get lost' to 'hope you have a lovely stay', shoved his hands in the pockets of his jeans and gave the room a glance.

'Jess has shown you where the bathrooms are, I take it?'

'Yes, and the kitchen and um ... common room. Very practical.'

'That's one way of putting it. Is that your family?' He inclined his head towards the photo.

'Yes.'

'Hmm.'

And? And? What the hell did 'hmm' mean?

'Long way from Cambridge, aren't we?' he said.

Gaby's hackles rose. 'Three hundred and twenty miles, actually. That's as the crow flies.'

His brow furrowed. 'That's not what I meant. I meant that this place is different to what you're used to. A big change.'

'That's why I'm here,' said Gaby firmly, determined not to show a moment's weakness.

He exchanged a glance with her, very like the one they'd shared when she'd teased him about his buns. This one lasted slightly longer but had the same effect: giving her a prickly sensation that was both pleasurable and a little bit worrying.

He glanced away first though. *Re-sult.*

'Right. I'll leave you to it,' he said, taking a strong interest

42

in the tassels on her bedside lamp for some reason. 'Oh. I've remembered the reason I wanted to pop in in the first place. I don't know if Jess told you. Training starts tomorrow. Seven-thirty sharp at the packing shed. Len will show you the ropes and we'll see how you shape up.' He smiled encouragingly as if he regretted his choice of words. 'I'm sure you'll be OK with the right training, is what I meant. We'll give you plenty of support.'

'Sounds terribly exciting. I can't wait.' She tried to keep the edge of sarcasm out of her voice and failed miserably.

Damn Will Godrevy, how dare he come in here being nice to her – because he *was* trying to be nice in his own blunt way, she was convinced. Whereas she was acting defensive because she was tired and suddenly horribly afraid she *had*, in fact, made a huge mistake in running away to this outpost where no one gave a monkey's that she had a PhD in poetry and only cared if she could pick a daffodil correctly.

'Exciting?' He gave the kind of tiny smug smile people do when they think they know some great truth about the world that you clearly don't and wait until you *do* ... 'That's one way of describing Len's training. I expect Jess'll be back later to see how you're getting on and you'll get to know everyone in the common room tonight. Enjoy yourself. See you tomorrow.'

Enjoy yourself? Gaby picked up the photo and sighed, then pushed up the corners of her mouth with her fingers. She was here. She knew what he was thinking, what they were all thinking: Grouchy Will, Scary Len, Gentle Giant Adam and

43

even kind-hearted Jess. Despite fixing the pump, they all thought she was an airy-fairy flake and that she'd crumble within five minutes.

Gaby ran her finger over Stevie's face. 'And, Stevie, forgive me, but I may well do exactly that.'

Chapter 4

After showing Gaby to her room, Jess was waylaid by Len to deal with a problem with the flower refrigeration room. Adam came to help her and when it was sorted they found Will in his office, tapping away furiously at the desktop computer and muttering curses.

'I decided to reorder some cardboard boxes because we're running low, but the order site keeps throwing me into a loop. Every time I think I've cracked it, I get thrown off the site and have to do it all again. I should be down at the quay now, helping to unload a new load of packing materials. And please don't mention it's a bank holiday.' He lifted his hands from the keyboard and sat back in disgust.

'Let me take a look. Maybe a fresh pair of eyes will help,' said Jess, bundling him off the seat. 'Why don't you make a coffee or something.'

Will hovered by her shoulder. 'I don't see how you can do any different. I've tried it five times.'

'Let Jess have a go, mate,' said Adam. 'We'll grab a coffee and you can tell me about the *Athene*. I've been to look at her. Do you think she'll be ready for us at the start of the new season next spring?'

Will seemed to perk up at mention of the *Athene*. 'I hope so. We need a crew for her first. We're two women short at the moment.'

'There's always Jess – she can step in if we're desperate.'

Jess glared at Will. 'Thanks a lot! And tough because I'm already committed to the Women's boat. You might enjoy rowing twice in a race meet, but not me. Now, do you really want this stuff ordered or shall I let you suffer?'

'It's your business too,' said Will with an infuriating grin.

Adam winced. 'Come on, mate. Let's make a drink before she takes you at your word.'

Jess heard them discussing the progress of the *Athene* in the kitchenette before the hiss of the kettle drowned out the conversation. She didn't mind a bit of teasing from Will and while he could be short-tempered and annoying, he was a loyal brother and friend. He and Adam had been mates almost since the first time Adam had set foot on St Saviour's. Although Jess's first encounter with him was when he'd delivered a bag of mail to the farm two summers previously, it was through Will that she'd got to know him better. As Adam had played rugby semi-professionally in his Cumbrian home town, he was soon roped in as captain of the Scilly Corsairs. Will had soon realised Adam would also be ideal rowing material and persuaded him to join the St Saviour's Men's crew.

The two of them had hit it off quickly and Adam had been grateful for the excuse to visit the farm to see Jess before he'd eventually asked her out. He'd confessed as much to Will, who'd rolled his eyes and complained he'd never intended to 'play matchmaker' and must make sure he never did it again.

Ah. Will. What on earth was Jess going to do about *his* love life – or lack thereof?

With his rowing in the summer and rugby in the winter, plus the farm, her brother's life seemingly was a full one. There hadn't been much time for relationships, although he had dated a few women over the years. The longest lasting one had been with a Belgian woman who'd come to work in the ferry office in Hugh Town. She'd decided to go back to Ghent to study, so that had been the end of that. Will had wandered around in a gloom for a week or two but soon snapped out of it when rowing season started in the spring, so Jess had suspected he wasn't too heart-broken.

Since then, he'd managed to acquire a reputation for being an impossible catch and even though he'd had a couple of flings with temporary visitors to the islands, he didn't seem to have fallen hard for anyone special. That wasn't *so* unusual because finding a partner among a small and ever-changing community was difficult in itself, not to mention when you were very busy and tied to a business, as Jess had also discovered over the years.

Before Adam, she hadn't had the best romantic track record herself. A couple of flings that had fizzled out; one with a doctor who'd inevitably left to further his career on the mainland, and one with a policeman: ditto.

She counted herself incredibly lucky to have met Adam. She knew that moving in to his place was on the cards and she was looking forward to making a life together, and fingers crossed, having a family of their own one day.

And then Jess thought of her best mate, Maisie Samson. They'd been friends since their schooldays, although Maisie was a few years older. All the children from the smaller isles boarded at the high school on St Mary's because it was too disruptive for them to constantly travel back and forth on boats every day. Maisie had taken Jess under her wing in the first year, and during the holidays when she'd returned from sixth form college on the mainland. As Jess grew up, they'd become firm friends.

Jess had supported Maisie through some dark times lately. Maisie had miscarried her previous pregnancy the Christmas before last. Far from being supportive, especially as Maisie has found it difficult to fall pregnant in the first place, her ex-boyfriend, Keegan had left very soon after, saying he couldn't handle having children anyway. Keegan also happened to be Maisie's boss at the brewery chain where she worked so after the trauma of losing her baby, Maisie had decided to come home to Scilly and help her parents run the Driftwood. How must she now feel, seeing her best friend, Jess, and Adam loved up? How would she react when Jess told her she would be moving in with Adam? And how would she feel when, hopefully, she and Adam had kids? Maisie would put on a brave face because she was a good friend, and Jess hoped that Maisie would find someone as sexy and just-plain-lovely as Adam, and they could all enjoy their families together. They could have their own little gig crew one day ... well, you never knew. Miracles could happen.

But this wasn't getting the cardboard ordered, and giving herself a stern talking-to, Jess refocused. Ten minutes later, she pushed away the keyboard in triumph and turned to the boys. 'There. Done and dusted, fingers crossed.'

Will groaned. 'Really? Thanks. Now I know why you run the operations side of things while I stick to the fields. I'll get back to Len and see if he's still freaking out about the flower refrigeration room.' He collected his phone from the table. 'Oh, I dropped in on Princess Gabriella before the system threw a wobbly. She's very smart, but I'm not sure she's right for the farm. I've no idea why she wanted to hide away in the middle of nowhere or where she thought a degree in poetry comes in. Maybe she's going to read to the Innisidgens.'

Jess recalled Gaby's quotation about the sea with amusement but decided not to share it with Will. 'It's actually a PhD in poetry, and apparently she wanted to try out a new lifestyle away from the city. Plus she did fix the pump.'

'A lucky break,' said Will. 'We'll see how she gets on.'

'People have a lot of different reasons for coming to Scilly. Some of them end up sticking around,' said Adam, shooting a knowing look at Jess that made her skin tingle. She didn't think she could wait much longer to drag him off to bed. 'I think she'll do OK,' he added.

'As long as you don't call her Princess Gabriella in front of Len and the others,' said Jess.

Adam laughed at Will. 'I reckon you've got a handful there, pal.'

'I don't know what you mean. Len will soon kick her into shape,' he said.

Jess got up and Adam slipped his arms around her waist. Jess put hers around his neck.

Will made a fingers-down-throat gesture. 'Do you mind not doing that holding hands and kissing thing in here? Why don't you get a room?'

Adam glanced at Jess, who was still gleeful at seeing Will so wound up by Gaby. 'Great idea. We might do that, hey, Jess?' They both loved teasing him. 'We ought to start practising for when we have kids. I think half a dozen would do for starters – you need a team of unpaid pickers.'

Will pulled a face. 'Eww. Lovey-dovey stuff. Puts me right off my coffee. I'm off to do some work while you two get on with it whatever it is.' He walked into the yard, shouting. 'Leonard! I've sorted the cardboard order.'

Jess gasped. 'Hey! I did it!'

Adam laughed. 'Leave him. He has to have some victories after losing that spat with Gaby. His face was priceless.' He pulled her into his arms. 'Let's forget about them. I've been dying to get you on your own.'

'Do I have a say in this brood of little flower pickers?' she said, guessing Will thought Adam was joking about the kids, whilst she wasn't so sure. Maybe they should have the conversation later at his cottage. Or now. 'Because two will do,' she said.

Adam laughed. 'Like I said, we'd better put in some practice.'

He slid his hand under the hair at the nape of her neck. Closing her eyes, she let her head tip back, anticipating the touch of his lips on hers as he gently pulled her in for a kiss. When it came, the kiss made her knees buckle and her whole body feel as if she'd been dipped in popping candy. It was the weirdest, but most wonderful sensation. No one had ever made her feel like that, not even when she'd been a teenager and had a Christmas kiss with the best-looking boy in the school. Now she was in her mid-thirties she felt she had no right to feel so intensely. She would have been scared by it but she was ninety-nine per cent sure that Adam felt the same way and that their relationship was about to move on to the next level.

Adam held her and she rested her cheek against his chest, enjoying the beat of his heart under the warm cotton and the scent of him. That was what was so amazing about being in love, she thought: being able to abandon yourself to a kiss, and to one person. Sod the world, sod the business, sod everything except the two of them: her and Adam, even if it was just for a few minutes or hours. She'd love to have that feeling of pure joy every day and for the rest of her life – but was it possible? It hadn't been for her mum and dad – or Maisie – but it could be for her and Adam.

'Did you mean that, about the room?' she murmured, looking into his eyes.

Adam's face was suddenly serious. 'Of course. We need to talk about it. Shall we go to my place or does Will need you here?'

'Sounds like the best offer I've had all day. Will always needs me here, but I've done my bit and it's technically my day off. I'll come back later tonight to see how Gaby's doing.'

Adam kissed her again and Jess thought she might take off with happiness. And lust. Things were going well: for the farm and finally for her love life.

'Come on then,' he said. He took her hand as they walked

to Thrift Cottage, which nestled behind a stony bay at the far end of the island.

The next couple of hours were lost in some deliciously wicked downtime before the shadows lengthened outside and Jess reluctantly started to get dressed. No matter how much she wanted to stay in bed with Adam or sleep over in the cottage, there was way too much to be done at the farm and she didn't want to abandon Gaby on her first night. Despite what she'd said to Adam earlier, running a farm meant she never really had a 'proper' whole day off.

'Sorry. Have to go back to work soon,' she said, pulling her T-shirt over her head. 'I can't leave Will on his own for much longer. It's not fair.'

Adam sat on the edge of the bed, still naked. 'We can spend more time together when you move in ... you'll be in my bed every night. Come here.'

Jess joined him at the bed and stood between his legs. Even now the sight of him made her long to jump straight back under the patchwork cover with him. In fact, it was crazy not to move in with him as she already spent plenty of nights here each week. There was no reason to wait any longer and it wasn't as if she had to move any further than half a mile from the farm. Everything could carry on as before, only much better. She held his head between her hands, leaned down and kissed him, feeling as if she could float on air.

'Let's talk about it tomorrow evening. Shall I come for dinner?' she said.

'Sounds perfect. Stay over and we can start moving your stuff in.'

'I hope you can find room for my extensive collection of fleeces and wellies.'

'Of course, but don't bother with any underwear, will you?'

'Ha ha,' said Jess, brimming with excitement while also wondering what her mother's reaction would be. Will would be happy for her, but her mum had dropped enough hints for Jess to work out that she didn't think an island postman was good enough for her daughter. Jess wasn't too concerned. She had long since ceased to care what her mother thought about her choice of partners and where Adam was concerned, she was resolved not to let her spoil her moment.

A buzzing came from underneath Adam's abandoned boxers.

'Yours or mine?' she asked.

'Sounds like mine. Probably Javid calling me about rowing practice ...' He glanced at his watch. 'Oh shit, is that the time? I promised to meet him down at the gig sheds ten minutes ago. See how you've distracted me. I'll call him to say I'll be late.'

Jess moved away as Adam picked up his phone and frowned at the screen.

'It's not Javid ... it's a text ... I don't know ...' His voice trailed off and he stared at the screen for a few moments. His smile evaporated and he scrolled down further.

Jess joined him on the edge of the bed. 'Adam? What is it?'

'Nothing. It's nothing.'

Her stomach turned over. 'It doesn't look like nothing. You've gone as white as a sheet.'

'I'm fine.' He threw the phone on the duvet. 'It was just a junk message. Sick of them to be honest.' Flashing a smile at her, he grabbed his shirt. 'I need to get down to the sheds. Sorry ...'

'Oh. OK, I should be getting home anyway. See you tomorrow?'

'Yeah. Sure.' Adam pecked her on the cheek before scrambling into his clothes.

Jess looked at the phone lying face-down in the folds of the duvet. Adam's reaction convinced her the text had been more important than he was letting on, but she certainly had no intention of checking his mobile. She trusted him to tell her if anything was amiss.

Adam saw her to the front door. He always stood in the porch watching her until she was out of sight of him – perhaps longer for all she knew. He still stood there today, but as she reached the point when she would lose that last glimpse of him, she turned around to find the porch empty.

She told herself she was being paranoid and she was tired at the end of a long summer of work ... and sex. Then she thought back to the hasty kiss, the eager removal of his hands from her waist and to the empty spot on the cottage porch and shivered. She was probably overthinking things but she had the feeling that whatever was in that text, it had shifted Adam's world on its axis and, with it, her own.

Chapter 5

Five and a half months later

Valentine's Day

The Flower Farm, St Saviour's

Well, it was one way to spend Valentine's Day ... Gaby took a swig of coffee from her mug as she and her fellow pickers enjoyed a quick break in the 'staff rest area', which was actually an old farm building with a couple of ancient sofas, a sink and kettle. It was the middle of the morning and she was more than ready for a break. Her back and arms ached already and it wasn't eleven a.m. yet. Her dungarees were damp and despite the rubber gloves, her fingers were almost numb as she warmed them on her steaming mug.

The stems had grown thigh-high and the fields were aglow with blooms. Beyond the hedges, the Atlantic Ocean was topped by frothy whitecaps whipped up by the brisk February wind, while the other isles were green oases in the silvery-blue sea.

It had rained overnight; in fact, it had been raining for a few days now and the fields were thick with mud that threatened to ooze over the top of her wellies. However, the skies had now cleared and she'd been able to forgo the bright yellow oilskins provided by the farm. They kept her dry but also swamped her and Gaby felt like she was in a TV ad for frozen fish fingers when she was wearing them. There was still a keen wind gusting so she'd kept on the extra layer of luxury thermals she'd been given by Carly when she'd gone home for the Christmas break.

Gaby still had to pinch herself from time to time, amazed she'd survived through the winter rain and gales and into the spring. When she looked around her, she stood in her own ocean: the flowers around her were a sea of cream, gold and green. She'd been harvesting two of her favourites: Daymark, with its creamy petals and bright orange cups and Yellow Cheer, a double-headed variety with a subtle but lovely scent.

Since arriving at the end of the summer, she'd alternated between the fields and sheds. She'd learned how to pick the tightly closed buds when they showed the merest hint of colour and carefully hold huge bunches under her arm before placing them in deep white crates called Proconas. They were then whizzed off to the packing sheds by quad bike and stored in a refrigerated room until the team were ready to arrange them. Over the months, she'd also learned how to grade and arrange the different varieties into bunches of tens and pack them in tissue-lined boxes ready to be transported to the St Saviour's quay and on to the airport.

She'd guessed she'd have to work hard when she first arrived but nothing could have prepared her for how tired she'd feel. Even after tending her own allotment at her college and working for the commercial nursery, harvesting the narcissi was knackering – especially in the run-up to Christmas and the previous week as they'd worked into the night to make sure all the Valentine's bouquets reached their recipients in time for today.

Gaby still remembered the look on Jess's face when she'd first landed at St Mary's airport almost six months previously – and the dismay on Len's craggy features when they'd been introduced: not to mention Will's horrified expression.

He was still brusque, impatient, and his jokes weren't anywhere near as funny as he thought they were. However, she'd soon found out that even though he was the boss, he was prepared to take as much banter as he dished out. In return, Gaby had been determined to give as good as she got and the two of them had earned a reputation for sparky exchanges.

Slowly but surely, she'd settled in at the farm almost without realising it. Many were the times when she'd been so exhausted, so stiff and cold that she'd thought of swimming home to Cornwall. But with the help of her mates at the farm and at home supporting her, and a bloody-minded determination, here she was, a fully-fledged member of the team. Besides, no amount of back-breaking work or taunts from Will could ever compare with the tough times that she'd been through at home.

She'd also fulfilled her other ambition to visit Tresco Abbey Gardens. In fact, she'd invested in an annual pass and been half a dozen times, as there was colour and beauty in the exotic plants all year round. She'd spotted the red squirrels and had become quite a fixture, making friends with some of the staff and meeting up with them when she could get away from the farm. She felt she was slowly building a life on St Saviour's – even though it was temporary – and although she still thought of her brother several times a day, there were times when hours passed and she realised he hadn't been on her mind and that the remembrance of him didn't come with quite such a sharp pang of loss as months before.

Thinking of Stevie and home she decided she would call her mum and dad after her shift today. Maybe they'd like a bunch of the narcissi she was harvesting. She could make up a special bouquet of her favourites and send them to her parents. The Carter family had an emotional day coming up soon so she had the perfect excuse to see how everyone was coping. It would have been Stevie's twenty-second birthday later in the month and Gaby was sorry to be away from home on a day that was bound to be hard for everyone including her.

Gaby started to walk back into the field and back to work cramming the remains of a Mars bar in her mouth. That was one thing: she could eat what she liked with all the physical work and though she'd put a bit of weight on, even Carly had said she looked 'miles better' when she'd seen her at Christmas, 'apart from the ruddy cheeks and farmer's tan; I'll send you some of my sunscreen, instead of that cheap rubbish you use'. She went back to her picking. Carly would be horrified if she saw her now: knee-deep in damp flowers with a wet crotch and hair like a scarecrow. She might take a selfie and send it tomorrow. Anything that could bring a smile to her family's faces was worth doing.

Chapter 6

Jess drank in the scent of the blooms she was helping to harvest. She'd been working in one of the lower fields since early morning. The farm had safely got through the week leading up to Valentine's Day with a healthy stream of orders that, thankfully, had reached customers on time without any major disasters. The days were lengthening and the temperatures slowly but surely creeping up. Spring was here.

She didn't normally work outside and Valentine's Day itself ought to be a time for a breather but the flowers kept on growing anyway and the farm had a large wholesale order for a supermarket to fulfil. Most of all, she was hoping that a busy day in the fields would help to blot out the event she'd wished would never come, but was actually happening.

That had been a false hope judging by the way her stomach turned over when she heard the low-pitched drone of the plane engine in the sky above her. That sound meant the end of long-cherished dreams that she'd clung onto against all the odds for months now.

Will was walking towards her down the row between the narcissi. She took a deep breath, filling her senses with the scent, hoping he wasn't going to offer her sympathy or she might actually cry. It was a forlorn hope because the first thing he said when he reached her was, 'That's Adam's flight.'

She nodded. Adam and Will had remained civil and met up with their rugby and rowing mates, but Jess realised their relationship had cooled too.

'How do you know?' she asked him.

'Patrick told me last night. Adam was in the pub and mentioned it. I'd guessed that Maisie told you too?'

She swallowed the lump in her throat. 'I think Adam *wanted* me to know he was leaving today.'

'You can't know that for sure ...' She felt Will's hand briefly on her shoulder, but then he removed it, probably not wanting to draw the attention of the nearby field workers. 'I'm sorry, Jess.'

She gulped back a sob and dug her nails in her palm. 'It's not your fault.'

'Maybe, but he is – *was* my friend. I wish I could have made him see what a dick he's being.'

'It doesn't matter now. It's over.' She brushed her knuckles over damp cheeks.

Will dug a handkerchief out of his pocket. 'It's clean,' he said as she hesitated.

'Thanks.' She took it and hastily wiped her face.

He grinned. 'Sorry. *Almost* clean.'

She laughed but another sob bubbled up. 'Oh, Will. Shit. Why am I bothered about him still? It was over last August, the day he got that text.'

'I did try to ask him what the fuck was happening but he made it clear it was between you and him.'

'That's no help because he wouldn't even tell *me* anything.'

She took a few deep breaths. When her mind had dwelt on why Adam had decided to end their relationship over the winter months, she'd tried to think of the good things like her family, her friends and her home. Many times, over the previous autumn and through the long dark nights of winter, she'd reminded herself how lucky she was to live in such a beautiful place.

The engine note changed as the Twin Otter climbed higher after leaving St Mary's airport. It banked, heading straight for the farm. If she looked up, she might be able to see the passengers in the windows of the tiny aircraft. She imagined Adam's face and wondered if he was feeling as devastated as her – or was he merely relieved to finally be out of her life for good?

'I keep trying not to care but knowing he's up there makes it feel so bloody final. The final nail in the coffin.'

'I'm sorry. Life is shit sometimes,' was all Will could offer, but he shaded his eyes and looked up at the plane too.

There was no possibility of a last-minute reprieve. He really was going. Already had *gone*. As Adam flew over, he'd be able to see the golden fields below and easily pick out the flower farm. He'd easily distinguish Thrift Cottage. Perhaps he would even spot her, standing in the middle of the field staring up at him. Would he be feeling as if his heart had been ripped out too? Would he be longing to turn that plane around and head back to Scilly and tell her that he'd made a huge mistake and ask if they could start again?

The plane was almost directly overhead. She was being silly. It wasn't likely Adam was looking out for her. If he cared that much, he'd be here on the earth not leaving, because they *had* been happy once. Everything had been perfect until that bank holiday in August.

Something had changed in the moment he received that text. That message had sent him racing home to Cumbria to deal with a 'family crisis' and when he'd returned, he was a different person, as if he'd picked up a burden overnight. It had started a chain of events – all still a mystery to Jess – that had gradually seen Adam loosen his connection with her over the autumn until last October he'd said he needed a break. His reasons had been vague and no amount of questioning by Jess had ever unearthed the real cause, just that 'he had to have some space.' She'd been upset, then angry, before finally accepting that she might never know what had happened. Will had tried to ask him what the matter was and met with a firm rebuff, and even Maisie had tried to find out and got the same stony silence.

With Adam living and working in the same tiny community, it had been impossible not to bump into him around the island and in the local pubs. On those occasions, they'd barely spoken, although they'd exchanged plenty of looks. Occasionally, Jess had thought Adam was about to speak to her but other times, he'd seemed eager to be out of her sight as soon as possible. He'd walked out of the Driftwood a couple of times shortly after she'd walked in, once attracting comments from the regulars about leaving his glass half full.

In November, Adam flew home to Cumbria and was gone

again for a few days at Christmas, presumably to see his parents. He'd visited them before and they'd stayed with him a few times but Jess couldn't help wondering why he was going back so frequently, as it was an expensive and time-consuming business. Even though she'd been angry and hurt, she hadn't stopped loving him, which seemed the cruellest thing of all.

'He's still renting the cottage. I know that much,' said Will, returning his attention from the plane to Jess. 'Maybe he does plan on coming back.'

'It's probably because he can't get out of the cottage lease. There's a few months left on it. I know that because he took out a year's contract on it last spring.'

'Hmm. If he was too much of a coward to even explain properly why he's leaving, then you're better off without him. Oh, shit. There's Mum.'

Jess groaned as they both spotted Anna crossing the yard at the top of the field. Fortunately she walked straight past the entrance to the field and headed in the direction of the barn where they stored the animal feed and other farm supplies.

'Phew, for a moment there, I thought she was coming over to give us the benefit of her views on Adam again,' said Will, toeing the soil with his Hunters. 'Not to mention our love lives, or lack of them.'

'Yes, she doesn't have the greatest view of men in general and Adam specifically. A postman was never "good enough" for me, according to her, and now her lack of faith in him has been proven.'

Anna had been quick to subscribe to the theory that Adam had a secret girlfriend or even wife and told Jess 'it was typical of bloody men' – in other words, she considered Adam in the same league as her ex-husband. Jess knew Adam wasn't the same as their father. At least she hoped he wasn't. But maybe her mother was spot on and Adam had been seeing another woman and his reluctance to explain himself had merely been guilt. There probably wasn't some great mystery behind his change of heart, just someone else who he cared for more than Jess.

Will heaved a sigh. 'Well, I'd better be getting back to work. If you need me, you know where I am. If you want to get out tonight, why not come down the Gannet for a few drinks?'

Jess had never felt less like going out, but maybe drowning her sorrows was better than moping. 'Thanks. I may just do that.'

'You can keep the hanky,' he said and, with a consoling squeeze of her fingers, he went back to supervise the harvest in the top field.

Jess tore her eyes from the plane and bent low to twist and pluck a stem from the earth. She had to get a grip. Adam had clearly moved on and it was time she did too. For the next half an hour, she threw all her energy into furiously plucking flowers. Yet she couldn't shake off the thought that something dramatic had changed while Adam had been away from Scilly in the dark nights of the previous autumn. Although she'd hardly spoken to him, his behaviour had seemed erratic to say the least. Over those autumn and winter months, she'd caught his longing looks, the moments when he'd been about to say something to her and stopped. If she could only have got through to him, reached him somehow but it was obvious that all meaningful communication between them was long over. And ... then in January, she'd finally found out that Adam was leaving Scilly for good.

In contrast, Maisie's life had changed dramatically over the past six months – for the better. Jess was delighted for her friend, although it seemed as if the two of them had exchanged places. She so wanted Maisie to be happy, although the contrast in their lives since last August couldn't have been bigger. Since then, Maisie had found love again with Patrick McKinnon, a handsome Australian who had come to work in the Driftwood Inn – and stayed. He and Maisie were now having a baby after a whirlwind romance and had moved in to a cottage near the pub.

Jess heard voices and laughter from the seasonal staff. They included Gaby who stood up and stretched her spine. Her oversized dungarees hung off her and her hair was caught up in an old-fashioned headscarf like one of those Land Girls you saw in wartime TV series. She was peering at the plane as if she knew Adam was on board too. Gaby caught sight of Jess and raised a hand in a half wave.

Jess waved back before pretending to inspect a bloom. Gaby didn't need Jess being a grumpy arse too. She had enough to put up with, with Will's scathing comments and grumpiness. For some reason, he behaved very strangely around her, although Jess was pleased that Gaby gave as good as she got. She'd surprised Jess with her resilience; that inner core of steel Jess had glimpsed had really shown itself and Gaby had become a valued member of the team.

Thinking of the staff reminded Jess of how many people depended on her getting on with things and that's exactly what she was determined to do. Besides, she had a family wedding to look forward to at the end of the month as her cousin, Julia, was marrying a guy who worked in the same hotel as her on St Piran's island. Will and Anna were going of course, and the farm was supplying most of the flowers for the venue. The wedding was set to be one of the biggest on the isles for years. Now wasn't that *exactly* what you wanted when the person you loved had just flown out of your life forever?

Chapter 7

Valentine's Day was already a memory when Gaby made her way from the staff house towards the fields, there was a hint of true spring in the air. They were into the final week of February and although an inch of snow had fallen in London, gridlocking the capital, the air on St Saviour's was mild and the sun warm on her back. She planned on calling her parents later, but for now, a day of work lay ahead.

She hoped the hard work would help to stop her from dwelling too often on the fact that Stevie would have been twenty-two today. Not only that, but the first anniversary of his death was only a month away. It would be a very tough time for the whole family and Gaby planned to go home for a long weekend to support her parents.

'Gaby!'

The shout came from Will who was about to waylay her as she was entering the top field. Her spirits lifted when she saw his outfit: a charcoal grey suit, with the trousers tucked into his wellies. Both the trousers and jacket looked brand new, teamed with a white shirt and tie, which also looked fresh from the box – unlike his trusty wellies. He carried a small narcissus buttonhole between his fingertips as he bore down on her. Gaby waited for him by the edge of the field, acutely aware of the contrast between Will's smart suit and her own outfit. Along with her dungarees, she was wearing a new hat: one of those patterned Norwegian woollen ones with a fleece lining that made her look like an elf. Resisting the urge to pull it off before Will saw it, she braced herself for a confrontation but had no idea why.

'Gaby, have you got a moment?' he said briskly.

'Yes, boss.' She peered at his clean-shaven chin, not sure if she preferred it to the usual stubble. Then decided she did rather like it and had to stifle a giggle.

He frowned. 'What's so funny?'

'Nothing. Nothing at all.'

He rubbed his chin. 'Have I got toothpaste on my chin or something?'

'No. Everything's fine.'

He rolled his eyes. 'Good because I've no time to fart about this morning. This wedding's come at our busiest time and I can't really afford a whole day off. Why do these events have to last all day?' He pulled a face, then poked his fingers through his hair which was still damp from where he'd rushed out of the shower by the look of it.

Gaby nodded enthusiastically. 'I totally agree. I'm never offended when I only get asked to the evening do. And those Save the Date cards give you no chance of booking a week in Outer Mongolia so you have a good excuse for getting out of them.'

He laughed. 'Well, as we're already in Outer Mongolia, I

never need an excuse to avoid the things on the mainland, but I've no get-out this time. Mum's close to her sister, so we have to go and, of course, we've provided all the flowers for the church and reception.'

'Yes, I did notice.'

Gaby had been called in to help pick and take the flowers into the shed, where Becca, one of the senior members of the design team, had worked with the wedding florists to create the table arrangements, displays and bouquets. There were jasmine-scented Paper Whites, sunny Hugh Towns and Daymarks, with added greenery and some other spring blooms from the mainland to add a splash of contrasting colour. The flowers had been loaded onto the boat at first light to transport to the wedding venue at St Piran's community hall.

'I really don't want to leave you, of course,' Will said, adding hastily. 'To cope on your own, I mean.'

'I expect we'll survive somehow.'

He sighed. 'Good ... I don't feel I can bring the boat back here straight after the ceremony, leaving Jess and Mum to get a lift later. The new group of pickers who arrived yesterday need supervising. Normally we don't take on new staff mid-season, but we need them for that new supermarket contract that Jess has managed to secure and Len's not well and can't come in today.'

'I heard Len was ill. Nothing serious, I hope?'

'Norovirus, apparently, but he needs to keep well away from everyone or it'll go through the whole team.'

'Poor Len,' said Gaby, and she meant it. Although Len could

be a pain in the bum, she didn't really want him to go down with Noro.

'He's stopped throwing up but he has to stay away for another forty-eight hours.' He shoved one hand in his suit pocket. Gaby winced. Stevie had always done that on the rare occasion he could be strong-armed into a suit like the day she got her Master's a few years earlier. She could hear her mum now, saying, 'For heaven's sake, Stevie, you'll ruin the cut of those trousers.' Stevie had rolled his eyes and shoved his hands deeper in his pockets. Gaby smiled.

Will didn't.

'The thing is. You've come on a lot. I despaired when you first started, but I'm beginning to think you might make a half-decent picker after all.'

'Why, thank you for the compliment, Mr Godrevy.'

He frowned deeply as if he was offended, then the corners of his lips tilted. 'I – we – need you to keep an eye on the new lot, just for today. You know what novices are like. We need to finish harvesting the Daymarks for a big wholesale order. I wouldn't ask but we're desperate, so if you could leave this and go up there and show them the ropes. I'll tell them you're the temporary supervisor and know it all inside out so they won't know any different.'

'Again. Thanks for the vote of confidence.'

He grinned. 'You're welcome. I like the new tea cosy by the way.'

'I like your new overalls.' She raised a cheeky eyebrow.

He glanced down and grimaced. 'Make the most of it. You're not likely to see me in a suit again.'

71

'I guess not. Um. You might like to cut the tag off before you go to the wedding.'

'What? Damn. Where?'

'The price tag's hanging down the back. Hold on.'

Gaby held the buttonhole so he could take off his jacket. She snipped off the price tag with the cutters she kept in her pocket and smirked. The jacket had obviously been ordered online from John Lewis and was actually a rather nice one. She tried not to smile too much while he shrugged it back over his broad shoulders.

'Don't forget this.' She offered the flower.

'Thanks.' He took the buttonhole from her, pulled a pin from his lapel and started trying to fasten it.

'Hold on. You're making holes in your new suit.'

She took the bloom from him, stuck the pin between her teeth and in seconds had fastened the narcissus neatly onto his lapel. With a gentle tweak to make sure it was at exactly the right angle, she stood back to admire her handiwork.

And him.

Wow. This was quite worrying. The way her hands weren't quite steady when she'd finished fixing the flower. The way her stomach did a routine to rival an Olympic tumbler at the feel of his suit under her hands. The hungry way that he was looking at her despite her tea cosy hat and her dungarees with the strange flask-shaped bulge in the pocket like she was nursing a baby kangaroo.

He lowered his chin and peered down at the buttonhole. 'I'm impressed.'

'Practice. I've fixed them lots of times for friends during

exams,' she said. When he looked surprised, she added, 'They liked to wear a different colour carnation for every day of Finals. It lightens the mood a little as you're going to the gallows,' she explained as his brow creased in puzzlement.

'That's how I feel.'

She laughed at his gloomy expression. 'Then again, this *is* a wedding, not root canal work.'

'Hmm ... look, thanks again, and if there are any problems, you can reach me or Jess on our mobiles. It might take a while for us to get here, but if it's an emergency, you must call.'

'Relax. Enjoy. Everything will be fine,' she said breezily. If only she meant it.

'I'm sure it will. And, Gaby ...'

'Yes?'

'Are you absolutely *sure* you'll be OK?'

He looked at her and lifted his hand as if he was going to touch her but then dropped it again. *He can't possibly know what today is*, Gaby told herself. No one outside the family knew. She wasn't sure he even knew about Stevie at all. She had mentioned the circumstances briefly to Jess not long after she'd joined the farm, but asked her not to tell anyone else. She didn't want anyone's pity, least of all Will's, but she did crave his respect ... Oh, who was she kidding? She fancied him like crazy, and the sight of him in a suit and wellies was fuelling a load of very unusual fantasies.

'I'll be fine,' she said, then cleared her husky throat. 'Just go to the wedding, Will. *Please*.'

Yet he made no move to leave her, and they held each

73

other's gaze too long for boss and employee. For a few seconds, she genuinely wondered if he might jump on her in his wedding suit in the middle of a muddy field.

'Will! What on earth are you doing? You'll ruin that suit!'

At the shout from behind him, Will turned sharply, but Gaby could already see Anna making her way into the field. Like her son, Anna was also wearing wellies, but any resemblance ended there. She was holding up the skirt of a purple shift dress while hobbling between the flower rows. She wore a fitted teal jacket over the dress and her immaculate blow-dry was topped by a fascinator of extravagant blue and purple feathers. She reminded Gaby of a very angry peacock.

She reached them, darted an accusing glance at Gaby and then rounded on Will, while keeping her tight dress above the level of her wellies.

'I've been looking for you for the past twenty minutes. What are you doing out here?'

'Sorting out some cover for the new crew. Mum, be careful or you'll get your dress dirty.'

'If I do it'll be thanks to you. We need to leave!'

'I'm ready now. Gaby's going to supervise the new crew while Len's out of action.'

Anna's eyebrows rose. 'Her?'

'Yes, Mum. Everything's fine.'

'Well, if you think Gaby's up to it. No disrespect to you, of course,' Anna said to Gaby, when she was clearly thinking something very cutting indeed. 'But you are new and it is a huge responsibility.'

Gaby opened her mouth to try and get a shot into this game of Godrevy ping-pong, but Will batted his response back too fast.

'Mum. It's only for a day and Gaby knows exactly what she has to do. She's been here six months and if there's a crisis, I'll have to bring the boat back, won't I?'

Anna pursed her lips. 'And wouldn't you just love an excuse to do that?'

'It's fine. I promise you there won't be a crisis.' Gaby finally jumped into the rally. 'So, you can all go and have a lovely time at the wedding. Don't worry about anything. Enjoy your day,' she said emphasising the word 'day', so Will knew he had to stay away.

'Thanks a lot,' said Will, his eyes gleaming with a mix of gratitude and exasperation.

Gaby grinned. 'You're welcome.'

'Well, as there's no one else, I suppose we've no choice,' Anna muttered. 'Now let's get on our way before you change your mind. I know how much you'd love to find another reason to get out of this. Your aunt fully expects you to find some way of wriggling out of it as it is, so we're going to show them, they're wrong.'

Anna stumbled. Will caught her arm and stopped her from slipping into the mud.

'Be careful, Mum. Now, come on or we'll be late for this damn wedding.'

'I've been telling you that for the past hour!' Anna shrugged off his arm and squelched off, holding up her hem and muttering about where Jess had got to now and hoping she'd have a lovely day as she deserved some fun after what that bloody postman had done to her.

Will turned to Gaby and mouthed 'thanks'.

Gaby watched him trudge after his mum.

She was pleased to be given the chance to show she could look after everyone despite the moths stirring in her stomach. All she had to do was show the rookie team how to harvest the crop and get it done by the time Will got back. That would show Len and Anna. Most of all, it would give her something to focus on, on a day that held such bittersweet memories.

Chapter 8

Gaby was glad the four new pickers couldn't see her churning stomach as they gathered outside the packing shed. They'd only arrived the previous day and most bore the same expression that she must have had on her first day: a rabbit in the headlights. They shuffled around, dressed in a jumble sale mix of hats, jumpers and gloves.

There was a slight look of the chain gang about them, Gaby thought, stifling a giggle. By now, they would have realised that, until tomorrow at least, there was no way off the island even if they'd wanted to leg it. Pickers were often native Scillonians but today there was only one local who was new to picking. The other two were from the mainland UK and one was Polish. Natalia was about Gaby's age and from a small town outside Krakow. She'd worked in various market gardens in East Anglia over the past couple of years and looked slightly less terrified than the others. She also knew Cambridge a little, which had broken the ice between them when they had been briefly introduced the previous evening.

Gaby straightened herself up to her full five feet one and a half and threw them all a confident smile.

'OK. You've already had your induction and health and safety with Len yesterday, so we're going to get straight to work,' she said. 'We need to pick the Daymark and Yellow Cheer today. This is a Daymark. You can tell it by the bright orange cups.' She held up the distinctive flower in one hand and a paler yellow one in the other. 'And this is a Yellow Cheer, but of course, we don't want to pick any that are already in bloom like this one. We look for tight buds that will be ready to open when they reach the customers. Don't we?'

Natalia nodded but the others seemed nonplussed.

'Come on! You can do better than that,' she said, feeling like an aerobics instructor faced by a Monday morning class.

'Yes, Gaby,' a faint chorus and a few smirks. She suspected they knew she wasn't used to being in charge and were obviously looking for signs of weakness.

She soldiered on. 'You don't have to worry anyway, because I'll show you the exact varieties we're going to be working on. You'll soon be able to tell which is which by their scent alone. I'll be around to help if anyone has any questions or problems.'

Although, by now, she could have picked and packed with her eyes shut, it was another thing instructing a group of newbies who were staring at her as if she was the fount of all knowledge.

She grinned. 'Come on then. Let's get on with it before this lot is already in bloom.'

The local pointed to the nearest field. 'That's the field we're doing?' he asked incredulously.

'What? All of it?' a skinny guy with a Scottish accent asked. He was called Robbie, appropriately enough, thought Gaby, resisting the urge to quote Burns. That really would freak everyone out.

'Yes. It's perfectly doable before the end of the day. Even for beginners,' Gaby added with a touch of sarcasm. Len would have been proud. Will must have carefully calculated exactly what the novice team could pick in the time allotted. So, she was damn well going to get it done, no matter how much they moaned.

Without giving them any more time to revolt, she marched them to the field, setting to with gusto and hoping to lead by example. However, it was frustrating work as she had to break off every few minutes to correct someone's technique or answer questions about whether the bloom was at the right stage. Normally, Len drove the quad bike full of crates back to the packing shed, but Gaby had to do it herself, which meant she had to leave her team for minutes at a time and wait while the crates were unloaded at the packing shed and collect empty ones.

By lunchtime, they'd only done a third of the field, but everyone, including Gaby, was desperate for a break and there was no way she would expect anyone to work through.

The moment lunchtime was over, Gaby led her crew back to the field, trying to work at double the rate. Ignoring her aching back, burning arms and sore fingers, she did her best to make up the difference. Her team were more experienced now; even though they were tired, they'd had a morning's practice and there were less interruptions. The general manager, Lawrence did her a favour by collecting some of the full crates on the quad bike and bringing empty ones back when he could spare a few minutes from the office.

By mid-afternoon, Gaby was starting to think they would come close to finishing the job but not quite. Her heart sank. She'd wanted to get it done, and show Anna, Len and Will that she could do it – and mostly, she relished the challenge. She had a feeling that Will wouldn't be disappointed if she didn't. Perhaps, he never really expected it, but for her own satisfaction, Gaby wanted to do it. Bizarrely, she also had the idea that she needed to do it for Stevie. There was no rational reason for this, although the analytical part of her brain suggested it was probably another way of coping with her emotions on a difficult day. It was certainly a way to keep busy and ensure she went to bed completely knackered.

The sun started to sink lower and, with it, the spirits and rate of the novices dropped significantly. They were all shattered and frequently standing up to stretch or moan, or both. Gaby knew how they felt. She was ready to drop and she knew they'd be stiff and aching for days until they got used to the constant stooping and the sore fingers.

She checked her watch. Arghh. There was only twenty minutes to go before she had to let everyone clock off.

'Come on. Not long. One more push!' she shouted, but knowing that they were very unlikely to finish the field now.

Most, but not all the workers, made a final effort, but what seemed like mere moments later, Gaby's alarm went off.

With a sigh, she stood up, her fingers numb and stiff from the extra effort she'd made.

'OK. That's it. You'll be pleased to know that's the end of your first day. Thanks for your great work and see you tomorrow.'

In seconds, the field was empty, apart from Natalia who patted Gaby on the back. 'Thanks.'

'What for? Cracking the whip?' Gaby was bemused.

'For not being a horrible boss.'

Gaby laughed. 'Thanks, but I'm not your boss. Will and Jess are.'

'I met Jess. She seems OK. Quiet but nice. Fair. Will is hot.' Natalia fanned herself extravagantly, then pulled a face. 'But he also walks around like he has a thundercloud over his head. He needs a girlfriend.' She grinned. 'Or boyfriend?'

Gaby had to smile too, but she was horrified that Natalia had sussed out in a moment that Gaby fancied Will, and inside a light bulb had gone on. What if Will looked stressed out because he wanted a boyfriend? What if she'd misread the moments between them – or just imagined them – and Will was gay?

'All Will cares about is getting these flowers picked,' she said, and that at least was partly true.

'We did our best,' said Natalia, pulling off her gloves. 'The rest of us will be here tomorrow. So will Len.' She wrinkled her nose. 'I've heard the others talking about him. I hope his sickness decides to stay with him for a while longer.'

Gaby stifled a laugh. She didn't want Len to be ill and his bark was a lot worse than his bite, but his reputation for drilling the new workers like a platoon sergeant *was* fearsome and well-earned. 'I doubt any bug would dare hang around Len for too long. I'm surprised that one's dared to approach him in the first place.'

'Hmm. I'm going for food in the common room. Then some of us should go to the pub. There is a pub here?'

'Yes. The Gannet. It's about ten minutes' walk away. You go and get cleaned up. I need to drive these crates up to the sheds. Then maybe I'll join you in the pub later if I haven't fallen asleep in my room!'

This was more than likely, thought Gaby as she trudged back to the staff house after unloading a batch of crates. She was very tired but secretly happy, even though she hadn't finished the whole field. She'd got the small team working well and encouraged them to keep going even when some looked like they wanted to chuck it all in. Maybe one or two would: she couldn't help it if they decided they'd made a big mistake. All she could have done was try her best to complete the task for the day without too many disasters.

The quad bike wasn't quite full. There were still a few empty crates. There was no point leaving them like that and it wouldn't take long to pick a few more flowers and fill them. Gaby took a swig of cold coffee from her flask, finished off the chocolate bar in her bag and set to again.

Ouch. Even stopping for ten minutes made it hard to get going again, but she wanted at least to fill the crates. Half an hour later she drove the quad bike into the yard, laden with crates. Everyone had gone from the packing shed, so she took the crates into the fridge herself, almost toppling over with the weight of them. Then she went back to the bike.

With a sigh, she looked at the one corner of the field they'd not got round to, still with the flowers in bud at the perfect stage. They seemed to mock her, saying, 'Pick me, pick me.'

It was five-thirty p.m. and the sun was hovering just above the horizon, the sea silvery in the early evening light. Although she'd been warm from the recent work, she'd been in and out of the fridge and now felt the evening chill. How long would it take, she thought, to finish that corner? How long before the Godrevys got back from the wedding on St Piran's? It depended on the tides, and even though Will and Jess were perfectly capable of piloting their boat after dark, perhaps they might want to be back before then. That didn't give her much time if she wanted to finish the job before Will's return.

Gaby drove the quad to the top of the field and sat looking at the tiny patch in the corner that was bugging the heck out of her. It was like a compulsion: she had to finish the field for Stevie, even though he'd have laughed and told her to go down the pub.

Oh, sod it. She could virtually finish the field, have a lightning-quick shower and still show up at the Gannet. She climbed off the quad, picked up a crate and marched across the field.

Chapter 9

Will and Jess tied up the boat and helped their mother onto the quay. It was around nine-thirty and the full moon had painted everything with a silvery sheen so you felt you could almost walk across its glittering path to the horizon.

Jess had swapped her heels for wellies and put on her waterproofs for the journey home from St Piran's because the open sea between the islands was choppy. The evening party had ramped up another gear as the Godrevys and a few others had to leave because of the tides, but Jess wasn't heartbroken to have an excuse to come home.

'Well, I'm glad that's over with. I'm knackered,' said Will, walking beside his mother and Jess.

Anna snorted in derision. 'Knackered? You've been to a wedding. This is your day off.'

'Didn't feel like it,' said Will drily.

'Well, I think it was a great do, but I'm glad to be back,' said Jess, trying to smooth things over between Will and her mum. She'd enjoyed catching up with friends and family, but there had also been a lot of awkward questions about Adam. No, she hadn't heard from him. Yes, he was in Cumbria with his family, as far as she knew. Will had also been interrogated, but not having been in love with Adam, he naturally found any questions easier to fend off.

'Hmm. The flowers looked great, though I wasn't sure about that qui-no thing they served with the salmon. What's wrong with the good old-fashioned potatoes that we all grow in our own backyard? Funny wedding all round, if you ask me. Did you see Cousin Alison's face when they said the vows? Looked like she'd swallowed a bottle of vinegar, but then she's always been a sour-faced misery.'

'I thought Maisie looked amazing,' Jess cut in before her mum started on the bride's dress which had been scarlet silk with a train that swept the floor. Jess had loved it, but her mother's eyebrows had shot right up when the bridal party had entered the church. 'Pregnancy suits her, even if she is only four months. I think the worst of the morning sickness is over and she looks great.'

'Yes, she does. I'll give you that,' said Anna. 'I still can't get over what happened with that Australian though. Fancy lying about his past to us all.'

Anna was clearly referring to Maisie who had looked radiant on the arm of her new partner, Patrick, at the wedding reception. Before the two of them had finally got together, Patrick had kept a major secret from Maisie and when the truth had finally come out, it had caused a lot of trouble. Far from being a penniless barman, Patrick had been unmasked as Hugo Scorrier's cousin, and was actually the wealthy owner of Petroc Island and resort. He'd had his own reasons for keeping this fact secret but the deception had hurt Maisie badly. However, he now appeared to have been largely forgiven by the community and most importantly, by Maisie. So while their relationship had started on very rocky foundations, they were crazy in love now. It reminded Jess that anything was possible and she could be happy again too ...

'Maisie and Patrick seem very happy now and I can't wait to meet Little Sprog and be his or her godmother,' said Jess.

Anna snorted. 'Fancy naming a baby that.'

'Oh, Mum. That's only their nickname for the bump.'

'I think it goes well with Maisie's surname – Samson,' Will piped up randomly. 'And it's better than Tarquin or Honey Boo Pie, or whatever the hell people call their kids these days.'

Anna turned to him. 'What would you know about it? I can't see myself being a granny any time soon.'

Behind their mother's back, Jess swapped a resigned look with Will. He held up his hands in frustration, but fortunately they were now at the gates of the farm. Even though it was early, she couldn't wait to get out of her dress and into her old trackies. She'd make a cuppa so they could all rehydrate, although she hadn't had that much to drink as she was 'driving home' in the boat. Then all she wanted to do was get to bed and enjoy some peace and quiet.

They walked into the farm and the security light clicked on as they entered the yard. It was more for safety and convenience than any security issue as no one was going to be able to get millions of flowers and equipment off the island even if they wanted to. Any minor thefts and the culprits could be narrowed down to about a hundred people, so it basically wasn't worth it.

The sound of laughter and chatter came from over the

hedge and, a few seconds later, half a dozen of the workers followed the Godrevys into the main yard.

'It's the newbies and some of the older gang. I think they must have been to the pub,' said Jess. 'Probably drowning their sorrows after their first day. Lucky for them that they had Gaby. I wonder if she's been as tough on them as Len is.'

'I doubt it.' Will scanned the group carefully. 'Although she isn't with them, so perhaps she really did play hardball. I'd have thought she would have gone along.'

A few of the old hands asked Anna and Jess about how the wedding had gone. Jess spotted Will having a word with Natalia, one of the rookies.

Jess joined them. 'How was your first day?' she asked Natalia.

Natalia did a shaky hand signal but smiled anyway. 'OK. It's hard work, but I've done worse. Gaby kept us in line.'

'Good. Did she not go out with you?' Jess asked.

'No. When we finished she said she had a few things to do and she might join us at the pub if she wasn't too tired.'

'And did she?' Will cut in to Jess's surprise.

'No. But we guess she was asleep in her room. I knocked her door, but there was no answer. She was tired after looking after us. We didn't finish the field. We tried and she tried even harder. I'm sorry.'

'It's OK. I didn't expect it from your first time,' said Will. 'Thanks, Natalia. I'll see you in the morning.'

With a grin, Natalia joined the other new workers and they headed off to the staff house.

'Gaby must have been too knackered to make the pub, but

it's quite unlike her – she's normally very sociable. I hope she's been OK,' Jess said, suddenly remembering that it would have been Stevie's birthday. Gaby rarely talked about the loss of her brother but Jess now recalled that she had mentioned about it being today. Jess's heart sank a little. It must have been a difficult enough time for Gaby, without the added stress of supervising the new recruits. However, Gaby had also asked her not to share any details with Will so Jess kept her misgivings to herself.

'She'd have called one of us if anything had gone wrong,' said Will.

'I guess so …' Jess felt guilty.

Anna bustled over. 'Well, I'm going to get out of this outfit and put the kettle on. Want a cup of tea?'

'Thanks. I'll have a quickie then I might go to bed,' said Jess.

'I'll be back in a minute,' said Will.

With a doubtful 'mmm', Anna nodded and left them in the yard. Jess was going to follow her, but Will lingered, a frown on his face.

'What's up?' she asked.

'I might go and check everything's OK in the packing shed and the day's harvest is safely in the fridge.'

Jess knew him too well. 'You just want some time on your own.'

He turned to her. 'Don't you?'

'Yeah. It's been a long day and I'm shattered too. It was tiring answering all those questions about Adam and knowing people were talking about us.'

Will patted her shoulder. 'They'll soon find something else to gossip about.'

'Thanks, bro.'

'You're welcome. Come on, let's go and set our minds at rest before we turn in.'

Jess followed him, not unhappy to see if Gaby was OK herself, but also wondering if he had an ulterior motive for checking the day's work. She'd seen him scrolling through his phone more often than he usually did. She'd had a few glances at hers during the wedding, but Will had been pulling his mobile from his pocket even during the church ceremony. While it hadn't been ideal leaving Gaby in charge today, Jess had every faith in her abilities. She was experienced and conscientious, and much stronger than she appeared. She guessed that Will wanted to reassure himself that nothing had gone wrong; perhaps he was even hoping to bump into her.

They walked to the work sheds and flicked on the lights but were met with silent emptiness, as expected. There were still a few rejected stems on the floor and some crates waiting to be cleaned in the entrance. Will opened the door of the refrigerated room where the picked flowers were kept prior to being arranged, and after they were boxed, to keep them fresh before their journey to the quay. Having looked inside, he closed the door behind him and joined Jess.

'There you go. Everything looks fine, doesn't it?'

His brow creased. 'I suppose so.'

'But?'

'Natalia said they hadn't finished the quota for today and

89

yet the fridge is packed with flowers. One of the crates was almost blocking the door as I pushed it open.'

'Will, it's late. If they've over-picked, it'll be OK because we have that big order to fulfil. Stop worrying. Now can we finally go home and chill out?'

'Suppose so.' He didn't look at all reassured.

'You're worried about Gaby?' Jess asked him.

'I'm not *worried*. I just wonder how she got on today.'

'If you like, I'll drop by her room and check on her. Either she'll answer or I'll hear her snoring or something and then you can relax.'

'There's no need for that.'

'No, but I'm going to do it all the same. You might as well come too.'

They set off for the staff house, Jess's mind working overtime. She'd suspected for some time that Will felt something more for Gaby than an employer's care for his workers, even though he denied it strenuously. She was now ninety-nine per cent sure he *did* have a thing for her. Jess already knew Gaby liked him and the teasing, the banter and the looks they shared when they thought no one else could see them had fuelled her suspicions for a long time. Will's eagerness to see Gaby now sealed the deal in Jess's eyes.

However, she also thought she knew why Will was reluctant to get involved with Gaby while she worked for him: it was too complicated. Putting a finger on her lips, Jess approached Gaby's door; Will kept a discreet distance. There was no obvious sound and no light spilling from under the door.

'She must be asleep,' she whispered to Will.

He showed her his watch face. It was past ten o'clock.

Jess put her ear close to the door, half expecting it to be pulled open at any moment and that she'd fall inside the room like in a sitcom. She thought she could hear the odd snuffle, but the walls were so thin, they might have been coming from someone else's room or even a mouse or night bird outside. Either way, without knocking and disturbing Gaby, there was nothing more they could do.

With a shrug, she indicated to Will that they should leave.

'You've worked her into exhaustion,' Jess said as they walked back to the farmhouse.

'I never meant that to happen!' Will exclaimed.

After Jess and Will had done their duty, had their tea with their mother, and listened to her appraisal of most of the guests' outfits, the food and the service, they went to their rooms. To mainlanders it might seem odd that they still lived 'at home', but the farm was their family business and staying on site kept costs down.

Besides, thought Jess as she brushed her teeth, the farmhouse wasn't a bad place to call home, even with its quirky plumbing and low beams that Will was forever bumping his head on even now. Jess had her own large bedroom with an en suite. Will's bedroom was slightly smaller but he had his own bathroom too.

There was a snug downstairs where she and Will retreated at various times, as well as a family sitting room and a room their mum liked to call the 'drawing room', which had been added back in Edwardian times. Space wasn't a problem but privacy was, and any relationship was conducted in the full glare of friends and family. As Jess got ready for bed, she thought about Adam's cottage. She hadn't been to look at it for months now because the memories of the happy times they'd spent together over the previous summer were still too painful to dwell on.

Her mother had urged her to be sociable at the wedding, which Jess took to mean she should look for a man. It was so bloody retro in the twenty-first century, but in one way, Jess agreed with her mother's advice: she couldn't mope forever. She'd danced and chatted with a Cornish guy who'd come to work as a chef at a local eaterie. They'd had a few drinks and he'd said he'd call her, but Jess wasn't holding her breath. He was nice and good-looking and claimed he intended to stay long-term on Scilly, but she hadn't clicked with him in the way she did with Adam. Maybe he would call ... maybe she'd give him a try.

She yawned and put her pyjamas on. It wasn't the best day to be dwelling on what might have been.

Before she climbed into bed, she went to draw the curtains. Her room overlooked most of the north side of the island and she could see the chimney on Adam's place on a clear day and the lights in his bedroom window at night. She peered out of the window, half hoping to see the yellow glow, but no matter how hard she squinted, all was dark. Cursing herself for being stupid, she was about to close the curtains when she spotted a beam of light wavering in the yard. She switched off her bedroom light and rushed back to the window. As her eyes adjusted, in the silvery gloom, she spotted Will making his way across the yard in his pyjamas.

Chapter 10

Gaby was riding pillion on the back of Stevie's motorbike. She was clinging onto him for dear life, her screams snatched away by the wind roaring past her ears. She didn't have a helmet on and she was begging him to slow down. He was crouched low over the handlebars, and her hands kept slipping from his leather jacket. The harder she tried to cling onto him, the more she lost her grip. A dazzling light blinded her and the next thing she knew she was flying through the air and landing with a massive thud in a clump of bushes.

Her first thought was that it was quite odd that she had survived a seventy mile an hour ejection from a motorbike when she wasn't wearing a crash helmet and her second thought was, *who is that man shining a torch in my eyes?*

'Am I in hospital?' she said in the croaky, panicky way people did when they've been woken up very suddenly and unpleasantly.

'No, but you were asleep on the floor!'

'Whaaaa?' She prised her lids open, flinching in the light. Her bottom was damp. In fact, most of her was damp and she was also very cold. She realised that she was lying on the rough concrete of the field workers' shelter. 'Ow ...' She rubbed at a sore spot on her thigh.

A light flashed in her eyes again, temporarily blinding her but she knew the voice instinctively.

'You must have been in here for hours,' said Will. 'Why are you on the floor?'

Gaby shaded her eyes. 'I dunno ... would you mind not shining that in my face?'

The beam disappeared and Gaby rubbed her eyes. It took a few seconds to get used to the twilight again. Meanwhile, Will was talking a *lot*.

'What happened? What were you doing in here? Did you pass out or have a fit and hit your head or something? Do I need to call the paramedics?'

'Oww ...' Gaby groaned. Her lower back throbbed. She tried to sit up, but two hands pushed her down, which probably wouldn't have been the best idea if she really did have a spinal injury, thought Gaby. However, they were Will's hands and as she was still dazed and confused, she decided to let him carry on for now.

'No, you'd better not get up. You might have broken something and I don't think you should move. That's what they tell us at rugby. You need to keep absolutely still. Shit, I'd better hold your neck still or something.'

Will got behind her and held her head between his hands. His face was upside-down from her point of view.

'No, I'm fine. Honestly, I'm fine ...' she said, feeling that things might have gone far enough, actually.

'You don't know that. Do Not Move. Do not bloody move! *Jess!*' he shouted over his shoulder towards the open door.

'Will. Please don't worry,' said Gaby. 'I fell asleep, that's all. I must have rolled off the sofa onto the floor.'

Slowly, Will removed his hands from her head. She was still wearing the tea cosy. 'Oh.'

'Now, can I please get up?'

Her back clicked as she pushed herself up to sitting. She was as stiff as a board. Will was crouched by her side. He shone the torch around the wooden building. Gaby became aware of creaks in the old timbers and the wind whistling through the cracks. She also noticed something odd about Will.

'Are you wearing pyjamas?' she asked.

'Yes, I went to the wedding in them instead of the suit.' He sighed. 'No one could find you earlier and we thought you were asleep in your room, but then I wondered if you'd had an accident out in the field or in the equipment sheds and I thought I'd check in here ... I saw the fridge was full of flowers and put two and two together. What were you trying to do? Finish the whole field on your own?'

Gaby tried to stand up. She did feel light-headed but that was only from getting up suddenly and having had no dinner. She decided not to share this with Will though in case he started CPR, although maybe that wouldn't have been a total disaster ... In fact, it was a shame that she no longer needed her head cradled in his hands ... On the other hand, what a prat she was to have fallen asleep and rolled off the sofa. No wonder she'd dreamed she'd fallen off Stevie's bike. By the look

95

of Will's pyjamas, he'd also got out of bed specially to look for her.

'What on earth were you doing?' he said, still kneeling beside her, but brusquer now he was sure she wasn't really hurt.

'We'd almost finished the field by close of play so I sent the team home. They did well for newbies, especially Natalia, but then I came back and thought there wasn't much to do and maybe I could carry on until the light had gone. I remember sitting down for a little rest after I'd done the last one and then ... absolutely nothing until someone shone a great big light in my eyes and started shouting in my face.'

'I thought you might be dead. You are completely mad, you do know that?'

'It has been said,' said Gaby proudly. 'And I'm not dead, as you can see.'

Will stood up and put the torch on the sofa. He loomed over her. 'But I might be after tonight. You almost gave me a heart attack when I saw you lying on the floor. There's no way I would ever have put you under pressure to finish that field. You should have clocked off at the same time as everyone else.'

'Probably,' said Gaby, embarrassed but not wholly disappointed that he'd been so worried. She certainly didn't want him to know the real reason that she'd stayed out to get the job done.

'Let me give you a hand up.' He reached out and pulled her to her feet. Still stiff and groggy, she overbalanced, so he steadied her with an arm around her back.

This was the moment when he should have let her go and she should have shrugged off his arm. There was no need for his help now she was upright and yet they were still connected. One hand in the small of her back became two hands on her waist, which swiftly turned into them both grabbing each other and kissing as if their lives depended on it. Even though the tassels of her hat kept getting in the way, it was an amazing kiss. Not too soft, not too hard, confident but not crushing – who knew he would be such a good kisser? The warmth spread through her face and arms, her back and right to the centre of her.

She moved her hands to the back of his pyjamas, resting her palms on his bottom through the thin jersey. He wore nothing underneath! Gaby suspected he'd only put the trousers on to come outside and the fabric did little to hide how his body was reacting to her. He slid his hands under her sweater and flicked the clasp of her bra which sprung open. His tongue explored her mouth deliciously and she pressed herself harder against him. Would he have a condom with him, she thought as he ran his warm palms over her back and started moving them around to her breasts. It was unlikely … they'd probably have to creep back to her room or be super careful. But how could she possibly wait, when she was already about to burst and Will was setting every nerve ending aglow and driving her insane with lust?

'Hello? Is there anyone in there?'

'Shit.' They both said the word at the same time and sprang apart as if they'd been stung.

Will waved his torch in the air. 'Jess! Gaby's here in the shelter. She's fine. She fell asleep.'

Gaby's cheeks burned. In fact, the rest of her, so cold before, burned for all kinds of reasons. Had she really grabbed a handful of her boss's admittedly lovely arse? Had he really stuck his tongue inside her mouth and enjoyed the best French kiss ever? Had they been minutes from shagging each other on the sofa in the barn in the dark?

It was hard to believe that any of that had happened given the way that Will was standing six feet away from her by the door as if she was Dracula. Any minute now, he'd be holding up a cross and garlic.

A torch beam wavered in the doorway and Jess materialised from the shadows.

'In the shelter? What happened?'

Will hurried over to her. Probably for protection, thought Gaby.

Jess was wearing a hoodie over her pyjamas which were tucked into wellies, like Will's. 'Is everything OK?'

Will blinked. 'It's OK. Gaby decided to finish the field and fell asleep and rolled off the sofa. Disaster averted.'

'I wouldn't have said it was a disaster,' said Gaby, fired up by his sudden change in attitude. 'Sorry, Jess. I didn't mean to worry you and Will.'

Jess stepped inside. 'Have you finished the *whole* field?'

'Sort of and then I must have nodded off.'

'Will?' Jess shone her torch right in his face as if he was a suspect she was about to interrogate.

He winced. 'It's not my fault. I never expected them to finish it all. And would you mind not pointing that light right in my eyes?'

Jess lowered the beam and spoke to Gaby kindly. 'We didn't

expect you to do that. They were a new team. No one expects miracles on the first day,' said Jess, obviously blaming Will for putting pressure on Gaby and her team.

'It's all fine,' said Gaby, joining Jess. She was anxious to put space between her and Will now he'd gone so cold on her. 'And I apologise for causing any anxiety and getting you both out of bed. Now, I'd really like to see mine, so shall we all go back inside?'

'Why don't you come into the farmhouse for a hot drink?' said Jess. 'Will, I think you'd better go inside and put the kettle on,' she said pointedly.

Gaby cringed. The last thing she wanted was to sit around the table playing happy families. The evening had turned awkward enough. 'No honestly, I *am* OK.'

'Let's get you warmed up first and then we can all go to bed. Will. *Kettle.*'

Still in two minds about accepting the offer, Gaby finally decided that it would cause more fuss if she refused. She walked with Jess and Will out of the shelter and through the back door into the farmhouse kitchen. The heat from the still warm Aga hit her immediately and she sat down on an old carver chair at the scrubbed table.

Will leant his bottom against the worktop, shooting glances at her when he thought she wasn't looking. His feet were now bare and he'd put on an old faded hoodie as well as the pyjama bottoms. She knew he had nothing on under the hoodie or pyjamas because she'd had her hands all over his gorgeous, smooth, bare skin. He probably slept in the nude, Gaby thought, and shifted uncomfortably in her seat.

'Tea or coffee? Or hot chocolate?' Jess asked.

'Chocolate, please.' The words came out as a squeak. With Will brooding sexily a few feet from her, Gaby thought it was all getting very *Cold Comfort Farm*.

'I'll get the biscuits,' Will muttered darkly. 'Or there's some fruit cake. If you fancy it.'

'I do fancy it,' she said. 'Thanks.'

There was a large scrubbed oak table with grooves and dents that testified to its many decades of use. Initials had been scratched in the table: WG, and a failed attempt had been made to polish them out. No prizes for guessing whose they were. Gaby imagined Anna or their father giving Will a telling-off for carving them. However, despite the slight air of shabbiness, the framed prints of old Scilly scenes and the vintage china on the dresser gave the room a cosy feel that perfectly suited the age of the building. Family history was ingrained into every beam and picture. The farm was clearly part of Will's DNA.

When Jess opened the fridge to get the milk, Gaby noticed a couple of photos of Will, Jess and their mother tacked by magnets onto the door. There were none of their father, as far as Gaby could see, which was hardly surprising since he'd left in acrimonious circumstances. Some of the experienced workers had long ago warned Gaby not to mention him.

While she sipped her chocolate and wolfed down a large slab of fruit cake, Gaby thought how much the kitchen reminded her of her family home. A blue glazed vase full of Yellow Cheer stood in the centre, mingling its fragrance with the faint tang of wood smoke from the chimney in the snug next door. Her family – oh God, she'd never got around to ringing them today. Her heart sank.

'I'm going to bed now the drama's over,' said Jess.

'There was no drama.' Will and Gaby said the words almost at the same time.

'OK. OK. But I'm still going to bed. Hopefully until morning this time.'

'I'll drink this up and turn in myself.' Gaby took a larger gulp, burning her tongue in the process. 'Ow.'

'Don't rush,' said Jess with a smile. 'We don't want any more injuries. Goodnight.'

'We won't be long,' said Will who had so far left his chocolate untouched. He'd kept as far away from her as possible too.

Jess shut the door to the kitchen and Gaby heard her footsteps as she climbed the stairs to her room. Gaby could still feel the tingle of Will's lips on hers, the strength of his solid body beneath her fingers and his hands seeking the fastener of her bra under her sweater. How had that happened?

There were footsteps on the stairs again. Jess must be coming back down, thought Gaby, but instead, Anna swept in, in a flowery cerise dressing gown.

She glared at Gaby but addressed herself to Will. 'What's going on?'

'Nothing, Mum. I found Gaby asleep in the field shelter and …'

Anna shot Gaby a horrified look that froze her mug halfway to her lips. 'Asleep in the barn? What on earth were you doing in there?'

'She was trying to finish harvesting the last of the Daymarks and lost track of time. Nothing to get worked up about. You can go back to sleep.'

Anna snorted. 'Sleep? That's what I was trying to do before I heard all this noise. I'm wide awake now.'

Will's lips twisted as he bit back his frustration and Gaby lowered her mug to the table. It was more than half full but she couldn't stand the tension any longer. 'I really had better go back to my room,' she said. 'I'm sorry for causing trouble.'

'Never mind. All's well that ends well.' Will pushed himself off the worktop. 'Finish your drink first. You must have got pretty cold out there,' he said gruffly.

She allowed herself a small smile. 'Actually, I've warmed up very nicely now. Goodnight, Will.'

'Wait,' said Will, but she ignored him and got to her feet too.

'Goodnight,' she said to Anna.

Anna nodded. 'Goodnight. And by the way, you'll be delighted to know that Len will be back at work in the morning. He texted me earlier.'

'I'm thrilled to hear that,' said Gaby.

'I'll see you out,' Will muttered then turned to his mother. '*Goodnight*, Mum.'

'See you in the *morning*,' she said, narrowing her eyes at Gaby.

She swept out of the kitchen but left the door open wide, presumably, thought Gaby, in case she attempted to leap on Will. Which, to be fair, she would have loved to do if he hadn't

102

made it so plain he wanted to keep his distance after his earlier lapse.

'I'll come with you to the staff house, in case you get lost,' said Will once Anna had gone. It was possibly an attempt at a joke but Gaby was too tired to play nicely.

'It's OK. I know my way out. You'd better get to bed,' she said before hurrying out of the kitchen door to grab her wellies from the porch. They were cold and damp but she struggled into them. She really needed some proper sleep but had a feeling that wasn't going to happen while her mind was still whirling from the night's events. Any triumph at finishing the field had evaporated: she'd convinced herself she'd been doing it for Stevie but she was now wondering if she'd also wanted to prove a point with Will – a point that he hadn't expected or asked her to prove. And she had to be up early again tomorrow. God, why did she go off on these mad schemes?

The security light clicked on when she was halfway across the yard. She heard the crunch of gravel behind her and seconds later Will caught up with her. He was in his wellies now and despite the hoodie, he hugged himself to keep warm in the damp night air. Perhaps it was a gesture of defensiveness too.

Gaby held her breath, wondering if he'd had a change of heart and wanted to reignite their moment in the shelter.

'Gaby. Wait. I must say this.'

'Yes?'

'We should probably forget what happened out there,' he muttered.

She nodded. Her heart plunged into her boots. 'You're right.'

'It was ... pretty good ... but I shouldn't have done that.'

Her blood fired up. Only *pretty* good? 'There were two of us involved, or have you forgotten?'

'Yes, but even so. Things could get way too complicated if we carried on ...'

'They *could*.'

'And our paths are headed in very different directions, aren't they?'

She was struck dumb for a few moments. He wanted her to confirm what he was thinking: almost as if *he* wanted *her* to tell him to back off.

'Yes, they are.' Her ironic smile wasn't returned by Will. His expression was impossible to fathom. Did she see guilt that he'd even started something with her? Or regret that it had ended too soon? If Jess hadn't come along, would they still be in the shelter, ripping each other's clothes off? 'Well, goodnight. *Boss*,' she said and left him without glancing back.

He was right: no matter how much she liked or lusted after him, how much fun the farm was, it was only a stepping stone on the road to her next destination. There was a life for her to live beyond Scilly eventually. Even though she loved it here, there was a whole world out there that she felt she had to live and explore, for Stevie's sake as well as her own. It was probably best they didn't take things any further. With Will so tied to the farm, she couldn't imagine a place for him on her journey.

Chapter 11

February turned to March, the days lengthened and the fields glowed with fresh hues of orange, gold and lemon as new varieties came into bloom. Almost a month had gone by since Adam had flown out on Valentine's Day and Jess had accepted their split was final, and that he might well be gone for good.

To cheer her up, Maisie had asked her to lunch at their favourite restaurant overlooking Hugh Town's harbour, so Jess wangled a few hours off to join her friend. They met up outside the clinic on St Mary's after Maisie's latest antenatal appointment and hurried to the restaurant under a shared umbrella as it had started to rain. Over a drink, their conversation had all been focused on how 'Little Sprog' was. The fact that Mother's Day was coming up in just over a week's time, seemed to add to the mood of anticipation of the baby's birth. He or she was set to appear in August and Jess was delighted to talk about something other than Adam, although she knew the topic couldn't be put off for long.

'So, how are *you*, hun? Heard anything from him?' Maisie asked once their starters had arrived.

Jess toyed with a prawn in her seafood salad. 'No, and I don't expect to ... I passed by his place the other day. He must still be paying the rent because his ancient curtains are still up in the windows and his bike was chained up under the lean-to.' As if he intended to come back for it, thought Jess, laying her fork on the plate.

'So, no sign of him moving out permanently. I don't know how he can afford to pay the rent and live somewhere else,' said Maisie.

Jess knew that her friend was trying to gently hint that Adam might have moved in with someone willing to provide him with a free home. It was tough love from Maisie, but Jess couldn't be angry. Adam must be living *somewhere*, and she had to face up to the fact it might not be with parents or mates.

'I'm sorry for raking it – and him – up again when we're meant to be having a lovely time. It's none of my business, but I want you to be happy,' said Maisie. 'Bugger, that makes me sound like your mum – and mine.'

'Well, you may as well get in some practice,' said Jess and they both laughed.

'True. Why don't you have another glass of wine? It's your day off.'

Maisie ordered a fresh white wine for Jess and a soft drink for herself and they moved on to talk about Patrick's plans to decorate the spare room of their cottage on Gull Island – or rather Maisie's reluctance to make any preparations until Little Sprog was almost ready to arrive.

Jess started to tell Maisie about Gaby falling asleep in the shelter and Will going out in his pyjamas to 'rescue' her. Everyone at the farm knew about it now and half the island too. Will hadn't teased Gaby half as much as Jess might have expected, and seemed pissed off when Jess joked about him cracking the whip.

'Will and Gaby have been winding each other up since she arrived last summer, though it's never gone further than teasing, as far as I know. Of course, I wouldn't dare ask Will directly. All I do know is that since the "shelter incident" the banter's cooled down and they're both trying to ignore each other.'

'Any idea what actually happened in the shelter, *if* you know what I mean ...' said Maisie, topping up her own glass with elderflower fizz.

'No idea. I interrupted them ...' Jess paused. Will and Gaby had seemed very startled, so maybe there *had* been something going on ... 'Will was obviously worried he might have worked her too hard. We both checked her room earlier in the evening and he seemed happy with that, but then he went out later in his pyjamas to look for her. Turns out she'd tried to pick the whole field and nodded off in the field workers' shelter. She came back to the house for a drink after. I don't think Mum likes her, which is a sure sign she thinks Will does.'

'Any particular reason?'

'Mum sees her as a threat and worries she might take Will away from the farm, though he'd never leave, of course. Gaby's lovely, but I don't really know why she's working for us. But then, as you've discovered, this is the sort of place that attracts all kinds of people for different reasons at different times of their lives.'

'You can say that again.' They both knew Jess was referring to Patrick.

The main courses arrived and Jess started her seafood risotto and Maisie tucked into her halloumi salad, while they chatted about the plans for Little Sprog's arrival. With the company of her best friend and a large glass of Sauvignon, Jess started to relax. It was fantastic to see her friend so blooming. When Maisie had met Patrick last autumn, she had found it hard to trust him because of their rocky start and especially his deception over being heir to Petroc. In a dramatic night in January, Maisie had had a fall and revealed to Patrick and her family and friends that she was carrying Patrick's child. Sadly, she'd lost one of the babies but the other twin had survived. Soon afterwards, Patrick had persuaded Maisie to give him another chance and since then they'd seemed blissfully happy, although she and Patrick were naturally anxious about the baby.

The scans today had shown all was well with the remaining twin, and now Maisie was eighteen weeks' pregnant. Her relief and bubbliness rubbed off on Jess, who realised that she herself felt, if not quite happy, then definitely not miserable for the first time in weeks.

After dessert, Jess and Maisie were enjoying coffee and amaretto biscuits when a new customer walked into the café. Many of the out-of-season crowd were twitchers, toting binoculars and huge camera lenses, but Jess knew this visitor wasn't here for the birdlife.

He'd obviously arrived by taxi because despite the showers outside, his charcoal-coloured suit was barely touched by raindrops. He wore no tie, just a fitted white shirt, and was carrying a laptop bag over one shoulder and a rugged leather holdall with Skybus tags in the other hand. Judging by his olive skin and beautifully cut suit, the stranger was either Italian or Spanish. He was also built like something out of an aftershave ad, complete with chiselled jaw and cheekbones you could grate parmesan on.

Jess and Maisie exchanged raised eyebrows and the waiting staff almost jostled with each other over who was going to serve him.

Maisie dabbed her mouth with her napkin in an attempt not to giggle. 'Who is he?' she mouthed, her eyes widening.

Jess shrugged and mouthed, 'Wow,' back, then frowned. She'd seen him before somewhere ...

'Italian?' Maisie mouthed over the top of her decaf cappuccino.

Jess raised an enquiring eyebrow and quickly took a sip of her Americano, while trying to check out the mystery man. Apparently oblivious to the stir he'd created, he selected a table near the door and scrolled through his iPhone.

The restaurant owner whizzed over to his table. 'Afternoon. What can I get you, sir?'

The man put his phone down and smiled at the owner who almost melted. 'Are you still serving the lunch menu?'

'Of course, sir,' she said. Maisie raised an eyebrow at Jess. They both knew that the restaurant normally stopped serving lunch at two.

'Great. I'm starving.'

'Have you just flown in?' the owner asked. 'I heard there were some flight disruptions so you've done well to get here.'

'That was at Exeter. Fortunately, I flew from Newquay but I had a very early start in London to get my connection, and so I'm starving. What do you recommend?'

'Hmm. Local goat's cheese salad to start and then the half lobster?' She practically purred at the customer. Any moment now, and she'll be fluttering her lashes, thought Jess.

He smiled. 'Sounds great.'

'And would you like to see the wine list, sir?'

'No thanks. Mineral water will be fine.'

Every eye in the place was on him, every ear straining. Jess knew what Maisie was thinking: that by evening, everyone would know what the 'Italian' had ordered for his lunch. Although he didn't *sound* very Italian with that BBC urban accent.

'OK. I'll get some bread in the meantime. Can't have you going hungry on Scilly,' the owner trilled and swept through the door to the kitchen after throwing pointed 'get on with it' glances at her waiting staff.

Maisie and Jess stretched out their coffees as long as possible in the hope of finding out more from the exotic diner. While he was waiting for his starter to arrive, he got up and headed towards the washroom.

'Who is *that*?' Maisie whispered once he was safely out of hearing.

'No idea. He looks Italian.'

'Whoever he is, he's here for a couple of nights at least, judging by the smart bag and suit. I think I can make a wild guess where he might be staying.' Maisie's eyes gleamed mischievously.

'Petroc?' Jess replied. 'It's the most luxurious on the islands, that's for sure. Did you notice his name?'

'No, but I did see his watch. That's a Breitling.'

As a bar owner, Maisie was used to assessing people in a glance. Jess's knowledge of gentleman's timepieces was limited, but even she knew that Breitlings could cost as much as a second-hand car.

'Wow. Well, in that suit and with a laptop, he can't be a birdwatcher,' said Jess. 'He must be here on business at the Petroc Resort. I expect he's here to see Hugo.' At her mention of Hugo, who still ran Petroc despite recently finding out that his cousin, Patrick was the actual owner, a light went on in Jess's brain. 'Oh, hold on a moment. I thought I'd seen our mystery Italian *somewhere* before.'

'What? You didn't say. Where?'

'At the airport last August bank holiday. I was picking Gaby up with Adam.' Jess pulled a face. 'That's why I didn't remember at first ...'

'Unhappy memories?' Maisie grimaced.

'You could say so ... but it was definitely him. While I was looking out for Gaby in the arrivals hall, this guy was waiting by the briefing area. He'd been chatting to Hugo and I only saw him for a few seconds, but I thought he was different from the usual passengers. I've not heard anyone talk about him on Scilly before so he must have made a flying visit.'

The Italian came back, carrying his jacket over his arm. He hooked it over his chair and thanked the waitress as she laid his salad in front of him. He speared a nugget of goat's cheese on his fork while he glanced at his phone. The cuff of his snowy shirt had pushed back to reveal a sprinkling of dark hair.

His gesture prompted Jess to check her own phone, but they both knew that if they didn't leave soon, she'd miss the tide for her boat trip home to St Saviour's and even though it was officially her afternoon off, she had plenty of paperwork to do at the farm.

'Argh. I'll have to leave you very soon,' Jess announced.

Maisie winked. 'Shame. Can't you find an excuse to stay?' she said, delving into her bag for her purse. Patrick was meeting Maisie shortly too.

'No, the tide's turning and I don't want to have to leave the boat in the harbour and hitch a lift back.'

'We could drop you on the way back to Gull if you want to hang around,' Maisie teased.

'Much as I'm enjoying the spectacle, I'd better go back because I've left Will holding the fort.' Jess stole another glance at the Italian who had a forkful of rocket poised while he scrolled through his phone again. Must be something important to distract him from his lunch.

Maisie paid the bill with her card and Jess gave her half of the bill in cash. They got up and Maisie made her way between the tables towards the door.

'Oh!'

Maisie stumbled and seemed to trip, throwing out a hand to steady herself on the back of the Italian's chair. Immediately he was on his feet, holding onto her arm. His eyes – espresso brown as Jess had imagined – widened in horror when he spotted Maisie's bump.

'Are you OK? Oh God, did you trip over my bag?'

'It's fine.'

'Maisie. Are you OK? Did you feel faint?' Jess asked, not afraid to interrupt where her friend's welfare was concerned.

'No. I just caught over the strap of the bag with my heel. I'm absolutely fine.'

'I'm great, thanks but sadly, we both need to go. Don't worry about it.'

'Well, please accept my apologies ...?'

'Maisie,' said Maisie, introducing herself. 'And this is my friend, Jess.'

'Nice to meet you, Maisie,' he turned his eyes on Jess. 'You too, Jessica,' Jess was taken aback. No one ever used her full name and it was odd that a stranger had, although perhaps he'd misheard. 'And again, I'm sorry if I nearly caused an accident. Have a safe journey to wherever you're going.'

With a smile that could have lit up the whole of Hugh Town on a December night, he gathered up the offending bag and stuffed it under his feet.

'Come on,' muttered Jess, noticing that everyone in the restaurant had homed in on them.

'Oh. Can you hang on a mo? I need to visit the bathroom. *Again*. Sorry.' Maisie grimaced. 'One of the joys of being pregnant, if that's not too much information,' she said to the Italian guy.

He smiled gallantly before retaking his seat. 'No need to be sorry– and congratulations by the way.'

Leaving Jess stranded in the middle of the restaurant, Maisie scooted off to the loo. Jess glanced back at their own table but the waitress was clearing it. She could have waited for Maisie outside if it wasn't now pouring so hard, raindrops were bouncing off the outside terrace.

The Italian smiled. Jess smiled weakly back, feeling cut adrift.

'When's the baby due?' he asked, taking her by surprise. His gaze was very direct, forcing Jess to meet his eyes which were the colour of the burnt caramel on her crème brûlée. 'Your friend's baby, I mean. Naturally,' he added, seeming to have lost interest in his salad entirely. Jess noticed the linen napkin, casually draped over one thigh. It really was a lovely suit, and a very nice thigh too. She refocused her attention on his face.

'Erm. It's August.'

'Not so far away then. Are you two sisters?'

'Oh no. We're just friends. Close friends. We were at school together on St Saviour's.'

'And you live there now?' he asked.

'Yes. I run the flower farm.'

'Wow. A *flower* farm. Sounds idyllic.' He heaved a sigh and Jess wasn't sure if he was joking or not.

She decided he was just making polite conversation. Maybe he felt obliged to chat to her until Maisie emerged from the loo, which Jess sincerely hoped she would as soon as possible. 'It might sound idyllic, but you wouldn't think so when you're thigh-deep in mud in the middle of a raging storm.'

His eyebrows shot up his tanned forehead. '*Thigh*-deep in mud. Now there's an image ...'

Jess's eyes were drawn to his lap again. She was becoming

fixated. 'I've exaggerated a bit. We're knee-deep, mostly. The mud doesn't always get that far up unless it's been really wet. Like today for instance.' Argh. Jess cringed at her unintended innuendo. She glanced towards the bathrooms, but Maisie was nowhere to be seen but she couldn't leave without her. That would look very awkward.

'Yes, I think I might get wet on the way down to the quay,' said the man. So he *was* getting a boat to Petroc, she thought.

'It might blow over. I have to leave soon though or I'll miss the tides for my boat.'

'You have your own boat?' He sounded impressed.

'It's my family's boat. Only a small motorboat but it's essential for getting around.'

'You must know the waters well around here.'

'I was practically born in a boat.' She smiled but stopped herself from adding that their father had taught her and Will to handle the vessel from when they were small children. He didn't need to know that, or anything more about her, in fact. While she felt awkward about making small talk with a stranger, he seemed unfazed and certainly not bothered about his food or his phone. 'No choice really,' she added. 'Oh, look. Here's Maisie. I'll have to go. Nice to meet you.'

'*Ciao*,' said the man. 'Maybe I'll bump into you again while I'm on Scilly.'

Jess flashed him a weak smile and moved swiftly towards the door before Maisie could come up with any more reasons for thrusting her and the man together, however easy on the eye and apparently charming he was.

'*Are* you OK?' Jess demanded as soon as they were safely

outside. There was still rain in the air, spotting their faces, but the black cloud that had unleashed its load was already being driven away by the brisk wind.

'Of course I am. It was only a stumble.' Maisie grinned. 'Luckily it happened in exactly the right place.'

Jess gasped. 'Oh my God. Did you do that on purpose?'

'Would I?'

'Oh my God. Maisie. We're too old for pulling stunts like that. It was OK when we were teenagers but not now. You're forty, remember?'

'Cheek! And you're never too old to take a chance, although it fell a bit flat. He didn't give his name, did he? Probably too embarrassed that he'd almost injured a pregnant woman.'

'More likely too scared we might stalk him!'

'I thought you were the adventurous one,' said Maisie teasingly. 'Remember when Patrick first turned up at the Driftwood? You chatted *him* up.'

'Only because I wanted to try and make Adam jealous. Oh, that sounds terrible, because Patrick's gorgeous and lovely, but ...'

Maisie laughed. 'Don't worry, hun. I'm not offended. I never could be offended by you, but I was only trying to find out more about the mystery man. *Did* you get his name?'

'No, I didn't.' But he knows mine, Jess thought, and where I live and work. Why did that slip out? The man had skilfully found out, without revealing a single thing about himself. He was probably just polite, to cover both their embarrassment at being manoeuvred together so unsubtly by Maisie.

'We can always ask the restaurant owner. She'll see his credit card.'

'You can't do that, Maisie!'

Maisie waggled her eyebrows. 'I can. And I might ...'

'Noooo.'

'I'm joking! But it's time you had some fun. Now's your chance. There was no wedding ring or even a pale mark where one might have been.'

'That means nothing. Not that many men wear rings these days.' Besides, thought Jess, she'd been too fixated on his eyes – and thighs – to notice his hands much.

'And besides, you're not interested because of Adam?'

'Not because of Adam,' Jess said firmly.

'Aha, you don't deny being interested then?'

Jess tutted. 'Being pregnant doesn't give you a licence to matchmake everyone on Scilly and behave like my mum.' Jess tried to sound stern but she was amused by Maisie's efforts even if she had found it excruciating to be thrown together so obviously at the time.

Maisie linked arms with her and gave a gleeful, wicked smile. 'Oh, it gives me a licence to do anything I want. Not that anyone could ever match your mother ... Now, he clearly travels here regularly from what we've already deduced. I'll see if Patrick can find out more from Hugo.'

'Patrick won't want to ask Hugo, will he?' said Jess, knowing the fraught relationship between Patrick and Hugo Scorrier. Even though they were cousins, Hugo had – understandably – not been impressed when Patrick had turned up out of the blue to claim ownership of Petroc. The island lay on the opposite side of the channel to Maisie's pub and they had to meet to discuss business but were hardly on friendly terms.

'He might make a few enquiries. If you're interested, that is,' said Maisie.

They'd reached the harbour now. Jess thought there were definitely more tourists around and once the Islander started its services at the weekend, Hugh Town would be bustling with life. Spring was here ... had it really been almost six months since she'd split up with Adam? Time seemed to race by quickly when your whole life was governed by the changing seasons.

Jess forced a smile for Maisie. 'Don't trouble Patrick for my sake. I doubt this new guy is staying more than a couple of days and he probably has a glamorous Italian wife and a brood of ludicrously attractive bambini running around his villa in the Abruzzo.'

'It would be fun to find out anyway,' said Maisie.

Jess spotted half a dozen people she knew queuing by the ticket office for the boats to the smaller islands and several more working on the quay. A handsome Italian wouldn't stay mysterious for long. 'Yes. Although the rumour mill will already be white hot,' she said.

'In that case, we'd better make sure we have the full facts. I'll message you or call if I hear anything. Have a safe trip back to the farm and I'll see you very soon.'

With a hug, Maisie walked off to meet Patrick in one of the coffee shops in Hugh Town, while Jess got a move on to untie her boat and set off for St Saviour's. In her world, time and tide really did wait for no man – or woman.

Chapter 12

It was a toss-up as to whether Maisie got the lowdown on the Italian first or Jess heard it on the Scilly grapevine as the rumour mill went into overdrive. Maisie won and the very next day was on the phone with everything she'd gleaned from one of the Petroc staff who'd dropped into the Driftwood Inn. As Jess had suspected, Patrick didn't have a clue about the newcomer and was more interested in how Will was getting on with the *Athene* and preparing the Gull Island gig ready for the island championships over the Bank Holiday weekend in May.

'He *is* Italian by birth. No surprise there, then,' said Maisie gleefully down the phone. 'His name is Luca Parisi but he's been living in London for ages, hence the accent. Most importantly, he appears to be single, although I haven't had that confirmed yet. The bad news, I'm afraid, is that he's only here for a few days, according to my source, because he's involved in some kind of marketing initiative with Hugo. Sorry I don't have more positive news.'

'You can't win them all,' joked Jess, enjoying Maisie's attempts to play Sherlock and Cupid at the same time. She hadn't really expected 'Luca' to stay or even to ever speak to him again, but he had been on her mind in the last twenty-four hours more often than she had expected. That was probably down to curiosity more than anything else. Adam was on her mind about fifty times more.

*

However, even Adam took a back seat over the weekend when a fog rolled in during the early hours of Saturday morning. The forecasters said it could last for days and on Saturday, all the planes to and from Scilly were grounded. There were never any flights on Sunday, so the farm was obviously used to that, but if none went out on Monday, a nightmare scenario could develop. Prolonged fog wasn't a great scenario at the best of times, but couldn't have come at a worse time with Mother's Day just around the corner. Orders were meant to be on their way to wholesalers and customers the length and breadth of Britain throughout the following week. Each bloom had been specifically nurtured to be at its best for the day itself, so Will activated the contingency plan. The picked blooms were carefully packed and stored into every corner of the fridge to prevent them from opening too soon, ready for dispatch the moment flying resumed. Fingers crossed that it did …

Jess said a silent prayer when strong winds blew in on Monday morning and cleared the mists sooner than forecast. Over the next few days, everyone busted a gut to make sure the backlog of orders was sent on its way, with endless trips to and from the quay and St Mary's.

By the end of the week, all of the orders for Mother's Day had left the farm and the exhausted crew were able to breathe. Jess took herself off for a long hot bubble bath and a large glass of wine and her thoughts turned to the handsome Luca again.

She allowed herself a few moments to wonder 'what if?' It was pure fantasy, but she felt she had to make herself think about relationships after Adam. It wasn't healthy to imagine she'd never meet anyone else. Maisie and her mother had urged her to get out and meet new people, even if they were only passing through, and Luca Parisi was easy on the eye. She shook her head. He was far *too* easy on the eye, and if he flew back and forth between London and Petroc Resort on business, he probably led the sort of glamorous life that meant he wouldn't be interested in a flower farmer. Besides, he was probably long gone by now and back in the metropolis.

*

Everyone heaved a huge sigh of relief when Saturday came and the staff took a well-earned weekend off. Jess and Will took their mother out for lunch on St Mary's on Sunday. She thought of Gaby who had flown home on Friday morning to spend Mother's Day with her family, and also to mark the first anniversary of Stevie's death. Jess felt desperately sorry for them all and wondered how they were coping, but she said nothing to anyone else, to respect Gaby's privacy.

On Monday morning, Jess needed to sort out the quarterly

VAT return so she took advantage of the lull to make a start, even though it was her least favourite task. She might treat herself to an afternoon at the St Saviour's hotel spa once she'd cracked this bloody VAT. She deserved it after their manic week. There was only Easter to get through in a few weeks' time and then the main narcissi season would be over.

'Arghh!' She threw up her hands in frustration when the figures she'd entered into the spreadsheet vanished inexplicably. Oh God, that was all she needed after all her hard work. After trying to recover the figures to no avail, panic had set in. She'd have to get the office manager, Lawrence, to help sort it when he came back from his trip to the flower farm co-operative on St Mary's.

'All things bright and bee-oo-tiful …'

Jess glanced up from the desktop. There was only one person who sang hymns on their way to work and it wasn't the vicar. Seconds later, the new post lady, Carmel, laughed and stepped inside, breathing heavily after carting the mail bag from the van to the office. Carmel brought the regular post from the airport to the smaller 'off islands' like St Saviour's. It still felt strange to greet a new face every morning instead of Adam.

'Morning, Jess. How's it going? Busy time? Those fields are glorious.'

'They are. With Mother's Day just finished and Easter coming around, it's pretty hectic. How about you? Enjoying your new round?'

'It's a contrast from Walthamstow, that's for sure.'

'You're not finding it too quiet?'

'Being on Scilly still seems like a holiday at the moment. The kids think so too, even though they're at school. They can't get over being able to run down to the beach straight from the school gates and they think it's the coolest thing ever that my round includes a boat and a quad bike. I must admit it's a bit of a shock that they turn off the street lights at night, but at least the kids can see the stars. I'm not sure they knew there were any in London.'

Jess laughed, remembering the wonder of some of the seasonal workers at the dark and beautiful night skies on St Saviour's where there were no street lights at all. Carmel and the rest of the Cooke family had moved to Scilly from the East End after Adam had moved away.

'I've a bundle for you today,' said Carmel, sliding the bag from her shoulder and onto the floor. A couple of the letters spilled out and Jess helped her pick them up. Jess handed the post to Carmel but kept a couple. 'I think you missed this one. It's for Gaby Carter.'

'Oh, thanks,' said Carmel. 'I'm still finding my feet here. Here's the rest of the farm mail.'

She handed a stack of mail secured with an elastic band to Jess. It held a mix of manila and pastel-coloured envelopes, plus junk mail.

'Do you have time for a cuppa? There's one in the pot,' Jess said. She hoped that some miracle with the VAT spreadsheets would happen while she took a breather, or that she'd come up with a way to recover them.

Carmel hesitated then said, 'If it's made, I'd love a very quick one. Milk and one sugar, please.'

123

Jess poured out a mug of tea, added milk and a spoon of sugar and handed it to Carmel who sipped it with a sigh of pleasure. Jess had seen Adam unloading the mail boat many times and dragging the trailer of post up the slipway to his van, so she knew it was hard work and Adam was twice Carmel's size and fifteen years younger. While Carmel ate a homemade flapjack brought in from the island café, they chatted about how she was settling in to her new life.

'I hope you're happy with the deliveries. Adam left big shoes to fill,' said Carmel.

Jess had heard this more than once from people all over the island. 'It's sometimes nice to have different shoes,' she said, wondering if Carmel had heard that she and Adam used to be an item. It was possible that the new post lady didn't know yet, which suited Jess.

'He *was* very popular,' Carmel said, a little unsurely.

'Yes, but you're doing a great job. I hope you'll stay. We could do with some new faces around here,' said Jess, guessing that Carmel must have found it more difficult to adjust to island life than she let on. Adam had found it a challenge at first too, he'd once admitted to Jess. She found herself wondering where he was now, and what he was doing. Was he working up in Cumbria?

'I plan on giving it my best shot and, anyway, we've burnt all our bridges. This has to work.' Carmel took a bite of flapjack and Jess sipped her tea. When she'd finished the cake, Carmel's broad smile was back in place. 'I need to get on with my round, but can I use your loo first?'

'Course you can.'

Carmel picked up her bag. 'I'll collect your mail now and see you tomorrow.'

'Thanks.'

After Carmel had left, Jess shut the door and separated the staff post from the Godrevys' family and business mail. At the bottom of the pile, there was a white envelope addressed by hand to *Jess Godrevy, Flower Farm, Scilly,* with *Personal* scrawled in the top left-hand corner and underlined so strongly that the ballpoint had almost pierced the paper.

It was Adam's handwriting.

Her heart almost jumped out of her chest. She pulled out two folded sheets of paper.

Dear Jess,

I'm sorry I've left it so long to send this letter. I've written and rewritten it so many times. I've thought about sending it almost as many times too, but I think I owe you some explanation for why I left. I ought to have said this stuff to you face-to-face, but please believe me when I say things have been difficult for me. I can't explain any more than that, but I swear, I've tried to handle things better but leaving seemed the only solution. There are things I have to sort out at home. Things only I can deal with and that I can't share for all kinds of reasons. I don't want you to take them on too.

If the good times we've had make you smile, then remember them. I'm so sorry there have been only bad ones over the past few months. It tore me apart to leave and I only hope that it's not as bloody awful for you and that, somehow, I'm wrong about the way you feel for me.

I <u>never ever</u> set out to hurt you. Knowing that I might be causing you pain makes me feel sick to my stomach. There's no one else. I can at least reassure you of that.

Unlike me, you're strong, so I know you'll get through this and I hope you'll find someone who deserves you a lot more than I ever have.

Adam x

She read it three more times and felt even more shaken and confused than before. Why had he sent it to her now? Over the past months, she'd longed for some explanation, but now she had the letter, it left far more questions than it explained.

Tears wet her face but Jess hastily wiped them away as she heard Lawrence outside the door, whistling as he crossed the yard. He didn't come into the office which was a relief but she still needed him to help with the VAT. Shrugging on her fleece as she left, she hurried out to speak to him and take the mail down to the fields. She might feel crap, but she could at least bring a smile to people's faces by delivering the post in person.

Chapter 13

On Monday morning, Gaby had gone straight back to work after getting the early morning plane from Stansted to Newquay and on to Scilly. Her parents had been delighted to see her, of course, and Carly had made the effort to come home too. They'd all visited Stevie's grave and laid some flowers, which Gaby herself had taken over on the plane. These first 'landmark' occasions – Stevie's birthday, the anniversary of his death, Mother's Day – were tough and emotional times when his loss was felt even more keenly. Some people had said that such moments would become easier to deal with but Gaby wasn't sure. Look at how she'd dealt with his birthday: by working herself into the ground and ending up in an awkward situation with Will.

Jess had generously let her have the morning off to get home so she planned on working extra hard to make up for the lost time. She hadn't been in the fields more than half an hour, however, when she spotted her boss making straight for her, with a bundle of letters in her hand.

She'd seen the postwoman arrive so guessed she had some mail. Jess nodded and smiled to some of the workers, but knowing her boss well by now, Gaby thought the smile hid a lot of pain. Gaby had seen Will talking to Jess in the fields on Valentine's Day and had heard on the grapevine that it was the day Adam Pengelly had flown off. Poor Jess. She and Adam had seemed so happy the previous August when they'd collected her from the airport. He seemed like a decent bloke and Jess was obviously loved-up at the time, but who knew what had happened between them since.

Gaby had heard plenty of rumours lately. The theories varied from feasible to plain nuts. He'd met another woman. He'd met another man. He'd inherited a lot of money and wasn't interested in Jess or the flower farm now he was rich. He'd gambled all his cash away and had fled because he was in debt. Gaby's personal favourite was that Adam had been forced to go into a witness protection scheme while he testified in a postal fraud trial.

The witness protection theory seemed to have taken particular root for some reason, but Gaby thought that was too far-fetched even for St Saviour's. Personally, she figured it was none of anyone's business, though she couldn't help but listen to the gossip. Even if she'd wanted to pry, although Jess was becoming a friend as well as a boss, Gaby definitely didn't know her well enough to intrude on her personal life. She also knew how it felt to want to keep her personal life private.

She tried to look cheerful as Jess reached her, holding out a bundle of pastel-coloured envelopes. Were Jess's eyes red or was Gaby imagining it?

'Hello, Gaby. Carmel's been. I've got some post for you.'

Jess's voice was suspiciously perky but Gaby was grateful

to have the post. 'Thanks,' she said, feeling a warm glow as she took the envelopes. She recognised the writing on all of them. Although she'd brought her close family cards and gifts back to Scilly with her, she was thrilled that her old mates back home had remembered too.

'It's my birthday,' she said, thinking out loud.

Jess's brow creased. 'Today? I'm sorry, I didn't know …'

'Please don't worry. Actually, it's tomorrow and I was sort of wondering if you'd like to come to the pub after work? A bunch of us are getting the jet boat to the Driftwood and I know you're friends with Maisie, so I thought you might like to come along?'

Jess hesitated. 'Um … tomorrow. I – I don't know. I think I'm coming down with something.'

Gaby looked closer at Jess and was taken aback. With her rosy cheeks and glossy nut-brown hair tied back with a scarf, she'd always reminded Gaby of the glamorous actresses in fifties movies. Today, she was pale with dark smudges under her eyes. She obviously hadn't slept well and looked like she was carrying the weight of the world on her shoulders and she looked skinnier than she did last August too.

'Are you OK?' Gaby asked gently.

'Yes.' Jess smiled. 'Why wouldn't I be?'

'You look rather peaky,' she blurted out.

Jess narrowed her eyes. 'Peaky?'

Gaby could have kicked herself. 'Well, you did say you thought you were coming down with something … I'm sorry.'

Jess groaned. 'Don't be. I'll live, but I don't want to spread my germs round. This cold is making me a right old grumpy-pants.

129

Look, I'd really love to come to the pub if I'm not a germ factory. Honest.'

Jess's smile was back in place but Gaby was still wary. She genuinely liked her boss but wasn't totally convinced by the 'cold' excuse, and usually when people added 'honest' onto the end of their statements, it was because they weren't being entirely honest in the first place. However, Jess didn't need any more negativity, so Gaby decided to keep up the cheery attitude. She'd already got a reputation as some sort of posh Girl Guide/plucky Enid Blyton type, so why not live up to it?

'That would be absolutely lovely. We're going in the fast jet boat at six. Meet at the gig sheds on the beach?'

Jess nodded. 'Great. I'll be there if I can ...' She touched Gaby's arm briefly. 'What about you? How was the weekend?'

Gaby almost lost it. Her throat was thick with emotion at Jess's sympathetic gesture. 'Mum and Dad were happy I went home. I'm so glad I did and it's another milestone we've got through. That's about all I can say. Thanks for letting me have some extra time off.'

'It's the least I could do.'

'Will didn't ask why, did he?'

'No. He just assumed you went home for Mother's Day and he knows you can hardly fly back on Sunday when we're all cut off.' Jess gave a small smile. 'Besides, he was far too caught up with working on the *Athene* with his mates.'

Gaby nodded, glad that she wouldn't have to discuss her weekend with Will, but slightly disappointed he'd obviously had no interest in her absence. Oh well, she couldn't have it both ways.

Jess moved a few yards away, examining some of the blooms to check the quality.

Meanwhile Gaby spotted Will at the top of the field, deep in conversation with Lawrence. Unless it was raining hard or unusually cool, Will could be found in all weathers in various old tatty T-shirts and jeans that had faded to muted greys and blues, with frays and tears at the knees and other places. Sometimes you could see hairs on his thighs through the threads. The pair with the tear at the top where his thighs met his bottom were her favourite – and don't even get her started on his Hunters.

She sighed to herself. The shelter incident had done nothing to cool her passion, even if relations between them were chillier than before.

Gaby had a sudden impulse. Which almost always turned out to be a bad idea, but she couldn't help herself. She trotted up to Jess.

'Oh, Jess …'

Jess lifted her head from the flowers and frowned. 'Everything OK?'

'Yes. Fine. It's only that I thought, if you happen to see Will, which you're bound to, him being your brother – ha ha – can you pass on an invitation to the pub? It's probably not his thing and he's always busy, but if he fancies a night out …' Gaby left the sentence trailing, fearing she'd rattled on too much already.

Jess's lips tilted briefly. 'I'll mention it to him, but I think he has rowing training with the men's crew so I wouldn't get your hopes up.'

'Oh. OK. No biggie.' She bit down her disappointment. She definitely wasn't expecting anything from Will after his brusque behaviour that night, so why had she even bothered asking? She'd have bet Will wouldn't come along. Even if it was her birthday and everyone else from the flower farm she'd worked with for the past six months was going along to the Driftwood. Ever since their passionate moment in the barn, he'd avoided spending more than the absolute minimum of time alone with her.

Jess checked her watch. 'It's coffee break time soon. You might see Will up at the packing sheds and you can ask him yourself.'

'Maybe. Thanks for the cards. I'll take them back to my room at break time.' Gaby pushed the cards down the large pocket at the front of her dungarees which she wore over a T-shirt with an oversize lumberjack shirt. Her outfit, which was practical and warm for working outdoors, was a source of amusement to Will, who'd managed to defrost sufficiently to ask her when she was going to chop down a tree. At least the mild weather today meant she'd been able to ditch the lumberjack hat with its fold-down earflaps, although she didn't care if Will did tease her. It had kept the cutting wind from freezing her ears on many days and was only one of the ingenious types of headgear that everyone – including Will – employed to keep themselves warm on cold days.

After work, Gaby spent the evening in the staff house, enjoying the preparations and chat about her birthday party at the Driftwood. The jet boat would take them over immediately after work, leaving enough time for a lightning-quick shower and change. It was early, but the tides were right and that dictated the evening out.

Even without Will, Gaby was looking forward to it. Nights out on Scilly were very low-key compared to London and even to Cambridge. Although Hugh Town had several pubs, the nearest clubs and cinemas were forty miles away across the Atlantic in Penzance, so home-grown entertainment and meet-ups with mates were doubly important. The hard work in the fields sent Gaby off to sleep quickly, as it usually did, even with the excitement of a party to look forward to.

Fortunately, Jess seemed to have brightened up a little by the next day when she called Gaby into the office at lunchtime. She opened a filing cabinet and handed over a shiny bottle bag and a card. 'It's from all of us,' she said.

Gaby ripped open the envelope and pulled out the card, which had a funny meerkat on it. It was signed from Jess, Will and Anna, all in Jess's handwriting. It made her glow inside to think that the Godrevys had sent her a card, even if it had probably all been Jess's doing. She found a bottle of fizz from the island vineyard in the bag, together with a bag of chocolate truffles from the deli on St Mary's. 'Oh, these are lovely. I'll enjoy sharing them later. I didn't expect anything. Thanks so much. This is a wonderful surprise.'

'No problem. You're pretty much a fixture now,' said Jess cheerfully.

Gaby put the bottle on the desk. 'Am I, really?'

'You've been here longer than most.'

Gaby hadn't realised she was starting to be considered as one of the 'OAPs' among the temporary seasonal workers. She wasn't quite sure how she felt about this 'accolade' as the flower farm was only meant to be a temporary stepping stone on her bigger adventures. 'Well, thanks. I'll go and drop these in my room. Will I see you later at the party?'

Jess nodded. 'Definitely. I'm not feeling grotty like I did yesterday. That cold decided to bother someone else.'

Gaby resisted the urge to ask any more about Will, and had decided not to bother to ask him to the party herself and risk being rebuffed in person. She took her present to join the others back in her quarters. Some parcels had arrived for her that morning, and she opened them along with the gifts from her parents, from Carly and a couple from mates from uni, plus a fresh bundle of cards. One present was missing, of course: Stevie's. She pulled out the *Gardens of the World* book again and looked at the inscription, even though she knew it would make her cry. It was a cruel twist of fate that her own birthday was so very close to the anniversary of his death so she was surely allowed a few tears today.

A few hours later, she, Jess and the rest of her workmates were rushing along the concrete track that served as the island's only road, and down the steep slope to the quay. Laughing and chatting, they waited for the jet boat, although Gaby couldn't help the odd sneaky glance to see if Will might put in a last-minute appearance after all.

They were all muffled in thick coats and hoods against the stiff wind. After all, it was still only March, and it was going out like the proverbial lion rather than the lamb. Gaby wrinkled her nose in apprehension at the choppy swell while she boarded, then gritted her teeth and held on tightly to the rope around the edge of rib. The rigid inflatable boat had a small cabin, but that was only to provide shelter for the skipper and crew. The rest of the passengers had to brave the elements. Spray hit her face as they bounced over the waves like a stone skipping along. She'd have to redo her make-up when they got to the pub, along with the rest of the girls.

There was a patch of open sea as they rounded the headland between St Saviour's and Gull Island that was out of the shelter of either island. Whitecaps tumbled over the surface and the wind howled. She braced herself and held on tight. Some people let out little shrieks as the boat bucked like a fairground bronco, but Gaby knew what to expect, even if she hated the rough ride, she wasn't going to let on how much. There was no way you could live and work on Scilly without using the sea, unless you intended to fly straight into St Mary's and never step off the island.

The time to worry, Jess had told her when she'd 'enjoyed' her first trip on the jet boat, was when Jerry, the grizzled skipper, started handing out the life jackets. At the moment, Jerry was smoking a pipe with one hand and chatting to Lawrence while also steering the boat, so things must be OK.

The sun was setting as they moored up alongside the Gull Island jetty and a few minutes later, they were squeezing into the tiny bar and warming themselves by the fire while Maisie and Patrick pulled the pints and handed round glasses of wine. The rich aroma of curry spices filled the bar area, making Gaby's stomach rumble.

Jess became a different person when she met up with Maisie. Her eyes lit up and she laughed out loud. Maisie was now almost twenty weeks into her pregnancy and on her slight frame, her bump was now visible. Gaby noticed Jess lay her hand on Maisie's stomach and let out a little squeal of delight, presumably, Gaby thought, because the baby had moved. Gaby had absolutely no idea when babies first started moving, but she was happy to see her boss in a sunnier mood.

Inevitably, she recognised most of the handful of regulars in the bar, although they were outnumbered by her own workmates: Lawrence and Becca from the office, Natalia and Robbie, the ginger guy who Gaby had thought wouldn't make it past the first day. One bloke had left from the rookie group, but everyone else had stuck it out. And so what if Will wasn't here? It wasn't often she had the chance of a night out, and she knew Stevie would certainly have made the most of it. She swallowed a lump in her throat, thinking of their final celebration together at home and later at the local pub. She gulped down the rest of her wine, trying not to get maudlin.

'Another drink?' Natalia pointed to her glass with a smile.

'Thanks.'

While Gaby started on her second glass of wine and chatted with her mates, Jess helped Maisie and her mum, Hazel, serve up the curries. Someone put on some music, old-school pop, and the noise levels rose as people got stuck into their kormas and jalfrezis, laughed and drank.

Jess joined her table. 'Enjoying yourself?' she asked. Pleased to have some time to chat away from work, Gaby made space for Jess on the sofa next to her.

'Yes. This curry is fabulous and Maisie looks well.'

Jess smiled as they both spotted Patrick kiss Maisie on the cheek. 'She is. Patrick too. I'm so happy for them.'

'You've known her a long time, haven't you?'

'Yes. Since we were at school. She was older when I started and I was homesick because the off-island children had to board on St Mary's. Maisie looked out for me in the first year until she left to do her A levels on the mainland. I spent two years at college in Penzance too, but I ended up back here when Dad left.'

'What about Will? Was he homesick at school?'

Jess blew out sharply. 'No. He couldn't wait to get away from the farm and have some adventures even if it was only on St Mary's.' Jess paused then added, 'School was tough at times because our parents' marriage was in trouble for years before Dad actually left.'

Gaby was surprised but pleased to be able to have a closer chat with her boss. 'I'm sorry about that,' she said, eager to listen now Jess had opened up.

'Thanks, but don't worry. Mum's much better off without him, even if she didn't think so when it first happened. It was hard work because Will and I were only twenty, but we've managed OK and the business has really taken off. Will found it hard at first ...' Jess stopped talking, clearly having caught sight of something behind Gaby. She raised her eyebrows. 'Well, well. Talk of the Devil.'

Chapter 14

Gaby's heart missed a beat but she didn't turn around.

'Is there any curry left or have you greedy lot eaten it all up?' said Will, appearing at the side of her table. It was funny to see him in the middle of his rugby/rowing mates. He was six feet tall, but next to the rest of the gang, some of whom were huge and had very little neck to speak of, Will was one of the slightest. He was in clean black jeans and his wellies had been replaced by chunky Timberland boots. His hair had been tamed a little and he was sporting designer stubble ... and was that a chunky new sweater under the waxed jacket? His rugged 'going out' look was so sexy that Gaby's mouth went dry. He held her eyes a split second longer than necessary and then grinned. 'Happy Birthday, Gaby.'

'Nice to see you made it,' said Gaby, trying to sound bored while still amazed to see him there.

'It's a coincidence. I didn't know I was invited.'

Jess gasped. 'Yes, you did. I mentioned it to you yesterday and you can't fail to have heard everyone else on the farm talking about it.'

'I suppose now you come to mention it, I might recall someone saying there was a curry night at the Driftwood.' There was a glint in his eye as if he'd planned to come along but Gaby was momentarily speechless. Why had he bothered to come if it was only to wind her up?

'Liar,' Jess said for him. She shook her head. 'He *did* know,' she told Gaby.

'How did you get here? Did you use one of the other jet boats?' Gaby asked him, knowing the Godrevys' boat had been tied up at the quay when they left.

'I got a lift with Javid after our rowing session. I was hoping to grab a lift home with you all.'

'No chance. We're almost full and you'd probably capsize us after you've wolfed down all the curry,' said Jess.

'Nice. Guess I'll have to swim then.'

Gaby smirked. 'I'd like to see that.'

'I bet you would,' Will murmured, that was directed at her alone. Jess didn't seem to have heard as Maisie had come over and was speaking with her. Will and Gaby met each other's eyes again for a moment before Will laughed and said to Maisie, 'So, is there any of that curry left? I could eat a horse after being out on the water.'

Maisie rolled her eyes. 'Ask my mum. She might possibly have saved you some in the kitchen.'

The moment had gone, but Gaby was unlikely to forget it. In those seconds, every other soul in the pub might have vanished. Will and Gaby were the only two people in the world, that look was so intense. He seemed to want to tell her something, or ask her something.

'Second helping?' Hazel Samson was by the table, with a shiny balti pot.

Gaby held up her hands in surrender. 'Erm. No, it was delicious but I think I'm stuffed.'

'I'll have it,' said Will.

'Pig.' Jess's attention was back on her brother.

'Only because I've been working so hard,' he said indignantly.

Patrick and Javid, who owned the Gull Island campsite, joined Will and soon Gaby was forgotten again as their talk turned to rowing and which teams would be their biggest rivals in the forthcoming championships.

Gaby did her best to finish the rest of the curry, even though her appetite had strangely deserted her since her 'moment' with Will across the crowded pub. Had the glance they'd shared meant anything at all? She'd probably read way too much into it.

'Attention, everyone! I know you're enjoying yourselves, but settle down. I've got an announcement to make.' Maisie's plea for quiet gradually hushed the hubbub. Gaby craned her neck, trying to see what was happening over the heads of people obscuring the bar. 'Oohs' and 'aahs' rang out and then people stood aside and a space opened up.

Maisie's mother, Hazel, walked out of the pub kitchen carrying a triple-layer chocolate cake topped with buttercream rosettes, chocolate stars, candles and sparklers.

'Happy Birthday, Gaby!' Maisie called and someone started singing 'Happy Birthday to you …'

Gaby's jaw was on the floor. She hadn't expected this.

Everyone sang and then there was a deafening round of applause. She was laughing but also felt like crying. It was her first birthday away from home since Stevie had died. Birthdays were a big deal at home and whoever's turn it was – Gaby, Carly or Stevie – was expected to come home for a big family dinner. Although she'd seen her family only recently, it still felt strange to be without them.

Her new friends from the farm and around the islands were funny and kind, but she suddenly realised they were all from a life post-Stevie. He would never meet them, get to know Will or tease her about him ...

His words in the garden book came back to her.

'Don't dream your life, live your dreams.'

Making a new life was necessary and healthy, but why did it have to be so painful sometimes? Why did sorrow come back to bite you in the midst of happy moments?

Gaby hid the pain with a cheesy grin while Maisie put the cake in front of her. 'Who? Moi?' she said.

Jess nudged her. 'Blow out the candles then!'

'Yeah! Come on, Gaby! All in one go!' the calls came from her mates.

'If you can manage it.' That was Will. The teasing smile was back on his face but his eyes were also intent on her. He was as infuriating as he was sexy. Gaby scrunched her toes up with lust and annoyance, determined to meet his challenge if it killed her.

There wasn't room for twenty-eight candles on the cake, but it felt like there were dozens stuck in the oozing chocolate icing. The heat almost scorched her face: that cake was a mini volcano. She took a deep breath in and blew out with all her might. Cheers echoed round the bar and there was a round of applause.

Damn it. One candle stubbornly refused to be extinguished.

'Oh, what a shame!' Will called in a delighted voice.

Gaby blew on it sharply and, finally, the flame faltered and died. More cheers and clapping rang out. Patrick approached her table with a tray of flutes filled with bubbly.

'Happy Birthday,' he declared.

'Are these for me?' Gaby asked in surprise. Everyone was doing their best to make her birthday special.

'There's a glass for everyone in your party. It's local fizz from the St Saviour's vineyard,' said Patrick in his Aussie accent. 'And though I hate to admit it, it's really not bad for a Pommie wine.' He laughed.

'This is very generous of you,' said Gaby, before realising she might have made a huge assumption. 'Oh, I mean, not that you ought to give it away. I'll pay for it.'

'No need for that. The cake was arranged by your mates from the farm. The fizz is a gift from a friend.'

Gaby lowered her voice. 'Who? Jess?'

Patrick winked. 'I'm not at liberty to say.'

'You tease.'

'Enjoy.' Patrick handed a glass to Gaby and went back to the bar where Maisie had poured out another tray of bubbly. Gaby could guess who'd bought the bubbly: despite the laid-back surf dude appearance, Patrick was a wealthy man known for helping out the islanders financially. It was typical of him to make the gesture.

As Maisie took away the cake to be cut, Gaby was congratulated by her friends and they asked her about her plans for Easter. Thinking of her family at Easter without Stevie made her suddenly sad. During a lull in the conversation she found herself staring into her wine glass.

Jess leaned in towards her ear. 'Missing home?'

Gaby's stomach flipped. She appreciated Jess's guess that today might be bittersweet.

She toyed with the stem of the glass. 'A little bit. I spoke to Mum and Dad earlier today.' She took a large sip of bubbly.

'How are they doing?' Jess asked.

'Pretty well considering ... or at least, they *say* they're OK and as for my sister ... Carly's always "absolutely fine and incredibly busy". She has a job as an accountant with a City tax firm.'

Jess blew out a breath. 'Sounds high-powered.'

'It is.' Gaby smiled. 'Carly thinks I've never had a proper job. She thinks a PhD in poetry is "as much use as a chocolate teapot" and I'm afraid she doesn't consider working at a flower farm to be work either. I think she imagines me floating around sniffing blooms and writing odes to nature.'

'She should come and try it, eh? Anyway, you've had plenty of work experience before you came here. I've seen your CV, remember? And I took up your references and that's how I knew you'd be a hard worker.'

'Yes, but working in a garden centre and a flower farm isn't a "career" to Carly. She was more impressed that I got a few hours supervising the undergraduates in my vacation, but that wasn't enough to support me during my PhD.' Gaby sipped the wine again. It really was delicious and hard to believe it had been produced half a mile from the flower farm.

'It's a wonder you got your degree at all, with all those extra jobs.'

'I wonder that too, sometimes.' Gaby laughed. 'One night when I'd been shifting growbags all morning in the garden centre, researching in the library in the afternoon and doing a late shift on reception, I drifted off on my bicycle riding home in the small hours.'

'Ouch!' Jess sympathised.

'Luckily it was only on the cycle bridge over the rail line so I didn't end up under a car, but I've still got the scars.' She pushed back the flared sleeve of her top and showed Jess the white slash across her elbow. 'But at least I'm in one piece.'

Jess picked up the bottle and topped up Gaby's glass. 'You've earned this. Sorry if I made you think about hard times on a happy day.'

'No. It's fine. Not many people know about it and I don't mind being reminded of Stevie. Unlike my sister, he'd love the idea of me working in all weathers in the back of beyond. Sorry, not that the flower farm is the back of beyond. It's beautiful.'

Jess shook her head. 'No. You're right, it *is* the back of beyond, but maybe that's why you came here?'

Gaby ran a nail along the tabletop. 'I guess it was. My brother was a big believer in following your dreams, even if that meant taking off with his mates at the drop of a hat.' Gaby decided not to share that the motorbike was one of the ideas that her parents hadn't wanted him to pursue. If only she hadn't become involved in *that* family row, Stevie might be here now ...

Jess was talking again, for which Gaby was grateful. Her thoughts were turning toxic and she didn't want to spoil the mood.

'The trouble is, a lot of people rock up here thinking they can escape from the world, and you can to some degree but troubles don't go away on a small island, they can be intensified,' said Jess, fiddling with the stem of her glass.

'And you find yourself under the microscope?' said Gaby.

'Exactly. There's no real escape. You can't disappear into the crowd and when things go wrong, in business or families, the fallout can affect everyone like ripples in a pool.'

Was Jess referring to Adam – or Will? Or even to her mother? Quite soon after arriving at the flower farm, Gaby had been told all the history of the Godrevys and how 'Roger ran off with a younger woman.' Was Jess warning her off Will, or merely reflecting on her own situation with Adam? Gaby wasn't sure.

There was a collective murmur of excitement and Gaby looked towards the door into the pub kitchen. 'Oh look. Here comes the cake.'

Maisie carried out a large platter piled high with slices of the cake. Despite having filled up on curry, most of the farm workers fell on it like gannets. Gaby licked vanilla buttercream from her fingers, enjoying the guilt-free indulgence after all her hard work outdoors. Her glass was topped up another couple of times by Jess before she excused herself to pop to the loo. The toilets at the Driftwood were situated in a lean-to that had to be accessed from the outside of the inn. Gaby was on her way to the ladies' when a red-faced guy she vaguely recognised barred her path.

'So, it's the lovely Miss Carter. Or should I say Ms?'

Gaby groaned inwardly. Jack Yarrow occasionally worked on some of the inter-island boats, when he wasn't hanging around the island pubs, and while she didn't have much to do with him, he had a reputation for being a pain in the bottom. Although he was only around Will's age, he had the jowly features and spreading belly of someone much older: not to mention a brain the size of a gnat. Probably other bits to match, thought Gaby, though he swaggered around if he was Ryan Gosling's hotter younger brother.

'Hi Jack,' said Gaby.

'Or, being accurate, maybe I should call you Doctor Gabriella.' He leered at her and she rolled her eyes. He was clearly drunk.

'Gaby will do and if you don't mind, it's actually pretty chilly out here and I'd like to go back inside.'

Ignoring her reply, he let out a whistle. '*Doctor* Gabriella Carter. I'm impressed. Not just a pretty face, then. Make that a beautiful face. Cute nose too. Actually.'

She smiled politely, resisting the urge to tell him she hadn't spent eight years at uni to impress Neanderthals like him with her nose. He leaned close enough for her to feel the heat of his breath on her face. God, she could pass out from the lager fumes.

'What's a hot babe like you doing in a place like this?' he said in a voice he clearly thought was gravelly and sexy but actually sounded like Russell Crowe with tonsillitis.

She took a step back and smiled sweetly while keeping her nostrils closed. 'Avoiding dinosaurs like you.'

'Ooh, touchy. Come on, don't play the ice maiden with me.' He laid his hand on her bare arm.

Growing annoyed now, she picked his pudgy fingers off her arm. 'Ice maiden? What is this? A prehistoric sitcom? And while you're living your 1970s fantasy, some Listerine wouldn't go amiss.'

She could have sworn his eyes crossed in puzzlement, but she'd already turned around and was on her way past him into the loo before he could think of a riposte.

When she came out, he was still hanging around the rear of the pub holding forth to a couple of regulars about his rowing prowess and how he could 'take anyone in Cornwall with one hand tied behind his back'.

Gaby wanted to walk right past him, but she didn't want any more hassle so instead she decided to return to the inn via the front door and the Driftwood's terrace.

She paused on the terrace before going back inside and took a deep gulp of the fresh air. The sun had now slipped behind Petroc Island on the western side of the channel opposite Gull Island. At almost eight p.m., some deep blue twilight was still visible on the far west horizon, but the sky to the east was velvet dark. Light spilled out onto the terrace from the lanterns of the pub. Twenty yards away on the beach, cigarette ends and a mobile glowed from a huddle of drinkers who'd taken their pints onto the sand. Gaby rubbed the goosebumps that had popped up on her forearms, wishing she'd brought her jacket out with her. Frosts were rare but the March evening was still pretty cool under the clear skies.

The beautiful scene had an 'edge of the world' feel, and made her feel very small and insignificant. She shivered again and thought of her parents in their Cambridge village where night would have fallen by now. They must miss her even though they'd told her to cut loose and 'enjoy her freedom' after the family had taken the agonising decision to turn off Stevie's life support. He'd slipped away without ever regaining consciousness, or even knowing what had happened to him. He'd left them with a sigh as quickly and silently as the twilight dissolving into darkness in front of her.

After weeks spent under the artificial lights of a hospital ITU, she'd been desperate to find sunlight and a place where she could immerse herself into new life, where things blossomed all year round and she was literally surrounded by nature. Like her poetry made real. She'd found comfort and a purpose here but she still couldn't escape the emptiness Stevie's absence brought.

'Gather ye rosebuds while ye may …'

The poet Robert Herrick's words slipped into her mind. Stevie wouldn't have had a clue Herrick had written them, or who the hell he was, but he'd have agreed with the sentiment: that you should make the most of every moment while you were able or there would come a time when your youth had gone and worse … The wind rose, chilling her face. She should go inside to the light and warmth and the extra bottle of bubbly waiting on her table. It was her birthday, after all.

'Gaby?'

Will's voice startled her from behind.

'Are you all right?'

Gaby sniffed and hastily wiped her nose before she faced him, hoping her hand wasn't snotty. That would be typical, wouldn't it, for Will to find her snivelling on the beach. That was all she needed. 'Course. Why wouldn't I be?'

It was dark but she could see his face, the shadows heightening his craggy good looks and the stubble on his jaw. She ached to reach up and kiss him. That brought a smile to her lips. Imagine his face! Imagine the shame. She smirked at the idea. That would mean she'd be on the first plane out of there. Even if Will recovered from the embarrassment, Gaby definitely wouldn't.

'Jack Yarrow been bothering you? I saw him giving you a hard time a few minutes ago.'

'No. I was fine and he wouldn't dare ...' She wondered exactly how long Will had been watching her. Had he seen her gazing mournfully out to sea and thought she'd been shaken up by Yarrow? 'Don't worry. I can handle him,' she said.

'I've no doubt you could handle anyone. I only meant that if he was bothering you or making a nuisance of himself, and you needed any help in getting rid of him, well, you know where I am.' He hesitated. 'If you need me ... you know what I mean ... As your employer, I don't like to see my workers hassled,' he said, almost tripping over his words.

'Your workers?' she repeated, dying to remind him of the fact that locking lips in the middle of the barn wasn't in either of their job descriptions.

'Staff, then. Team. I mean I'd have done the same for anyone,' he said, still awkward. 'Look. I didn't have to step in. You sent him packing on your own. But I'm speaking now as a mate.'

'*A mate?*' Gaby was amused. Will was clearly out of his comfort zone.

'Yeah. It's your welfare I'm concerned about.'

Will folded his arms. His biceps bulged. A hot shiver of lust shook her and she hugged herself. Why was he acting as if he cared, then trying to undercut his concern by claiming it was only an employer's looking out for his workers? Talk about giving out mixed signals ... but then, wasn't she doing exactly the same? Will could be infuriating but she wanted him too, a lethal combination when you were trying to act cool. Emboldened by the wine she'd drunk, she took a risk.

'Shall we walk a bit? I'm cold.'

'Here. Have this.'

Oh no. she hadn't intended him to offer his jacket. 'I'm fine.'

'Don't say no or I'll be very hurt,' said Will in a small voice.

Despite herself, Gaby laughed and tugged the jacket around her, feeling the warmth from his body infuse into hers. They started to walk down onto the beach in front of the Driftwood, making their way between the stones and bleached wood by the last remaining twilight. She stopped and gazed out over the channel towards the twinkling lights of Petroc Island.

'*She walks in beauty like the night*
Of cloudless climes and starry skies ...'

The words were out of her mouth without thinking then she winced inwardly, expecting Will to snort in derision or laugh at her.

'Who wrote that?' he asked.

Gaby glanced at him in surprise. 'Byron.'

'Right.' He scuffed the sand with the toe of his boot and started to mutter some lines.

'Full many a flower is born to blush unseen
'And waste its sweetness on the desert air.'

Gaby held her breath. Was she really on the beach, wearing Will's jacket and listening to him quote poetry?

'Or something like that,' he muttered, hands deep in pockets again, clearly cringing with embarrassment

'No. That's perfect. I didn't know you were into Thomas Gray,' she said.

He laughed. 'I'm not! I can't even remember the exact title. Something about a Country Churchyard. They're the only lines of poetry I know because of the flowers.' He stopped, scuffing the sand with his boot, a classic sign he felt ill at ease.

'Did you learn it at school?' Gaby asked gently, not wanting to discourage him.

He snorted. 'God no. Dad liked that poem. He read a lot and naturally anything about flowers stuck in his mind. He was – *is* – a cultured, thoughtful man. Too bad he saw fit to forget all his thoughtfulness and behave like a shit and leave us.'

He started walking again, as if he wanted to leave bad memories behind.

'I'm sorry,' said Gaby quietly.

'Yeah, it was a long time ago.'

It might have been, thought Gaby, and despite the brave

151

face, she guessed the memories were still raw in Will's mind and still affecting him now.

'I still don't understand what that poem means,' he said.

'What do *you* think it's about?' she asked, feeling slightly like she was coaxing more info from a nervous undergraduate.

'That there are a lot of ordinary people getting on with their daily lives in the face of all the odds. Doing things that don't get on the news. Working at their jobs, making things, art ...' he shrugged.

'Creating beauty. Like growing flowers? Heroes in their own quiet way?' she prompted, slightly taken aback by his sensitivity. Perhaps she shouldn't be. She'd often suspected deeper layers underlying the bluff farmer's exterior. Perhaps he'd had to suppress such 'softer' thoughts to be able to make a success of a hard business.

He laughed. 'I don't think that flower farming can be called heroic by any stretch of the imagination.'

'No. Possibly not, but you and Jess did save the farm against the odds. You kept it going in very tough times and now you have a thriving business and employ lots of people.'

'Lots is a relative term.'

'Don't hold your achievements that lightly. You both gave up a lot to keep a home and livelihood going for you and your mother.'

He shoved his hands in his pockets as they strolled along the beach. So close but not touching. 'It's no more than anyone else would have done. Anyway, we had no choice.'

'Then what you did is certainly heroic in its own way. I bet you missed out on a lot of stuff to stay here and run the place.'

'We're very fortunate to have a house and income to be able to stay here. I don't feel I've made sacrifices compared to many. Most people from the mainland think we live in paradise.'

'It is very beautiful but ...'

'But?' he gave a wry smile. 'I'm sensing a Gabriella bombshell here?'

'It can be quite claustrophobic at times. I know it's your world, but it is a very small one all the same. I should imagine that sometimes, you might like to break free and see what else is out there and not be tied to the business twenty-four seven.'

He looked at her. 'But I *am* tied to it. I'm rooted in the soil whether I want to be or not, so there's no point wishing otherwise.' He fell silent for a few seconds as if he was carefully considering his next words. 'While we're into analysing people's motivations, what are *you* really doing at the flower farm? With your education and your PhD?'

Her throat clogged with emotion. This was a moment when she might have told him about Stevie but she knew that if she let her real feelings out now she'd probably make a massive fool of herself. She didn't know Will well enough for that. Despite the kiss and the tentative steps towards each other this evening, she couldn't make herself that vulnerable. It was her birthday party, he was her boss and she'd had way too much wine. It wasn't safe to open up to him, even a little bit.

'I fancied a change. You must know how that feels, from what you've said about having no choice but to stay here and run the business.'

He laughed bitterly. 'Yes, perhaps I quite fancy swanning off round the world and dabbling in this and that here and there.'

Gaby fired up. 'Is that what you think I do? Swan off and dabble?'

'Not exactly. But poetry … I'm not sure what practical use it is in terms of making a living.'

'A moment ago, you seemed to be enjoying it,' she said, annoyed by his comment.

He smiled. 'That might have been the beer.'

'The *beer*?' Gaby felt as if he'd thrown a bucket of icy water over her. 'For a moment I thought that you might actually have a soul inside that horny-handed son of toil façade you like to cultivate, but obviously I was wrong. You know what you are sometimes, Will Godrevy?'

He folded his arms, challenging her again. 'I've a feeling that you're going to tell me.'

'You're a – a – pig-headed boor.'

His mouth formed an 'o'. 'Did you call me boring?'

'No. I said *boor*. B-O-O-R. Although you can have it both ways if you like.'

He folded his arms. 'Wow. Why don't you say what you really think?'

'I just did.' Gaby felt shaky but she wouldn't back down, even though she was already wishing the insults back. She wasn't sure he was genuinely annoyed but she regretted her insult. Oh, God … 'I'm going back inside.'

She didn't stay to see Will's expression and if he replied to her insult, she didn't hear it. Even as she walked back into

154

the pub, she was regretting her words which had touched a raw nerve. He'd had a point: Why *was* she really here?

How could she ever explain that to Will when she'd never voiced her deepest fears to a living soul? That's why she was here in a remote outpost surrounded by flowers. Not to heal herself but to run away. And, the dark monster that lurked in the darkest corner of her mind whispered: Stevie's accident was partly her fault.

Chapter 15

The bar was much quieter now, with only a few locals lingering around, chatting to Patrick. There was no sign of Jess, or any of the other farm workers apart from Natalia who was waiting by the front door.

The moment she spotted Gaby, Natalia knocked back the dregs of her lager and beckoned her over. 'Where've you been? The boat's here for us. Everyone's already gone to the quay.'

'Sorry. I was in the loo,' she said hastily, not wanting anyone to know the length of time she'd spent with Will.

'For so long? We need to leave.' Natalia frowned then handed over a white cardboard box to Gaby. 'Don't forget the rest of your cake.'

'Thanks!' she shouted to Maisie, Hazel and Patrick, but Natalia tugged at her arm and in seconds they were hurrying through the beer garden towards the track that led to the jetty. Natalia was bubbling with excitement and giggling over being chatted up by one of the St Saviour's locals who was twice her age.

'That was a great night,' said Natalia. 'Good food and a good laugh. Have you had a nice time?'

'Great,' said Gaby, holding onto the cake box and trying to

focus on everything that happened up until her row with Will.

'And Will's not all bad, is he?' said Natalia as the boat came in sight.

Gaby stumbled in her heels. 'What do you mean?'

'He bought all the champagne.'

'What? How do you know it was him?'

'I overheard Maisie and Jess talking about it … I think it was meant to be a secret but I guess it isn't now.' Natalia hiccupped. 'Whoops. That was the curry. Oh, Jess is freaking out. They'll go without us if we're not careful. Come on.'

She grabbed Gaby's arm and practically dragged her towards Jess who was waving her arms and shouting: 'Come on!'

Gaby's head swam as they slithered over the stones of the jetty to laughter from her waiting mates in the boat. She'd had too much to drink, but she could remember *exactly* what she'd said to Will. Buying champagne and knowing a bit of poetry didn't mean he wasn't a boor … But still. Oh, shit … she'd let him get to her and probably overreacted. She could blame the wine, of course, the wine that Will had paid for, but that would be a cop-out.

She practically fell into the boat, to sarcastic whoops from her friends and – oh God – a stony-faced glare from Will. Damn. She'd forgotten he'd asked to hitch a ride home. She kept stealing sneaky glances at him when she thought he wasn't looking at her. Their conversation on the beach had begun so promisingly. Where had it all gone wrong? Oh wait, he'd started the path downhill with his boorish remarks about poems … She'd called him a few choice names, but they were accurate at the time and she wasn't going to apologise.

157

Anyway, she was starting to feel too queasy to worry too much about the row. She tried to keep her eyes on the horizon, but even that was moving up and down with the boat. Every few seconds, the low dark shapes of other islands would come into view, along with a flash from the lighthouse at the western edge of the isles, before disappearing as the boat rose and fell.

She tried to distract herself by listening to a conversation that had started up about gig rowing and the Mixed team that St Saviour's were hoping to enter in the island championships when the *Athene* was seaworthy. With the noise of the wind, the roar of the engine and the smack of the hull on the waves, it was conducted in shouts. Although that didn't seem to matter after all the fizz. The cake box bumped around in her lap so she had to keep two hands on top of it and her stomach was jumping in time to the boat's lurches.

'We're still two people short for the Mixed boat,' Jess was telling Will. 'Even if I do row, we only have you, Natalia and Lawrence. I heard that Petroc's gig already has a waiting list of people who want to join.'

'That's because the resort on Petroc has dozens of staff who don't want to let their boss down; I wish my staff had the same attitude,' said Will. 'I'm prepared to row in the Men's crew as well as the Mixed, so I don't see why we can't find two more. I was thinking of asking Robbie; he turned up to the Men's practice and while he's a complete novice, he seemed keen. After all, the Mixed event is only a bit of fun.'

Jess snorted. '*Fun?*'

'What about you?' Natalia screeched down Gaby's ear.

'What about me?' said Gaby as the boat thumped its way over wave after wave. She hoped she could make it home without throwing up.

'You could join the St Saviour's gig crew. We need another female.'

'Great idea.' Lawrence leaned forward. 'Gaby?'

'No, I can't row.'

'Yes, but we *are* desperate,' said Will.

Under normal circumstances, Gaby would have been pissed off at Will's comment but she felt too nauseous to care.

'Gaby may be small, but she's strong and very fit. Isn't she, Will?' Natalia said, teasing him.

Gaby got her answer in before he could reply. 'However, you're not *that* desperate.' The boat lurched again and she rescued the cake box from flying off her lap. She wished her stomach would be tamed so easily.

'Oh, go on. You must have rowed in a boat when you were at Oxford. Everyone does, don't they?' Lawrence shouted from opposite. His fine blond hair was blowing so hard in the wind, Gaby was worried it might be ripped out.

'It was Cambridge, actually. I'm not big enough to row in an Eight and if I'd been a cox in the races I'd have probably caused a massive pile-up on the river.' Even if she'd had the courage to overcome her fear of the boat overturning, the after-race ritual of throwing the cox in the slimy river petrified her.

'In that case we're not even going to be able to raise a boat,' Will muttered.

'You'll find someone else,' said Gaby, standing firm. 'Trust me, you do not want me in that boat.'

159

Jess intervened. 'Look. Gaby's said she doesn't want to do it, so let's leave it at that.'

To her enormous relief, Gaby spotted the St Saviour's jetty ahead. The roar of the engine faded to a dull throb and the swell subsided as the jet boat nudged into the shelter of the quay. The sickly whiff of diesel made her stomach turn over, but they were back at the quay.

Everyone started to clamber out of the rib. Feeling light-headed, Gaby's foot slipped as she stepped off the bobbing boat in the semi-darkness. She swore and before she knew it, Will was pulling her onto the quay.

'Are you OK?' he said, letting go of her hand.

'Fine. Thanks. Too much wine,' she said, instantly regretting it when she remembered it was the wine *he'd* bought.

Everyone was laughing and talking around them so she didn't think they'd noticed her lose her footing, thankfully.

'It is your birthday,' he said. 'By the way, Jess is right. I don't want you to think I was forcing you to row. No one's going to make you do anything you don't want to, even if we might have to pull out of the race.'

Gaby searched his face. Was he trying to make her feel guilty again or trying to apologise in his own clumsy way?

'I accept that getting hot and sweaty with a bunch of us isn't your thing,' he added, with a glint in his eye.

Unsure if he was teasing – or if the hot and sweaty remark was an innuendo – Gaby decided to call his bluff. Now she was safely on dry land, she felt a lot more equal to the task. 'You don't think I could handle that?' she asked.

'I think you could handle the hot and sweaty part but like

I say, I don't want to be accused of bullying you – or of being a *boor* ...'

He was the most infuriating man on the planet and a fire of anger and pride shot through her. 'Look. As it obviously means *so* much to you and everyone else, I'll have a go, but I can tell you now that you'll regret it.'

His lips parted and she was delighted to see she'd taken him aback. His eyes met hers and he raised an eyebrow. 'Is that a threat or a promise?' he said in a low, husky tone that turned her on despite her annoyance – and her still queasy stomach.

'You decide, *Mr* Godrevy.'

They locked horns a second longer until Jess bustled up to them, preventing Will from getting his reply in.

'Are you two coming or not?' Jess demanded.

'Yes,' said Will and a triumphant smile tilted his mouth. 'And I have some good news. Gaby's agreed to row, so we have a team for the championships.'

Jess frowned. 'I thought you didn't want to do it? Are you sure? Will hasn't badgered you into it, has he?'

Gaby glared at Will. 'Believe me, Will could *never* make me do anything I didn't want to.'

Will's eyes gleamed wickedly. 'As if I'd try.'

Chapter 16

Almost as soon as she opened her eyes the next morning, Gaby's spat with Will flooded back to her in all its toe-curling glory. She'd called him a boor. Pig-headed might have been in there too.

Each of those words was accurate ... yet it didn't make it right that she'd flung them at her boss. *And*, she now knew, he'd bought the fizz for her birthday toast. *And* he'd wanted that to be a secret, which was both a nice thing to do and peculiar, considering he'd been trying to avoid showing her any special attention for the past couple of weeks.

Why had he wanted to keep his generosity under wraps? Because he didn't want her to know he cared?

Wow. Turning over the permutations felt like dragging a rake through her brain.

Dringgggg.

Ow. She reached out and bashed the cube alarm until it bounced off the table and onto the rug. It was time to get to work ... unless, of course, Will had sacked her.

She sank back onto the pillows.

Never mind, she was sick to death of flowers anyway.

162

Yeah, right. Who was she kidding? She'd never be sick of flowers or the farm. She loved working here and she loved Scilly. She liked her down-to-earth gang of mates, the glorious views and colours and scents. She liked Jess, and she still – arghhh – even 'liked' Will. Even though she hated him too.

She turned over and pulled the pillow over her head. Why did life have to be so bloody complicated? Why had she let her emotions get the better of her?

Wait a minute ... Will had had a lot to drink too. Would he even remember what she called him? With that flicker of optimism, she hauled herself out of bed and washed down two Nurofen with a black coffee. She was hauling herself into the shower when another of the evening's highlights came back to her: she'd agreed to join the St Saviour's gig team for the island championships.

*

Any hope that Will might have forgotten their sparring contest was extinguished by mid-morning when he strode down the field towards her, whistling and looking fresh as a daisy. His hair was a little tousled, there was a hint of stubble on his chin, but he was still infuriatingly gorgeous and clearly not hung-over – unlike her.

He stopped halfway to exchange a few words with Len, sending him into gales of laughter, which was disturbing in itself for Len's default setting was miserable git. Gaby didn't think she'd ever laugh again because her head might literally explode. The painkillers had helped for a short time, but now she needed more. She threw two more down her parched throat and glugged down some water from the flask in the pocket of her dungarees.

Will and Len were still laughing and joking. Were they talking about her? Would Will have shared their row with his mates? No. He'd never do that. She surprised herself by how definitely she answered her own question. Will was blunt and outspoken, but she'd never known him to be nasty or petty about anyone. He might join in general teasing and workplace banter but never talked about the other staff's personal lives when they weren't present.

They were probably sniggering at the prospect of her joining in the rowing championships, which Gaby had googled to make sure that in her semi-drunken state last night, Will and her friends hadn't been making the whole thing up.

She'd heard enough talk about the event during her time on Scilly but never having planned on being part of it, and not being interested in sports, had let the talk pass over her head. It was a deadly serious event if you were a gig rower, involving boats not only from the isles but the whole south-west of England. She'd only put herself forward out of pride and sheer bloody-mindedness – and because she hadn't been able to resist Will's challenge to get hot and sweaty. In the cold light of day, she might have read more into his comment than he'd meant.

Len had stopped laughing now and Will was coming straight for her. The pills would help numb her headache but her tum was still doing a gymnastic routine to rival Beth Tweddle.

'Morning.'

They both grunted the word at the same time. Great start.

'Will, I think I may – possibly – owe you an apology.' Gaby's voice came out as a squeak. It hurt her to say sorry, but she felt that one of them had to offer a crumb of peace. Since he was her boss, and she didn't want to leave yet, she had to be the one to back down first.

Will grunted again – whether he said yes, or thanks, she had no idea – then he peered at her. What the hell was up with him now?

'What is it?' she asked.

'Your jumper's on inside out.'

'What?' She pulled the fabric out of her dungarees and spotted the seams. 'Was that all you came to tell me?'

He shuffled around, unable to meet her eye. 'No. Um. I might have said some stuff that was out of order last night.'

Wow. Was that an apology? 'Ditto,' said Gaby quietly.

He prodded a clump of soil with the toe of his welly. 'Probably best not to rake it over.'

Gaby picked at a loose strand of wool on her jumper. 'Probably ...'

'And besides, we're not going to have to put up with each other much longer, are we?'

'Oh?' Shit, he *was* going to sack her or at least ask her to leave, she thought.

'I assume you're going to quit after the narcissi season ends next month ...'

Gaby was relieved that he hadn't said 'I assume you're going to quit *now*,' but put on a show of bravado. 'That's what it says in my contract.'

'That's what I said to Jess, that there was no point asking

165

you stay on for the summer to help with the farm work and chalets.' He lifted his eyes from the soil and searched her face hopefully.

'The chalets? I don't understand ...' Gaby genuinely thought she'd misheard his offer. Her stomach danced around again.

'We need some help with the holiday lets and uplifting the bulbs and Mum can always do with a hand with the goats. But I'm assuming you've made plans?'

'Swanning off round the world type plans, you mean?' she said, unable to resist a little light teasing.

A smile briefly hovered on his lips before he grunted. 'Yeah.'

Gaby recalled her vow to her parents to see the world and live life to the full in memory of Stevie. She hadn't planned on staying at the farm beyond her contract, so why would his offer change that? Suddenly she realised that, for some reason, she had been putting off her plans for after Scilly since that kiss with Will. The temptation to spend more time here with him was strong, but she also wanted to see the world, the gardens ... live her dreams before it was too late. One kiss shouldn't have changed that but somehow ...

She tried to stall for time. 'I *do* plan on going travelling at some point, but I haven't actually arranged anything specific *yet*, so I suppose I could stay on for a few months *if* you really need me to.' Her heart was beating very fast and she knew she was only adding fuel to the fire by tormenting him. 'But please, no goats. I'm not a goat person.'

He actually smiled. 'OK. No goats. Tell you what, think about it and let me have your answer as soon as you can, but I can put you on a senior picker's rate if money's an issue.'

Gaby almost passed out. An extended contract *and* more money? Had Will had a lobotomy? She didn't dare tease him further though. 'Um ... thanks. I'll give it serious thought and come back to you later.' However, she pretty much knew there would only be one answer.

'Good. We'd better both get back to work.'

He turned to leave but Gaby called out. 'Will. Thanks for buying the fizz at my party last night. I appreciate it.'

His head snapped up. 'Who told you about that?'

'One of the girls overheard Maisie and Jess talking about it.'

He blew out a breath. 'Shit.'

Gaby cringed that she'd managed to put her foot in it again just as things had eased between her and Will. 'Is it that bad that I found out?'

'No. But you can't keep anything to yourself round here. It's so bloody small and claustrophobic. I'm sick of it.'

Wow. Gaby was too surprised by this outburst to reply.

'I have to get back to the yard. The crate washer's up the spout again.' And with that he stalked off, hands shoved deep in his pockets. He hadn't even mentioned the one thing she'd expected him to: the rowing. Had he forgotten? Then she realised: he'd been having her on! Her shoulders slumped in relief. It had been a wind-up, thank God.

Yet alongside her amazement at being asked to stay on and the hope that she wouldn't have to row, Gaby was puzzled. What had prompted such a strong response to the fact she'd heard about the wine? Granted, he sometimes railed about various issues to do with the farm business: the market, the weather, et cetera, but they were always in the context of 'that's farming'. She'd never heard him say he hated island life itself or that he was sick of flower farming. He loved his mates and gig rowing and rugby and his family. What could have prompted him to suddenly speak so bitterly – and be so unguarded? And was his offer of a summer contract at the flower farm strictly business or was there more to that too?

Chapter 17

With her head throbbing from too much wine and lack of sleep, Jess washed down a couple of paracetamol with a tepid cup of coffee. She'd enjoyed seeing Maisie, and everyone – apart from Will, perhaps – seemed to have enjoyed the party, but putting on a show of being cheerful in public had left her knackered.

She'd managed to grab Maisie in the pub kitchen and tell her about Adam's letter. She'd lain awake half the night wondering whether to get in touch with him, then reminded herself that he'd walked out on her and the letter had told her to forget him anyway.

Why send it though? It wasn't as if she'd had any contact with him since he'd left or tried to make him come back. She'd been much too shocked and proud for that, so it seemed cruel of him to get in touch now ... and she was still convinced that Adam wasn't callous, despite what he'd done to her. He had said there was no else ... or was that a lie?

Maisie couldn't make any sense of it either and thought Adam must have been racked with guilt. She'd also gently suggested Jess shouldn't raise her hopes that he'd changed his mind and was coming back, but Jess had already dismissed that possibility herself. The letter felt very final.

Will walked into the kitchen as she was staring into her coffee. 'Morning. You look like death warmed up,' he said cheerily.

Jess wondered whether to tell him about the letter for a split second, then decided it wouldn't help either of them if she did. The fewer people who knew, the better and it wasn't as if there was anything she could do because Adam had made his decision and she just had to get on with life.

'Thanks. I've got a headache.'

'Not surprised, the way you were knocking back the wine.'

'You had enough beer yourself,' Jess threw back, wishing she hadn't risen to the bait. Her tetchiness over the letter was making her extra sensitive. 'And what do you think you were playing at last night, forcing Gaby to join the gig team?'

Will snorted. 'I haven't forced her to do anything. She volunteered.'

'More like she was press-ganged. Sometimes I despair, Will Godrevy. You can see she's terrified of rowing and also, I might add, it's obvious she has a crush on you.'

For once, he didn't fling back a sarcastic remark. 'She insisted on joining the crew. I even tried to dissuade her, and she can back out any time she likes. As for having a crush on me, you're living in cloud cuckoo land.' He turned away and leafed through a pile of mail.

Jess moved next to him. 'OK. Maybe I'm willing to give you the benefit of the doubt as far as the rowing is concerned, but you won't get off the hook so easily otherwise. I know you too well and I know Gaby. She likes you. She specifically asked me if you were coming to the pub for her birthday party.'

He picked up an envelope and peered at it, even though Jess knew it wasn't even addressed to him. 'Did she? What did you say?'

'That I'd mention it, though I thought you were out with rowing practice ... So, you did actively turn up at the Driftwood "unexpectedly" because it was Gaby's birthday? And what about buying the wine?'

'Firstly, I like the Driftwood. Secondly, Gaby is one of the team. I felt it was my duty to show my face and the wine was meant for everyone. Not that I wanted to take the credit for it, but some people can't keep their mouths shut.' He gave her a pointed look.

Jess gasped. 'I didn't realise it was that much of a secret and, as for Gaby, you can't claim you were only doing your duty for one of the team. I know you like her, though you've got a funny way of showing it. Well, be careful.'

Will snorted. 'Be careful. You're sounding exactly like Mum.'

'And you should watch you don't turn into Dad.'

He folded his arms. 'Four girlfriends in twelve years makes me Casanova?'

'There were five actually, with the woman who came to service the tractor.'

'Jesus. Are you counting? You should set up a blog.' Will sat down in the swivel chair, put his arms behind his head and rested his stockinged feet on the desk. He knew Jess hated him doing it but, on the upside, it meant she'd got him on the defensive. 'For your information,' he continued, 'I took the tractor technician out for a meal in Hugh Town, we had a passionate debate about the merits of various power take-offs and then she went back to her hotel, not that it's any of your business. There have only been four other women you could possibly count as actual girlfriends who I was involved with for a couple of weeks.'

'Hey. I'm joking. Sort of, but I do like Gaby and I don't want her to be hurt and there to be trouble in the ranks. The last thing we need is upset staff and gossip and bad feeling,' she said in a softer tone.

'Neither do I, which is one of the reasons I'm not going to get involved with Gabriella Carter ...' He pulled his arms from behind his head and took his feet off the table. 'Anyway, she's not my type.'

'No, she's out of your league, or ought to be,' Jess said, knowing this would jolt him into a response.

'Out of my league? What's that supposed to mean?'

'Only that she's clever and educated,' said Jess, teasing him.

'And I'm some thick boor who's not fit to kiss the hem of her dress?'

Disquiet flickered in his eyes and Jess thought she'd misheard what he'd said. 'Did you say *bore?*' she said.

'No, boor. B-O-O-R. Don't look so surprised.'

'I'm not surprised. It's only that it's a funny word for you to use.'

He bristled. Jess was starting to regret teasing him because Will was taking her comments more seriously than she'd expected. She'd obviously touched a raw nerve.

'Funny in what way, exactly? Because my vocabulary is so limited? Or that I had to abandon my own plans to save this place from ruin?' he asked.

Jess groaned inwardly. The last thing she wanted was for Will to go off on one, but he really did have a bee in his bonnet. 'That isn't what I meant. I was surprised that you used that word because it's so old-fashioned, like in an old book ... Oh, hang on a minute. Did Gaby call you a boor?'

Will snorted and folded his arms again as he often did when threatened or upset. The way their father had when their mum confronted him over 'the other woman'. Perhaps, Jess thought, it was best not to point that out right now.

'Will, I might be wrong here but I'm getting the impression you care more about what Gaby thinks of you than you let on. But I'm not sure she's the ideal person for you,' said Jess, feeling torn between Gaby and her brother, but feeling she had to speak honestly or risk causing more damage to them both.

'Why not?' he said tetchily. 'Because she's out of my league?'

'That was meant to be a joke. I just don't think she has any plans to stay on the isles long term. Even if you did get involved with her, it could never be more than a fling because she'll be off round the world or something. I don't want you to be hurt – or her.'

'How do you know that she's definitely going to go off round the world?' he demanded.

'She told me shortly after she arrived, but she wanted it kept quiet because I think it was too painful for her to talk about. Her brother, Stevie, had a motorbike accident last year, and ended up in a coma. Gaby was devoted to him and her parents and helped them care for him until they made the decision to end his life support. Now he's gone, I think she's working on all the things she didn't do when she was studying and looking after him. I think he was an adventurous type and he encouraged her to travel and do all the things she always wanted to ...' Jess softened her voice. 'Yesterday was her first birthday since he passed away.'

Will sat down on the chair next to her. He was silent for a few seconds and she could tell he was genuinely shocked. She wondered if she'd done the right thing by finally sharing Gaby's personal history with him, but, damn, it was too late.

He toyed with a knife left over from breakfast and sighed deeply. 'I didn't know that about her brother. Jesus. That's tough. I wish you'd warned me.'

'Why? Would it have made any difference? To be honest, I'm not sure I should have shared it now, so don't let on you know.'

'I won't ... but it makes sense now you mention it,' he said thoughtfully. The revelation had obviously subdued him. 'You needn't worry about me and Gaby. I've not even asked her out, and I've told you that I'm not going to hurt her, as you put it; I can see why she wouldn't want to stick around here for too long ...'

'I might be wrong about her. She might want to stay, but I don't want another person I care for hurt the way that ...' her voice trailed off. She looked away from him, half wishing she'd never started the conversation but recognising it was probably one that they both needed to have. Discussing stuff like this – relationships – was rare between them.

'This is about Adam, isn't it?' His voice softened.

'I don't know what it's about,' she said, wondering even now whether to mention the letter, then deciding it changed nothing and might only anger Will.

'I'm sorry. I wish I could change what Adam did. He was a mate and he still is, but I don't like him taking off like that any more than you do.'

'Thanks ... I probably shouldn't be asking this, but have you heard from him?' she asked, feeling slightly guilty.

'Once. He texted me shortly after he arrived back home. He said he was in Cumbria and sorting stuff out.'

So, that much was consistent with the letter.

'Did he say ... anything about me? About *us*?' Jess couldn't help asking, even though the question showed Will – and her – how impossible she found it to simply switch off her feelings for Adam.

Will shook his head. 'Sorry, Jess, but no.'

'Or anyone else?' The words were out before she could stop herself.

'If you mean another woman, then no, but I doubt if he would. I'd tell you if he did.'

'Even if he asked you not to?'

Will sucked in a breath. 'That's not fair.'

'So that's a "no". Sorry, I can't help asking. The way things ended between Adam and me was so sudden, it's hard to forget and move on no matter how hard I try.'

'If Adam asked me not to tell you something, I'd ask him not to share it with me in the first place. That's all I can promise, but there's no point fretting because I don't know why he pissed off to Cumbria any more than you do other than it was something to do with a family crisis. We didn't exactly pour out each other's hearts over a pint, although I thought I knew him ...' Will sighed. 'We were obviously both wrong. Now, can I get on with my coffee?' He smiled to show there were no hard feelings between them after their heart to heart.

Having reassured herself that Will was unaware of the letter, Jess nodded. 'Sure. I'm going to Maisie's after work and I'm staying over. Can you manage without me?' she asked.

Will smiled and gave her a brief hug. 'I suppose I *might* cope. Um. The *Athene*'s ready for her sea trials and now Gaby's on board, we have a full crew so I need everyone to come along to the evening Mixed sessions when I've organised the schedule.'

'Great. Just what I need. Test-driving a leaky old relic with a scratch crew: that's how I want to spend my evening after a hard day on the farm.'

'Leaky old relic? I'll have you know we've lavished months of work on that vintage craft. She's in mint condition.'

'I'll believe it when I've arrived home without getting drowned. Where are you planning on taking it for the first outing?'

'Only up and down to the Shag Rock. Javid and I have already had a few short trips in it to make sure everything's safe and watertight, so you needn't worry, but we need to test it with a full crew.'

'So you really *are* hellbent on entering the Mixed in the championships, then?'

'There's no point having a beautiful craft like the *Athene* and not using it.'

'I suppose not.'

He drummed his fingers on the table. 'Hmm ... By the way, Jess ...'

The hairs prickled on the back of Jess's neck. 'Yes?'

'I hope you didn't have plans for Easter Saturday?'

'Only to lie in bed all day, drink gin, stuff my face with chocs and recover from the busiest time of the year at the farm. Why, what had you got in mind, dear brother?'

'Well, I thought that we ought to have a bit of fun after all the slog of the past few months. Kind of a party, so I might have agreed to a small race as a sort of trial run for the championships, just in case we do take part. After all they're not that long away now.'

'A *race*? In an untried boat? Are you out of your mind?'

'Don't panic. It's only a friendly bit of fun, and the booze and food are the main point of it all. Javid's managed to put together a Mixed crew from Gull Island and they're rowing over here in it. The thing is that Hugo Scorrier got to hear of it. Javid was going to say no, but then Patrick found out too and decided that Gull should rise to the challenge, so Javid gave in. It's turned into quite an occasion and we thought we'd have a party on the beach afterwards.'

'Oh God. This gets better and better. A party and a race between us, Hugo and Patrick? You know they can't stand each other and we'll all be completely knackered,' Jess said. 'Hold on. Does Gaby know about this trial race?'

'She'll find out. Me, Patrick and Javid only decided to do

177

it this morning. Look, there's really no need to worry. We're only doing it to test the boat but we might give the Gull lot a run for their money if you pull your weight and Gaby doesn't chicken out or throw up.'

Jess hit him on the arm. 'You're horrible, Will!'

'No, I'm not and I do want Gaby to enjoy it. I was kind of hoping that you'd give her some coaching with the Women's crew over the next couple of weeks to help get her up to speed. As I said, I'll work out a formal schedule of practice sessions for the Mixed too. I should think we could fit in four or five before the trial race.'

'*Five* Mixed sessions in just over two weeks? Plus Ladies' sessions on top? I won't blame Gaby if she gets the first plane home! Maybe I'll join her. Will Godrevy, sometimes I have no clue as to how we can possibly share any DNA at all, let alone be twins.'

'You know you love me really,' said Will, dancing out of the way of another swat in time. 'And it'll be a great day out. You might even enjoy it.'

As Will left, crunching on a piece of toast, Jess very much doubted that.

Chapter 18

Late on Easter Saturday afternoon, Jess reluctantly made her way through a path in the dunes to the gig sheds. The sun-bleached timber boathouses were situated on a long sweep of bay near the quay. It was five o'clock and a fine fresh evening. Chilly, of course, because it was barely into the second week of April but gin-clear and beautiful too.

The *Athene* had been towed down to the shed and Jess found Will, Natalia and Lawrence busy transferring it into the water from its trailer. The Petroc crew and the Gull Island boat, skippered by Javid, had already rowed over from their islands, followed by a motor launch of supporters that included Maisie. Hugo had followed on in his own boat, the *Kraken*, to cheer on his team.

With all the rowing practice and the business, it had been decided that the Godrevys had enough to deal with without preparing for a party too, so everyone was heading to the Gannet Inn for hot food after the race. They'd probably need a few stiff drinks with it, if Gaby's body language was anything to judge by. Jess spotted her emerging from the public toilets by the gig sheds where Will and some of the other crew were wheeling out the *Athene* on a small trailer. She looked as white as the sand and seemed to be doing some deep breathing exercises between the sheds and the toilets.

Poor Gaby, thought Jess. She'd done well to turn up for this 'trial race' at all, after her initial training session and her first row in the St Saviour's Women's boat. The island ladies had enough regular – and better – rowers than Jess to make up a crew for the championships but were happy to help train a novice. Natalia had rowed before while she'd been working in Newquay so she was at home quite quickly. Understandably, however, Gaby had been very nervous. Getting the hang of the stroke rhythm had been a big challenge and her fingers had rubbed raw despite the cycling gloves Jess had handed out. Most of the crew had started rowing when they were in their early teens and no matter how low they kept the rate, it was still too fast for Gaby. Then, to top it all, once they'd finally ventured out into the bay, a swell had blown up and Gaby had thrown up over the side.

But, to give her credit, she'd been determined to carry on and had soldiered on through another Ladies' session, which had gone better and she hadn't even moaned about her blistered fingers. By the time she had her first outing with the Mixed crew, she was starting to get the hang of the timing and didn't feel as sick. To Jess's amazement, Will had been surprisingly patient, encouraging Gaby and curbing Len's worst excesses of tyranny with the scratch crew. After their most recent outing, a few days before, they'd managed to complete a trial run of this evening's course, but they were far from ready for an actual race, even a 'fun' one with their friends and neighbours.

Deciding that there were enough people to handle the boat, Jess went to meet Maisie who was walking down the slipway from the jetty. Maisie's partner, Patrick, was somewhere among the melee of crew. Before she could reach Maisie, Gaby spotted Jess and jogged up the beach, almost slipping in the powdery sand in her haste to reach her.

'Have you seen ... the new g-guy in the P-petroc crew?' she said between breaths.

'What new guy?'

'That one,' said Gaby, pointing to the crew. 'You can hardly miss him.'

Jess almost didn't believe her own eyes, but even from the back, the dark-haired guy laughing with the Petroc crew was unmistakable, even without the business suit. His espresso-coloured hair brushed the top of a pair of deeply tanned shoulders while his vest and shorts showed off muscular limbs and sculpted calves. You could easily have mistaken him for a professional athlete and he stood out even among the fit members of the Petroc crew. But what was Luca Parisi doing in the Petroc rowing crew?

'He's very buff, isn't he? Looks like one of the Boat Race rowers,' said Gaby. 'Though he'll probably turn out to be a complete idiot like Gaston in *Beauty and the Beast*.' Jess laughed, relieved to see Gaby had found a distraction from the impending ordeal – and just as intrigued to see Luca there herself.

Will walked over, following their gaze as Luca checked the oars on the gig.

'Then again,' said Gaby loudly, 'just because he looks *incredibly* hunky and gorgeous doesn't automatically mean he is stupid. You shouldn't judge on first appearances, should you, Will?'

Jess stifled a giggle. 'I think he's a businessman, actually.'

Will snorted. 'He's a bit of a tool apparently.'

'And you know this, how?' Jess demanded while Gaby tried hard not to dissolve into hysterics.

Will shrugged. 'Patrick told me that he works for Hugo.'

'That doesn't necessarily make him a tool,' said Jess.

'He's some kind of marketing guru from London. He only arrived two days ago by private helicopter and he's been holed up with Hugo ever since,' said Will.

Maisie arrived and must have just caught the end of Will's comment because she joined in the conversation. 'Let me guess? You're talking about Luca Parisi. It's not the first time he's been here.'

Will's eyes widened. 'How did you know that? And when exactly did you see him?'

'I thought everyone knew about him,' said Jess, enjoying herself. 'Maisie and I bumped into him when we were having lunch a few weeks ago ... but I don't really understand why he's in the Petroc boat.'

'He used to row for one of the Oxford colleges,' said Maisie.

Gaby punched the air. 'Told you! I knew it. He has that rower's physique. Broad shoulders, great big guns and powerful thighs. My friend went out with a Cambridge Blue rower, so I got invited to a lot of their socials. Shame Luca's from the Oxford but ...'

Will groaned. 'That's bloody typical of Hugo to bring in a ringer. We've got no chance now.'

'I thought this was meant to be a bit of fun,' said Jess, watching Luca at the centre of a group of rowers of both sexes from his own crew and the rival Gull Island boat, including Patrick. Everyone was gathered round as if some kind of superhero had landed in their midst, although, judging by his stony expression, Will was less impressed.

'I think we may as well give up,' he said.

Jess slid a look at Luca's impressive thighs. She wanted to agree with Will.

Gaby gasped. 'No. No way. Even if we're last, we're not giving up. You're not going to let the *tool* put you off, are you, Will?'

Gaby had clearly hit a raw nerve with her jibe.

He snorted in derision. 'Of course not. I was joking. Javid might have been winding me up about him anyway. Just because he's rowed in a sliding seat on a city river doesn't mean he'll have a clue about gig rowing. When he gets out on the open sea, he's in for a hell of a shock.'

*

'I think that went pretty well,' said Will gloomily, as he locked the gig shed door a couple of hours later.

Jess patted him on the arm. 'At least no one drowned,' she said, wondering if her arms could have been pulled out of their sockets. Thirty-six was still young, but the Petroc crew had an average age of around twenty-five, not counting Luca, who was thirty-one, according to Gaby.

'He really has rowed for the Oxford reserve Eight in the

Boat Race,' she told Will. 'And for a gig crew in Salcombe. His family have their UK holiday home there.'

'According to Javid, he rows for a famous Thames club when he's not in Devon,' said Will gloomily.

Javid arrived and slapped him on the back. 'Hard luck, mate. No shame in coming last. We were miles behind the Petroc boat too. I reckon they would have won even if Luca had been in the boat on his own.'

'Everyone did their best,' said Jess. 'Although I think you'll have to carry Gaby to the pub.'

Will followed her gaze to the forlorn figure lying on the sand and staring at the sky. The rest of the crew were sitting around her looking like they'd been steamrollered too.

'She did well for a novice,' he said.

'She was amazing. I think she was almost sick at one point.' Jess stretched her shoulders and there was a distinct clicking sound. 'I'm not sure my shoulder muscles will ever recover and by the looks of the others, I think productivity will take a nosedive for the rest of the week.'

'I'd better see how everyone is,' said Will.

'I'll come with you,' said Jess, hurrying after him as he jogged down the beach towards Gaby, but Luca was also making a beeline for her, running over the sand like a *Baywatch* lifeguard.

Luca arrived a second before Will and crouched next to her.

'Are you OK? Do you need a hand? Come on, let's get you up. You need some hydration and carbs.'

Will stood over them both, hands on hips. 'I can manage. She's my crew member.'

Gaby waved them both off. 'I'm perfectly capable of walking to the pub on my own,' she said, sitting up. 'I was only having a rest.'

Luca's deep brown eyes were full of concern. 'Are you sure?'

'Of course, but thanks for asking.' Gaby threw a smile at Luca. He had gorgeous eyes, thought Jess wondering if she should say so to Will just to wind him up a bit more. No, that would be *too* cruel on top of Gaby's comments about how handsome Luca was. Will was taking the race far too seriously, but he'd probably heard enough about Luca today.

Luca smiled. 'No problem. I'll leave you to your skipper, then. See you at the pub?'

'Great.' Gaby smiled back. Jess wondered if Gaby was flirting or just being polite.

Luca seemed to have second thoughts about leaving. 'Oh, for what it's worth I thought you did an amazing job in your gig. I heard you hadn't been in a boat until last week.'

'I once crashed an Eight into the banks of the Cam,' Gaby added, wincing as she rubbed her legs.

'You were at the Other Place?' Luca laughed. 'Oh well, no one's perfect, but if you've been to Cambridge, we must see if we have any mutual friends.'

Gaby seemed to brighten instantly. 'Oh, we must have.'

'I can tell you're an experienced rower,' he said to Jess, almost as if he'd sensed she was being ignored.

'I wouldn't say I was *that* experienced,' she replied, and he gave her a knowing smile that implied she was only being modest. She *had* been slightly miffed but she'd also been fascinated by the rapport between Luca and Gaby. She sensed

185

a definite frisson between them, unless Gaby was only responding to wind up Will. If that was the case, it was working because Will muttered in her ear, clearly not impressed at Gaby and Luca's pally use of Oxbridge jargon: 'Excuse me while I puke. Patrick's right, he is a tool.'

Poor Will, thought Jess. Luca had backed off now but hovered by Gaby's side, a concerned expression on his face. Will offered Gaby his hand again, but she waved it away and got to her feet. Jess thought her legs still looked on the wobbly side.

Some words were exchanged between Gaby and Will and judging by Will's thunderous expression, they were probably rude ones.

'Shit. I hadn't meant to intrude on a domestic,' Luca said in a low voice to Jess.

'What do you mean?' Jess asked, wondering how he could look box-fresh after bringing the Petroc crew home twenty yards ahead of anyone else.

'Will and Gaby. I was only trying to help but I can see he's protective of her. I didn't know they were a couple.'

'They're not,' said Jess, watching Gaby stomp off up the beach, with Will in tow.

Luca arched an eyebrow. 'Oh. OK. It seemed as if they're more than just friends.'

'Actually, they're both single.'

Luca's gaze drew back to Gaby who was marching determinedly after the rest of the rowers. He had a smile on his face.

'Hmm. I see.' He turned to Jess, and her stomach did an

annoying little flip even though she'd been left in no doubt that his interest lay with Gaby. 'Shall we head for the pub before the bar runs dry? I should probably get the first round in too. I suspect I need to build some bridges with the other crews.' His dark eyes twinkled and Jess realised he was probably perfectly aware that his brilliance in the gig hadn't made him the most popular man on St Saviour's. He smiled and Jess decided that not only was he fit and rather gorgeous, she rather liked his sense of humour too.

'You know, I don't think that can do any harm at all ...' she said.

Chapter 19

It took two large gin and tonics in the Gannet to numb the aches and pains in Gaby's arms and legs or at least make her not care about them. At times over the past few hours, she'd half-wished she'd volunteered to be cox, not row, but the prospect of steering the gig between rocks, reefs and sandbanks made that a non-starter. At least she couldn't actually kill anyone but herself by rowing.

She looked down at her hands and winced. Jess had loaned her a pair of cycle gloves but she still had blisters on the insides of her fingers and wasn't looking forward to the next day in the fields. On the other hand, she'd really enjoyed the sense of camaraderie with the other members of her own crew and their rivals and a quiet but deep sense of satisfaction was gradually filling her veins. Then again, that could have been the gin.

Everyone – even Will – was laughing and joking as they milled around the pub terrace which had glorious views over the lagoon towards St Mary's. The evening was cool but clear, with flat-topped pink clouds hovering on the horizon, almost like ghost islands above the real ones. It was on nights like these that she contemplated the idea of staying on Scilly for more than a mere summer, even if it meant abandoning the promise she'd made to her family and herself to see the world while she could.

Around two dozen rowers were gathered around her, tucking into hot pasties. As it was Easter Saturday, there were also trays of Easter brownies studded with mini eggs. After all that rowing, the crews attacked the food like a pack of seagulls let loose in a chip shop.

Luca came over a second after Gaby had taken a large bite of a pasty.

'Gaby, you were incredible.'

She nodded and tried to smile while chewing furiously, spraying him with pastry crumbs. She pointed at her mouth and tried, 'Sobby.'

'It's fine. Please, finish your dinner.'

Gaby gulped down the chunk of pasty, wincing as the hot meat lodged in her throat. She started coughing.

'Drink this.' Luca shoved a pint of lager at her and she managed to dislodge the pasty and cool her throat at the same time. He patted her on the back. 'Sorry. I've almost caused you to choke. I came over to see how you were. Great effort today by the way.'

'It was nothing, really.'

'Not at all. You performed extremely well.'

Gaby's cheeks heated up and the volcanic pasty had nothing to do with it. Her fellow crew members – including Will – must have been able to hear. In fact, she could see Will out of the corner of her eye, holding a half-eaten pasty and scowling in her and Luca's direction. Jess's attention had been caught too, but her eyes were mostly on Luca.

'I was rubbish,' she said, embarrassed by Luca's effusive praise. 'And no, please don't say otherwise. It's only thanks to the others that we even made it over the line before dark.'

Luca smiled indulgently. He really was incredibly handsome, with gleaming black hair straight from a shampoo ad. She half-expected him to have arrived in a vaporetto with a supermodel or Hollywood actress on his arm. When he lifted his pint, the muscles flexed in his biceps very distractingly. Having a thing for the male bicep, Gaby couldn't help comparing Luca's with Will's. Actually, she thought, sliding a very sneaky glace at Will, who was lifting a tankard of ale, her boss came out rather well, considering he wasn't an athlete and must be five years older than Luca.

'What part of Italy are you from?' she asked, before Luca could praise her rowing skills again and annoy Will even further. She could still see him, casting glances at her and Luca. To be fair, Will had been less frosty of late, possibly because she'd agreed to be in the crew and stuck at it.

'The Amalfi coast. My grandparents are Sardinian, but Mum and Dad moved to the mainland near Salerno when they got married. That's where I was born. They started a small vineyard when I was a baby but it's grown since then.'

'You don't have an Italian accent at all,' said Gaby.

He smiled. 'No. I went to boarding school over here because my parents wanted me to have an English education. My mother had some romantic notion about England gleaned from Jane Austen novels, but I picked up a taste for rowing and soccer rather than fencing and horse-riding and I ended up staying here for university.'

'Don't you miss home?'

'That depends on the weather.' He smiled. 'I find excuses to visit my parents and grandparents as often as I can, especially in the English winter. Those opportunities have become fewer, sadly, since I set up on my own as a marketing consultant. I'm based in London normally, but I'm working freelance for the Petroc Resort for a few months. Enough about me. What about you? You said you were at Cambridge. What did you study?'

'I went to St Aldhelm's and I have a PhD in Flower Poetry.'

'Wow. How romantic ... and what a coincidence that you were at Aldhelm's. You might know my sister, Sophia? She's a few years younger than me and she was reading English there?'

Cogs turned in Gaby's brain as she pictured a dark-haired girl who was much quieter and more serious than her brother seemed to be. 'Oh, yes. Sophia Parisi. I do remember her. She was in the year below me. How is she?'

'She's doing very well, thanks. In fact she went to RADA after Cambridge. She's an actress now. She was in that new Italian crime series on the BBC, but she uses another name.'

'Wow. How exciting,' said Gaby, amazed that the shy Sophia was now a performer.

After telling her a bit more about his sister's work, Luca moved on to ask Gaby more about her job at the flower farm and somehow another G&T miraculously appeared in her hand. The evening grew cool so Gaby put her hoodie on over her T-shirt.

'Have you been to Italy?' Luca asked.

'No. I've always wanted to go. I went to France and Portugal while I was a student, but never made it there. Terrible, isn't it?'

He tutted and sighed. 'I'm afraid it is. *Never* been to Italy?'

'No. Bella Pasta is the closest I've come. I'm clearly a very bad person.'

Luca laughed and Gaby laughed too, while sneaking a look at Will and finding him engrossed in a conversation with Javid. She returned her attention to Luca's question. Although she made light of not having been to Italy, Luca wasn't to know he'd opened up a wound. She'd actually had a rail trip around Italy planned out with a friend, but Stevie's accident had meant she'd had to cancel. She hadn't cared at all; nothing had mattered to her but hoping he might recover and come out of his coma. She'd have given up every material thing in her life to see him wake up and have some quality of life, but it wasn't to be.

To all of this, Luca was, of course, oblivious. He carried on smiling. 'We'll have to put that right. When you get some time off, message me and I'll make sure our holiday place in Amalfi is free. My parents don't use it much these days with the vineyard being so busy and Sophia's always working. You'd be welcome to stay there any time. With your friends, of course,' he added.

Gaby didn't know what to say. She'd only known him an hour and he was offering to let her stay in his parents' villa? Then again, she did know his sister – sort of.

'Thanks,' she said, not sure if she'd ever take him up on it and starting to question his motives for paying her so much attention.

'Hold on. Keep absolutely still,' Luca suddenly said.

'What?' Gaby squeaked.

Luca brushed her shoulder. 'There. It's gone.'

'What?'

'A rather large flying beetle of some kind.'

'How large? I'm used to creepy-crawlies in my job but I do prefer them of manageable size. Thank you.' She smiled, wondering if Will had noticed Luca remove the insect from her top.

Luca looked down at her. 'No problem.'

'Sorry to interrupt, but I think Hugo wants to row back to Petroc.' Will's gruff voice made them both turn suddenly. He'd detached himself from Patrick, Maisie and Jess and now loomed a few feet away.

Luca glanced at his watch. 'Thanks for telling me. I totally lost track of the time.'

'Luca's invited me to his villa in Amalfi,' said Gaby. 'After I've finished working here of course.'

Will's eyes darkened. Gaby hadn't been able to resist it, but then wondered why she'd provoked him at all.

'It's my parents' villa, actually, but Gaby's welcome any time.'

'Sounds great. Look, I hate to spoil anyone's fun, but if you don't leave shortly, mate, the tides will be against you and you'll be stuck on St Saviour's for the night.' Will sounded neutral enough but Gaby knew him too well to miss the edge of sarcasm in his voice.

Luca shot Gaby an amused look. 'You know, that might

not be too bad, but Hugo's in charge, so I'd better do as he says. Hopefully our paths will cross again soon,' he said to Gaby. 'Will you be doing the Mixed race in the champs?'

'I doubt it, but Will's our skipper so it's his call.' She turned to him, feeling slightly bad about mentioning Luca's villa and hoping to smooth things over a little. 'What do you say, boss?'

His expression was cool. 'It's up to you,' he said. 'I don't want to force you to do anything.'

'Oh, you should definitely do it, Gaby. Tell you what, if Will can't find a place for you in his crew, you can join the Petroc II gig. We'd be delighted to have you and, in fact, there's a training evening on Wednesday night. I could come and collect you in the island jet boat.' He smiled indulgently, probably to show he was only joking.

'Hmm. That's a very kind offer, Luca, but if I do row again, I ought to stay loyal to St Saviour's.' Luca was engaging and easy on the eye, but she didn't want to give him any ideas.

'You don't owe me anything,' Will interrupted. 'However, I'd hate to sound like a *boor*, but technically Gaby is part of our team now, so it wouldn't be the best idea if she switched sides ...'

'I'm not going to switch sides, and I'm sure Luca's only being polite,' Gaby cut in, annoyed with Will. 'I'm committed to the St Saviour's boat and it's my decision. Goodbye, Luca. Nice to meet you. I'm off inside to join the others. It's getting cold out here.'

She walked off, leaving Will and Luca to battle it out on the terrace if that's what their game was. Luca hadn't actually done anything wrong, whereas Will had acted like an overgrown schoolboy. Gaby didn't want to flatter herself that Luca had been trying to chat her up; he struck her as the kind of charming marketing whizz-kid who'd talk the hind leg off a donkey to use one of her granny's favourite phrases.

As for Will, Gaby despaired. Since their kiss all those weeks ago, his moods had been as unpredictable as the weather. Anyone would think he was suffering from teenage hormones, but that was no help to her. Maybe Luca had the right idea about not hanging around. Why bother staying on for the summer, let alone longer? Perhaps she should take Luca up on his offer and head to Italy.

Later, as she followed the rest of the St Saviour's crew to wave off the Petroc and Gull Island boats, Gaby thought she wouldn't leave *quite* that evening, but she was having serious doubts about remaining much longer. She hadn't given Will an answer to his question about staying on for the summer and he hadn't renewed the offer. Perhaps he, like her, was having second thoughts about her staying.

Chapter 20

After a barbecue at the Driftwood on Easter Sunday and a lazy family lunch on Monday, it was back to work for Jess on Tuesday. The farm was still busy, but there was a lull in the frenzy of activity so she caught up on some admin while some of the workers took a well-earned break. Anna had gone to the mainland on the Islander, which was now making its daily journey full of tourists to and from Scilly.

You could tell it was still holiday time for some of the schools by the amount of families enjoying the mild spring weather on the beaches of St Saviour's. Jess loved to see the kids chasing around the beaches and dipping their nets in the rockpools at low tide, although the sight had taken on a bittersweet edge lately. She'd started to imagine how it would be to start a family with Adam, before their relationship had broken down. But as quickly as such rogue thoughts intruded, she shook them off again, throwing herself into her work and the comforting rhythm of life at the farm.

The cycle of the seasons and its never-ending stream of tasks had always been her solace when times were tough, especially over the past few months. There were still a few late narcissi to harvest: Silver Chimes, Golden Dawn and Winston Churchill – each with its own distinctive hue ranging from white through orange-flecked cream to paint box yellow. Even though she'd lived at the farm for thirty-six years, Jess still found it hard to believe that in a few days, they would all be gone and the whole cycle would start again in preparation for the next season's crop. The team would shortly be digging up and replanting bulbs to give them space to grow and flourish over the summer so they could produce the best flowers when autumn came again.

She meant to do so much, but as was always the way, once she took her foot off the gas pedal at this time of year, she felt listless and lacking motivation. Her mind kept wandering to almost anything else but the business.

Maisie's latest scan had shown Little Sprog developing well and Maisie was starting to think about letting Patrick clear out at least the spare room in their cottage. Will was reasonably cheerful and had organised another rowing practice and formally entered the Mixed team for the championships after a slightly more promising session the previous week. He planned to row with the St Saviour's Men's crew which was held on the Saturday of the bank holiday weekend and then take part in the Mixed on the Sunday, which was the final event of the schedule. This was now less than a month away, which meant they could realistically only get in three more weeks' practice.

And, of course, there was Adam's letter. Jess had read it so often now that it had become crumpled, grubby and in danger of tearing along one of the creases. She stood by the window of the office now, looking out over the fields. 'Why did you write it?' she murmured.

'Write what?'

Jess turned around to find Luca in the doorway. She thought again how striking he was. No one on the islands – not even Patrick or even Adam himself – came close to that level of male beauty. He was wearing a shirt and suit today but no tie. Italian, of course, she guessed, judging by how perfectly it fit him.

'Hi there. Hope I'm not interrupting,' he added, saving her from having to answer.

She blushed at her appraisal of him, hoping he couldn't detect her admiration in her pink cheeks. 'As a matter of fact, you are,' she said.

'Oh. OK.'

It was fun to see his confident smile fade, but Jess couldn't keep up the pretence for long. 'But that doesn't mean the interruption isn't welcome.' Any excuse to avoid the latest directive from the health and safety executive she should have been reading. 'Are you looking for Gaby?' she asked.

His brow creased. 'No. Why would I be looking for Gaby?'

'I don't know. I thought you two were friends.' More than friends, judging by the way they'd been flirting at the pub after the rowing 'race'.

'No. Actually I was hoping to find you.'

'Oh?' Jess was so surprised, she couldn't think of a witty reply.

Luca perched on the edge of her desk. 'I've been to the St Saviour's Hotel.'

'For lunch?' she asked, noting the firmness of his thigh encased in Italian wool. It was hard not to, when he was only a foot away from her.

'I did eat there but my primary purpose was to check out the competition. Spying, I suppose you could call it.'

She smiled at his honesty. 'And?'

He brushed a stray thread off his trousers before replying. 'Great food. Incredible view. Decor needs bringing into the twenty-first century, but the service was top-notch.'

'Glad to hear they looked after you. Some of my friends work there.' But what had any of this got to do with *her*?

'I also passed the Gannet Inn on the way home. There's a notice outside saying there's a band playing there on Thursday evening.' He glanced up at her. 'I wondered if you wanted to have a bite to eat there and then give them a try.'

She couldn't tear her eyes from him. He was beautiful in the way of statues she'd once seen on a school visit to Rome. Sculpted and chiselled. That fanciful thought made her want to laugh. He was only human, but what the hell was he doing asking her out? Her heart rate picked up. This had been the last thing she'd expected to happen ...

'Are you *sure*?' was all she could manage.

He laughed softly. 'Would I ask if I wasn't? Of course I'm sure.'

'OK ... but I'll admit you've taken me by surprise. I wondered if you and Gaby were interested in each other ...'

'No. There's nothing going on.' He smiled again, showing a perfect set of white teeth. 'It turns out that she knew my sister, Sophia, at Cambridge, though. It's a small world, isn't it? And anyway, I also kind of assumed that Gaby and Will were an item, despite what you told me after the rowing.'

'What made you think that?' she asked, grateful to have a few moments to try and work out how she felt about Luca asking her out.

'Will's always looking at her as if he wants to jump on her; she's always looking at him as if she wants him to leap on her ...'

Jess laughed.

'... And then there's the verbal sparring between them of course. Even if I *had* been interested in Gaby in that way, I'd have picked up the signals that she's crazy on Will within about five minutes.'

Jess nodded. 'Hmm. I've suspected this for a long time and I thought they'd get together months ago, to be honest, but Will thinks it's a bad idea to get involved with a member of staff. As for Gaby; she's very independent underneath the charm. She knows her own mind and she's probably decided to steer clear of him.' She shut her mouth suddenly, regretting her words. 'Hold on, why am I telling you all this? I hardly know you.'

Luca tapped the side of his nose. 'Ah. That's the thing. People always tell me things they don't share with anyone else. It's my secret superpower.' He climbed off the desk. 'So is seven o'clock OK? I assume you never really finish work with a business like this?'

'You're right ...' Jess realised she hadn't even said yes and he was offering a time. Classic salesperson's tactic: leave no room for a 'yes' or 'no' answer. She shook her head in amusement and decided to fall for it. She needed a boost. 'Seven should be fine.'

Luca blew her a kiss and left.

Jess hung around in the doorway and watched him saunter across the yard and out of the gate towards the quay before taking a deep breath. Wow. That was unexpected: Luca asking her out and her agreeing. What would Will say? She could picture his face when she told him she was going out with 'the tool'. She smiled to herself. It could be quite funny, but her mother's reaction wouldn't be as amusing: her mum would be breaking out the champagne and planning the flowers for the wedding. Erlicheer if it was spring: Gran's Delight if it was a summer ceremony.

Maybe she should keep the date quiet until she rocked up at the Gannet with Luca, after which word would no doubt spread ... after all it was no one's business but their own. She took another calming breath: going out with Luca was exactly what she needed after the gloom of the past six months: he was witty and handsome and, most of all, he wasn't Adam.

*

On Wednesday lunchtime, Jess walked back from the St Saviour's Hotel with a spring in her step. She'd splashed out on a cut and blow-dry at the hotel spa, and splurged on some new coppery highlights at the same time, then gone mad with a manicure that she hoped might last until the following evening, if she could avoid all manual labour until then. She couldn't remember the last time she'd indulged: not even for

201

her cousin's wedding, when her nails had been a DIY job and she'd trimmed her own fringe.

The price had made her wince but she reckoned she deserved a treat after a gloomy winter. She doubted Will would even notice. She still hadn't told him about the date and he'd gone to St Mary's to talk to some of the other narcissi farmers about selling more of their crop to the flower farm to meet demand in the autumn. They'd managed to secure a deal with a big supermarket and they couldn't grow everything they wanted on their own patch. Her mother was still safely away on the mainland, so Jess wouldn't have to endure her scrutiny either.

Jess's route home took her past the market garden, with its vegetable stall and 'honesty box' selling assorted misshapen but perfectly edible veg. Despite the dark times over the past few months, it always made her smile. She and Adam had once spotted a large willy-shaped carrot on the stall and fallen about in hysterics. She remembered Adam saying, 'Wow. That gives a new meaning to the phrase meat and two veg.'

Even now, the happy memories gave her a bittersweet pang. He'd bought the carrots and cooked the rude one and presented it on a plate to Jess, with a couple of strategically placed Brussels sprouts. It was very silly but had had them rolling about with laughter ... and shortly afterwards, rolling about on the floor of his cottage.

Which unfortunately, was only minutes away down the path to her left. She'd managed to walk past the track several times in the past couple of weeks and thought she was doing well, but today ...

Today she could bear it. Today was the first day of the next stage of her life without Adam and she needed to put her hand near the fire and prove to herself that she really had moved forward.

She turned off the concrete road and down the sandy track towards the bay. Two minutes later she emerged from the high hedges and out onto a cobbled slipway that led into the shallow water. Several boats were afloat off shore with more pulled up on the beach and secured by chains to metal rings on the cobbles, which glistened with bright green weed.

Thrift Cottage hunkered down below a gentle hill, fifty metres back from the sand. It was one of a row of four that had once belonged to fishermen. Three were now holiday cottages and the other owned by a Scillonian family on St Mary's who rented it out to long-term or permanent residents like Adam was – or had been. Jess kept her distance for a while, and calmed her racing heart. Adam's bike was still outside but leaving stuff behind meant nothing: few people could afford to ship all their possessions with them when they left. Adam's furniture would probably be sold at a 'garage' sale or given away soon.

She thought back to how she'd reacted to him when he'd first turned up with the post at the flower farm two years before. She'd thought he was a gym bunny – like Luca – but soon realised that he was naturally built like that. She hadn't been able to stop thinking about him and slowly but surely, she'd fallen for him. He'd taken out a long-term rental contract on the cottage, bought a boat and shown every sign that he was here to stay.

203

Jess's gaze was pulled like a magnet to the silent cottage with its blank windows and the bike already showing signs of rust in the sea air. Damn. It had been a mistake to come here. It wasn't helping her focus on the future or on tomorrow's date, and anyway rain was rolling in from the far west if those dark clouds were anything to go by.

She gave the cottage a last glance and was about to leave when she heard the crunch of gears and groans as an ancient vehicle turned off the road and down the track to the cottage. It sounded like the Yarrows' Land Rover ... Jack probably. He lived on the hill above and his boat was pulled up on the beach, probably waiting for the turn of the tide so he could go fishing.

Jack was a loudmouth and know-all. The last thing Jess wanted was to be spotted moping outside Adam's cottage, so she decided to make herself scarce. She hurried across the top of the slipway towards a 'rabbit run' path through the hedge opposite the cottage. She could make her way from there back up to the main road without being seen. She'd slipped behind the hedge when the Land Rover laboured onto the top of the slipway. Jack was in the driver's seat, but he wasn't alone. She heard voices and recognised two of them.

Her heart thumped as loud as a drum as a heavy door slammed shut.

Jess edged towards the exit of the path, desperate to have her fears – her hopes – confirmed but not daring to move any closer in case she was seen.

'Thanks for the lift, mate.'

''S'all right. How long are you back for?'

'I'm not sure.'

'OK. See ya. Do you and the ladies want a hand with the luggage?'

'No, thanks. We can manage from here.'

That northern accent, even the ring of his boots on the cobbles. It was impossible to mistake.

Adam was back – and he wasn't alone.

Chapter 21

Seconds later the engine rattled into life and the rumbling diesel and grinding gears drowned out any other sound. Jess could stand it no longer. She had to risk it.

She stepped out of the hedge and onto the slipway, just far enough to see Adam with a huge rucksack on his massive shoulders, a flowery suitcase in one hand and a leopard print one in the other. Behind him, a blonde woman in a pink fake fur jacket teetered up the path in high-heeled boots. Her arms were almost pulled out of their sockets by several Co-op bags. She barely looked out of her twenties. A girl of about eight or nine wearing a unicorn backpack trailed behind her, running her fingers through the plants.

The woman dumped the carrier bags onto the porch and let out a huge sigh of relief. Adam put down the suitcases and fumbled in his pocket for the keys. He muttered something, but Jess didn't catch it because all she could hear was the thump of her heart in her ears.

The woman planted her hands on her hips and stared out to sea. Jess's heart rate spiked further, and she flattened herself against the hedge, ignoring the nettles brushing her hands.

She heard the key scrape in the lock and the door, unused for weeks and stiff with damp, creak open. From the porch it was unlikely they'd spot her, but still. Her heart thumped and she strained to listen to the conversation.

'My God. I thought we'd never get here. I thought we were going to crash into the cliff as we came in to land and then the sea was so rough. Jesus, Adam, you really do live in the middle of nowhere.'

Jess wasn't great at accents but she recognised the Scottish lilt clearly enough.

The woman joined the little girl who was looking at the waves breaking on the beach, while keeping tight hold of her backpack straps. Meanwhile, Adam had opened the door of the cottage but hadn't gone inside. He stood watching them for a few seconds.

With her heart still beating like a drum, Jess brushed away the fine drizzle that had blown in on the sea breeze from her face.

'Mummy. Are we really staying here?'

The woman heaved a sigh. 'It looks like it, pumpkin.'

'For how long?'

'Only until the end of the Easter holidays.'

The girl turned her face to her mother. 'But not forever?'

That word 'mummy' sliced through Jess like a knife. Jess could see Adam's face even though the mother and daughter couldn't. It was set like granite.

'No, Emmy. Of course not. We all have to go home when term starts. Unless you really like it here and then we could see about moving.' The woman kissed the little girl on top of her head.

'You'd better get inside. There's rain in the air,' said Adam.

He was right. The slate-coloured clouds had already marched closer, and the first spots were falling. Jess's newly trimmed fringe was already starting to stick to her forehead. She pulled her hood up.

Emmy skipped ahead of her mother into the cottage.

Adam walked down the path, picked up another bag of shopping but stayed at the gate, gazing out at the horizon, his bicep muscles bunched as he lingered.

Jess stepped out of the hedge so she could see him better. Which also meant he would see her. She wanted him to. Wanted him to know that *she* had seen him, seen all of them.

Her lips moved. 'Adam.'

He *had* to see her. If he so much as glanced towards the path beside him, he *would* see her. Instead, he turned away from the sea and trudged up the path with the shopping.

As he neared the door, the woman appeared in the doorway. 'Shall I put a cup of tea on? Good job I bought some milk. Did you know you left some in the fridge? Jesus, I'll have to deep-clean the whole kitchen. Emmy! Don't touch anything until I've given it a good scrub. Emmy!'

Jess couldn't see Adam's face but she heard his words before the door closed.

'Sorry, Keri. It's been shut up for months. I'll help you clean it up. It'll soon feel like home, I promise.'

*

208

'Jess? Are you in the house? Jess? Je-essss!'

Will's voice seemed to penetrate the walls. His shouts almost shook the building and he sounded desperate, but Jess still didn't answer. After spotting Adam, she'd been wandering around in a daze, trying to process what she'd seen and heard before going straight up to her room and locking the door.

In his letter, Adam had said there was no one else, but Jess had always struggled to believe that and wondered if he'd just been trying to be 'kind'. The sight of this woman and her daughter, obviously so close to him, seemed to back up her worst suspicions.

Emmy had Adam's dark curly hair and straight nose, so she could very well be his daughter. Keri must have contacted him or Adam had decided to contact her and rekindle a past relationship. Now he'd decided to bring them back to Scilly for the holidays to see how they liked the islands. Maybe Adam even intended them to live with him full time. Had he known all along that he had a little girl or had Keri only dropped that bombshell on him in the text last August? My God, she might even be his wife ... he could have married her while he'd been away. No: he might have been married *all along* and now Keri had come back to him and needed him. That was it. End of.

If Adam hadn't been willing to share the truth with her, then she really was better off without him. It was no use staying with a man she couldn't trust. She'd seen the damage that could do to a relationship within her own parents' failed marriage, and if he *had* been committed already, he should never have started a relationship with Jess in the first place.

Thoughts, some reasonable and some wild leaps of speculation, continued to gallop wildly through her brain, but Jess didn't try to stop them. She was in no state to think straight or reasonably.

'*Jess?*'

Will's voice was quieter now and his knock softer.

'Are you in there? Are you OK? I've been looking for you and you weren't answering your calls. I know you're in there ... I can hear you. I'm going to open the door so I can make sure you're OK.'

Jess sat up. 'No. Hang on. I'm not decent.'

She gathered up a pile of damp tissues from the bed and chucked them in the bin.

'Hold on. I'm coming.' After a deep breath, she opened the door.

'Great. Found you.' He frowned. 'What's up? Your face is red. Have you been crying?'

'Of course not. Don't be silly.' She tried not to sniffle.

His eyes swept the room behind her as if she might be hiding someone. 'Are you OK? It's not like you to be up here in the middle of the day.'

'I'm fine. Thought I might have a migraine coming on so I lay down on the bed, but luckily it was only a headache. I've had some pills and I was coming back to the office.'

He peered at her. 'Yeah, you do look pretty rough.'

'Thanks a lot,' said Jess, realising her brother hadn't even noticed her hair. Mind you, it must be a right mess since she'd come back from Thrift Cottage in the drizzle and lain on the bed for half an hour. 'Let me sort myself out and I'll be down in five minutes.'

He turned away but Jess's stomach lurched. She had to tell someone, and if she couldn't tell her own brother and Adam's friend, who could she tell?

'Will?'

He frowned. 'Jess? What's up?' His voice softened. 'If anything's the matter, tell me.'

'It's Adam,' she said.

'Fuck. I knew it. It's still upsetting you. Jesus, I wish he'd never bloody come to Scilly, mate or no mate. I can see you've not been yourself since he left.' Will leapt straight into protective big brother mode.

'But I *was* getting over him and I was determined to leave it all behind. But that's just it. I can't leave him behind because I saw him this lunchtime. He's back.'

Will's jaw dropped. He cursed softly, walked back inside the room and closed the door behind him.

'Did you know he was here?' Jess asked.

'Isn't it obvious from my face that I didn't? Where did you see him?'

'At Thrift Cottage. He was getting out of Jack Yarrow's Land Rover.'

'Did he see you?'

'No ... and that's not all.' She took a deep breath. 'He was with a woman and a little girl. I think they might be his girlfriend and his daughter.'

'Shit. Are you sure?' Will rubbed his hand over his mouth.

'No ... but I can't think who else they *can* be. The woman's called Keri and the daughter is Emmy. They both have Scottish accents and I think this Keri must be his ... partner because they seemed really close and when they went inside ...' Jess could hardly get the next words out, as her throat clogged with emotion. 'Keri mentioned something about being here for the holidays but that they might consider staying if Emmy liked it and ...' She swallowed down a sob. 'Adam told them that the cottage would soon feel like home. And the little girl even looks like Adam.'

'Fuck.' He rubbed the top of Jess's hand. 'I'm sorry. I never expected anything like this. I thought Adam was a mate. I had no idea he was a Grade-A tosser.' He turned and headed for the door but stopped before he got there. 'I'm not going to let him get away with hurting my sister like this. I'm going over there now to have it out with him.'

Jess grabbed his arm. 'Don't be stupid. That won't solve anything, and besides, he's a free man. He can do what the hell he likes. I don't want you fighting my battles.'

*

It was with difficulty that Jess pulled herself together and returned to the office to try and get some work done, or at least appear to be doing some work. Seeing Adam, Keri and Emmy had certainly thrown a bucketload of cold water over the sunny mood she'd been in after her visit to the spa, which reminded her – she had a date with Luca the next evening. She wasn't in the mood for that either, but thank God she had a night to try and calm down and get over the shock.

She knew that news of Adam's return wouldn't take long to spread round the island. In fact, she wouldn't have been surprised if the whole of St Mary's had known about it before she'd even spotted him at the cottage.

It had definitely reached Gull because a text came from Maisie before Jess had closed down the office laptop for the day. She'd been about to call her friend, but now she didn't need to. Not content with a phone conversation, Maisie asked Jess to come over to the Driftwood and, the tides being right, Jess took the boat over for a quick visit after work.

'Why has he come back *now*?' she asked Maisie as they shared a coffee in the kitchen of her cottage.

Maisie shook her head. 'I don't know, hun. Only he can tell you. You *have* to ask him.'

'Speak to him? Over my dead body!' Coffee spilled from Jess's mug as she put it down on the table harder than she'd meant to but her earlier shock and hurt had now turned to anger. 'Shit. Sorry, Maisie. I'll clear that up.'

Maisie covered Jess's hand with hers. 'Forget it. This has been a big shock and you need to find out what's going on if you can, but most of all, you need to keep on with your own life. By the way, your hair looks great and the nail colour is gorgeous. Is there something I should know?'

Jess looked at her nails. A couple had already chipped, probably when she'd been hiding in the hedge. Damn Adam.

'Jess?' Maisie probed.

'I'm supposed to be going out for a meal with Luca tomorrow night. I've been meaning to tell you. I even had my hair done today.'

Maisie let out a whoop. 'I thought you looked different. I love it ...' She eyed Jess sharply. 'Hun, I sincerely hope you're not going to let Adam's reappearance change your mind?'

'Obviously, I'd said yes to the date with Luca before I found out Adam was back. Not that it should make any difference.'

'It absolutely should not make a difference but I do understand how you must feel. Bugger, why has he come back now with this woman and little girl? Have you found out who they are?'

'No. But I bet everyone will be sure they're his girlfriend and daughter. I can't think they're anything else or why would they be living with him?'

Maisie pressed her lips together. 'Being honest, I don't know either ... I could punch Adam on the nose myself for doing this to you. I am sorry, hun, but you must carry on with your plans, especially now. Show him you don't care, even if it's hurting like hell,' said Maisie fiercely.

Jess nodded. Maisie was right, but it was going to be hard to put on a front with everyone watching. 'When I first saw Adam was back, I was so shocked I didn't know whether I would keep the date. Then I thought Adam hasn't come home to beg me to come back to him, has he? Not that I ever would, after the way he left, so I'm going to go out with Luca. But I haven't told Will yet ...'

'Why not?'

'Will can't stand Luca. He calls him "the tool".'

Maisie winced. 'Oh dear. Patrick may be partly to blame for that, but actually, Luca seems OK to me.'

'Will thinks he spends far too much time looking in the mirror.'

Maisie let out a squeal. 'Yeah, well he is pretty hot, if you like that sort of thing. And you *do* like that sort of thing, don't you, Jess?'

'I must admit, he's gorgeous and charming. I get the impression some people think he likes himself a bit too much but he seems pretty normal when you talk to him. Besides, Will's prejudiced.'

'He probably worries that Luca's going to do a runner like Adam.'

'Or a runner with Gaby,' said Jess.

'But he's asked *you*, not Gaby, and you, madam, are going out with him if I have to carry you there myself. Now, come on, let's dive into this chocolate cake that Patrick made and talk about it.' Maisie stood up but suddenly let out an 'oh'.

'What?' said Jess, her heart beating fast at the grimace on Maisie's face. It soon turned into a smile.

'Little Sprog's obviously going to play Aussie Rules like her father. I'll get the cake tin and we can hatch a plan of action.'

Maisie had always put on a brave face and cheered Jess up, no matter what had been going wrong in her own life over the years. She was a true friend who Jess could always rely on.

Maisie pointed to Jess's nails. 'I think I can help with one thing. I've got some varnish that colour in a Christmas gift-pack and, more important, what are you planning to wear for this night out with the tool?'

Chapter 22

On Thursday evening, Gaby checked her face in the new mirror she'd bought for her room. It was on the small side, but it worked well enough. She twisted round, trying to catch a glimpse of her bum in the new dress she'd ordered from an online store. Stuff took longer to arrive but she hadn't been able to resist. It was a fit and flare with a subtle flower print, appropriately enough, and considering she hadn't been able to try it on, she was quite pleased with the fit which skimmed her bottom and ended a couple of inches above the knee. It wasn't too tight, was it? Or too short?

She was wearing thick opaque tights and suede ankle boots with it which kind of made it OK, and the cropped military jacket over the top, which she hoped to cut through the girliness of the dress. That had been a vintage buy from a craft market when she'd gone home to see her parents at Christmas.

'Hello.'

She nearly jumped out of her skin. Will stood in the doorway. Her cheeks heated up. How long had he been watching her twirling this way and that? She planted her hands on her hips. 'Do you have a problem, Will? Only you're staring at me in a most peculiar way? Do I have spinach between my teeth?'

'You look fine to me,' he muttered, then added, 'Exciting plans?'

'Yes, we're going to the St Saviour's Hotel.'

He did one of his 'humphs'; as if she'd supplied precisely the answer he'd been expecting, then shuffled awkwardly.

'Was there anything you wanted in particular?' she asked, with a smile.

'I was wondering if you'd given any more thought to my offer of a summer job.'

He just came straight out with the request without hesitation or jokiness. Wow, he must be serious. She caught her breath. She'd thought of it most of the time since he'd initially asked her. In one way, she wanted to stay longer, mainly because the thought of leaving Will was very depressing, even if nothing had really happened between them or was likely to.

He folded his arms and she wasn't sure if he was impatient for an answer or bracing himself for disappointment. At times he was very easy to read and at other times, impossible.

August wasn't that far away and there was work to do here. He wouldn't have asked her if he didn't want her here ...

'If you really need more help with the summer chalets and you can't get anyone else, I suppose I *could* hang on a bit longer.'

'I'm not forcing you,' he said sharply.

'I know that.' Gaby softened her tone. 'Honestly, I didn't mean to sound ungrateful.'

'You don't have to be grateful. We need staff and you're already on the books and you know the way we operate. It makes good business sense to take on someone we can rely on, that's all ...' He hesitated, then spoke firmly. 'But of course, if you want to leave, then I'd appreciate it if you'd let us know so I can make other arrangements.'

'There's no need for that,' said Gaby, her spirits sinking at his eagerness to let her know he wasn't bothered if she stayed or not. Was it all an act and he was only trying to clumsily cover up that he wanted her to stay? Every sensible instinct told her to take him at his word and say she had to go. Hell, she ought to leave. That had been her plan: come to Scilly, live here and then go and see the rest of the world, landscapes, wildlife, gardens ... That had been her pledge to Stevie and herself ... She looked at Will and saw something flicker in his eyes: hope? Need? He *did* want her to hang around, she was almost sure of it.

'I'll stay,' she said.

His jaw dropped and his eyes lit up with surprise.

'Until August,' she added. 'But then I really ought to go. I have things I want to do, *need* to do ...'

'Of course you do ...' He sighed and looked her up and down. 'You look nice ... you'd better get your skates on. He's on his way.'

It was Gaby's turn to be taken aback. 'Who's on his way?'

He frowned. 'Luca, of course. I was in the top field and I saw the Petroc boat pull into the jetty ten minutes ago. Bloke got off it looked an awful lot like him. I expect he'll reach the farm any moment.'

'Oh,' said Gaby. 'You mean Luca as in "Luca The Tool"?'

Will folded his arms defensively. 'That was a joke. I never started it. Patrick did and, yeah, there is only one Luca it could be, isn't there?'

A light bulb went on in Gaby's head. Aha. So that was it. Will had seen Luca, seen her getting ready and put two and two together. He obviously thought she was going on a date with Luca, when she was actually going to a hen party for a girl from the St Piran's rowing club. Will was so frustrating, blowing hot and cold, so she decided not to put him right *just* yet.

'Hmm. I suppose it would be way too much of a coincidence that there were two hot Italians called Luca on Scilly ...'

He grunted. 'Well. I'd better leave you to it. Don't want to cramp your style.'

Before she could have second thoughts about enlightening him, he stalked off, leaving Gaby staring after him in puzzlement.

That left another mystery. Why was Luca on his way to the farm? Maybe Will was mistaken and he was headed somewhere completely different like the hotel or the pub. Whatever Will had assumed, Luca most definitely wasn't coming for her.

Or was he?

Grabbing her bag, she went out to the front of the staff house where Natalia and a couple of the other girls from the farm were waiting. She hoped Luca wasn't going to ask her out and would be very surprised if he was. Although he was fun to talk to and some people thought he was the hottest guy on Scilly, she didn't want to get involved with him. He was witty and charming, but he was too aware of his own appeal for her tastes. She liked her men a little ragged round the edges, and a pair of muddy Hunters would always trump Burberry boots every time.

Chapter 23

Whereas Jess would have been happy to throw on a clean pair of jeans and tug a brush through her hair for a night at the local with Adam, her date with Luca had turned into a mini makeover. On Thursday after work, she'd had to do repairs to her nails with Maisie's varnish and blow fresh life into her new haircut. That was even before she spent half an hour deciding what to wear. In the end, she'd unearthed an as-yet-unworn pair of heeled boots from their box, squeezed into her slightly too small skinny jeans and plumped for a leather bomber jacket that she'd bought in a sale and hardly used.

Normally, her only make-up indulgence was moisturiser and sunscreen: she ordered that by the bucketload from the internet and never stinted. As for the rest of her bag of tricks, it wasn't too hard to stick with a natural look since her highlighter wand and mascara had dried out long ago. She resorted to sneaking her mother's best YSL from her room and adding a slick of natural lip gloss from a rather nice gift pack Maisie had given her for Christmas.

She gazed at herself in the mirror on the back of the

wardrobe door. Another activity she wasn't in the habit of doing. She was quite tall at five feet six and as she spent her days on the go, even if some of it was in the office, she didn't need to diet. She had to admit the jeans, boots and new jacket went well with the silky vest top underneath.

She checked her watch and realised Luca should have been here by now, but a quick glance out of the window showed no sign of him. Jess took her chance for a final check in the mirror. Having spent the past few months in overalls, wellies and waterproofs, it was weird to see this alternative version of herself. The outfit was probably still too smart for the Gannet, but she guessed that coming from London, where everyone seemed to dress up all the time, Luca probably wouldn't even notice she'd made an effort.

When he'd first suggested they meet at her local pub, Jess had almost suggested changing the venue. She was sure he would have done if she'd asked, and she'd wrestled with the dilemma. What if Adam saw them together?

So what if he did? She owed him nothing. She owed him even less now he'd returned with another woman and a little girl and not given her any explanation or warning. She had every right to be here with Luca. It would probably be the best thing that could happen.

Through the open window she heard the gate open and shut, and saw Luca strolling up the drive ... and Will marching to head him off at the pass. Oh no, by the way Will was hurrying, Jess half expected him to whip out a shotgun and threaten to throw him off his land. That was partly a joke but she didn't want him to scare Luca off. She snatched up her bag and flew down the stairs, bolted out of the door and trotted over to them.

Was that relief or pleasure on Luca's face when Jess reached them, breathing heavily.

'Hi there. Sorry, I'm running slightly late ...' Luca said. The comment was aimed at Jess but Will cut in.

'Don't worry. She hasn't gone without you. She's still up at the staff house,' he muttered.

'Oh?' Luca glanced from Will to Jess, as if Will had made the most random statement and Luca was hoping someone would enlighten him. In an instant Jess realised what had happened: Will had thought that Luca had come to pick up Gaby.

'Luca's taking me for a meal at the pub and we're going to see the band at the Gannet,' she said, moving closer to him.

Luca gave a beaming smile. 'Ciao!' he said, holding her shoulders and kissing her on both cheeks. 'You look fantastic.'

Will gawped like someone had slapped him in the face with a wet haddock. Jess braced herself, determined not to put up with any hostility.

'You and Jess are going out?' Will sounded incredulous.

'Yes. Me and Jess,' said Luca, slipping his arm around Jess's back.

'We're off to the pub.' Jess could have kicked herself for not warning Will but also rather enjoying his amazement. 'Sorry I forgot to mention it. See you later.'

'Bye,' said Luca.

Jess took his arm and practically dragged him away. 'Come on, it can get quite busy in the Gannet on a band night,' she said, lying through her teeth.

While Luca walked ahead of her to open the gate, Jess risked a glance over her shoulder. Will had stopped halfway up the yard and was watching them with a dour expression. She held up her hands and mouthed 'Sorry.' Then, to her surprise, his scowl turned into a smile and he lifted his hand in a little finger wave.

'Coming?' Luca asked.

'Yes.' Jess smiled to herself and not only because she was excited about the evening ahead. Will had a face like thunder until he'd realised that Luca had come for *her*. He must be very jealous of Gaby if he was *that* relieved that she wasn't seeing Luca, which actually made Jess's life a whole lot easier. Now all she had to do was try to relax and enjoy the night.

Five minutes later, Jess and Luca made their entrance into the pub.

Jess had expected heads to turn when they walked into the bar together and a few glances – and greetings – were directed their way but most were more interested in their pints. The Thursday folk evening had attracted a few new faces, who were probably guests from the hotel, but the other half a dozen customers were islanders, all of whom she knew and nodded to. More people would surely arrive later when the band started up. Their speakers were already waiting on the makeshift stage in the far end of the bar.

Luca rested his hand on her back as they waited to be served. There was nothing wrong with that and she guessed that several of the women in the bar were probably longing to be in her place, but it was strange. It had been eight months since she'd been in there as part of a couple: Adam had been gone a long time and no one would have blamed her for starting afresh with someone else. No one seeing them this evening could have mistaken them for 'just good friends'.

Even so, Luca's hand on her back felt weird, however lightly it rested. She couldn't quite explain why. It was like waking up to find familiar fields carpeted in an exotic new flower you'd never seen before – but a change was what she needed, right?

They ordered a bottle of local Prosecco and took a couple of menus over to a table in the corner. The conversation was all light-hearted, about the rowing gigs, Luca's impressions of Petroc and how the flower farm was going. After they'd ordered their meals, their chat turned to Gaby and Will.

'It was so funny when I realised Will thought you'd come to take Gaby out,' Jess said. Even funnier, she thought, because she'd expected Luca to come looking for Gaby at the farm the day he asked her out.

'Gaby's a great person, but we're definitely only friends,' he said, pouring fizz into their glasses. 'And besides, I think Will would fight any man who dared to come within six feet of her. I felt like I'd entered the lair of a guard dog who hadn't been fed for a week when I saw him heading across the yard for me tonight.'

'I'm surprised he wasn't foaming at the mouth. Sorry,' said Jess, trying not to laugh. 'I maybe should have mentioned we were going out this evening, but somehow I never seemed to find the perfect moment. It's none of his business really, but he is my brother and I thought he should hear it before reports of tonight reached him on the island grapevine.'

225

Luca glanced around him and lowered his voice. 'A baptism of fire for a first date. Maybe it wasn't the best idea.'

Jess shrugged. 'There has to be a first time.'

Luca raised his eyebrows and his glass. 'You can say that again. Are you and Will very close? It can't be easy living and working with a sibling.'

'It's not always ideal.' She smiled. 'There are some positives: I'd trust Will with my life and we both know we're always acting in the farm's best interests but it's hard to live on top of one another and the personal lives can get tangled up with work life. When there's conflict within either aspect of your life, there's no escape.'

Luca gave a little grimace then smiled. 'He's not my biggest fan, that's for sure.'

Jess laughed and she realised it was becoming a habit with Luca. It had been a long time since she'd laughed so genuinely, so often.

He topped up her glass with Prosecco. 'Shall we have another bottle? This really isn't as bad as I expected.'

'The wine or the company?' Wow, where had that come from, thought Jess the moment the words were out of her mouth.

'The wine, of course.' He leaned in closer, over the table, so that no one could overhear, treating her to a subtle hint of some expensive cologne. 'The date is everything I'd hoped for and a whole lot more. You look great if you don't mind me saying.'

'I think I can allow it.' He looked pretty good himself, dressed down in jeans, boots and a long-sleeved T-shirt that

226

nonetheless showed off his physique. Jess was pretty sure the jeans were more Armani than Primarni.

After a glass and a half of fizz on an empty stomach plus a long day at work, she was finally starting to relax. Only now did she fully realise how tense she'd been since finding Adam's letter and seeing him return with Keri and Emmy. She wondered what they were all doing now, but instantly tried to refocus on Luca who was telling her about the lemon grove at his parents' villa in Amalfi. It sounded wonderfully exotic.

The landlady's son brought over their meals, a plain steak for Jess and less exotic fish and chips for Luca and they fell to it. Easy, relaxed chat continued while they ate, although Jess felt she was talking way more than Luca, who definitely had a gift for drawing people out. Or perhaps for drawing *her* out.

After a few mouthfuls of his meal, he nodded in appreciation. 'You know, this may be only a pub, but the food's great for what it is. The Rose & Crab attracts all the plaudits, but I haven't had a bad meal in Scilly since I arrived. Apart from the ones I've made myself of course.'

'I thought Italians were meant to be great cooks,' she teased.

'Not this one. Luckily, I'm almost always being wined and dined while I'm here.'

'Can't be too much of a hardship.' Jess liked his easy self-deprecation even if she wasn't totally convinced by it. She had a feeling he was probably a much better cook than she was, no matter what he claimed.

'Petroc's definitely a *very* comfortable place. I can see why the business is doing so well.'

227

'Are you still staying in one of the holiday cottages?'

'Yes. It's much better to have my space rather than lodging in the hotel. The cottage gives me a little more privacy, not that there is much of it on Petroc.' He nodded at the bar where a new group of customers were giving Jess and him the once-over.

'You get used to the scrutiny after thirty years,' said Jess.

'Hmm. Maybe. It's weird how we met in the garden restaurant isn't it?' he said, pouring some more wine into his glass. 'I was horrified when Maisie tripped over my bag. I'd never have forgiven myself if she'd fallen.'

'All's well that ends well, eh?' said Jess, her already warm cheeks heating up further at the reminder of Maisie's subterfuge.

'She seems like a good friend. Patrick too.'

Jess's cheeks were burning now. Luca was far more generous towards Patrick than the other way around. She wished he and Will wouldn't call him a 'tool'. Maybe she'd tell Will later, not that she dared say too much or Will would start to read more into their relationship. It was only one date, after all but she did like Luca and she would definitely repeat the occasion, if asked. Or perhaps she should ask him?

She drained her glass faster than she'd wanted to.

'Finish it off?' Luca waggled the bottle and poured more in before she could even protest. 'I think I'll order a brandy with coffee. It's great never having to drive and the Petroc water taxi's picking me up later.'

Jess was enjoying herself too much to think about the end of the evening at this stage but there was still plenty of time before Luca had to leave. As darkness fell outside, the band came on stage and started their set. They were a Cornish band who also occasionally played at the Driftwood too and they weren't bad at all, mixing folky stuff with mellower chart hits. Luca's arm snaked around her shoulders and Jess settled against him happily enough, although she still kept thinking how strange it was to have another man's arm around her and that it felt like wearing a coat that didn't quite fit, even though everyone said it looked great on you. Or was that her simply readjusting to the new 'normal'?

During the band's break, they had a couple of coffees and Luca had his brandy. Jess had turned down a brandy herself, feeling she was mellow enough. They chatted easily about anything and everything. The farm, life on Scilly, Luca's parents' villa and his grandparents' place on Sardinia. He told her a little about his work in London and with the Petroc Resort but didn't mention a significant other or any recent relationships. If Luca knew about Adam, he didn't let on either. Talking about ex-partners was meant to be a no-no on first dates anyway, and Jess was certain neither of them wanted to sour the mood.

After the band had done their final number, Luca suggested they leave before last orders. Jess was feeling chilled and hopeful. If she could have a good time after the shock of seeing Adam with Keri and Emmy, she must be more resilient than she'd thought.

As soon as they were outside on the pub terrace, Luca turned to her, his face lit by the light spilling out from the windows.

'I hope you've enjoyed this evening ... And if you can bear to repeat it, there's an Italian Gourmet evening at the Rose & Crab on Saturday night.'

Jess's stomach fluttered, as she realised how much she'd subconsciously hoped there would be another date. 'Sounds great.'

He gave a wry smile. 'I expect it'll be about as Italian as a chicken tikka pizza but if you fancied joining me for dinner, that would be great.'

Funnily enough, she couldn't think of a single reason to say no to a handsome, fit Italian asking her for a gourmet dinner at one of the islands' top restaurants.

'OK,' she said boldly. 'But I'm not letting you pay.'

He grinned. 'Oh, I've no intention of paying. I'm the marketing manager. I'll put it on expenses. And you can take this any way you want to, but please stay over if you want to instead of worrying about rushing to get the boat home. I can get you a room at the hotel,' he added.

'The hotel?' She wasn't quite sure what he meant but his next comment made it clearer.

'If you're more comfortable with that. Although there's always the sofa bed in the cottage ...'

She went shivery. Wow. This handsome, sophisticated man was asking her to stay the night ... in his own subtle, charming way. All she had to do was say yes.

'Thanks. I'd love to come to dinner.' Let him make of that what he would. It let him know she was interested in taking things further but not how far. She wasn't certain herself yet.

'Great. I think I have to leave. Keith the boatman texted

me to say he's on his way and if I miss the tides, even he can't get me back to Petroc. I had a great time tonight. It was fun, even with the eyes of a whole island on us.'

'So did I.'

Smoothly and before she'd even realised it, he leaned in for a kiss and she was in his arms. She tried to relax into the kiss: no peck on the cheek this time but the full-on variety.

Her first kiss in eight months.

It was so different. So expert but maybe more insistent, more demanding, than she'd expected. He even cupped her face with his hands like they did in the movies. He made no attempt to end it, but pulled her closer against him. Jess tried to relax and enjoy the moment as much as she ought to have done: being kissed in the moonlight by a gorgeous Italian wasn't a hardship after all. Just as she thought she needed time to breathe and think, his phone beeped.

He swore softly, let her go and glanced at the screen.

'That's my carriage,' he said with a rueful smile. 'Sorry.'

'Don't want you turning into a pumpkin,' she said, still reeling from the kiss, but trying to keep things light. She didn't know how she felt about the way things were moving and she definitely didn't want Luca to know.

'I'll be in touch about times when you've decided whether you want to stay over or not? Is that OK?'

'Fine.' She sounded far more blasé about the decision than she felt.

'Goodnight then.'

He walked swiftly off, but Jess lingered on the path that led up to the pub. The wine was wearing off as the cool night air hit her lungs and made her feel as if the whole situation was slightly more surreal than before. She doubted she'd sleep that night as she tried to make sense of the evening. The highs, the lows, one new experience after another, the kiss and the offer: *come to my place, stay over, no pressure but I'd really like you to sleep with me*. He may not have used those exact words but she wasn't naïve.

She had to think about it and even if she did stay, maybe he really did mean she could sleep on the sofa bed.

Hey, get real, Jess. That's what Maisie would say to her. For God's sake, they were way more than grown-up and he was absolutely gorgeous. What possible reason could she have for not staying over with him? Or sleeping with him? She certainly didn't care what anyone thought: it was none of their business. Not even Adam's, not that he could have any idea how her evening had gone.

She zipped up her jacket as the cool air chilled the exposed flesh of her cleavage. She deserved a bit of fun and Luca Parisi was surely the man to provide it?

The clouds had parted to reveal the moon over the sea, laying a silver pathway to the other islands. The wind rustled the branches of the trees and a bird called from the shadows. Jess quickened her step, hoping to clear her head with the brisk walk home. She heard footsteps behind her and thought Luca had come back down the path or someone from the pub was out, but when she turned, a figure detached itself from the shadows.

She'd lost count of the times she'd rehearsed what she was going to say to Adam if she ever came face to face with him again. She was going to be casual, relaxed, polite and as normal as it was possible to be. She was going to be *fine* with him having left without a reason and arriving back on the island with a woman and child in tow.

All her resolve flew away in an instant to be replaced by an anger that seethed through her and made her feel like a stranger to herself. Why did he still have the power to upset her like this, even after a lovely evening with a new date? She barely allowed herself a second's glance at him before she almost ran off in the opposite direction.

'Jess! Wait!' Adam caught her up and took her arm.

She was shaking and felt sick – and shocked too. My God, he was thinner and diminished somehow. She was almost too shocked to speak. Almost.

'Please get out of my way,' she said.

'Jess. Please don't do this. Let me explain.'

'I think it's a bit late for that. I've nothing to say to you and I don't want to hear anything you have to say to me. I'm going home.'

Adam stayed put. A shadow on her path to a new life.

'Move out of my way,' she said.

'OK. OK. But you must understand I never—'

'*Please* don't say you never meant to hurt me. Please don't be that disappointing. You did hurt me, but now I'm over it. Keep away from me.'

He didn't say anything and it was hard to see his face in the twilight. The moon slipped behind a cloud and only the lights from the pub cast any light at all. Jess hurried away, hoping she wouldn't trip in the darkness.

233

'I saw you with him.' Adam's voice followed her down the path.

Jess's chest tightened and she turned back. The moon came out again, illuminating him in silver light.

'And I saw you with *them*, Adam.'

Before he could answer again, Jess was off, running down the road, by the light of the moon, towards home.

Chapter 24

'You won't find the answers in that tea, you know.'

Jess glanced up from the breakfast table the next morning as Will pushed a rack of toast towards her.

'Eat up. We've a busy day ahead.'

'Yeah.' She sipped her tea and scraped butter onto the piece of toast, and nibbled the corner.

Will lavished butter on another triangle and crunched a corner. He washed it down with a glug of tea and then speared a rasher of bacon from the dish to add to the fried egg and tomatoes on his plate. She'd noticed he'd cooked it how she liked: crispy, but she couldn't face any of it and the excess of Prosecco from the previous evening wasn't wholly to blame.

Will started to cut up the bacon. 'How was your date?' he asked.

'OK.'

'Only OK?'

Jess smiled. 'It was good. Luca's a lot nicer than you give him credit for. You should get to know him better.'

'Yeah. Maybe. So, is he going to be my brother-in-law?'

Jess rolled her eyes. 'Don't start that. I'm waiting for Mum to start planning the floral arrangements. Have you told her I saw Luca last night yet?'

He grinned. 'No. I thought I'd leave that pleasure to you.'

'Thanks, dear brother. I love you too.'

Jess nibbled her toast while Will tackled his full English, debating whether to tell him she'd seen Adam. She'd lain awake for ages after she'd got back to the farm with Adam's words ringing in her ears. '*I saw you with him.*' The irony and injustice of it had seared into her. How dare he judge her for seeing another man after he'd left with no explanation and turned up with an unknown woman and child? What kind of arrogance made him think he was entitled to do that? How could he care who she saw or what she did after such a betrayal of trust?

Will was pouring out the remains of the tea from the pot. It was rusty orange and strong, but he didn't seem to mind.

'I think you ought to know that I saw Adam yesterday,' he said. 'I bumped into him walking from the quay to Thrift Cottage. I – um – was on my way for a pint in the hotel bar; I didn't want to cramp your style by hanging round the Gannet.'

Jess opened her mouth to speak but Will got in first.

'Before you ask, he was on his own and, no, I didn't ask him about this Keri and Emmy.'

'Did you speak to him at all?' Jess asked.

'He muttered "hello", I grunted something back and then I went on my way before things got any more complicated. Put yourself in my shoes. He was my mate once and then he dumped my sister and has apparently turned up with a wife

236

and child in tow. Some people say that men have short memories when it comes to friends, but there's no coming back from what he's done. Family always comes first, Jess. No matter what you think.'

'I do know that. Thanks.'

'By the way, you looked very er ... smart last night. Even though Luca doesn't deserve you, either.'

'Why don't you like him?' said Jess, amused and quite touched by Will's attempts to be nice.

'Because he likes himself too much. If that bloke was an ice cream, he'd lick himself to death.'

Jess had to smile. 'You're only jealous that he beat us in the gig race.'

'Yes I am. I'm completely pissed off. However, it gives me even more motivation to work you all extra hard. Don't forget there's a practice session for the Mixed tonight.'

Jess groaned. 'You really are cracking the whip. We're all shattered.'

'No excuses,' said Will with a grin, then hesitated before adding, 'For what it's worth, I'm glad you're seeing someone else, even if it is the Tool.'

'Hey, thanks,' said Jess, a little peeved at his comments about Luca but knowing that his heart was in the right place. 'Now you can stop worrying that he's seeing Gaby,' she added.

He snorted. 'What gave you that idea?'

'The delight on your face when you realised he'd come to take me out.'

'Don't be silly,' he said but Jess knew he was squirming.

'You can't fool me. I'm your twin sister, remember.' Jess

took an inner breath before she spoke again, worried about Will's reaction. 'By the way, you're not the only one who saw Adam last night.'

Will's mug paused halfway to his mouth. 'Where?'

'Outside the Gannet after Luca had gone. He was in the bushes and stepped out in front of me.'

'Jesus. He hasn't hurt you, has he?'

'Of course not!'

Will thumped his mug onto the table. 'He'd better not come near the farm. Do you want me to warn him off?'

'No. I can fight my own battles, though thanks for the thought. Adam would never hurt me – not in that way – but he didn't like seeing me with Luca. He made that plain enough.'

'It's none of his fucking business.'

'That's what I told him.' Jess winced as she remembered her exchange with Adam. 'Sort of. Neither of our love lives are perfect, are they?'

'Mine's non-existent.' Will put a piece of toast on her plate. 'Eat up. I agree with Mum on one thing. You need feeding up. You deserve to be happy.'

She was touched. 'Thanks. I mean it but sadly the world doesn't owe us happiness. We have to go out and find it ... not so easy when your world is as small as ours, no matter how idyllic other people may think it is.'

*

Jess was relieved to have no more sightings of Adam before her date with Luca at the Rose & Crab. Despite its name, the place was far more like a posh restaurant than a pub, so she'd decided to go for the short-sleeved wrap dress that she'd bought for her cousin's wedding. With a leather jacket over the top instead of the cropped cardigan she'd worn to the wedding, it was a good compromise between smart and casual.

She'd accepted Luca's offer to have the Petroc jet boat meet her at the jetty and as she waited on the quay, alone, butterflies stirred in the pit of her stomach. This wasn't her first date with Luca so she knew what to expect, but there was also a big difference: her overnight bag sat on the quay beside her, reminding her that she wouldn't be home that night.

She tried to calm her nerves by walking up and down in the evening sun, enjoying the sight of seals playing just off shore. They popped up their heads and watched her curiously before diving back down under the waves, almost as if they knew where she was going and how she was feeling. The only signs of human life were a fishing boat out in the bay and the chug of a tractor from one of the fields behind the beach.

Jess checked her phone and strained her ears: the jet boat would be here soon. She'd feel better once she was on her way.

She picked up her bag, anticipating the low throb of the high-powered engine barrelling across the sea, but her heart sank when Adam appeared from between the gig sheds. It was inevitable she'd see him again, but why did it have to be now?

'Jess ...' He waited a few feet away from her and the evening sun highlighted how gaunt he looked in his face.

'Adam, I don't want a row.'

'I'm not looking for one.' His eyes strayed to her bag and back to her face. 'Are you going out?' he said warily.

'Isn't it obvious?' Jess gripped her overnight case. She felt like a criminal trying to get away with the loot. 'I don't think that's any of your business.'

He nodded then took an interest in the cobbles on the quay for a few seconds. 'I'm sorry for the way I kicked off the other night. It was wrong of me.'

'I don't care. What's past is past.' Jess tried to keep her tone firm but calm. The jet boat was now in sight and she didn't have long before she could escape. What a horrible thought that was: yearning to escape from the man she used to long to be with.

'I can see that.' He inclined his head to her overnight bag,

She cracked. 'If you had something to say to me, you should have said it long ago. No matter what your reasons for going, and it's obvious what they were, it doesn't matter now. If you'd told me you had a partner and a child, I'd have hated it, but I'd have accepted it. It was the ... the *silence* that did the real damage. There's no coming back from that. Your place is with Keri and Emmy now. They need you and and I need to move on.'

The jet boat engine quietened as it approached the quay.

'Sounds as if you've already made up your mind about me,' he said.

He sounded so forlorn that she almost felt sorry for him but her pity passed quickly. 'Leave me alone, Adam. I'm going for dinner and I don't want my evening ruined.'

'I don't intend to. I've caused enough trouble ...' He hesitated. 'But sometimes things aren't as simple as they look.'

'Please, Adam, no excuses, no more lies.'

'I haven't told you any lies.'

'Right now, I feel as if our whole relationship was a lie.'

He pressed his lips together but didn't deny it and fortunately the boat pulled up alongside the quay. She approached the boat, trying to pretend he wasn't there. She had to put down her bag as the skipper shouted and threw a rope to her. She caught it and looped it around the cleat.

'Evening, Jess. Your chariot awaits,' he said. 'Evening, Adam.'

'Evening, mate,' Adam replied, and handed Jess her bag. 'You'll be needing this.'

She took it, her fingers brushing his knuckles. 'Thanks,' she muttered and immediately gave it to Jem before climbing on board.

Adam untied the rope and threw it to Jess. She muttered a thanks, wanting Jem to see her and Adam on civil terms. He was one of the more discreet people around, but she didn't want to wash any more dirty laundry in public than she already had.

She sat in the stern with her bag on her lap. It was impossible not to see Adam as the skipper pulled away from the quay. He watched her, his arms folded across his broad chest, like a stone statue that had been there for centuries. It was difficult not to sense he was judging her, yet he was the one in the wrong.

She calmed her breathing as the boat speeded up and Adam grew smaller. She had to forget she'd even seen him tonight, but kept turning his words over and over.

'Sometimes things aren't as simple as they look.' Perhaps she should have listened, but she didn't have time and she hadn't

wanted her evening ruined. Besides, nothing he could say would change her feelings of anger and hurt. Could it?

She swore under her breath and turned away from him, holding onto the rail as the spray flew over the bow and Petroc came into view. She wouldn't think about Adam. Luca didn't deserve that and she didn't deserve to have the evening ruined. She was more determined than ever that tonight would mark a new phase in her life.

*

'How's your fish?'

Jess glanced up from the table to find Luca watching her. 'Sorry?'

'I asked how your bream was.'

She pushed her fork into the white meat of the fish and forced a smile. 'It's delicious.'

'Phew. Good because I was wondering if it was off. You've hardly touched it.'

She saw the fillet lying in its bright saffron sauce on the white china plate, still almost intact. 'Sorry. I guess I'm a bit nervous.'

The truth was that she couldn't shake off her encounter with Adam, no matter how hard she tried.

Luca had acted like the perfect gentleman in the cottage, leaving her bag on the sofa and suggesting they go for a cocktail in the Petroc Bar before their meal. As they'd sipped pre-dinner mojitos on the deck of the bar overlooking the channel between Petroc Island and Gull, she'd tried to relax.

She could see the familiar sight of the lights twinkling on the terrace of the Driftwood Inn opposite. Maisie, Patrick and all her friends didn't seem so far away. She'd spent many nights in there with Adam before it had all gone wrong. Laughing, joking, singing along to bands …

'I think our table's ready.' Luca cut into her thoughts and a waitress approached with two menus.

'Great. I'm starving,' said Jess, pushing her memories away with a smile and hoping that her appetite would improve once she sat down to dinner.

'Are you sure you don't want to order something else?' Luca's voice was tinged with concern as he spoke to her across the table a while later.

'No. No this is fabulous. I'm sorry. I was miles away.' She carved off a chunk of fish and shoved it in her mouth. It was a lovely meal but she was still not that hungry despite what she'd told him. 'Mm. This sea bream is really delicious.'

Looking happier, Luca topped up her glass with the New Zealand Pinot Gris he'd chosen. She'd almost choked when she'd seen the price but didn't want to seem unsophisticated by protesting. Besides, hadn't Luca said he was on expenses? And Maisie would love the thought of Jess dining and drinking at Hugo Scorrier's expense. Not, strictly speaking, that Hugo was the owner of Petroc, but he was certainly responsible for its profits. Jess had to stifle a laugh and started coughing as she found a tiny fish bone.

'Are you OK?'

'Y-yes.' She reached for the water glass but it was almost empty.

He filled it swiftly from a jug, his face concerned. He really was ridiculously handsome. She hadn't been too nervous to miss the envious glances from the other people in the Rose & Crab's dining room. She stopped coughing and dabbed her mouth with the napkin.

He shook his head, still worried. 'Man, I'm going to have to stop asking women out for dinner if I put them off their food and almost choke them.'

Jess felt a rush of sympathy for him. 'I've hardly been the best date so far, have I? But this is new for me. It's the first time since I split up with my ex.'

'Ah, I see. Would that be the postman?'

She gasped. 'Oh my God. The gossip round here is terrible!'

'I'm sorry. Hugo told me ...' Luca lowered his voice. 'This is very unprofessional and he may be my client, but I do take what he tells me with a large pinch of salt. On the other hand, I'd also heard a whisper about this Adam Pengelly from a member of the gig crew. I'd no idea that you hadn't been out with anyone since he left though. It must have been tough to go through a break-up in the full glare of the Scilly spotlight.'

'Tell me about it.' Her courage rose: she knew almost nothing about Luca's personal life so now was her chance. 'What about you?'

'I split up with my ex a few months ago,' he said. 'Actually, we're getting a divorce.'

'Oh. I didn't know you were married.'

'It was over some time ago and we've finally decided to make a clean break after several trial separations. Rachel's virtually moved in with another guy now in London. You

244

won't have heard, because I don't discuss my private life if I can possibly help it ...' He glanced round him and grimaced. 'So maybe asking you to your local and now mine wasn't the best idea.'

'I don't really know where we could have gone for any privacy, short of jetting off with a takeaway to some windswept corner of one of the uninhabited islands,' said Jess, slightly taken aback by the news that Luca was still married, even if the relationship was obviously over from what he'd told her.

Luca raised an eyebrow. 'Sounds like a great idea to me ... by the way you look gorgeous. Again.'

Warmth flushed from Jess's cheeks down her neck to her cleavage. She took a glug of the Pinot Gris and realised the bottle was almost empty. 'I don't think my own mother even recognised me out of wellies,' she said, making a joke of the compliment.

'I don't know. I rather like you in wellies too. Shall we get another of these overpriced bottles of white?' Luca said and lowered his voice. 'Familiarising myself with all aspects of Petroc's customer service is all part of my job.'

She laughed, feeling the tension ease. 'If it's work, and Hugo's paying, then why not?'

*

'Coffee? A nightcap? I've got some very good grappa in here ... I can even rustle up some decent coffee and amaretti.'

Luca stood behind the counter in the open plan kitchen of the holiday cottage that was his temporary home. Although it was called a cottage, it had actually been recently built to match the local houses dotted around Petroc's rolling countryside and tiny harbour. It was situated at the end of a row on a headland whose pink granite rocks glowed in the setting sun. Even by Scilly standards, the views were incredible from his patio, with no sign of human life other than a lighthouse on a rocky islet a mile away: just the open sea and islands inhabited only by seabirds.

Jess sank back on the sofa, almost swallowed up by the squidgy leather cushions. 'I shouldn't. I'm so full after that wonderful meal.'

He rolled his eyes. '"I shouldn't" almost always means "I want to but I feel burdened by some misplaced sense of Anglo-Saxon guilt." I'll put the machine on and get the drinks.'

Half an hour later, the only trace of the grappa was the hint of amber in the bottom of the glasses, glinting in the soft light of the table lamps. 'I shouldn't' had turned into 'I should have two' and Jess was sitting with her feet up on the sofa in Luca's lap. One of his arms dangled over the arm of the sofa, bare below his rolled-up shirt sleeves. His other hand rested on the top of her bare feet. The heels she'd changed into after getting off the boat lay on the rug. She hadn't noticed how she'd come to be in that position, and watched in surprise as he started to massage her sole gently.

'How does that feel?' he asked, circling his thumb around the ball of her foot with just enough pressure to relieve the tension but not hurt. Her legs gleamed in the lamplight, the result of an eye-watering home wax session and a tub of luxury body butter Maisie had given her for Christmas. Her toes were painted in a shell pink. If only he could have seen those feet the previous day, encased in fishermen's socks and wellies. She giggled. 'OK?'

'Mmm. It tickles a bit.' She shifted in her seat. Luca laughed. Jess laughed too.

'Try to relax,' he said, caressing the blade of her foot in languid, deft strokes. Jess had the feeling she was being handled by an expert ... even after the wine and grappa, he knew exactly what he was doing. Knew what *she* was doing too.

Adam hadn't intruded into her thoughts since she'd left the restaurant: a good hour. That surprised her ... and she was disappointed that he'd found his way into her mind now. She lay back on the cushion and closed her eyes as Luca's fingers circled her ankle and his hand skated over the smooth skin of her shin.

She tried to chill out and just let things happen while his fingers skated higher, resting on her thigh under the hem of her dress. She tensed slightly but she was definitely turned on. He slid his hand down her leg to her shin again.

'Jess. Do you want to take this upstairs?'

Her eyes opened and she burst out laughing.

Luca stared at her. She felt the pressure of his fingers increase slightly. 'What have I said?'

Jess flushed deeply, not that she wasn't already warm. 'Taking it upstairs ... Oh ...'

'What?'

'I c-can't say.' She stifled a giggle.

Luca grabbed her ankle and started tickling her foot.

247

'No!' she shrieked, trying to wriggle away.

His fingers danced over her sole.

'No! Please!'

'Sorry. No can do.' He ran a finger from toe to heel and Jess squirmed and cried out.

'OK. OK! It's the innuendo. Like something we used to say at school. Take it upstairs when you were talking about what a boy wanted to do.'

'Ah ...' Luca kept hold of her foot but stopped tickling. 'I see.' He gently pushed her feet off his lap and pulled her to her feet. 'Well, however you want to look at it, as a euphemism or not, I do want to take this upstairs. I want – very much – to take you to bed and I hope you feel the same way.'

Pulled to her feet so unexpectedly, she felt a little light-headed and swayed. Luca had his arms around her waist. She realised that she felt shaky, and not only from the wine. He leaned close to her face, took it in his hands and kissed her softly and carefully. He smelt as gorgeous as he looked. Just a hint of some sinfully expensive aftershave, of Italian digestif and a freshly laundered shirt.

'Well?' he said.

'I think I want to ...'

'Think isn't enough. And if you're still on the rebound from the postman ...'

'Don't call him that,' she said, slightly hurt by his tone.

'From Adam, then. I'm sorry, I didn't mean to belittle him and I'm not going to be the one to tell you to move on. Only you can know when it's time, but it has been many months, Jessica. And *he* left you.'

'I don't need you to tell me that. I know how long it's been ...' He was right about it being a long time since Adam had gone and about him leaving her and being back with another woman, Jess was insane to even hesitate about tonight. About *all* of tonight.

She removed Luca's hands from her waist and stepped back from him.

His face fell – momentarily, disappointment and surprise filled his eyes – but then he held up his hands as if in surrender and said, 'Fair enough. I'd never put you under any pressure. I'll take the sofa. You can have my bed.'

'No. I don't want your bed,' said Jess, a new tide of boldness rising within her. 'Not unless you're in it too.'

He raised an eyebrow and his eyes glinted. 'Wow. I'm not going to object to that.'

She took Luca by the hand and led him to the twisty staircase off the sitting room. He didn't say a word, but allowed her to lead him into the bedroom. It was lit softly and the curtains were open, giving a view out over the dark sea beyond their own reflections in the glass. There was nothing out there but the moon and the beam of the lighthouse on Round Island winking a mile across the sea. No one to see them or know what might happen over the next few hours, no matter how much anyone speculated or gossiped. This was between her and Luca – and she was in control.

Chapter 25

'Coffee?'

Jess blinked awake to find Luca next to the bed, with a fluffy white towel draped low around his hips, and bearing two mugs of coffee. The morning sun highlighted his nut-brown skin. Tiny droplets of water glistened in the springy hair around his nipples and in the trail that arrowed from his navel beneath the towel.

'Oh, thanks.' She pushed herself up onto the pillows, trying to keep the duvet above her own nipples, all too aware she was naked under the cover. The blinds were still open from where they'd had sex in the moonlight and although no one could see into the room – apart from the seals – it felt strange to be naked in the full glare of day.

Luca handed her the mug and sat on the edge of the bed. 'Sorry, I can't stay for breakfast with you. I've an early meeting with Hugo.'

'Breakfast? Oh my God, what time is it?' A drop of coffee spilled from the mug and splashed onto the white duvet cover. 'Sorry.'

He smiled. 'Relax. Housekeeping will clear that up and, anyway, it's only half past seven.'

'Half seven? I should be at the farm by now. Will wants me to help with the bulb replanting.'

'Surely he knew you'd be a bit late after your night here? It is Sunday.'

'Well, I didn't exactly spell out the details of my plans for him, but I guess you're right.'

Jess hadn't spelt out anything at all to Will because she hadn't decided one hundred per cent to stay over until she'd got on the boat after her confrontation with Adam. As for sleeping with Luca ... that had been a decision she'd held off until right until she was certain he hadn't expected her to be a sure thing. Now, with him smiling contentedly by her side, like a cat that had got the cream, she wasn't convinced she really had been in control, only that he'd carefully managed the situation – and her – until she'd thought she was making all the running.

Oh God, did it really matter? She'd enjoyed her evening *and* what had followed.

As the heat stole into her cheeks, she hoped Luca would put it down to the searing coffee. She tried not to wince as she sipped hers. It might be Italian and authentic, but it was also strong enough to strip the enamel off her teeth.

Luca asked her a little more about what her day held, during which the duvet slipped down. It was odd having a conversation about uprooting bulbs and tractor maintenance while you had nothing on, she thought, while trying to appear as if she did that sort of thing every day.

Luca put his mug on the dressing table. He kissed her and sighed. 'Unfortunately I need to get dressed now. I can call the jet boat for you, when you're ready?'

'No. Don't worry, I'll catch the scheduled morning boat.'

'If you're sure.'

'Yes, thanks.'

He turned away to open a drawer opposite the bed and dropped the towel from his hips onto the floor. His very fit bum – almost as tanned as the rest of him – was feet from Jess's face. She gulped the coffee. It had been one thing being naked in the dark with Luca, but in the cold light of day, his nudity – and hers – brought the memories of what they'd done together back in Technicolor detail. Nothing weird ... Luca had been considerate, but he'd also been very energetic and quite creative. She sank back against the pillows and closed her eyes, holding her mug with both hands.

'OK?'

She opened her eyes a slit. He was now wearing a pair of tight-fitting Armani boxers and shrugging on a snowy white shirt. Will's comment came back to her: if he was an ice cream he'd lick himself to death. She breathed out discreetly. That phrase would live in her mind forever now.

'There's juice in the fridge and some pastries ready to be warmed up in the oven. I'm gutted I have to leave you. Shall I call you later?'

'That'd be good.' She put her mug on the bedside table. His eyes lingered on her breasts.

Luca paused, halfway to buttoning up his shirt, and let

out a breath of appreciation. 'Wow. Maybe I should reschedule this meeting with Hugo. It is a Sunday after all, not that Hugo cares.'

'Oh, don't do that on my account,' said Jess, burning under his scrutiny. The momentousness of what she'd done last night was dawning on her more every minute. Most women wouldn't care but ... surely, she could forgive herself for feeling a little disoriented after her first night with a new guy? Especially one like Luca Parisi.

Luca zipped up his suit trousers, gave a theatrical sigh and kissed her lips. He tasted of espresso and smelled of the same aftershave as last night. 'I *will* call you,' he said. 'I hope you aren't regretting what's happened between us?'

'Regret? No. No of course not.'

'It's a big step after you know who, but I'm very pleased you took it. I hope we can have some good times together while I'm in Scilly.'

While he was in Scilly. Another subtle but unmistakable hint that this was a temporary arrangement. That should have suited Jess. It did suit her and yet ... Luca's words had the whiff of a business transaction.

He took his jacket off a hanger in the wardrobe and picked up his sunglasses from the dressing table.

'See you later, then. Ciao.' He put his fingers to his lips and blew the kiss her way.

Then he was gone, humming a tune Jess didn't recognise as he shut the door and left the cottage.

*

253

A little while later, Jess stepped off the morning boat at St Saviour's quay. A few locals were on board too and she nodded politely but stayed largely huddled up in her coat, nursing her hangover and trying to process the previous evening.

If anyone gave her overnight bag more than a quick glance, she didn't care. She'd also ignored two texts from Will, asking if she was OK, but replied to one from Maisie enquiring how it went with a winking smiley and a 'wow' face.

She'd changed back into her jeans, boots and coat after Luca had gone, an action that had added to the feeling that the whole evening had been an hallucination or that a different woman than 'Jess Godrevy: flower farmer' had had hot and steamy sex with an Italian businessman last night.

She walked along the quay, rehearsing what she'd say to her mother who was bound to give her the third degree and texting a quick answer to Will, at last, saying she was on her way up to the farm and was fine.

The handful of locals who'd disembarked at the same time had walked the opposite way to the small village that served as St Saviour's main 'town'. Jess was alone as she meandered along, texting with one hand, her bag over the crook of her arm. She needed to get back to work, but a few minutes of extra breathing space wouldn't do any harm and it would give her a chance to compose herself.

She decided to take the beach route but hadn't got more than a few yards when she spotted Emmy running over the sand in her direction. A bucket swung in one hand, a spade flailed in the other.

Keri and Adam were behind, chatting to each other.

Jess's heart thumped. The last thing she wanted was to speak to them, but she could hardly turn around and walk off. Why, why, why did he have to come across her now, fresh from Luca's bed?

Emmy was only a few yards away and stopped suddenly. She poked at a gelatinous mass on the sand with her spade, then pulled a face and let out a cry of disgust. 'Mum! There's a jellyfish on the beach!'

Keri and Adam looked up and Adam saw her. Jess had no choice but to stop.

The jellyfish was iridescent bluey green with long tentacles that sparkled in the sun. Emmy leaned down and poked it with her spade. 'Eww.'

'Don't touch it,' said Jess hastily. 'It's dead but those tentacles could still pack a mighty sting.'

Emmy jumped back. She really did have Adam's features and his curly hair.

Keri jogged over, with Adam close behind.

'Leave the wee creature alone,' said Keri, glancing up at Jess with a smile. 'You haven't touched it, have you?' she asked her daughter.

'No,' replied Jess, 'but I thought I ought to warn her because it's no ordinary jellyfish. It's a Portuguese man o' war.'

'Oh my God. Is it still dangerous?'

Adam cut in, 'Not if it's left alone.'

'It'll have washed up in the last storm, but it can still deliver a painful sting,' said Jess, deciding not to frighten Emmy by saying that a small dog had died after getting tangled in one earlier in the year.

Emmy kept a safe distance from the creature. 'What's a Portuguese man o' war?' she said.

'A bloody big jellyfish you don't want to mess with,' said Keri, with a grimace. She had delicate features and her hair was scraped back off her face in a high ponytail. She wore Ugg-style boots that had sand clinging to them. She didn't seem Adam's type, Jess thought, but what did she know about him any more?

'Do you live here?' Keri asked as Emmy ran off to investigate some shells on the tideline.

Adam and Jess exchanged glances. Her heart beat faster.

'Yes. I run the flower farm.'

'Oh,' said Keri and then her mouth opened wider. She looked at Adam. 'My God. You're *the* Jess.'

The Jess. What did that mean? Jess was dumb with shock.

'Keri. This is Jess Godrevy. Jess, this is Keri,' said Adam hastily. 'Keri, do you mind if I have a word with Jess?'

'No problem.' Keri seemed relieved. 'I wish he would talk to you, to be honest. Look, I'll take Emmy back to the cottage so you can have a chat.' Keri smiled at Jess sympathetically, but Jess's emotions lurched all over the place: what the hell was going on? Did Keri want Adam to tell her about their relationship – if so she had a very direct way of going about it.

'I'm not sure we've anything to talk about,' she said as neutrally as she could, while seething inside.

Keri shook her head. 'Adam. You *have* to tell her. Nice to meet you, Jess. Maybe I'll see you later. Emmy!'

Keri jogged to Emmy, leaving Jess and Adam alone.

Nice to meet her? What kind of comment was that?

'What does she mean, *have* to tell me?' Jess demanded as soon as Keri was gone.

'Don't worry. I'm not going to ask you to come back to me,' he said bitterly.

Something snapped. 'Good, because I wouldn't. After what you did to me.'

Adam visibly winced as if she'd slapped him. Jess was reeling. How had it come to this? How had it come to the point where she deliberately wanted to cause pain to the man she loved? *Had* loved. Wanted not to love or feel anything ever again and yet the way her whole body was shaking, she did feel for him. Hate and pity and love and longing surged through her, even more powerful for having been suppressed. What had been the point of last night if Adam still had the power to make her so angry and upset?

'I – I can see how this looks. I don't blame you, but you only know part of the story,' he started.

'What is the whole story, Adam? And if there's a whole story, why didn't you put it the letter?' She wanted to hear what he had to say even though it would almost certainly cause her more pain.

'I couldn't. I can't.'

'Why not? What's so mysterious? Tell me!'

'It's not mysterious. It's – Jess, please understand me, I never meant to hurt you.'

'Why did you turn up here with Keri and Emmy?'

'Because ...' He stopped talking abruptly. 'What's the point?'

'None at all. I need to get back to work.' This was getting

her nowhere. Adam seemed to want to get his confession off his chest but kept skirting around it. Was it a game to him or was he genuinely finding it impossible to tell her?

'Wait. Whatever you've assumed about me, you should know that Keri's not my partner, she's my sister-in-law and Emmy's my niece.'

Jess caught her breath. 'I don't understand. They can't be. You don't have a brother or any siblings ... unless ... are you trying to tell me you're married to someone ...?'

'No. I'm not married. Not to Keri or anyone.' He sighed. 'Please. Walk down the beach with me?'

Jess glanced around her. People were gathering at the quay ready for the freight boat to call. It was only a matter of time before someone from the farm arrived with the first flower load of the day. The beach was deserted ahead of them. She steeled herself for whatever might be coming, however painful. 'OK. I'm listening.'

They walked steadily and were soon out of sight of the quay as Adam began speaking. 'I do have a brother, or I *did*. I had a half-brother called Blake, but he died last year. He was Keri's husband and Emmy's dad.'

Whatever Jess had been expecting to hear, this wasn't it. She thought back to the first time she'd seen Emmy, holding tightly to her mum's hand, asking if they were staying on Scilly for long. To the little girl running along with her bucket and spade. She was so young ... Jess's heart went out to her and to Adam for the loss of his brother. 'Oh God, no. I'm so sorry for you both. That's terrible and Emmy's so young. She can't be more than eight?'

'She's almost nine. She's had a shit time, yes. She's been through stuff no kid should have to go through and seen things no one should have to.'

'I'm very sorry about your brother but I always thought you were an only child.'

'So did I ... This whole business really started the day I got the text ...'

'I knew it. You were so shocked. What did it say?'

'A few weeks before, I'd been contacted by one of those heir hunting companies. They kept calling me and leaving messages saying I might have inherited some money. I thought it was a scam and ignored it.'

'I remember you getting texts but I took no notice and you never mentioned what they were about.'

'Because I thought they were just scam texts. But eventually I answered one of their calls by mistake and they said I was named in a legacy. I was angry they'd hassled me and I cut the call short but when I checked out the company later, I realised they might be genuine. I still didn't say anything because I didn't think their claims would amount to anything much. I phoned my dad and he couldn't think of anyone who might have left me money except some distant cousin of Mum's who'd emigrated to Canada years ago, but it wasn't her ...'

Adam paused and they stopped walking.

'Things turned weird then. The company called again and said that I had people claiming to be my family who said I might be entitled to a substantial sum. They said that a man called Peter Garrison had died without leaving a will and I

259

might be entitled to a share in his estate. I'd never heard of him and thought they were wrong or he was some long-lost uncle or cousin, but no, they said, Peter Garrison was my father. His own family had told them that I was his son, but I might not even know that – but they did.'

He had to stop and take a breath. Jess's instinct was to reach out and comfort him, but she held back.

'Go on,' she said gently.

'I said they must be wrong and were talking rubbish and my dad *was* my dad and I told them to fuck off, basically. I tried to forget about it, though it niggled at me, I didn't want to ask Mum or Dad – how could I on the off chance it was true?'

'I can see why you were shocked when you heard. If it was true, it meant that your mum had had an affair,' said Jess.

'And how could I come out and ask her that? I tried to ignore it, but then that text came. It was from Keri. She managed to get my number from a guy at the heir hunting company. The message said that her husband, my brother – my half-brother, Blake, had died recently and then ...'

Adam clammed up, as if he was struggling with something.

'I eventually agreed to meet Keri,' he said. 'I went back to Cumbria before Christmas as you know. I couldn't bear anyone near me. It's as if I wanted to crawl inside a cave like an animal and never come out. Deep down, I knew it was all true. Why would Keri lie to me? So, I confronted Mum at Christmas.'

'Your poor mum. Did your dad know?'

'Yes. He knew. Mum had had an affair while they were going through a bad patch when he was working away on the rigs. Peter Garrison was the deputy head from the school where she was a teaching assistant. He left straight after the affair ended and went back to his wife. She'd moved in with her sister in Scotland. Dad knew that I couldn't possibly be his son, so Mum told him the truth and he stuck by her and brought me up as his own. They loved each other and didn't want to hurt me by telling me.'

Jess was horrified by the pain in Adam's face as he struggled to compose himself. She thought he was about to burst into tears and she'd never seen him cry. She touched his arm but withdrew it. She felt sorry for him but she didn't understand why he hadn't told her this at the time. Then again, he'd had a series of terrible shocks. Finding out he had a father and brother, losing them both. 'Oh, Adam. I would have helped you if only you'd told me.'

'I did try. After my real dad and then Blake passed away, I wasn't thinking straight. I had a lot to deal with. You too. You were supporting Maisie while she got back on her feet and her father was poorly. I didn't want to lay this on you.'

'Maisie? I love her to bits, but I could have handled this too.' Jess was puzzled, but Adam was right about one thing: he hadn't been thinking straight and she could understand that much. 'I'm sorry you lost your dad and Blake in such a short time. That's terrible. What happened to them?'

He swallowed hard and seemed in agony. The grief was still raw and he obviously couldn't bring himself to rake up the details so soon. 'Natural causes. For both of them.'

'Adam. I'm very sorry about all the horrible things that have happened to you. No one should have to deal with so much in such a short time, but if you loved me, you could have shared this with me. I loved you.' The words were out before she could stop them and Adam's mouth opened in shock. His eyes clouded with pain but it was too late to unsay them. Her stomach lurched.

'I agonised over whether I should, but I was overwhelmed by the shock of finding out that Dad wasn't who I thought he was, and that I had another family and a brother I'd lost before I even had a chance to meet him. I needed some space and time and the longer we were apart, the more I thought you were better off without me. Coming back and seeing you with Luca only confirms I was right.' His shoulders slumped, and he looked utterly defeated.

'But ...' Jess was about to say it was early days with Luca but stopped short. The state Adam was in, his determination to have no more to do with her, told her she shouldn't try and change his mind. She wasn't sure she wanted to, no matter how sympathetic she was towards his recent traumas. It would surely only invite more pain and hurt for both of them. 'Even if you'd explained this in the letter, I'd have understood more.'

'If I'd told you all this, you might have asked if you could come over and I didn't want to drag you into my problems, especially when you needed to be here for the business at the busiest time of year. I'm sorry I even sent the letter. It was a bad idea.'

It's too late now, Jess thought. She was in turmoil at hearing he'd gone through so much pain and was still obviously traumatised. Hearing his reasons for leaving had also left questions unanswered but she didn't want to push him too far in his fragile state of mind. 'I'm not sure why you've come back here now ...' she murmured.

'Because all hell broke loose at home since the new year. Blake's death had thrown everything up in the air. Emmy's had a terrible time at school ever since he died. She's been bullied, can you believe that? Even after losing her dad and granddad? Keri was desperate to get away, so I thought the best thing was to bring them here for some peace and quiet over Easter while things settled down. I kept up the lease on the cottage and I've been paying the rent.'

He stopped and for a few moments they both looked out over the sea. Jess tried to process what he'd told her but one huge question remained.

Adam broke the silence first.

'You know that this doesn't change anything between us?'

Jess's throat dried at hearing this. She couldn't even reply.

'I'm not the man I was. I can never be the old Adam again. I'm sorry but I can't see us ever going back to the way things were.' His voice was breaking with the strain.

Without thinking, Jess touched his arm. 'Don't say that. Even if we can't be together you can get through this. No matter how much you're hurting now, people can help. Get some counselling, talk to someone. I'm here if you need me. As a – a *friend*, if nothing else.'

He shook his head. 'You're kind and you're beautiful and I care for you, but you have a new life now. With Luca or whoever.'

Jess held her hand to her mouth to stop a sob. She'd finally had her explanation, for what it was worth, but she felt even worse than before.

'Adam ...' her words trailed off. She didn't know what she'd been going to say. She'd once had so much to say to him and now nothing whatsoever seemed to help in any way.

Adam carried on, 'And if you're worried about seeing me around, I only plan on staying until I've sorted out a few things. I need to arrange for my stuff to be shipped back to Cumbria and I've some financial stuff to deal with. Keri and Emmy are staying until Tuesday; Emmy has to go back to school on Wednesday. I'll be staying on here for a few weeks and then I'll be leaving for good too ... but otherwise, we'll try to keep out of your way. I hope you'll be happy with Luca.'

'It's early days, Adam. Last night was only our second date.' Jess had chosen her words carefully but Adam's jaw dropped and she realised that he fully understood what the date had entailed. Even if she hadn't spelled it out, her overnight bag and some sixth sense would have told him that she'd slept with Luca for the first time the previous night. His fingers clenched in a fist – not in physical rage because that wasn't Adam, and never would be – but because he was desperately trying not to reply to her. She felt a fresh surge of pity for him.

'I should never have even tried to speak to you outside the pub, or last night – or now. I'm sorry.' His voice broke as he said it and Jess's own heart broke a little more too.

'I'm glad we've spoken, at least.' No matter how painful for both of us, she thought. Something about this conversation felt very final; even more final than the day Adam had flown out of Scilly.

'Does anyone else on Scilly know about your situation?' she said.

'No one, but if it's easier for you, I'll tell them about Keri and Emmy. I wanted you to be the first to know.'

'I need to share it with Will.'

Adam closed his eyes. 'He must hate me for what I've done.'

'Will doesn't hate people. You're still his mate, but he was confused and angry. Like me.'

'I'm sorry. I am a coward. I couldn't handle what happened – I still can't handle it ...' The agony was etched on his features. Jess wanted to reach out to him. He looked as if his world had ended.

'You're *not* a coward. Don't say that.'

'It's *true* ...' He swallowed hard and tears glistened in his eyes. 'I have to go.'

'No, wait.'

'Goodbye, Jess,' he said, turned around and walked briskly down the beach before she could say another word. She stopped herself from following him, realising that he couldn't hold in his emotions any longer and that he needed privacy.

Jess lingered on the beach, unable to move. Tears spilled out and ran down her own cheeks. She definitely couldn't go home yet. Her mind and heart were full to bursting with Adam's revelations about his family. He was overwhelmed with grief and probably depressed too. Over the past fifteen minutes, so many things about their break-up had fallen into place but it still felt as though he hadn't told her everything and while he refused to trust her, she was as helpless as ever.

Chapter 26

Gaby pulled the duvet back over her head. No matter how much she'd wished it away, the day of doom had finally arrived: the final day of the championships. It was sunny May Bank Holiday Sunday: a day when she could have been visiting the Abbey Gardens, or lazing with her friends on one of the uninhabited island beaches with a picnic and a coolbox full of beers.

Instead she found herself jolted from a fitful sleep by Will banging on doors and barking like an Army sergeant to check that everyone was awake and reminding them to 'assemble at 07.30 in the farmhouse kitchen for a pre-race breakfast and briefing'.

The championships were taking place just off St Mary's harbour and there was only one way to get the gig over to the start from St Saviour's: row it themselves. Luckily the swell was gentle and the winds light because the conditions would have had to be storm force before the race was cancelled.

Having managed the crossing without incident, and feeling her nerves abating a little, Gaby helped to drag the *Athene* onto the harbour beach in Hugh Town alongside the other boats.

The butterflies took flight as soon as she saw the crowds in the harbour and town. The three-way race with Petroc and Gull had been one thing, but this was on another scale. Scores of rowers in shorts, vests and flip-flops swarmed around dozens of gigs from all over Cornwall and the south-west. Hundreds of supporters and onlookers milled around the harbourside so any cock-ups would be conducted in the full glare of the crowds.

Everyone was laughing and chattering with excitement. It was obviously regarded as the party of the year and the smell of barbecues and beer filled the air, as rowing clubs and spectators made a day of it. At least the weather was reasonable. High winds and seas the previous week had subsided, although Gaby had been secretly hoping for a mammoth storm and the whole thing to be cancelled. She was petrified of letting her crew down by collapsing with exhaustion, capsizing the gig or both.

Because of Will's paranoia, the St Saviour's boat was one of the first off-island boats into the harbour. Their race was over an hour and a half away, which gave her a break, but also far too much time to think about the impending ordeal.

Will bustled about making sure the gig was undamaged, registering with the marshals and checking everyone was OK. Petroc's boat rowed in shortly after, with its long-limbed athletic crew hopping onto the sand, as fresh as if they'd been for a Sunday picnic on a boating lake. Gaby recognised a lot of the rowers, a mix of veterans, newbies like herself, plus the odd scarily fit hunk like Luca.

The rest of the St Saviour's team was made up of Jess,

267

Natalia, Will, Robbie and Lawrence with Len as the cox. Although he didn't row these days, and was harsher on the crew than Captain Bligh, Len knew the waters around the isles like the back of his hand.

Gaby couldn't help comparing their boats. The vintage *Athene* had been carefully restored and was a thing of beauty, but she also showed her age next to some of the modern vessels. Not that she had the slightest delusions of winning the race: she fully expected to come in last, but hopefully not embarrassingly far behind and preferably without needing the aid of the orange RNLI boat moored in the harbour. Despite enjoying the banter and bonding between the crew members, she couldn't wait to get it over and hopefully give up rowing once she'd fulfilled her promise.

Jess caught her grimacing at the lifeboat. 'We'll be fine, you know,' she said, patting her on the back.

'I hope so. Don't tell Will, but I'll be so bloody glad when it's all over.'

'Me too,' said Jess, 'but it means a lot to Will so I have to show a bit of enthusiasm.'

'I don't,' said Gaby, thinking how well Jess looked lately. Her cheeks glowed and she'd lost the haunted look she had since Adam left. Even though he was back, she was still smiling more often than not and Gaby was sure that must have a lot to do with Luca. He'd been up to the farm numerous times and it had been hard not to notice – or hear – that Jess had been staying over on Petroc.

'Gaby? Feeling OK?' Jess asked.

268

Gaby smiled, glad Jess couldn't read her real thoughts. 'Actually, I feel crap, but I'll get over it,' she joked.

Jess smiled back encouragingly but her attention was quickly diverted away from Gaby by Luca. They exchanged waves before he said something to his crew, and left them to haul their gleaming craft onto the beach while he joined Jess.

Not wanting to play gooseberry, Gaby wished Luca good luck – though she didn't really mean it, of course – then left them to it. Checking she wasn't needed, Gaby took her chance to join the queue for the Portaloos that had been stationed on the green behind the beach.

When she'd finally made it out of the loos, Natalia was waiting for her on the steps above the beach. They could see Jess and Luca on the beach. A few yards away on the promenade above it, were Keri, Emmy and Adam. It was common knowledge by now that they were Adam's sister-in-law and niece, and that there had been a family tragedy involving a long-lost brother and his father. Jess herself had mentioned very brief details to her but not elaborated, although Gaby suspected she knew more about the situation than anyone else on Scilly.

Seeing Adam with his new family, Gaby felt deeply sorry for his loss. From his haggard appearance and remarks from people who had known him well, she could see he had been, and was still suffering from, the double bereavement. If she'd known him better she might have gently hinted that he could talk to her about the loss of his brother but she was nowhere near close enough to him to even offer.

Emmy held her mum's hand tightly and Adam was crouched

down beside her, pointing out the ferry in the harbour. The little girl giggled at something he'd said. At least his niece had brought a smile to his face, she thought.

'I bet Luca doesn't like him being back,' said Natalia in a loud voice.

Gaby watched Luca run his hands through his hair like he was in a shampoo ad. He put his arm around Jess who laughed.

'He's lucky to have Jess,' said Gaby loyally.

'Her ex isn't very happy about it.'

Natalia was right about that. Adam was too far away to be able to hear his conversation, but Gaby could see that his body language had changed as soon as he noticed Jess and Luca. A shriek of laughter came from the beach as Luca swept Jess into his arms and pretended to dump her into the Petroc boat. Adam's mouth was set in a hard line, then Emmy tugged his sleeve and he smiled broadly. He said something to Keri, took Emmy's hand and headed off into the crowds with them both.

Gaby checked her watch. There was still an hour to go to the race, but time would fly by as they made their final checks, listened to Will's pep talk and rowed out to the start line.

'We'd better get back to the boat before Will starts panicking,' she said.

Natalia sighed. 'I wish we could skip the race and go straight to the pub.'

'Great idea, but Will would never forgive us. Let's get down to the boat. The sooner we get this over with, the better.'

They hurried down the steps from the harbour to the beach,

threading their way through the rowers. A small crowd had gathered by one of the beach tents and judging by the green uniforms, they were paramedics.

'Someone's had an accident,' said a man next to Gaby and Natalia. 'I think it's one of your crew. Looks like your race is over before it's begun.'

'What?' Gaby and Natalia were forced to push their way past people to reach the *Athene*, where a small crowd had gathered.

To their horror, Lawrence was being loaded onto a mobile stretcher, wincing in pain.

Will was next to him, patting his arm. 'Sorry, mate. Hope it's not too serious.'

Natalia rushed to his side. 'Oh my God, is he going to die?'

'No, I'm bloody not,' Lawrence called. 'But it feels like it.'

One of the medics planted a mask on his face. 'Breathe this. It'll help with the pain.'

'What happened?' Gaby asked Jess.

'Lawrence was fooling around on the harbourside, lost his footing and fell. He might have broken his ankle but he landed on sand, so it's not too serious,' said Jess. 'Very painful though. Poor Lawrence.'

'Does this mean the race is off?' Natalia asked, with a hopeful smirk.

'I guess so ... Lawrence, I'll come with you to the hospital!' Jess said as the paramedics started to drag the trolley off the harbour sand.

Lawrence ripped the mask off his face. 'No, you bloody won't. You've got a race to win.'

'We can't carry on without you, mate,' said Will, walking alongside him.

Gaby and the others joined him by the ambulance. Gaby bit her lip. Relief that she wouldn't have to row after all was tinged by guilt as Lawrence yelped in pain. Did it make her evil that she was glad their race was off?

'We have to get Lawrence to the hospital,' said the medic. 'He needs an X-ray asap.'

Lawrence groaned.

The paramedic patted his arm. 'I'd use that gas, if I were you mate. It's going to be a bumpy ride up the quay and through these crowds.'

'I will once my team promise to carry on,' said Lawrence.

'But we're one oar short,' said Robbie, his red hair standing on end.

Lawrence clutched Will's arm in a vice-like grip. 'Find someone!' he said, pulling some horrible faces. 'We've worked too hard to quit now. Ow ...' He clamped the mask back on his face as the medics finally loaded him into the ambulance.

Jess watched him leave, and held up her phone. 'Poor Lawrence. I've called his girlfriend. She's going to meet him at the hospital.'

Will shoved his hands through his hair while the ambulance sounded its siren a few times to warn people to get out of the way. Gaby thought he looked beaten, but then he suddenly clapped his hands. 'Right, you lot. We have thirty minutes to find another rower to take Lawrence's place. Everyone get out there and try and persuade someone from another crew to join us in the Mixed race.'

Gaby's heart plunged. Surely they weren't still going to row. Oh God, what if they couldn't find anyone and Will made them join in with only five crew members? She might have an actual heart attack.

'But all the veteran men are already racing today, Will. They won't want to join us after that. They'll be knackered,' Jess said patiently.

'Even if there's time to find someone,' added Gaby, 'which there isn't ...'

Will's mouth was set in a determined line. 'I don't care. *Try*.'

'What about Luca?' Jess asked after a pause. 'I suppose I could ask if he'll swap sides and put one of the Petroc veteran men in the Mixed.'

Will groaned. 'No way. He won't do that. Petroc are hoping to win and he won't jeopardise their chances. Hell, they *will* win, but I at least wanted to give him a bloody run for his money. And so does Lawrence,' he added quickly.

'What about Patrick and Maisie? They might know someone,' Robbie piped up.

'Good idea ... I'll go and ask them. But everyone who can row is already rowing. It's a long shot, but let's at least try and find someone,' said Will desperately.

Len stood by and folded his arms. 'We're doomed, but I knew this was a crap idea in the first place.'

'I'm not sure that's helpful, Len,' said Gaby, even though she partly agreed.

'Yeah, shut up, Len,' said Will.

Len's jaw dropped. 'Suit yourselves. I'll keep an eye on the boat while you lot waste your time.'

'What he really means is he'll have a fag,' muttered Jess as Robbie and Natalia scooted off.

'I don't know anyone who could help,' said Gaby, feeling sorry for Will. 'Look. Luca's coming over.'

Luca joined them on the slipway. 'I just heard about your crew member. Is it serious?'

'Suspected broken ankle,' said Jess.

He pulled a sympathetic face. 'That's hard luck. You worked so hard to get fit to compete too.'

'We still intend to compete,' said Will curtly.

Luca gasped. 'You don't mean with only five of you?'

Will folded his arms. 'If we have to, yeah.'

Gaby saw Jess cringe. 'Don't be stupid, Will. You know we can't.'

'Bad luck, mate,' said Luca, patting Will on the arm. 'Unless you're strong enough to take the place of two of your crew.'

Gaby winced but Will looked up at the crowds on the quayside, a smile of grim determination appearing on his face. 'I may not be strong enough to row for two, but I know a man who is.'

Chapter 27

Will had homed in on Adam who was chatting to his family on the promenade a few yards away. Jess was surprised to see Keri and Emmy but guessed they must be visiting for the holiday weekend, but her main concern now was that Will clearly intended to persuade Adam to make up their crew.

'No ... You wouldn't ...'

'I'll be back in five.' Will patted her arm and headed off in Adam's direction.

'I have to go after him!' Jess told Luca and darted off before he could even reply. However, Will was already halfway up the steps to the prom about to be met by Adam at the top. Jess threw her hands in the air. 'Fuck. Fuck. Fuck.'

A few rowers glanced at her but immediately went back to the business of preparing their boats. Jess was surrounded by more people than she'd ever seen on Scilly, yet felt completely alone. She should go back to Luca: could see his head at the centre of a knot of Petroc rowers. She'd left him abruptly and rudely and he didn't deserve that.

But having Adam in their crew? It was too much.

She'd seen him around St Saviour's several times since their conversation on the beach. It was impossible not to have come across him, but they hadn't spoken again beyond a nod or a muttered hello and he hadn't said anything about Keri and Emmy coming back. Not that it was any of her business now. Over the past couple of weeks, she'd carried on seeing Luca, and stayed over on Petroc several times. Luca was as charming as ever and had listened thoughtfully when she'd told him who Keri and Emmy really were. It was tough on Adam, he'd said, but if he'd wondered if the situation might affect their fledgling relationship, he hadn't shared his fears with Jess.

Knowing Adam was on the island had made it harder to 'carry on as normal' with Luca, but Jess kept reminding herself that her relationship with Adam had effectively been over since the previous autumn. Life had to go on: for everyone's sake, Adam had been clear enough about that when he'd spoken to her. Adam joining the crew for one race shouldn't have meant anything but it *did* and it felt way too close for comfort.

In despair, she turned away and trudged back to the boat. Luca was still there.

'I didn't mean to snap. It's a fraught time with Will so hellbent on us doing this race and Lawrence's accident and ...'

'And seeing Adam again.' He slipped his arm around her. 'It must be strange to see him back here.'

'Everything changes. I have to accept that.' She smiled. 'I'm a grown-up.'

'Not *everything* has to change ... I plan on staying the rest of the summer until my contract runs out and then ... I was

276

going to tell you this after the race, but Hugo's been hinting at a permanent position as marketing director for the resort. I could take it.'

Jess was taken aback that Luca might want to stay on. She'd been enjoying their fling but never expected it to go on any longer. 'But your home's in London. Even working at Petroc can't be as prestigious or lucrative as your freelance business.'

'It gives me more security and it's further away from Rachel. Not that I need to run away, but perhaps the balance in favour of a fresh start has shifted recently.' He trailed his hand down Jess's back.

Out of the corner of her eye she saw Will and Adam engaged in heated conversation.

'You wouldn't be happy in this small place, Luca. You belong to a big sophisticated world.' She didn't *really* know him, she thought, despite their nights at the resort.

He laughed. 'Sophisticated? The truth is, I don't know where I belong since Rachel and I split up. My whole world and future were turned on their heads and I'm guessing yours were too, but we should both focus on the here and now.'

He was right, thought Jess, but it was the wrong time for this kind of conversation.

'If we're focusing on the now, I'm supposed to find another crew member and I'd rather it wasn't Adam. You can't help, can you?'

'If I wasn't committed to our boat already, I swear I would, but it's not possible. My own crew are all taken too and keen to win the race. And I can't think of anyone else. I don't know the other crews like you do.'

Jess scanned the crowds. Some were pushing their boats towards the water ready to row to the start line.

'Damn. Will wanted to do this so much, even though ...' She was about to say, we'll be thrashed ... 'Oh, God, no.'

Adam was kissing Emmy on the cheek. She looked excited but Keri looked confused. Will slapped Adam on the back.

'What?' asked Luca.

'I think Adam's actually agreed.'

'You're joking.'

'I wish I was. I really do. Bloody bloody men.'

'All of them?' Luca pulled her to him. 'Don't answer that.' Before she could stop him, he kissed her. A wonderful passionate kiss but one she'd have preferred to happen in private and not under the eyes of scores of rowers and half the island. Not under the eyes of Adam, who couldn't possibly have failed to see it.

Jess broke away. 'We both have to get to our boats,' she muttered, confused and angry, with Will, with Luca and with Adam – and herself for still giving a toss what Adam thought.

'Good luck!' he called. 'See you after the race.'

Jess didn't reply, but ran to the boat as the water seethed and splashed with gigs and rowers rushing to the start.

*

Adam had disappeared temporarily – presumably to borrow some rowing kit – as Will jogged back to the boat.

Jess grabbed him. 'What have you done?'

'It's either that or we quit,' he said brusquely.

278

She dug her fingers in deeper. 'Then we'll have to quit.'

'We can't do that. You don't have to even look at him, let alone speak to him.'

'Then I'm not rowing. You'll have to find another woman for the boat.'

He gasped. 'At twenty minutes' notice? Don't be daft.'

'I'm not being "daft". It's you that's being silly, putting me and Adam in the same boat.'

'If I had any other choice, I wouldn't, but please, can you put up with him for this race and then I promise that will be it. There's no chance of us winning anyway so you won't have to step up and get a trophy with him and I doubt very much if he'll join us at the pub, do you?' Will said in a gentler tone.

Jess knew she was overreacting. She also knew that Adam being in their boat might give rise to speculation. She glanced over to the quayside where Keri was handing an ice cream to Emmy. The little girl took it carefully, a huge smile on her face. Jess saw that Luca was deep in conversation with his team. No one was taking any notice of her or Adam.

'OK, but only because it means so much to you and everyone else. I'm sorry for lashing out at you.'

'It's fine and I am sorry it had to be him. Now, I have to go and see how the team are. Adam's borrowing some stuff from a mate. He'll be here any second.'

Jess said nothing. 'Gaby's wetting herself with nerves. You should have a word with her.'

'She'll be OK.'

'She's only doing it for you.'

'If I believed that then I'd pull us out of the race myself. But she's done well to get this far.'

'Better than you expected?'

'No. I always expected her to make it through. After the way she's fitted in here, I've learned not to underestimate her.'

It was the frankest admission Jess had heard about Gaby. 'Will. Be careful ...' she said.

'I'm not sure what you mean and anyway being careful never got anyone anywhere, did it? We'd never have stuck with the farm. You'd never have taken a chance on Luca. Forget it now, we have to push off.'

There was mayhem as crews climbed into their gigs and pushed off from the shore. The loudspeakers blared out announcements and, on the quay, Emmy danced excitedly. Will herded everyone to their seats and scrambled aboard himself, but Jess lingered on shore as the boat bobbed at the edge of the water. Gaby's face was white with terror as she gripped her oar. Robbie and Natalia were glancing around them nervously. Len was muttering to Will. Everyone was now ready for the off except her and Adam, who was shin deep, holding the boat steady, and waiting for her to move. They had to leave this instant.

'Jess. For God's sake, can you get in so Adam can push us off?' Will bellowed from the boat.

Snapping out of her trance, Jess splashed into the water, the surf lapping her ankles. She tried not to even glance at Adam in his rowing kit, lean and long-limbed but she couldn't help but note that even though he'd lost weight, he still had a powerful effect on her. Will roared instructions to the other rowers, warning them about the conditions. Len piled in with helpful comments about how they'd need to row for their lives to be in with a fighting chance. Will tried to calm things down while Jess struggled to scramble on board.

'Careful,' Adam warned as he held the boat to stop it from bucking in the waves created by the wash of a marshal's jet boat.

'I don't need a hand.'

'I know that.' He lowered his voice, and spoke close to her ear while Will and Len had a heated debate about the course. 'I didn't ask for this. I told Will it was a shit idea, but he wouldn't listen. I should probably have backed out, but he put me in an impossible position.'

'I could have pulled out too when I found out, so we're quits on that. We're both doing this because Will's desperate and we don't want to let anyone down.'

Adam hesitated, struggle etched on his features. 'Look. You told me not to hassle you and I didn't want to start something I dreaded finishing. I've wrestled with this, but there's something else that I should have told you on the beach. I *wanted* to tell you ...'

The loudspeakers blared.

'Something else? What do you mean?' Her heart thudded like mad.

'For fuck's sake, we have to go *now*!' barked Will, switching his attention to them. 'Get in or we won't make the start line!'

Jess finally scrambled in and grabbed her oar. Adam gave the boat a push and jumped into the seat in front of Jess. She hadn't even rowed to the start yet she felt drained of energy.

'Good luck!' Luca shouted from the next boat. He blew her a kiss.

Jess threw him a quick smile that vanished the moment they were off. She started rowing.

'Pull!' shouted Len. 'Can we please have everyone actually bloody rowing at the same time!'

'What's the matter? What don't I know?' Jess called down Adam's ear. She knew she should focus on the race but Adam's words echoed through her mind.

'Slow!' Len ordered as they made their way carefully between other crews.

Adam twisted round for a second. 'I wanted to tell you before but I didn't have the courage, but now, seeing you around, I can't leave you in the dark. When Will asked me to join the crew, I realised it was fate that we're together in this boat.'

Jess thought back to her taunt and felt sick. Adam was – used to be – the kindest, bravest man she'd ever known. 'What do you mean, *fate*?'

'Right. Let's at least make the start,' Len barked, shooting Jess and Adam an evil glare. 'And can you *all* please save your breath for the bloody race.'

They rowed away from the shore. Soon Jess couldn't speak, as they made their way towards the buoy that marked the start line. But she could think, and only one thought swirled through her mind: what other bombshells did Adam have in store?

Chapter 28

By the halfway point of the race, Gaby could barely breathe and her lungs were ready to burst. Every muscle in her arms and legs felt as if it was on fire and yet, incredibly, when they rounded the buoy, St Saviour's weren't last. According to Len – who admittedly might have been lying – they were fourth out of eight.

'Pull! Come on! Put your bloody backs into it! Row, you buggers, row!'

Len had used every swearword Gaby had ever heard and few she hadn't and she was ready to get out of the boat and strangle him, but with Adam on board, they'd managed to keep in the middle of the pack. Of course, one person alone didn't make a team, but Adam's skill, power and timing had rubbed off and everyone else felt they had to step up to the mark.

Nonetheless, Gaby wanted to stop rowing more than anything else in the world. Spray stung her eyes, people were breathing heavily and grunting, but no one was going to let the boat behind catch them.

'We're closing the gap on the Gull boat!' Len screamed.

Gaby didn't know where Gull were. She only knew she had to keep going if it killed her. She gritted her teeth and pulled harder.

'Come on!' shouted Will from the rear. 'Petroc aren't that far ahead.'

Gaby knew that *was* a lie, but she hadn't the breath to argue then the boat bucked a little, throwing her off her stroke, but she recovered and pulled with all her might.

'Bit of chop as we round the headland. Come on!' screamed Len, then burst into a coughing fit. No wonder he'd given up rowing, with the number of fags he smoked, thought Gaby wickedly.

'We can get third!' Will yelled. 'We're almost on Gull. More effort. Bloody come on!'

Gaby thought she couldn't pull any harder, but Will and Adam had upped the stroke rate and she had no choice but to ignore the fire tearing through her limbs and try to keep up.

'We're getting there. We can do this!'

'Len. Shut up!' shouted Jess.

'Oh my God,' Natalia screeched.

'What?' shouted Will.

Len's face was purple as he glanced to the side of them. 'What the fuck is going on ... Petroc are heading for St Piran's. Jesus, what is their cox doing? They're going to collide.'

'Whaaaa ...' Gaby mouthed but didn't have the breath to finish the sentence.

'Fucking hell!' Len shouted. 'They're going to crash into each other.'

284

'My God!' That was Jess.

'They've clashed oars. Great! Don't you bloody dare slow down. Ye-ess! I think we can win this.' Len was grinning in delight.

'Nooo. I c-can't.' Gaby let out a howl, but it was too late. The stroke rate picked up again and she had to keep up.

'We're past Gull!' Will yelled in delight.

Between gasps, Gaby caught sight of Patrick and his crew alongside them to the right, faces contorted with effort and despair. Seconds later, she spotted the Petroc and St Piran's boats off to the left-hand side. They'd come to a halt and were almost on top of each other with their crews shouting and swearing. Then they were gone as the *Athene* sped past, powered by six demented lunatics and an evil despot called Len.

'Row! Row until it kills you!' he shouted.

'It will!' said Gaby and wished she hadn't because speaking meant she'd missed a vital chance to snatch some oxygen.

'Line coming up. Faster. Faster. Gull are closing again.'

Gaby almost wept as the spray battered her face and her muscles screamed. Then there was a horn blast and cheering and shouting. The boat slowed dramatically and Will was screaming down her ear.

'We bloody did it!'

Gaby slumped over her oar, gasping for air. Around her, the crew were going nuts, whooping and shouting as she did a goldfish impression.

'You were fantastic!' Will slapped her on the back and she started coughing.

'Whoa! We won! We actually won!' Jess cried.

'Course we did. We're bloody fantastic.'

'Not half bad for novices,' said Len.

Gaby supported herself on the oar, wondering if she would make it to shore without throwing up. She managed to glance around to see Will punching the air and Jess with her arms around Adam. He twisted round and hugged her.

No one else seemed to have noticed, however. Len and Natalia were singing '*We are the Champions!*' as the Petroc boat limped alongside, looking like it was the end of the world.

'Congratulations!' Luca called sportingly from his boat, though his smile faded as he caught sight of Jess with her arms around Adam, laughing. Gaby didn't have time to dwell on them because Len was bawling at them to pick up their oars once more and row back to the shore, before they drifted into any other boats.

Once they were close enough to the beach, Gaby hauled her aching limbs over the side of the boat and stumbled through the shallows. Jess leapt out of the boat and splashed onto the beach, without speaking.

'Jess. Wait!' Adam called, dashing round to the other side of the boat to follow her.

Will pulled him back. 'Leave her, mate.'

'It's prob-bably for the b-best,' said Gaby, whose legs felt decidedly wobbly.

Adam let out a groan. 'You don't know ...' he began. 'Jesus. What a mess.'

Will was sheepish. 'I asked you to row. It's my fault.'

Adam's face was agonised as he saw Jess run towards Luca who was helping to haul the damaged Petroc gig onto the sand. 'Not the rowing. Everything ... I have to go. Emmy and Keri need me. It's been a long day ...'

Glancing up, Gaby saw Keri and Emmy making their way through the crowds on the quay. Keri waved at him and Emmy broke free of her mum, heading for the slipway and Adam.

'See you,' said Adam and hurried off towards her.

Will groaned. 'Shit. What have I done now? I'm a total idiot.'

'At last. The penny drops,' said Gaby.

Will glanced down at her, shook his head and sighed. 'I'd better go after Jess and apologise for asking Adam.'

Gaby touched his arm. Will glanced down as she kept her fingers on his skin. His arm was very sweaty, salty and hairy: a heady cocktail that ought to be gross but, perversely, sent a shiver of lust right through her. Besides, she was hardly fresh from the box herself. Her hair had escaped its scrunchie and tendrils were sticking to her face, which was probably as red as a beetroot.

'I was joking about you being an idiot, but you should leave Jess and Luca alone,' she said. 'The last thing they need is you sticking your oar in. If you'll excuse the pun.'

'I'll excuse anything today.' He looked at her intently in a way that made her feel deliciously shivery. 'You gave everything in that boat.'

The moment was interrupted by Len slapping Will on the back so hard, he almost staggered forward. 'Come on, skipper, there's a large pint of Tribute waiting for you.'

Will nodded, but his eyes lingered on Gaby. 'I can't wait,' he said and she might have been imagining it but she wasn't at all sure he was referring to the pint.

Chapter 29

Jess had been torn between wanting to find Luca and wanting to hear what Adam had to say. However much she wanted to speak to Adam, she owed it to Luca to see how he was doing after the crash. She soon found him talking to Hugo at the edge of the beach. Or rather Hugo was talking *at* Luca, and ranting about the damage to the Petroc boat, judging by the way his arms were flailing. Luca was holding up his palms and trying to calm Hugo down as the rest of the crews argued over the two boats. The St Piran's gig had clearly come off worse, from what Jess could see, but the brand new Petroc boat was also scraped all down one side. Splintered oars lay on the sand, but thankfully no one seemed to have been hurt.

It was obviously a bad time, so she headed away from the shore to calm her mind, but Luca caught up with her.

'Jess. Wait.'

'Are you OK?' she asked.

'Fine. Everyone's unscathed apart from bruised egos.'

'I'm glad you're not hurt. It was a nasty clash and I saw Hugo kicking off about the boat?'

288

'Yes. The resort sponsored and paid for the boat, which means he's going to have to foot the bill for the damage.'

'I'm sorry,' said Jess because she couldn't think of anything else to say and was bracing herself for the real confrontation to come.

'Sorry? What for? Beating us? It was our fault we ran into St Piran's. I don't blame Will for taking advantage of the situation. I'd have done the same.'

He flashed a smile at her but there was no kiss. 'Congratulations on winning.'

'Thanks. Luca ... I have to say this; that thing with Adam you saw. The hug. It happened in the heat of the moment, it didn't mean anything.' Jess's heart sank even as she said the words. 'You do understand?'

He shrugged. 'There's nothing for me to understand. It's your life.'

'It was an impulse. A reaction ... relief.'

He smiled knowingly. 'Why do I think you're trying to convince yourself here?'

She fired up. 'I'm not. It did mean nothing. I'd forgotten what had happened between me and Adam for a few seconds.'

Luca arched an eyebrow. 'I have to sort out the damage to the boat with the St Piran's captain, then let's find somewhere quieter if possible and talk properly. It's been a hell of a ride for us all today. Can you give me half an hour to deal with the gig and then meet me in town? By the deli café on Hugh Street?'

Jess nodded and headed off, scouring the crowds. Adam was no longer on the beach, and she couldn't see him or Keri and Emmy among the throng. She wandered further along the promenade above the beach but they all seemed to have vanished. Her mind was racing and her emotions were all over the place, what she really needed was time and space to think.

She'd reached the furthest end of Porthloo beach, so she decided to follow the path behind it, around the headland and up to Harry's Walls, an old fort that looked over the harbour. It was a tucked-away haven and she was relieved to find herself alone when she reached the grassy space within the ruined stones. She perched on a fragment of wall and looked down on the chaotic scene in the harbour. Other gigs were still racing and people scurried over the beaches and lined the quayside. Snatches of the loudspeaker announcements drifted up on the wind.

Jess realised she'd miss the prize-giving for the winning Mixed crew, but that wasn't a bad thing. She couldn't face being hauled onto the podium anyway.

She hugged her knees, glad she'd put her hoodie on over her racing vest.

Luca had seemed to accept that her embrace with Adam was an impulse. It was true, it *was* an impulse – she hadn't even thought about it as Adam threw his arms around her in the euphoria of winning the race. And yes, in those few seconds, the past eight months might never have happened. She and Adam were one again; a team: pulling together and joined together, as she'd always felt they were.

Yet it was all an illusion: as if she'd dreamt the rowing race and woken up now to cold harsh reality. She and Adam could never be together.

She shivered. The heat of the race had gone and she was growing cold in the wind, despite her sweatshirt. She could try and find Adam and ask him what he'd meant by 'fate', but time was running out. She'd promised to meet Luca, and she should really find Will and the rest of the crew too. No chance of calling any of them: her phone was in the dry bag in the locker of the *Athene* but there was nothing she could do about that. Anyway, her crew would surely be in one of the pubs, celebrating their victory: Adam wouldn't be so easy to locate.

She coaxed her stiff limbs into life and walked down from the fort to join the quieter back road into town. She hadn't got far when she saw Adam walking up the steep path towards her. Jess stopped and readied herself. It was relatively quiet here, no one else could hear them and most of all they had to stop running from each other.

'Jess?'

She waited by a bench. 'How did you find me?'

'One of the marshals said they'd seen you heading this way a while ago. I guessed where you might be. We used to come up here. Do you remember?'

She smiled at the memory. 'Of course I do. We were here last August after the beach party.' The week before he got the text, she remembered. 'It feels like a lifetime ago now.'

'It does for me too. I'm not going anywhere now. The question is: are you?'

'No. No I'm staying. I want to hear what you have to say, even if I won't like it. Where are Keri and Emmy?'

'Keri's taken Emmy to a pottery painting café in town. She's mad on art and crafts. I have an hour before I have to meet them and take the boat back to the cottage. I wanted to talk to you straight after the race, but I had to tell Keri where I was going and what I was doing. Then I saw you with Luca ...'

'He saw us together in the boat. I was explaining that it didn't mean anything.'

'No ...' said Adam, a little wistfully, thought Jess. 'If he's worth anything, he'll know that. It happened in the moment. It was a mistake.'

Her heart plunged. 'I wouldn't have called it a mistake. More an impulse. We forgot who we are – who we are *now*.'

Adam stared at her. 'But that's the problem. I *can't* forget who we are or what we were to each other and what you still mean to me. I've tried so fucking hard, but I can't let us go that easily. I thought I could get away without explaining anything, but now I know it was impossible. There's something I wish I didn't know but I do and I can't keep it a secret from anyone I care about or love and especially not you.'

Jess had promised herself that she would stay calm and hear him out without ranting or getting upset. She shoved her hands in the pockets of her hoodie to stop them shaking.

They had to step back almost into the hedge then to let a large group of walkers pass them on the path. Adam cursed under his breath, but he and Jess smiled and returned the group's greeting, though Jess was ready to scream in frustration. How bizarre that they had to observe all the niceties when they were both bursting to talk.

'Up here,' said Adam and they climbed the path back onto the top of the ruined walls out of the way of passers-by. Adam looked out to sea and took a deep breath of air, almost as if he'd been dying of oxygen starvation. 'You have no idea how I've missed this.'

'Me too, but what's going on? Why haven't you told me the full story?'

'Oh God. I panicked. I knew I should trust you, but I was so afraid. I still am more afraid than I've ever been in my life ...'

Jess had heard the phrase 'my blood ran cold' and never known what it meant, but that's exactly how she felt now: as if an icy fluid had been injected into her veins and frozen her solid. She couldn't move and could hardly breathe.

'Are you ill, Adam? Is it something terrible?'

'It's not great,' he said and smiled: but it was a smile that made Jess want to cry. 'Sit down,' he said gently.

She sat on a broken piece of wall, and Adam joined her.

'I need to go right back to the beginning. To last August, the day we fetched Gaby from the airport.'

And the text. That awful text. Jess knew that was the start of it: the misery.

Adam closed his eyes, as if he was trying to blot out a terrible memory.

Jess wanted to hold him, but those days were gone. She felt completely helpless. 'Go on,' she said quietly.

'After you'd left the cottage that evening, I called Keri back. She didn't only contact me to tell me about my real dad. Keri phoned to say that Blake had passed away from the same condition as my dad, Peter, had died of six months before.'

Adam took a breath before he carried on.

'Keri told me Blake had had an inherited neurological

disease and she was very sorry to have to tell me but I might carry the gene. She said that there was a test for it if I wanted it but that many people didn't want to know. But she said it was my choice, a horrible choice, but better than no one warning me at all. I wish she hadn't told me though, because there's no cure for it and a fifty-fifty chance I have it too.'

'Oh my God.' Jess threw her arms around him instinctively. She held him. Felt his body shake a little, then he gently pushed her away. His eyes were bright. Jess felt as if her heart was crumbling away, piece by piece. 'You should have told me. Why didn't you trust me before?' she murmured, finally releasing him.

'I refused to believe any of it. I feel well. I'm young and strong. How could I possibly have this … this horrible thing? So, I buried all the bad stuff and tried to ignore it, but the fear ate away at me. I could barely function and I know I pushed you away.' He held Jess tightly. 'I'm so sorry, but I couldn't tell you. Even as I slowly began to face the truth, I couldn't face dealing with my feelings, let alone yours.'

Adam gently let Jess go but stayed close to her. Jess bit back tears, clinging onto the realisation she had to stay strong for Adam.

'Have you told your mum why Keri contacted you?'

Adam put his head in his hands. 'I just told her it was about the money Pete had left. I didn't want to add the worry of this disease onto the stress of her having to tell me she'd had an affair. I still haven't told her.'

Jess thought of the little girl holding her ice cream and her stomach knotted. 'What about Emmy? Does she have it?'

'No. Thank God. Keri had her tested at birth and she doesn't. Jess. I still love you but the situation is impossible. The thing is that even if I don't have it, our children might also carry the gene. And I know how much you love kids. One of the reasons I finally decided to leave was when we all found out that Maisie was having a baby. You were so happy for her, I overheard you saying how much you'd love a family. Even though I'd hung on here because I couldn't bear to actually leave the island, that was the final straw.'

'What an awful burden for you, Adam. I'm so sorry ...' She hardly dared ask the next question but had to know the worst. 'What is the disease?'

'It's a neurological condition caused by a faulty gene. It's something like Huntington's but even rarer. We joke it must have been made specially for us.' He actually smiled briefly and Jess realised that no matter what he said about not having come to terms with it, Adam had already gone a long way down the road to accepting things.

'Is there really... *no* cure?' She had to stop her voice from faltering.

'There's lots of research, but no cure on the horizon. Some treatment to manage the symptoms and they're working hard on the genetic cause, but it's about as grim as it gets. It affects your central nervous system until you're completely unable to move or breathe on your own ...' his voice trailed off. Telling her this terrible news must be agonising for him.

She picked up his hand and squeezed it. 'Adam, I would have stood by you.'

'That's exactly why I left. I knew you'd want to help me,

but I don't want your pity and for you to end up as my nurse.' His jaw was tight and the strain etched on every feature. 'I'm sorry, but I've tried not to get down. I've tried to be strong. I've debated night and day whether I should find out if I have the gene too, but I can't find an answer.'

'But if you *don't* have it—'

'*If* I don't. But as I said, it's genetic: I could also pass it on to our kids. And I *wanted* kids with you. I still do, but I can't possibly allow that. I was petrified you might be pregnant for a while, even though we'd taken precautions. You know the worst thing about all of this?'

Jess squeezed his hand.

'I've been a coward. A coward to leave. Not to be able to deal with it, not to face up to it.'

'Stop saying it or thinking it. You're *not* a coward ... but you need to get some help. This is too much to bear on your own. Have you had any counselling?'

'No. I don't want to talk about it. I know the options: do the test or not. Die or not. Be with you or not.' His voice firmed. 'So you *have* to leave me. You have to be with Luca – or anyone else. Or on your own, but not with me. It's driven me half insane seeing you with Luca yet at the same time, I'm relieved. I want you to be happy with him: with anyone but me. I love you, Jess. I love you so much and that's why I'm the last man on earth you should be with and why I left you.'

'You can't tell me this and expect me not to care!' Jess cried. Especially now that he'd told her he still loved her, and he always had, yet he was leaving for good. He'd given her every-thing she'd longed for and snatched it away again, even though she knew he couldn't help himself. She felt as if she was fighting to keep her head above water as one wave of agony rolled over her after another.

'But I *do* and it's why, after today, I can't see you again. I've decided to end my lease on the cottage and move back to Cumbria permanently.'

'What if you get the test and it's clear?'

'I *won't* get it. I can't. I'd rather not know, and lots of people choose not to find out. And even if I did, and it was OK, I can never make up for what I've done to you. A clean break now is best. Forget me forever.'

'Oh Adam.' Tears ran down her face. She couldn't see him any more but she could feel his arms around her. He was holding her and soothing her. He brushed his hand over her damp cheeks. 'Jess, my lovely. I can't lay this burden on you. You have to believe me that I feel the same way about you as I did when I got the text, the same way I did when I flew out. Every day we've been apart I knew I loved you. I raked over the decision endlessly. It was Keri who wanted me to tell you the truth. She confessed to me last night that she badgered me to bring them here to Scilly, not only for Emmy's sake but because she wanted me to come clean with you and she's been on at me ever since. She said it would be more painful if you were left in the dark. Then when Will asked me to join the crew, I couldn't hold back any longer.'

'Keri was right but ...' Jess trembled in his arms. 'It doesn't matter now. Nothing does but you getting help.'

He shook his head. 'There is no help.'

'I want to help, I'd support you whatever happened. Let me, please, Adam.'

He shook his head. 'No. Stop trying to persuade me. I've made my decision. I can't do this, Jess.' He let her go as if he suddenly needed to escape from her. 'I need to find Emmy and Keri. I'll see you ... I'm sorry for everything but it's hopeless.'

'Wait!' Icy shivers ran through her as she felt the loss of his arms around her.

He jogged away from her. Jess followed but he was already scrambling down the path. She could chase after him but he was so hurt, he wouldn't have listened.

She closed her eyes and steadied herself on an old wall as the wind gusted around her and snatches of music and cheers filtered up from the harbour. She'd never felt so desolate in her life. If Adam told her that Keri was his girlfriend and he wanted to marry her and live on Scilly, it would have been a hundred times better than the truth. Her heart was breaking all over again.

Chapter 30

After collecting the trophy, Gaby and the rest of the crew trooped into the Galleon Inn behind the harbour, along with Patrick and Maisie and the Gull team. They had to fight their way inside, through the crush of rowers and supporters, before they found a corner.

Gaby was now squished against the side of a wooden settle. 'Well, that was a first for the championships. Only five of us turning up to collect the trophy,' she said, as Will shifted a few inches closer to her.

'Lawrence has a great excuse,' said Natalia.

'And Jess probably needed some time on her own. I hope she's OK,' said Gaby.

'Me too, and I'm not sure where Adam got to, either,' said Will quietly then cheered up. 'I'll get the first round in.'

After he and Robbie had returned with the trays of drinks, he resumed his place next to Gaby. Every now and then his arm would brush the back of her shoulders as he held forth on the famous victory. Gaby felt his laughter resonate through her body and saw his brown eyes light up with pleasure. She didn't think she'd ever seen him so happy.

'Sorry, mate.' Will grinned broadly as Patrick and Maisie joined them at the table.

'Yeah and you look sorry,' said Patrick. 'About as sorry as a bloke who's won the lottery twice over.' Patrick grinned. 'Captain of the winning crew buys the drinks for the rest of the day and that seems to be you, mate.'

Will laughed. 'I'm happy to get the next round in too. Your crew looks as if they need consolation.'

'Did you see Hugo's face?' added Len with a cackle.

Roars of laughter rang out as more drinks were brought to the table and every aspect of the race was raked over again and again. Gaby tucked into a bag of crisps and her wine, amused by how the details grew more colourful with every retelling. It now sounded as if the clashing crews had capsized *Titanic*-style and Petroc had been seconds from being rescued by the lifeboat. So that was how oral myths spread, she thought with amusement. She suspected the day would pass into gig rowing legend for decades to come.

The banter flew between the crews, and soon the table had vanished under glasses and empty crisp packets. There were so many excited and well-oiled people in the pub now that they could hardly hear themselves speak. Gaby had only had a couple of drinks but the effort of the race had taken its toll and she had no idea how she was ever going to peel herself out of the booth.

'Anyone heard how Lawrence is?' Patrick asked.

'His girlfriend called me. Badly bruised ankle but no break, thankfully,' said Will. 'She says he'll be discharged soon and she'll take care of him in her flat at Old Town.

Means that we'll be one short on the row home though.'

Gaby let out a squeak.

'You'll be fine. I'll be gentle with you.' Will spoke softly into her ear. A hand rested lightly on her back. It wasn't Len's so it had to be Will's. His fingers were warm and he inched a tiny bit closer to her, until their bare thighs beneath their shorts were touching. She shifted in her seat and Will's leg muscle tensed next to hers. The tension was agonising but delicious. 'What's so funny?' he whispered while Len related a tale about a previous gig disaster to the rest of the crews. 'You have that secret smile on your face.'

'Who? Moi?'

'Yes. You often have it. Usually when I've done or said something that amuses you.'

'Really?' She arched an eyebrow.

'You're doing it now. As if you know something about me that I don't. It's ... disturbing.'

'Shall I stop doing it?' she whispered back, pleased they were enjoying this light-hearted banter again. Fortunately the others were distracted by the disgruntled St Piran's crew marching into the bar, bemoaning their misfortune.

'No. But later I want to know exactly what it is about me that you find so funny. I won't let you go until I find out.' There was a definite glint in his eye.

'Is that a threat or a promise?'

Will leaned a little closer. 'Both ... I hope.'

She felt his breath against her ear and a very pleasant shivery feeling shot through her. The camaraderie and euphoria after the race seemed to be turning into something far more enjoyable.

'Will!' Len shouted.

'Yes, mate!' Will turned to Len.

Len raised his empty glass. 'Shall I get the next lot of drinks in? It's my round.'

The table fell silent in shock at Len's offer.

Will put a hand to his ear. 'Erm. Is my hearing going or did Len just offer to buy a round?'

Len snorted. 'You cheeky sod. I can always change my mind.'

'No! I'll have a pint,' said Will.

Natalia held up her glass. 'Rattler for me.'

'A Coke and a lime and soda!' said Maisie.

'*Gaby?*'

'Um …' Gaby glanced up to find Will looking at her enquiringly. She licked her lips. Her 'mind had been more agreeably engaged', as Jane Austen once wrote, though she'd been thinking of Will's fit arse rather than his fine eyes. Probably best *not* to share that with either him or the rest of the crew.

Will's mouth quirked in amusement which did nothing to cool Gaby down. 'Be quick because you'll never get this chance again,' he said huskily. Argh. Everything he did and said seemed sexy to her, which was *very* disconcerting.

'Another white wine spritzer please,' she said finally.

Len gasped. 'Don't get too carried away. We've got to row home.'

'In that case, I'll have a large G&T too,' she replied.

Everyone burst out laughing.

302

'You asked for that, Len,' said Robbie. 'I'll have a whisky, as you're paying.'

Muttering curses, Len scuttled off to the bar.

'I hate to spoil the party, but won't we be two rowers short on the way home if we can't locate Jess?' Gaby said to Will and Maisie, while Natalia went to the bar with Len.

Will winced. 'Maybe she's decided she won't get in the same boat as me. I could hardly blame her. I don't know what came over me asking Adam to row with us.'

'Ruthless determination to beat the rest of us at all costs?' Patrick chipped in.

'Ha ha,' said Will. 'The truth is I didn't want our hard work to go to waste and it seemed like a good idea at the time.'

'A lot of things seem like a good idea at the time, mate,' said Patrick, winking and kissing Maisie.

Will pulled a face. 'I do worry about Jess, though. Adam made himself scarce as soon as we'd got back to shore ... I know asking him put Jess in a spot, but I didn't know what else to do. Although they were friendly enough just after we'd won.'

'At least they weren't arguing, which is a step forward, and no matter what happens, you can't solve Jess's problems for her,' said Maisie. 'But perhaps we should call her after we've had this next drink. We all need to make a move soon anyway. The state of some of you, it could be dark before you get those gigs back to their sheds and I'm not towing you home in the *Puffin*, that's for sure.' Maisie hesitated. 'I've been wondering whether to go after Jess myself but she probably needs some time to herself.'

'Luca made himself scarce too. He was nowhere to be seen at the prize-giving,' said Will. 'Typical.'

Maisie rolled her eyes. 'Hold on a minute. We don't know if Jess is with Luca. I'll give her a bit longer and then I'll try to call her myself.'

In the end, Gaby only managed half her drink before she decided she'd had enough booze, mindful of the prospect of the journey to St Saviour's. She could tell Will was growing genuinely worried about Jess. She was concerned herself but she couldn't help feeling a real pang when they all squeezed out from behind the table and she was parted from Will.

'I won't let you go until I find out …' His words echoed in her head. It had been a delicious hour and she hoped the spark that had been had kindled in the post-race euphoria wouldn't fizzle out on the journey home.

Chapter 31

After Adam had left her at the fort, Jess had stayed alone for a few minutes, trying to calm down after hearing his devastating news. He'd told her that she should forget him. That was impossible ... she had to try and speak to him again, but how and when? The sound of laughter and voices disturbed her and a group of rowers clambered up to the ruins with cool boxes and a disposable barbecue. Jess recognised them and had to feign a smile when they congratulated her on the victory.

Their presence made her decision and she walked down the path to go and find Luca and the rest of her crew. She needed to let them know she was OK before she decided what she could possibly do about Adam.

To her surprise, he was sitting on a rock at the bottom of the path. He jumped up as soon as he saw her and Jess joined him.

'I thought you'd gone to meet Keri,' she said.

'I need to soon, but I didn't want to leave you like that ...' Uncertainty clouded his eyes. 'God, Jess, you'll have to forgive me. I don't know where I am at the moment.'

She touched his arm. 'I'm glad you waited for me.'

He smiled at her tenderly. 'Me too. Come on, people will be wondering where we've got to.'

They walked side by side onto the road that led into town. If it had been tough not knowing why Adam had taken off, knowing why was even harder. Adam *did* love her. He always had and that should have made her float on air, but the revelation that he might carry the gene for this terrible disease eclipsed any happiness. She'd rather have never seen him again and never known as long as he'd only take the test and it prove negative, but now she knew all she wanted to do was be by his side.

He didn't look at her as they walked and they didn't say anything. Every time Jess thought of something to say, it seemed trivial or hopeless.

They passed the boat shed bistro and the streets were still very busy even though the last race had finished. Jess stopped when she saw a figure detach itself from the crowds and head straight for her.

'That's Luca. I'd arranged to meet him at the deli café and I'm late.'

'You should go to him.' Adam touched her arm briefly.

'I don't want to leave you on your own.'

Jess was still torn.

'He'll be worried if you don't show up at all but please, don't tell him what we've talked about.'

'I won't, I promise, but it's nothing to be ashamed of.'

'It shouldn't be but that's how I *do* feel. Ashamed that I might have it and that I'm too scared to find out. Ashamed of how me being cowardly has hurt you.'

'Please don't torture yourself any more than you have. I'll stand by you. If you need me, you know where I am whatever you decide.'

Luca spotted them and jogged towards them before Jess could cut him off. His smile faded briefly but was back in place quickly enough. He was used to hiding his feelings, thought Jess, who suspected he was jealous but didn't want to let on.

'Hello, Jess. I was starting to worry, but I now I know why you're late. Congratulations, Adam.'

Adam's brow furrowed. 'Congratulations?'

'On winning the race. We handed it to you on a plate, eh?'

'Yeah. Thanks.'

Jess flashed him a hasty smile to cut off a conversation that was turning awkward. 'Sorry I was late.'

Luca kissed her on the cheek. She felt as if she'd been branded. It was agony in front of Adam, knowing what she knew now, even if he'd insisted that nothing had changed between the two of them.

'I'll go and find Keri and Emmy,' Adam muttered.

'Family comes first, eh?' said Luca.

He exchanged a momentary glance with Jess and in that split second, she shared his agony. 'Yes. It does. See you around, Jess.'

Jess wasn't sure if that was a question or a dismissal but daren't say any more to him in front of Luca. He turned away and strode off towards an alley that led to the pottery café.

'Bet you wondered where I was,' said Jess, struggling to inject some chirpiness into her voice while every cell screamed at her to run after Adam.

Luca smiled. 'It's OK. I guessed where you were.'

'Really? How could you?'

He put his arm around her. 'Just an instinct. I suppose you two have things to work out.'

'It's not what you think.'

He smiled wryly. 'Sure.'

Jess stopped dead in the street. 'It really isn't.'

His expression softened. 'Do you want to talk about it?'

'I c-can't. Adam told me something in confidence. It's private, and it doesn't make a difference to us.' As much as she wanted to believe her statement, what Adam had told her had turned everything on its head. How on earth was she supposed to carry on as if nothing had happened?

He frowned but Jess could see he knew she was serious. 'OK. I won't push you,' he said.

With Luca's arm around her, once more Jess was conscious of envious glances from some of the other rowers. Of course Adam's confession made a difference but Jess didn't know exactly how yet. While she'd thought Adam didn't care about her, she'd made the decision to move on. Now, she was caught in some terrible limbo.

'I've been thinking hard about the future and Hugo's offer of a job here for me.' Luca's voice brought her out of her reverie. 'If I don't accept it, have you thought of an alternative? I won't be on Scilly forever, but you needn't be, either. While all your memories, good and bad, are so rooted in this place and Adam is here, how will you ever leave them behind? Isn't it time you saw the big wide world and let go?'

'That's ...' Jess was too stunned to respond.

'I can see I've surprised you.' Luca moved smoothly on while she tried to process what he'd said. 'And of course, I'm not suggesting you move in with me in any formal way. We hardly know each other, but if you wanted to make a fresh start or even have a long break, you'd be welcome to stay in my apartment on any terms you feel happy with.'

Jess laughed in disbelief. 'That sounds very exciting, but what would I do in London? I'm a flower farmer.'

'I don't know. Study? Work? Travel?'

'Wow ...' His intense expression showed her that he was serious. Jess allowed herself to imagine the possibilities for a moment, then shook her head. 'I know we have a good time, but as you say we've only known each other a short time.'

'Long enough to know you're a breath of fresh air. This is a no-strings offer. No promises. No expectations.'

'Except I'll have left Will and my mother to run the farm on their own. I can't do that to them.' *I'm not sure I can do that to* me, thought Jess. *Or Adam.* Yet it sounded so glamorous and exciting, so far from what she'd ever imagined for herself. So far away from the simple life she and Adam had once hoped for but which was now never going to happen. Was Luca's idea so far-fetched? It might be the best thing she could do: leave all the bad memories behind and explore all the opportunities out there. Then she thought back to Adam, his head in his hands, and her stomach lurched. Why did life have to hurl these huge great curveballs at them all?

'The offer stands. No pressure, but I know we'd have a great time.'

'Jess!' Will ran up, waving frantically. Her shoulders slumped in relief at the interruption. She needed time to tame her raging emotions. 'Thank God we found you. We have to leave in the next ten minutes. Unless you're staying here?' Will looked pointedly at Luca. 'But if you don't come, there will only be four of us rowing and I don't think Gaby will make it. We'll have to leave the gig and hitch a ride with someone – *if* there are any boats free in this chaos.'

'You'd better go.' Luca kissed her. 'I'll come and see you at the farm tomorrow afternoon and we can talk more about it?'

Jess was frozen, her mind was so full of Adam's confession and Luca's offer that she could barely think, let alone speak.

'*Jess*,' Will hissed at her.

She snapped out of her trance. 'See you tomorrow,' she said to Luca and then to Will, 'OK. Calm down. I'm *coming*.'

After the tumult of the past few hours, she was desperate to get back to the flower farm and have some peace and quiet – if that could ever be possible again.

Chapter 32

Twilight was falling when Gaby, Will and the victorious Mixed crew finally wheeled the *Athene* into the gig shed on St Saviour's beach, where the Men's and Women's crews were holding a barbecue. The other members greeted them with cheers, although Len had complained that they'd rowed home like 'a bunch of drunken snails'. Gaby was just relieved to have made it back before dark and discover if the electrifying frisson she and Will shared at the pub was still alive. It certainly was for *her* and the prospect of taking things further with him was the only thing that had got her through the exhausting journey home.

Will hung back with her while everyone else headed off to the farm for a shower, followed by more partying. A few yards away a fire glowed in the dusky light, and flickering flames lit an intense and hungry gleam in his eyes that told her all she needed to know. She looked into his face and a shiver of desire made goosebumps pop up all over her skin.

'I might be about to crash and burn, but I can't stand this any longer,' he said.

'Stand what?' she asked innocently, fizzing like a bottle of champagne.

'All this teasing and sparring. It might be post-race endorphins or the beer that's taken hold of me. I don't know, but I think I'll go mad if we don't get together. I thought you felt the same way in the pub. I could hardly bear to be that close to you without ... Arghh. This is so difficult to say, but I really want you and it has to be now.'

'Right *now*? Here on the beach?' She pointed to the sand, buzzing with nervous anticipation. 'There are a lot of people around who might object.'

'Back at the farm. Where else?' His smile melted away. 'Or have I misread the signals completely, because if so, I'm an absolute tit and I'll never trust my instincts again.'

Gaby couldn't stand it any longer either. She raised herself up on tiptoes and whispered in his ear, 'For once, your instincts are spot on, Mr Godrevy. Let's both grab a shower and I'll wait for you in my room.'

Despite their exhaustion, they almost sprinted back to the farm. After her shower, Gaby lay on her bed, waiting ... Under her fluffy purple bathrobe, hardly the sexiest thing she owned, she didn't have a lot on.

A soft knock on her door and a low voice saying, 'Gaby,' sent her into meltdown.

She was so sore and exhausted, she could hardly get off the bed to open the door, but nothing would have stopped her from letting Will in.

'Hi ...' His face appeared around the crack in the door.

She giggled and closed the door behind him as quietly as she could. 'You realise that everyone will know what's going on with you coming to my room?'

'I don't give a fuck.' He pulled her into his arms and almost before she had the chance to breathe, he kissed her.

Her whole body fizzed like a bath melt in hot water. Shaky already, the warmth of his body against hers turned her limbs to liquid. She kissed him back, greedily, and started to pull his T-shirt up.

He tugged the belt of the robe.

'Oh my God.' He rested his palm on her bare bottom. 'A thong? I don't think I can stand it.'

'I wondered if you'd think it was a bit of a cliché, a lacy bra and a thong.'

'A cliché?' He let out a huge sigh. 'You are absolutely bloody going to kill me. I don't know how I've survived this long.'

'What's changed?' she asked, warming her hands on the smooth skin of his back.

'I have. I realised today that I've wasted far too much time already. Sitting behind you in that boat, and next to you in that pub, I thought: I can't keep this up a moment longer.' His face became serious. 'If you've changed your mind about this, please say now.'

Gaby put her finger to his lips. 'If I didn't want it to happen, you'd have known about it long ago.'

Will opened his mouth and gently drew the tip of her finger in. Wow. He ran his tongue along the underside of her finger. She nearly took off through the roof.

He slipped the robe down her shoulders. 'Do you have any idea what you've done to me?'

'S-so y- you keep saying.' His touch stole her breath away.

'Because it's true,' he said. His eyes had an intensity she hadn't seen before.

Every nerve tingled and she stood on tiptoes to kiss him. The cool air whispered over her bare skin as the robe fell to her feet. Will ran the back of his hand down her spine and kissed her again, exploring her mouth with his tongue, his hands on her waist. She could feel the imprint of every finger, and warmth radiated from his body to her own skin. His hand caressed her back, as he deepened the kiss. She scrunched up the robe between her toes as she kissed him back.

'Who'd have thought it?' she whispered, looking up into his face.

Holding her close with one hand, he trailed his hand deliciously along her spine. Gaby shivered. 'Who'd have thought what?' he said, his eyes unsure, expecting to be teased. She loved the way he didn't know what she might say or do next. It made her feel powerful.

'That the farmer was such a great kisser,' she said.

He frowned. 'Are you being sarcastic?'

'Would I?'

'Always,' he said and unexpectedly swept her up into his arms.

'Whoa!' she cried, holding onto his neck.

He dropped her gently on the bed and knelt beside her. 'You're beautiful,' he said.

A lump formed in her throat. She believed him completely. She smiled up at his rugged handsome face, at the brown eyes flecked with amber, and the tiny lines around them. He was real, no-bullshit sincere and she might possibly love him for it. She reached up and touched his cheek, the rasp of stubble making her fingertips tingle, a buzz that radiated through her whole body.

'You might laugh, but I think the same about you,' she said.

He kissed her again and lay beside her. 'Actually, I don't mind.'

And before she could say any more, Will was showing her just *how* much he didn't mind.

*

It was completely dark when Gaby woke up and a dim glow from the radio alarm on the bedside table told her it was almost midnight. After they'd had sex, they did it again and finally, the exhaustion and wine took its toll. She was still lying with her head across his arm. Will was breathing softly with his lips slightly parted, as innocent as a lamb.

Gaby smiled to herself, recalling the languid, delicious sex they'd enjoyed after the first febrile round. Will had been everything she'd hoped: considerate but confident. She'd surprised him too, and had worried that everyone would hear when he cried out. As for that single bed, the way the headboard had clattered against the partition wall must have left her housemates in no doubt of what was happening. Will had said he didn't care who knew what they were doing. Would he feel that way in the cold light of day – or night?

With a snuffle, he threw out an arm and the photo of Stevie

on the bedside table fell with a clatter onto the floor. She flinched.

'Whaaaa?' he muttered, blinking awake with a start.

Gaby turned on the lamp and he screwed up his eyes.

'What was that?' he said, again, wincing in the light.

Extricating herself from beneath his limbs, Gaby clambered over him and lowered her feet to the floor. 'Ouch!'

She fell back on top of Will, a sharp pain in her toe.

He pushed himself up, suddenly wide awake. 'Are you OK?'

'Yes.' She winced, and held her toe.

'You've cut yourself.' Will grabbed a handful of tissues from the box by the bed and then groaned. 'I've broken your photo and you've cut your foot.'

'It's not bad. Only a nick in my toe.'

'Hold on.'

'What for?'

He got out of bed and examined her foot. 'Keep still.'

Gaby gritted her teeth, then let out a little squeal.

Will held out a thin sliver of glass. 'More tissues. Quick,' he said, taking the handful from her and holding them against her toe. Splotches of red appeared.

Gaby sank back on the bed, while he pressed tissues against her foot.

'I'll get another frame. I'll order one the same. I am sorry.' He was full of remorse. It was strange to see his softer side.

'It really doesn't matter,' she said, trying to be kind. The broken photo was more painful than her foot.

'It does. The man in the photo, with you and your parents? That's your brother, Stevie, I assume?'

316

'Yes.'

He sighed deeply. 'Jess told me a little about it but asked me not to mention it and upset you. I'm really sorry.'

'Absolutely no need to be. It's been over a year now.' Gaby sat up and examined her foot which had stopped bleeding. How romantic, she thought, but Will was looking at her tenderly.

'What happened?' he said gently. 'Only if you want to tell me more.'

He lifted her hair off her face. Tears stung the back of her eyes, coming out of nowhere like a clap of thunder on a summer's day. She took a big breath.

'He was involved in a motorbike accident, shortly after his twenty-first birthday, for which I feel partly to blame. We'd had a row ...' She paused before going on. 'He already owed Mum and Dad for a car they'd bought him and he still wanted the bike even though they hated it. It was second-hand off a mate; a great deal for cash, he said. He didn't dare ask them to sub him the rest of the money, so I loaned him it from my savings.' Her voice became roughened. It was hard to voice fears she held back from everyone else.

He held her hand. 'You can't blame yourself.'

'All I know is that if I'd stuck to my guns and refused, he wouldn't have had that fucking bike and he wouldn't have been fucking killed. Oh shit.' The bitterness and anger in her voice shocked her so what must Will think? She tried to soften her tone. 'I've never told anyone that before. Bad timing. Sorry, when we've just ... you know.'

Will held her. He didn't say: 'It's not your fault. Don't beat

317

yourself up,' as she might have expected, not that she'd planned on ever pouring out her heart like this. He simply listened and held her and stroked her hair until she stopped wanting to cry and her toe started hurting again.

'What am I like?' She smiled through her tears.

'A normal person?' he said. 'A semi-normal person, anyway.'

'Ha ha ha!' Gaby picked up the pillow and hit him, eager to chase her tears away with laughter. She hadn't asked or expected to talk about Stevie, but Will had somehow drawn feelings out of her that she'd never shared with anyone else. Her stomach fluttered. This – her feelings for Will – was becoming serious ... dangerous and throwing up all kinds of possibilities she hadn't planned for. Like staying longer than the summer ...

Outside the door, they heard voices.

Will grimaced. 'Arghh.'

Gaby sighed. 'Too late now.'

'This saves us creeping round and pretending. People may as well know.'

Her heart rate picked up. What was he going to say? 'Know *what?*'

He swallowed hard. 'This is probably the worst idea ever, but if I don't say it, I don't think I can handle it any more. Jesus, what am I doing? Shit. It's just, I think I might love you.' Immediately Will buried his head in his hands and let out a groan. 'Oh God.' He dragged his hands over his face. 'Did I just say that? Scrub it. Forget it.'

Goosebumps had popped out all over Gaby's skin again and she didn't feel quite steady. The man of her dreams was finally in her bed and had just said the three little words that she'd least expected. Other words, perhaps: *let's do this again. Let's start behaving like adults for a change.* But not *I love you.*

'Judging by your silence, I just did an incredibly stupid thing.'

'No. It was an incredibly brave thing.' And the loveliest, most amazing thing anyone had ever said to her. But though her heart screamed to say the words back, how could she give him false hope when she knew she had to leave?

'Brave? It's that bad, then?' He jumped up. 'I'll go.'

'You'd probably better put some shoes on first or you'll cut your feet and drip blood everywhere.' Gaby smiled tenderly, even though her heart was aching. She pulled his arm. 'Sit down.'

Will obeyed and sat next to her, looking as if the sky had fallen in on him. 'I'm not the first person who's said this to you, am I?'

'Hmm. I'm afraid not. There have been a couple more.'

'I knew it,' he said gloomily. 'And did they crash and burn too?'

'It didn't end well. Henry tried to kiss me straight after he'd told me and we both ended up in front of the head of Year Four. Then there was a man at the garden centre who wanted me to move into his sheltered bungalow, but I had to decline.'

The look of complete confusion on Will's face gave way to a disbelieving shake of the head. 'You never stop joking, do you?'

Gaby rested her hand on his thigh. 'It's no joke. I can see you're serious. Is this the first time you've said it to anyone?'

'What do you think?'

'I heard there were other girlfriends in the past. I don't know if any of them were serious.'

'There was one I cared for a lot and maybe I thought it was love, but I wasn't sure at the time. Now I know for certain that it wasn't love because I know how I feel about you ... I'm making a tit of myself again, aren't I?'

'No. God no. It's amazing to have a guy say that to me. To hear you say it.'

'But you're not saying it back. That's understandable.'

'No ... It's not what I expected. That's all.'

He covered his head with his hands and blew out a breath. 'This has been a fucking disaster. I knew it was a stupid thing to do. Finally, we get together, have amazing sex ...'

She touched his chest, felt his thumping heart under her fingertips. 'It *was* amazing. Wonderful.'

'But then I have to bring the whole thing crashing down. Stick my size-twelve boots in it and destroy it.'

'I rather like your boots. In fact, it was your wellies that first attracted me to you.'

He frowned hard. 'What?'

'I love them. I love your boots and your knackered old jeans and your grouchy grumpy ways. Even when you're being an awkward, perverse bastard, I love it all but ...'

'*But* ...' he echoed, his eyes pleading with her.

'*But* I don't see how it's going to work, Will. No matter how I feel about you – even if I let myself feel the same way and believe me, I want to – I don't see how we're going to be together. Your life is here. You're rooted to this soil. You thrive on it and me – I love it here too – but I can't make it my home.' *Not forever*, she thought. *Not yet*. If she didn't escape now, she might never do all the things she'd promised herself and sworn on her brother's memory. She wasn't ready to let those dreams go yet. 'It's so beautiful here, but it's just one patch of earth,' she said as gently as she could. 'It may well be that I see some more of the world and still realise that this is the best place on the planet and the place for me. But I have to see those other places, experience them. I owe it to Stevie, to my parents and to me.'

Will shook his head and heaved a sigh. 'I know. Jess tried to warn me, but I think she was as worried about me hurting you as vice versa.'

Gaby thought for a moment, surprised that Will had gone so far as sharing how he felt with Jess. Her next words were quiet and tentative. 'You know, I *could* ask you to come with me.'

'I can't.' The response came back as swift and sure as an arrow.

Straight to her heart. She should never have tried. How was it that in a moment she'd got everything she wanted, yet she'd managed to throw it away? She'd spent so long hoping he'd show that he wanted her, that she hadn't thought that he might feel more than just physical attraction – that he might *love* her.

Will laid his hand on her thigh. Every muscle, every bone ached to say she would stay. She longed to say she loved him too, but she couldn't stay here in one place forever. There many places to see, so much life to experience elsewhere, and she wished she could live it with Will.

'Will you still stay for the summer?' he asked.

'I was going to, but now I'm not so sure it's the greatest idea.' She spoke softly. 'Part of me thinks if I hang around too long, I'll never go and staying here wasn't part of my plan.'

He pushed his hair out of his eyes roughly and let out a groan. 'I never expected to feel this way, but it's too late now. I can't change the way I feel or that I've told you.'

She kissed him on the lips but couldn't think of a word to say. He'd tossed all her expectations and plans in the air.

'The way I see it, we have two choices,' he murmured. 'Go for it while we can. Even if that's for a week. Or pretend this never happened.'

'We've already tried the pretence. I don't think it was working, do you?' she said. 'Oh!'

Without warning, he tipped her down onto the bed. His eyes were fierce as he looked into them. 'In that case, time's running out and we haven't got a moment to waste.'

As she gave herself into the kiss, Gaby knew he was right, but she just wished it didn't have to be that way.

Chapter 33

Jess hadn't expected to sleep the night after the race. Even though she was more physically exhausted than she'd ever been in her life, she knew Adam's confession would keep her awake. She sat up for a while, watching the moon lay a silvery path over the sea through her window. Imagining Luca sitting in his apartment on Petroc, maybe cradling a glass of brandy. Thinking of her? Or still consoling his crew and trying to schmooze Hugo?

Then there was Adam. She was on surer ground with him. He'd be with Keri and Emmy. Emmy would be in bed by now and Adam and Keri would be together in the sitting room. Would Adam be thinking of her or worrying about the axe hanging over his head – or both? How had he coped these last few months with that burden?

Jess had finally closed the curtains and lay in bed staring at the ceiling, trying to imagine it was the sky above her and count imaginary stars as she used to when she was at the school boarding house. When she was homesick or alone, she'd lose herself in the huge great blue bowl above her. She knew how to solve her problems these days and keep them in perspective: devise a plan for tackling them. But Adam's problem was too big. Too big even for 'grown-ups'. She could run away from it if she wanted to: take Luca's offer and leave ...

She closed her eyes.

A hundred and one, a hundred and two, a hundred ...

*

Their mother was sipping from a teacup when Jess entered the kitchen the next morning. The table was set for three but Will's place was untouched.

Jess sat down and reached for the teapot. 'Will not up yet?' she said.

Her mother pursed her lips. 'His bed's not been slept in.'

Jess put the pot down, wishing she hadn't asked. 'Ah.'

'Is that all you can say?'

'I'm not his keeper, Mum. It's his life.'

Anna's voice rose. 'He's with *her*, isn't he?'

Jess knew her mother meant Gaby and struggled to keep her reply calm. 'I don't know. That's his business.'

'He went out to the yard after he'd had a shower when you came back from the racing. I didn't hear him return. Did you?'

'I was spark out as soon as my head touched the pillow,' Jess lied as she poured tea into her mug.

Her mother tinkered with the teaspoon in the saucer. 'She's not right for him.'

'You don't know he's been with Gaby and, anyway, at almost thirty-six, he can do what he wants.' *We both can*, thought

324

Jess, hoping Will was going to seize every opportunity to be happy, even if she couldn't.

'She'll entice him away from the farm.' The cup hit her saucer with a loud chink. Her mother's eyes were moist.

Jess took her hand which wasn't quite steady. 'I know you're scared of losing us, but if Will wants to leave, there's nothing we can do and nothing we should do. It doesn't mean our lives would stop; the farm would go on.'

'I'm sorry.' She pulled a tissue from her pocket and dabbed at her eyes. 'I'm being very selfish, but after your father left, I thought the world was over; the business, your futures and my life. We all worked so hard to build it up and I'm so proud of you both.'

Jess got up and hugged her mum. She was surprised and touched by her honesty. 'No one's going to abandon the farm or you,' she soothed, but she was thinking of Luca's offer at the same time. How could she leave if Will *did* go? He had no plans as far as Jess knew, but their mother had clearly seen something that Jess had missed: something between her brother and Gaby way beyond physical attraction.

'You're right though. I can't stop either of you doing what you want. I have no right to. The closer I try to cling, the more you'll want to go free.'

'I love the farm. I love the isles. I don't want to leave,' said Jess. And it was all true, she suddenly realised, but it meant staying in limbo even if Adam left too.

Chapter 34

Gaby knew it was late by the angle of the sun through her room. She and Will spent much of the night trying to make up for lost time and now it was past the hour when she should have been up and about in the fields. Past the time when Will should have been out in the yard, calling for Len, carrying his coffee and crunching on the last of his toast. She'd fallen asleep last, wondering what to do, and woken first, having made her decision. She carefully extricated herself from his arms and managed to dress without waking him.

He opened one eye and blinked in the light. 'Gaby?'

Her smile was small and fleeting. She knew he'd stir eventually and was surprised that he'd taken this long, given the noise she'd made while she was emptying the drawers.

'What are you doing?'

Seconds were all it took him to see her, and the packed bags at her feet.

'Shit. No. Why now? What have I done?'

He jumped out of bed. Still rumpled and gloriously naked. Gaby felt a wrench of misery like someone had placed a vice around her heart and turned it harder and harder.

'It's better this way.' Her voice faltered as she squeezed out the words.

'Better for who? Fuck, why did I say those stupid things? Why did I have to ruin it all!' He shoved his hands through his hair, spiking it. 'Damn it. Why not wind it all back to before I said that crap?'

'You don't mean that. And it wasn't crap.'

Will threw up his hands in despair. 'But it *was* a disaster. Can we just forget it?'

'I'd like to, believe me ...' She held him, instantly worrying she might not be able to let him go again. 'But that's not what you want. I told you that I have to leave.'

'And I have to stay here. I have responsibilities. I owe it to the farm and all the work we put in. It would break Mum's heart if I quit. She went to pieces after Dad left. It nearly finished her and if I leave, Jess would have to shoulder all the burden herself.'

'That's why I'm going *now* before I *can't* leave and you start to hate me for making you feel as if you *should* leave.' She told herself she was trying to be strong, she'd made her decision and it was for the best all round even if it felt wrong.

He held her by the shoulders. 'I want to be with you. I can't imagine life without you,' he sighed, 'but my life is here and yours is wherever you need to go. I know you want to explore what's out there in the world. So do I, but we can't always have what we want.'

'I wanted Stevie to get better and I'd have done anything, but that was impossible. You seeing the world isn't and while I want you to come with me so much it hurts, I care too much about you to make you leave your family and the farm. It's your life – how can I take that away from you by issuing an ultimatum? It has to be your decision.'

'And that's why I won't ask *you* to stay,' said Will. 'This – you leaving – is why I tried so hard until yesterday not to even get involved. Not because I didn't want you to stay, because of how much I *did*. After that kiss in the shelter, I thought – hoped – that you felt something for me, but I was afraid that if I started something, I didn't know how I could end it. I've seen how miserable Jess has been because of Adam and I guess I couldn't face that.'

Gaby was sick with misery. 'I've been thinking. I can come back here. Some time. In a year maybe ...'

'A year! I don't think I can survive the wait.' He kissed her and she realised she was crying. His arms felt so safe and tempting and solid, but she backed away and picked up her bags.

'There's an early boat. I have to go.'

He shook his head and grabbed his jeans from the floor. 'I'll come with you to the jetty.' He struggled into them.

'Please. No. No goodbyes. You go into the fields or the packing shed and let me walk away, just as if it's a normal day. I can't face a goodbye again.'

'Because of Stevie ...?' he asked.

'Not only him.' She could hardly get the words out. 'See you, then, boss.'

'Yeah. I'll get some Earl Grey in,' he muttered. 'For when you come back.' His words were laced with a bitter despair that made Gaby's heart crack in two.

'I'll hold you to that.' And with that she walked out, forcing her eyes to focus on the walls, the corridor, anything but what she'd left behind her.

On her way out, she walked past the door to the kitchen where Natalia and a few of the others were filling flasks with coffee. A sob caught in her throat and Natalia must have heard or seen her, and rushed to the door. The others looked at her as Natalia asked if everything was OK.

'Fine,' said Gaby but carried on walking. No goodbyes. No long agonising decision-making, no time to dread the inevitable or change her mind again and again and go over and over the decision she'd helped her family make to end Stevie's life. Just a quick clean break and off to pastures new ...

She wanted to turn around. Every bone in her body, every sinew told her to go back and run to Will, but somehow, she forced her eyes to focus on the driveway and the farm gate and her feet to keep on moving towards them. The latch on the gate felt like lead, but she opened it and kept her eyes down while she closed it behind her. Tears poured down her cheeks as she hurried down the road towards the jetty, her backpack propelling her onwards, further and further away from the farm.

A small voice kept nagging at her. Was she leaving to honour Stevie's memory or had his loss affected her more profoundly than she'd thought? Was she really afraid of admitting she felt the same way about Will as he did about her – and losing him too if it didn't work out? Too late now. She couldn't agonise any more. Her decision had been made and she had to stick to it.

Chapter 35

After leaving her mother at the breakfast table, Jess decided to work out her worries in the fields until Luca arrived. She still had no idea what she was going to say to him. Would it be a good thing to take Luca's offer and spend some time away from the farm or should she try again to help Adam or accept his decision and get on with her life?

On the way to the top field, she came across Will and could tell by his face that something disastrous had happened. He didn't even want to speak to her but eventually told her that Gaby had decided to leave sooner than expected. Jess was shocked: he and Gaby had seemed so happy as they'd rowed home and Jess was pretty sure that they'd spent the night together. She had no luck in finding out what had gone on though, because Will angrily refused all attempts to elaborate beyond 'she has other plans and they don't include me'.

So on top of her turmoil about Adam and Luca, Jess was now fretting about Will but there was obviously nothing she could do about it, so she tried to concentrate on replanting the Innisidgen bulbs for the rest of the day. The late afternoon sun was mellowing when Luca arrived.

She spotted him walking up the road from the tractor and, wiping her hands on her old jeans, she jumped down from the cab and went to meet him in the yard before he started to traipse into the muddy field. She'd almost reached him when Will whizzed past on his quad bike. Luca waved at him, but Will didn't even lift a hand and zoomed off towards the lower fields, with a face like thunder.

Luca raised an eyebrow. 'Oh dear. Something I said?'

Jess thought there was no point hiding the news. 'No. I'm afraid Gaby's left the farm unexpectedly.'

'Oh … I see. Do you know why?'

'She didn't tell anyone, just packed her bag and walked out earlier this morning. Will won't say why. He won't talk about it.'

'So, I was right about those two?'

'Apparently so. I knew he liked Gaby and that she fancied him. I suspected there was more to it, but judging by the mood Will's in, it must have been more serious than a fling. I'd no idea how deeply he felt about her.'

'And yet she still left?' Luca said.

'Yes. Something major must have happened and from the state he's in, she's the one doing the heart breaking. He's devastated. He might be a grumpy awkward git at times, but he's very loyal and now he's fallen for someone at last, it's hit him very hard. It's going to be tough on him and I don't know how I can help him.'

Luca sighed. 'I'm sorry to hear it. Love is shitty at times. It's brutal and dirty and there are always casualties.'

Jess swallowed hard. 'Yes.'

'Have you thought about what I said?' he asked.

'I haven't thought about anything else,' Jess replied. It was half true.

Out of the corner of her eye, Jess saw her mother making her way over, an anxious expression on her face.

Anna smiled briefly at Luca before turning to Jess. 'There's no water. The pump has stopped again.'

'Where's Len?' said Jess, exasperated that she could do without any more problems. Still, the farm didn't stop just because its owners' love lives were broken beyond repair.

'He should be back from the quay with that delivery any moment.'

Jess sighed. 'OK. It's probably the trip switch and, if not, an airlock.' She thought of Gaby working her magic the previous August.

'I don't want to disturb Will, after you-know-what,' said her mother, lowering her voice when she referred cryptically to Gaby. 'But the goats need fresh water now, not to mention the rest of the farm.'

'OK. You go and start feeding the goats and I'll check the pump house. Hopefully it's nothing serious and we'll have water again soon. If not, we'll have to fetch some from the market garden.'

'Thanks.' She treated Luca to an apologetic smile. 'Oh, and while you're up there, could you bring some hay for the goats from the barn?'

'Yes, sure.' Jess waited for her mother to leave, then sighed at Luca. 'I'm sorry, I have to go. Life at the farm never stops. You'd think the goats would have more respect for family dramas.'

He brushed his lips over hers. 'Goats, eh? No empathy. Look, I'm meeting someone at the St Saviour's Hotel in a little while. Shall I call in again on my way back, hopefully after you've got this – and the goats – sorted?'

Jess touched his arm. He was funny and charming, but he did look odd in his smart chinos and jacket, standing in the middle of her muddy yard while she was dirty and scruffy. Their worlds were so far apart.

'Thanks, see you later,' she said and summoned a smile for him. She watched him exit the farm gate before she trooped off to the pump shed.

As she'd expected, when she checked the control panel and listened to the pump juddering, the problem was an airlock. She opened the vent, waited for the motor to start running smoothly again and when she was satisfied that things were working properly, she left the shed. Just in time, she remembered to go into the barn and collect the small bale of hay for the goats' feed.

The hay was at the far end of the barn and as she bent to pick the bale up, she heard Will call her from behind.

'Jess?'

'Will? Are you OK?'

'I'll survive. What about you? Are you all right?'

'Like you, I'll survive,' said Jess, reminded once again about Adam's terrible dilemma. She would have to share the news with Will soon. He was her brother and Adam's friend, but now was definitely not the time. 'The pump stopped but it was another airlock,' she said, wincing at even this loose association with Gaby. 'And Mum asked me to get some more hay.'

333

'I just came in for some oil for the tractor.' Will hovered by the wooden partitioned-off area where they kept the oil.

Jess had never seen him so beaten down, not since their father had left. She knew she was risking having her head bitten off, but she had to try and help him.

'I'm so sorry about Gaby,' she began.

'Yeah. Life's shit sometimes, but we just have to get on with it ...' He paused. 'What did Luca want?' he asked, switching the focus to her. It was typical Will and reminded Jess how closely he guarded his feelings and how badly he must be hurt.

'Just to talk, but I was a bit busy.' She didn't dare tell him that Luca had asked her to move to London.

'Tell me to mind my own business but did you speak to Adam yesterday? I'm sorry I asked him to row.'

'It doesn't matter now,' said Jess. 'That's gone.'

'And is it over between the two of you?'

'Yes, but there's more to the situation than he's let on. Adam spoke to me in confidence yesterday and it's ... well, it's complicated. I know he thinks of you as a close mate and I'm sure that, in time, he'll talk to you about it, but for now, let him dictate the pace.'

Will blew out a breath. 'Sounds serious.'

'It is, but only he can tell you. At the moment, though, he doesn't know what to do with himself.'

'Jesus. Poor Adam ... but I'll leave it unless he says anything. We were good mates once, as close as brothers I thought at one time. It saddens me he can't trust me now.'

She touched his arm. 'I hope he will soon. It's not been the greatest time for any of us.'

'No. So what about you and Luca? Where does this leave the two of you?'

'I don't know about that either. He was offered a permanent job by Hugo but I think he plans to leave Scilly for good.'

'Are you going with him?'

She smiled. 'How could I leave the farm? We'd be out of business in a week.'

Will's lips tilted in an ironic smile. 'Same here. If I left you on your own, we'd go under in five minutes.'

Jess gasped, but her heart surged with affection for him. So that's what had happened, had it? Gaby had issued an ultimatum to her brother.

'Both of us are pretty crap at this stuff, aren't we? Love, relationships ...' he said.

'So it seems,' said Jess, allowing herself a smile. 'I'll talk to you later about Adam if I can. And I'm always ready to listen. I can't promise to be any help, but you know where I am.'

'*Will!*'

A bellow reached them through the far door of the barn and the smell of cigarette smoke made Jess's nostrils twitch.

Will rolled his eyes. 'Great. That's Len. Last thing I need. Want a hand with the bale?'

'No, it's fine.'

'*Will, are you in there? I need you!*'

Will picked up the bale anyway, calling, 'OK. No need to go off on one, Len.'

Jess turned away, trying to compose herself before she had to go back to tell her mother the water was fixed. Will was right: they were both pretty rubbish at relationships. Perhaps that had something to do with falling in love with the wrong people.

She took a deep breath and followed Will towards the door before a huge bang lifted her off her feet and she was flying through the air.

Chapter 36

Gaby was about to step off the last boat of the day onto St Saviour's quay when there was a loud bang from the middle of the island. Everyone turned at once to stare at a plume of grey smoke curling into the sky.

'What the hell was that?' said the skipper, shouting from the wheelhouse.

'Looks like a chimney fire,' said a man, cradling a huge camera lens.

The boatman was on the quay, helping the passengers disembark. 'That's not a chimney fire,' he said.

The smoke plume was rapidly growing thicker and darker.

'That's a house fire and something's gone up like a rocket judging by the noise,' the boatman shouted to the skipper. 'I'll tie up, then I'm going to see what's happening.'

He tied off the boat, then ran down the quay towards the road, leaving the passengers talking and staring at the smoke. Some people were debating whether to go after him as the smoke billowed higher and blacker. A flame flickered within the grey cloud and Gaby's legs turned wobbly. No, it couldn't be ...

337

She dropped her bags on the cobbles. 'It's the flower farm!' she shouted and ran after him. She raced up the slope, her heart pumping hard. It had been a last minute decision not to get the ferry back to Penzance half an hour earlier. She'd actually walked into the ticket office on the harbour ready to buy the ticket before walking out again.

If she hadn't decided to stay, she wouldn't even be on St Saviour's, and now it looked like some disaster had befallen the farm: the farm she couldn't bear to leave because she now knew for certain she was in love with Will. Those few hours she'd spent wandering around Hugh Town, trying and failing to buy a ticket and leave Scilly, had made her realise that sometimes the greatest adventures could lie in familiar, well-loved places. One day she hoped to see other parts of the world, but she now knew for certain that she could never enjoy any place unless Will was by her side.

Even from a hundred yards away, the bitter reek of smoke was strong and she could hear people shouting from the yard. Though her lungs were bursting she didn't stop until she'd overtaken the boatman and reached the gate.

Then. Oh God. It was total chaos. One end of the storage barn was in flames, with smoke blown across the yard by the wind. Anna was screaming while Natalia, Lawrence and the other staff ran in from the fields, yelling for people to fetch water and call the island fire service. There was no sign of Will.

Gaby heard Lawrence shouting that the part-time fire crew had already been alerted and would be on their way once they could gather at their base at the other end of the island and get to the farm with their appliances. She shielded her face as a gust of wind blew a tongue of flame in her direction. The heat, even from yards back, was fearsome.

She caught Lawrence by the arm as he raced past with a fire extinguisher which seemed pathetically inadequate for the blaze. 'Oh my God. What happened?'

Sweat glistened on his face. 'Don't know but the fire crew are on their way.'

'That blaze could spread in this wind. I'll run down to the station, to make sure they know it's desperate,' said the boatman. 'Anyone unaccounted for?'

Anna ran up to them and clutched at Lawrence. 'My son and daughter! Jess and Will.'

'Everyone's out except for the twins,' Lawrence confirmed, holding Anna.

Jess … And Will … Gaby's legs buckled. Tongues of orange and red flicked up one side of the barn. If they were trapped in that part of the building, there was no hope.

Len ran up, coughing, his face bleeding. 'I was walking past. I heard Will talking and then there was a bang and the far end exploded. It threw me back into the hedge. Is everyone OK?'

'Will's in there. And Jess?' Gaby repeated, almost dazzled by the dancing flames.

'She was fetching some hay for me. I asked her to! It's my fault,' Anna sobbed.

'We have to do something!' said Gaby, taking a step closer to the blaze.

'No. We have to wait for the firefighters. We can't put anyone else in danger.'

Ignoring Lawrence, Gaby darted forward but had to stop. Sparks and ash flew into the sky and the heat was unbearable. Hands reached for her and dragged her back.

It was Len who held onto her tightly. 'Don't be so stupid. Wait for the fire brigade!'

'They'll be dead by then!' Gaby twisted free of his grip and dashed in the other direction, around the back of the barn. She ducked low to avoid the smoke but the flames were blowing away from her now and she was by the small outbuilding that housed the pump. She heard shouts above the crackle of the flames and the hiss of splitting wood.

There was a small door at the intact end of the barn. The smoke made her gag and the heat was still fierce, but it wasn't as intense as standing in front of the flames. She snatched a damp rag from the pump house and pushed open the wooden door into the barn. The contrast between the dark at one end and the blinding orange and red at the other hurt her eyes and the smoke caught her throat even through the wet cloth.

She took it off her face and called, 'Will!' then immediately started to cough violently. She was going to be sick. God knows what horrible stuff they kept in there.

With the rag back over her mouth, she spotted a figure on the floor a few feet away. It got to its knees and crawled towards her. It was Will. She didn't dare take the rag from her face again, so she fought her way to him and with one hand clamped to her mouth, tried to drag him towards the door. He was struggling to move, so she abandoned the cloth and used both hands to help him to his feet. With an arm under his shoulder, she half dragged, half pulled him to the door. He was so heavy, and acting like a drunken man, staggering around, Gaby thought she might collapse under his weight. Her lungs burned worse than they even had in the race and her throat was on fire, but suddenly light and air hit her face. In seconds, Lawrence and Len had come round and taken Will's weight and pulled them both outside into the sunlight.

Natalia was waiting, and helped Gaby onto the yard where Anna let out a scream. She'd spotted Will, but in the same moment, realised that Jess must still be inside.

'Where's Jess? Someone find Jess!' she wailed.

A fresh explosion burst from the far end of the barn.

'Get back! There's oil and diesel for the pump at the back,' said Len.

Will was sitting on the grass, coughing his guts up, but he kept muttering, 'Jess. Jess ... have to get her.'

Anna screamed and ran towards the barn, but Len held her back. Through her tears Gaby saw Lawrence trying to stop Will from crawling on his knees towards the barn.

Will choked. 'I have to go to her.'

Len was with him. 'No. You can't even stand up.'

'I have to.' He crawled forward.

The smoke billowed and a gust blew it across the yard, covering everyone momentarily. When it cleared, there was a new face in the yard. It was Adam, breathing hard. 'I saw the flames from the cottage and knew it was the farm. What's going on?'

No one spoke for a second, then Anna tore at Adam's clothes. 'Jess is in there. In the barn.'

'Jess is in *that*?' His hand flew to his mouth. 'Christ, no ...'

The smoke had blotted out the sun and the flames were brighter. The fire lit up his face. Gaby could feel the heat on her skin. Adam seemed frozen with terror.

'Where exactly?' he asked, suddenly snapping into life.

'I don't know.'

'She was only a few feet from me but the explosion might have knocked her back.' Will managed to speak and grabbed Adam's arm as he tried to head towards the building. 'It's hell in there.'

'I don't care what happens to me. I may be dead anyway,' Adam replied defiantly.

'There's a door at the back where I found Will,' said Gaby. 'Opposite the pump room, but be careful. There's oil and diesel in there and stuff in the barn too.'

Gaby held onto Will while Adam shot off towards the barn. A first responder Gaby vaguely recognised ran up then and started to check Will. They told her that the ambulance boat was on its way from St Mary's. Then another paramedic ran into the yard, followed by the fire tender. Through her streaming eyes, Gaby thought of Jess lying unconscious – or worse – on the floor of the barn among the flames. Adam had already vanished into the smoke.

The fire crew jumped out of the tender. A woman in fire kit – one of the receptionists from the hotel – ran over. 'Hey. Hey. More fire crew and ambulance boat on their way from St Mary's. How many people are in there?'

'Everyone's out, but Jess. Adam just went after her,' Gaby answered.

342

'Adam Pengelly?' said the woman, obviously recognising the name.

Gaby nodded.

The woman left and the rest of the crew, aided by locals from all over the island, began to connect up the hoses and start to douse the flames. Several questioned Len and Lawrence while putting on breathing apparatus, while others looked after Will and Gaby and Anna.

There was a crack as a timber collapsed inside the barn and Anna screamed, 'Jess!'

After what felt like hours but couldn't have been more than a few minutes, Adam came around the front of the building as the fire crew ran towards him. He was staggering with Jess in his arms. She was as limp as a rag doll.

Gaby saw two of the fire crew catch Adam just before he collapsed, and he and Jess were surrounded by people.

Anna broke free and ran to them.

Will held onto Gaby. 'J- jess! Is s-she OK?' he said, half choking on his words.

'God, I hope so,' said Gaby, but she could only glimpse Jess, lying like a deadweight on the ground by Adam, until they were both completely obscured by medics and fire crew.

Chapter 37

Jess didn't know exactly how long had passed since she'd arrived at the hospital on St Mary's. She couldn't remember much at all since the explosion had lifted her off her feet. All she knew was that she must have swallowed wire wool. Her throat was so sore, it hurt to breathe even with the oxygen mask over her face. It could get worse before it got better, the doctors told her, and also that she was very lucky to have survived. The end of the barn had collapsed minutes after Adam had carried her out ... she remembered that much, even if everything else was now a blurry haze, like an image that kept coming in and out of focus.

Adam had been in the inferno and she had no idea why.

After the explosion, she must have passed out for a few moments. She'd been hurled onto the bales of hay at the far end of the barn and opened her eyes on hell. Even though she'd been thrown away from the blaze, the heat had been unbearable. She was sure she was burning, but by a miracle, she'd escaped any actual burns. She'd seen a figure in the doorway, thought it must be Will, tried to shout to him, but gulped in smoke and passed out again.

The next thing she remembered clearly was waking up in the yard with a mask over her face and Adam next to her, tears streaming down his face and ash in his hair. People were talking to her, over her, about her – she heard someone tell her that Will and Gaby and everyone at the farm was OK – but her entire energy had been taken up by just breathing in and out.

The journey to the island hospital was a jumble and she didn't have much recollection of being assessed and admitted. They'd kept her overnight, monitoring her lungs for any long-lasting damage. She'd slept or felt woozy for much of that time and vaguely remembered visitors passing in and out of her room, but now, on the following morning, she was finally more awake and alert.

Adam was sitting by her bed, stroking her hand.

'Y-you ... OK?' she said to him, pulling her mask away

'Shh. Talking's going to be hard for a while.' Adam smiled and Jess knew he was trying to joke but without expecting her to laugh.

She squeezed his hand hard and he winced.

'You're burnt.'

Adam held up his hand, bandaged around the palm. He wiggled his fingers. 'It's not serious. It should heal quickly.'

'Oh, Adam ... thank you.' There was so much she wanted to say, but nothing seemed enough, even if she could have squeezed out the words.

He put his finger gently on her dry lips. 'Just lie there and take it easy.' He coughed again. 'Keri and Emmy have gone home, but they sent their good wishes and hope you'll be better soon. Jess ... I can't believe I almost lost you.'

'W-was it my fault? I turned the valve on the pump and soon after there was an explosion. I don't know why ...'

'Shh. The fire was nothing to do with the pump. Len caused it by accident.' Gently, he replaced the mask on her face, his eyes bright.

He told her more about what had happened. There would be an investigation, but Len had already admitted throwing a cigarette end outside the barn. He thought the cigarette was out, but it must have smouldered and eventually set light to the sacks and the dry timbers of the barn. They weren't sure what had exploded, possibly some fuel for the generator.

Jess shed a few tears when she heard how Gaby had dragged Will out. She wanted to say so much more to Adam, but she knew she had to keep breathing the oxygen. Her only way of communicating how she felt was to squeeze Adam's good hand with all her strength.

Adam stood up. 'I have to go. Your family want to see you again now you're more in the mood for visitors but I'm so happy you're OK. I don't know what I'd have done if ...' He didn't finish, but kissed her briefly on the forehead and left before she could respond.

Will and Anna came in and Anna burst into tears. When she eventually left to get a cup of tea, urged by Will, Gaby joined him. Gaby looked pale and had steri-strips covering a graze on her forehead. Will kept having to stop to cough and his voice was almost as hoarse as Jess's own. How close they'd come to losing each other, she thought. She shivered despite the warmth of the hospital room.

Although she was already exhausted by all the visitors, she

was so relieved that everyone was safe. She couldn't believe the horror of what had almost happened. Jess took the oxygen from her face. There was something important she needed to say. 'Thanks for saving Will,' she told Gaby.

'Someone has to,' said Gaby, with a cheeky smile, while nudging closer to Will.

Jess's eyes widened as Will slipped his arm around Gaby's back. Wow. That was a big step forward, but what did it mean? Gaby had been leaving that day. Was she now staying on the island? Come to think of it, how was she here at all? She and Will looked so happy – so comfortable – together – which was wonderful but made her think again of Adam and how he'd risked his life for her. Even though they were both safe, he still had a spectre looming over him that wasn't going away. How must he be feeling now?

'Do you know where's Adam gone?' she asked.

'Back to Keri and Emmy.' Gaby exchanged looks with Will. 'This probably isn't a great time, but he said something weird before he ran after you.'

'Weird?' Jess started coughing again.

'He said he didn't care if he died in the fire because he might be dead anyway.'

Jess nodded. 'Oh.'

Will patted her arm. 'Don't worry about it. Rest up for now ... and Luca wants to see you but he said he'd wait until you were home.'

Jess nodded. She needed to rest, but all she could think about was Adam risking his life to save her and what he'd said to Gaby. She was safe and she was grateful for that, but while he was suffering, if she had to drag herself out of bed and crawl, she would find him and try to comfort him again.

Will and Gaby sat by her bed and chatted to her for a few minutes, but seeing that she was tired, they left shortly after. Jess didn't want to sleep even though she was exhausted because she wondered when – or if – she would ever see Adam again. The future was as uncertain as it had been before. But no matter how hard she tried to stay awake and think things through, she couldn't keep her lids from closing.

*

Jess's stomach turned over when she got out of the pick-up in the farmyard the following afternoon after she'd been released from hospital. One end of the barn was a blackened ruin, while the remaining half was intact but cordoned off with makeshift tape. Charred and water-damaged equipment and rubbish was piled up a few yards away.

'It's a bit of a mess,' said Anna, holding onto Jess's arm as she helped her out of the car. Jess didn't need a hand but she wanted to please her mother. She suppressed a shudder and turned away from the barn. She'd thought she – and Will – wouldn't get out of that place alive until Adam had appeared.

Jess breathed in carefully. There was a slight tang of ash on the air, but the fresh breeze was still miles better than the hospital. The doctors had said her lungs would continue to improve and there seemed to be no long-term damage, although she'd have to have regular check-ups.

She took a moment to look at the bare brown earth in the

348

fields. The scent of the sea and late spring wildflowers was carried on the breeze. A tractor rumbled its way along the bottom field where some of the workers were lifting up the bulbs. They lay in piles along the ridges, drying in the sun before they were replanted again to give them fresh room to grow in a different field.

On her mother's arm, she walked into the house, where the scent of baking bread hit her. The kitchen table was covered with cards and gifts from friends and neighbours. No one had sent flowers, of course, but homemade cakes, boxes of chocolates and a crate of vegetables from the Barton sisters' garden waited for her. Maisie and Patrick had visited her in hospital the previous evening and were coming over the next day, after she'd settled in.

'Do you want to go upstairs for a rest?' her mother asked her.

Jess sank into the carver chair, still marvelling at the gifts waiting for her on the table. 'Thanks, Mum, but I think I've had enough rest for a while.'

'Cup of tea? Or would a cold drink be better?'

Jess smiled. 'Cold will be good.'

She pointed to a cottage loaf on the table. It had a wonky top. 'I made some bread. I thought the smell would disguise the other one, but my baking skills are very rusty.'

'Thanks, Mum.' Jess squeezed her mother's fingers, touched by the comforting gesture.

Her mother stood behind her chair and put her arms around Jess's neck. She kissed the top of her head and then went to get a glass.

Jess started to open her cards, smiling at the messages. One envelope was obviously written by a child and she opened it. It was from Emmy with a drawing of a narcissus on the front. Keri had added her name too.

'The little girl and her mum came over with that before they left,' said her mother, setting a glass of squash in front of Jess. That made her feel about five years old, but the cool liquid was soothing for her throat. 'Keri and Emmy seem quite pleasant.'

'They're both really nice,' said Jess, still unsure what her mother knew about Adam's family.

'You can tell she's his niece, can't you?'

Jess nodded.

Her mum sat opposite Jess and toyed with the ribbon on a jar of homemade cookies. 'Keri told me a bit about Adam's troubles.'

'What did she tell you?' Jess caught her breath, wondering what was coming.

'Not much more than you'd already mentioned. I do feel sorry for her and the little girl. She's a brave woman because she seemed more concerned about Adam. She said it had been very tough for him. Is that why Adam took off? The shock of finding out about his new family and his father and brother dying so young?'

Jess nodded. 'It's been very hard on him.'

'Yes, I can imagine. I wanted to do the same after your father left. I wanted to get on the first plane and never come back, but I knew that I had to stay or we'd all lose everything and I loved you both too much to destroy your future. At

350

times, on the worst days, it was hard to carry on, knowing everyone was talking about me and that my husband loved another woman. I almost stepped off a cliff a few times.'

'Oh, Mum! I knew you were unhappy but I didn't realise how awful you were feeling.' Jess coughed, horrified at this confession.

'No. Don't get upset.' Her mother patted her arm. 'You and Will kept me going. You kept me alive and now I only want you to be happy. I saw what Adam did for you and for me too. He risked his life for you. I was always worried that he was wrong for you. I thought he wasn't good enough at the start and then I thought he was a bastard like your father.'

'He's not,' Jess asserted.

'Yes, my love, I know that now and I'm so glad he's back. If you want to be with him, if you want to leave the farm with him, not that you need my permission, you go ahead, with my blessing. Nothing matters but you and Will and you both being happy.'

Jess smiled but inside she was crying. Her mother thought everything was hunky-dory now. She'd given her blessing to Will and Gaby, and to Jess and Adam. Gaby and Will probably thought the same thing. Everything had changed for them and yet for her and Adam, nothing had changed.

*

After she'd settled in, a visitor arrived. It was Luca, smiling and bearing a large hamper of goodies from the Petroc deli.

351

A variety of emotions hit her. She was relieved that she was even here to see him again and genuinely pleased to see his smiling face. But she felt a tinge of regret that she would have to deliver news that might make him unhappy.

'Hi there. I hope this is OK. Flowers were out of course, and I wasn't sure champagne was appropriate so here you are.' He handed over his gift and Jess baulked a little at the weight of it before putting it on the kitchen table. The basket was wrapped in a blue silken bow. Even through the cellophane she could smell the tantalising aromas of chocolate, coffee and spices. 'Thank you. They're gorgeous,' she said, smiling at his thoughtfulness.

He kissed her on the cheek, then his expression became serious. 'My God, Jess, I can't tell you how relieved I am to see you looking so much better. That day will be etched on my memory forever. I heard the explosion at the hotel and ran up to the farm, but by that time you were already with the paramedics. Adam saved you. I wish I'd been there to help.' Guilt edged his voice.

'Don't beat yourself up,' said Jess, about to add that she needed to confess something too but Luca carried on.

'I do feel guilty, but it's not really about not being there to help you out of the barn.' He dragged his hand over his face. 'Something's happened. I don't know how to tell you. I came to the farm yesterday to break the news ...'

She frowned. 'What news?'

Luca shook his head. 'Shit, what a mess.'

He took her hand and Jess let him speak.

'It's my wife. It's Rachel. Her new partner has left her and she's in a bad way. She called me ... Jess, I have to go and help her. I'm sorry.'

'Don't be. Don't be sorry. You love her and it's natural.' Rather than feeling crushed with disappointment, as Luca was obviously worrying she might be, Jess wasn't hurt. She knew more than anyone that feelings for someone you loved couldn't be switched on and off easily, or ever. Luca and Rachel had shared their lives and there was clearly still something there between them.

'I'm sorry. I thought it was all in the past. I don't know if this will be the start of anything between us, but you're right, I do love her and I'm sorry if you've been hurt.' He ran his hands over the table, unable to look at her momentarily before he met her eyes again. He obviously hated doing this to her. He was a good man.

She shook her head. 'Stop trying to be someone you could never have been. It's been fun, you came along at a time when I needed something fresh, an escape. You made me see that there was a chink of light on the other side of a dark place, but we were never going to be long term. We live in two different universes.'

Luca held her and kissed her lips. But it was a chaste kiss, a farewell kiss, and Jess was flooded with a sadness that was tinged with relief. He'd saved her from telling him she didn't want to go to London with him. Every moment that passed, the load on her mind eased. She had barely been able to cope with the idea of Adam being desperate, and hurting Luca too.

Luca shook his head. 'I have no idea what's wrong with Adam, but I hope that almost losing you forever finally brings him to his senses. I know how much you care about him, but in my opinion, he's out of his fucking mind.'

Jess couldn't help but smile.

He stayed a little while longer, talking about how relieved he was that she was safe and a little bit about Rachel and then he got up. 'You must be tired. I'll probably be back to see Hugo now and then on business but I won't be moving here. My life's in London now though I'll always be there for you if you need a friend. More than a friend.'

'I really hope it works out for you and Rachel.' Jess hoped he could tell from her voice that she genuinely meant it.

'Yeah. I need to help her get straight before I can even think of starting anything with her again, but thanks. Thanks for everything.'

She saw him off at the gate and they embraced. Her mother was feeding the goats but had stopped to watch her say her goodbyes to Luca. Jess turned away once Luca had gone out of sight and walked back to her mother.

'It's Adam, then, is it?' her mother said.

'Not unless a miracle happens,' said Jess, stroking the goat's head as it tucked into its feed.

'He'd be mad not to snap you up.'

'It's not that simple,' said Jess. 'But please, Mum, don't ask me any more about it now.'

Chapter 38

'What are you thinking?' Will was propped up on one elbow watching Gaby. They were in his double bed in the farmhouse.

She turned her head and smiled. 'You know I don't think any man in the history of the world has ever asked a woman that.'

'You know me. Full of surprises.'

She raised an eyebrow. 'You can say that again. I thought you were meant to be taking things easy while you recovered.'

His answer was a sexy, knowing smile that made Gaby want to hit him with the pillow and dive on him at the same time.

'Actually, I was thinking that it's amazing to sleep in a proper big bed for the first time in months.' She pushed herself up.

'Funny. I'd been thinking how it seemed way too big for one.' He danced his fingers over her collarbone. 'I still can't believe you came back for me.'

'Good job I did. You can't be trusted on your own.'

'I don't just mean that you helped me out of the barn – which was incredibly brave and bloody stupid by the way – but that you came back to the farm.'

'I can always go away again.'

'No! Stop winding me up. But you wanted to leave.'

'Not as much as I wanted to stay, clearly.'

Will laughed then grimaced.

'I think you should rest your throat.' She grinned.

He pulled a face and shook his head in frustration. 'I don't want you to feel you *have* to stay,' he said, resting his hand on her thigh. 'Did you really almost buy a ticket for the ferry?'

'Yes, but I couldn't bring myself to actually set foot in the ticket office. I went back four times and walked away again. Now why do you think that was?'

'I don't want you to make a compromise for my sake.'

'But *someone* has to.'

He took a deep breath. 'Not necessarily.'

Gaby's heart beat faster. 'What do you mean?'

'I've made a decision. Life's too short for not doing what you really want, once in a while. I'm going to talk to Jess and to Mum, and try to make them understand that I'd like a sabbatical from the farm. A year so I can travel – with you – and see the world, just as I planned to before Dad left us.'

'I'm not going to force you to leave here. I'm happy to stay because I want to be with you,' said Gaby, slightly horrified that she'd triggered Will into such a major decision.

'You don't have to, because this is what I want. I've always wanted to, but I've never thought it was possible. Now I've decided that I can get a manager in. Lawrence could do it, with Len's help, as long as he doesn't set the place on fire.' He grimaced. 'If Mum and Jess agree, then I'd like to do that and we can see where it leads us.'

She hugged him and he kissed her softly. 'Will ... I'll be with you whatever happens, but if travelling the world together is what you really want then you've earned it, and that would be wonderful. But I'm not going to be the source of a massive family rift. Families count. We need them and they need us.'

'Let's leave it a few days, let Jess recover and Mum get over the shock and then we'll talk to them,' he said, paused then added, 'And your own parents? How will they feel about us being together?'

'I already know how they feel because I called them after the fire and had a heart to heart. I've told them I plan to stay here at the farm. I spoke to Carly too and she said she was just glad I was safe and wanted me to be happy. She agreed with me that Stevie would be pleased to see us together and happy too. You two would have got on so well ... he'd have loved rowing with the gig team and all the banter ... loved the farm ...' She blinked back a tear and Will put his arms around her. 'I'm sorry.'

'Don't be. I wish I could have known him.'

'Me too ... but that can't be and that's why I need to focus on what's in front of me now. After everything that's passed, my family are happy with me doing what's in my heart, which seems to be you.' She smiled. 'Stevie told me to live my dreams and actually, there are far worse ones than the one we have now, don't you think?' she asked, looking into his eyes.

Will pushed her hair off her face and smiled. 'You know, for once, I really might have to agree with you.'

357

Chapter 39

A few days later, Jess walked down the track to Thrift Cottage. It was one of her first outings after coming home and she took it very easy as the effort still made her short of breath. Adam had phoned her once to see how she was and they'd arranged to meet at the cottage. He'd offered to come to the farm, but Jess was going stir-crazy and being fussed over by her mum, Will and Gaby, and even Len, bless him, was getting a bit much.

She stopped a few times on her way, to remind herself how beautiful the island was and to compose herself before she met Adam. He'd said nothing about their relationship since the hospital and she'd no idea what to expect when she saw him.

Adam must have been watching out for her because he was halfway down the path before she'd even opened the gate, an anxious look on his face.

'Hi,' he said, opening the gate for her. 'How are you? Should you be up and about?'

'Well, I won't be rowing for a while, but I'm definitely a hundred times better than I was and I was going mad at home.

They're lovely, but you can have too much of a good thing.' She touched his arm. 'I wasn't able to say thanks properly when I was in hospital, but I can now.'

Adam shook his head and glanced away; typically shy at anyone who praised him. 'Forget it.'

'That's going to be tricky. You did save my life.'

He shrugged. 'I was in the right place at the right time and I was lucky. We both were.' He allowed himself a smile. 'Although I'm apparently "a bloody stupid prat", according to my old boss at the fire station.'

'I expect running into a burning building with no kit on counts as bloody stupid.'

He looked straight at her and his voice was fierce. 'I'd do it again. A hundred times if you were in there.'

'Or anyone you loved?'

'Maybe ...'

Jess laughed and coughed.

His brow creased in concern. 'Come inside.'

Jess went ahead of him into the cottage and sat down on the battered sofa in the tiny sitting room. With his bandaged hand, Adam picked a furry unicorn dressing gown off the armchair.

'It won't fit you,' she said as he draped it over a dining chair.

'Shame. I quite like the idea of turning up to rugby training in a furry robe with a silver horn. Emmy left it behind,' he explained.

'Perhaps she wanted an excuse to come back for it,' said Jess, noticing the dining table was covered with colouring books, pencils and sharpie pens. Other signs of the 'old' Adam were scattered about: his jacket on the peg in the hall, a coffee mug she'd bought him on the table, still half full. He often drank the rest cold ... but this wasn't the 'old' Adam and she suppressed a shiver at the reminder of that sobering fact.

'I haven't had a chance to clear her things up yet. Emmy likes it here. She's made a few friends and she loves the beach. She's done a lot of paintings of the sea and pirates.' He smiled. Despite her misgivings, Jess thought he seemed calmer, and more at ease with himself since she'd left him after the rowing championships.

'I'm glad. They deserve some peace and quiet after what they've been through.'

A few seconds of silence ensued, and Adam seemed to struggle to know what to say next. He finally sat next to Jess on the sofa and held her hands tightly.

'I thought I'd lost you forever.'

She looked down at his injured hand. 'You haven't.'

'But what about Luca?' His eyes searched hers.

'He's gone.'

'I should say I'm sorry, but I'm not. I'm glad ... and that's so selfish of me. Has he upset you?'

'No. It's by mutual consent.' Jess reached up and touched his face, the trace of stubble under her fingertips sending a rush of longing through her. 'The issue being we both still love other people.'

Adam's lips parted in disbelief. 'Is that true?'

'He's gone back to his wife and I'm here with you now. Does that answer your question?'

Adam pulled her tightly to him and Jess kissed him, hardly able to believe she was in his arms after so long. His mouth and skin, the solidity of his body, felt so familiar and yet so wondrous at the same time. Luca had been a lovely interlude during a dark time in her life but she'd known, deep down, that she'd wanted Adam all along.

'I still love you too,' he said when they broke apart finally. 'Every day we've been apart I've loved you more, but how can I expect you to share the burden of what might happen in the future? I can't stand the thought of you worrying about me all the time, or worse, having to give up your life to care for me – or worrying about our kids inheriting this condition?'

Jess held both his hands, her heart full to bursting. 'Listen to me. You found the courage to run into a burning building and rescue me. You told Will it was because you were already dead, but you're not. Even if your brother and dad were unlucky, there's still a very good chance you'll live to be as ancient as the old-timers propping up the bar at the Driftwood. Now tell me, if you didn't know about this disease, would you still have rushed in to get me?'

He didn't hesitate. 'Yes, of course I would.'

'So, if you really love me – why throw away my life now?'

'That's not fair.'

'None of what's happened to you is fair. Not finding out your father was a stranger, not him dying, or your brother – or this disease.'

'Oh God, Jess. I want to be put out of my misery, but it's a gamble that terrifies me. Many people in my situation don't

361

even get tested because there's nothing to be gained from it other than peace of mind. It's a living nightmare that I didn't want to drag you into.'

He took a deep breath and seemed calmer again. More resigned.

Jess held him and said, 'What you don't understand is that I'd rather live in a nightmare with you than a dream with anybody else. I love you, Adam. I always have.'

There were tears in Adam's eyes.

'I know. I tried to make myself believe that you didn't feel the same way, but deep down, I knew you did and that I'd hurt you so badly because I couldn't handle my own problems.'

'Then let me help you. Either as a friend or more.'

'A friend?' He shook his head firmly. 'I can't stay here with you as a friend. It's all or nothing.'

A kernel of hope lodged in Jess's mind. 'I think we tried the nothing. It wasn't working for either of us or you wouldn't have come back, would you?'

'I thought I was coming back for Emmy's sake and to break off my ties with St Saviour's, but now I realise I was being selfish. I couldn't stay away. Jess, I'm so sorry ... But if I *do* stay, I don't have a job any more, unless you'll give me a job as a flower picker.'

'That's easy. I can give you a job, but I have a reputation as a really tough boss.'

'I know that. I want to stay so much ...'

'Then, let's just be together in this moment. Forget everything that's happened or might happen. We have now and I want to make the most of it.' She rested her hand on Adam's

362

chest, almost as if she wanted to show how strong and steady it was and that she could cope with anything life threw at them, however long that life might be. 'Haven't you missed that?'

'*Missed* it?' Adam groaned. 'It's been agony. When I saw you with Luca the night before ... and the morning after ... Not that I blame you, but it ripped me apart.'

'I don't want to talk about Luca. Only you and me.' Jess spread her hands over his thighs and touched her face to his. His body tensed and she wasn't sure if it was desire or uncertainty.

'It's too soon, isn't it?' he said softly. 'For you, after the fire?'

'I won't know until I try.'

He touched her cheek. 'I don't want to hurt you.'

'Neither do I.' She smiled at his bandaged hand. 'What a pair we are. I guess we'll just have to be extra careful with each other.'

With no more hesitation, Adam took her hand and led her to his bedroom and they lay down on the fading patchwork quilt she'd seen and loved so many times before. It took a while for him to undress her with one good hand, though she found it surprisingly easy to help him out of his jeans, T-shirt and boxer shorts. The breath she had left was taken away by the sight of him naked. He had scars from old rugby clashes and fresh bruises that must have come from his dash through the barn. He was definitely leaner than he had been but still beautiful and magnificent in her eyes. When he touched her, it was as if popping candy had been sprinkled all over her body. He lay beside her, kissing her and touching her until she bunched the sheet in her hands and cried out.

Afterwards, Adam lay staring at the ceiling, his hand covering hers, the tips of his fingers circling her nails.

'I think we should tell people,' he said.

Jess hardly dared to breathe. 'Tell people what?'

He turned his head. 'That we're back together.'

Jess had to bite back the tears. 'So, you're going to trust me?'

He rolled over and traced his fingers over her breastbone, making her shiver with pleasure. 'If you're sure ... but everyone will want to know why I left.'

'They can carry on wondering. I don't care about anything other than having you back in my life. Unless you *want* to tell them the truth, and I don't see why they're entitled to know anything beyond the fact that you've had a tough time. That should be enough for them until you're ready to say more. Even on St Saviour's, we're entitled to some secrets but I'd like to tell Maisie if I can? Is that OK?'

'Yes. Will should know too.'

'Yes. He should.'

'And your mother?'

Jess grimaced. 'I don't know. She's had enough shocks in the past few days. Perhaps she's not quite ready to hear it yet.'

'Maybe when I know for certain.' He checked himself. '*If* I decide to find out.'

Jess nestled under his arm and looked him deep in the eyes. 'Whatever you decide, and whatever the outcome, I'll be here by your side always. I love you.'

*

They walked hand in hand back to the farm, smiling at the handful of people who saw them together, enjoying the gobsmacked faces. When they got home, Gaby and Will met them at the gate.

Will gawped at seeing them together, but Gaby broke into a smile, as if she'd guessed what might happen. As soon as they were all within hearing distance, everyone spoke at the same time.

Gaby almost skipped up to them. 'We've got something to tell you!'

'So have we, but you go first,' said Jess.

Gaby held up her hands. 'Oh no. You first. Absolutely you should go first.'

Will and Adam exchanged glances. Jess suspected Will still didn't trust Adam and that only the whole truth would help him understand.

'Jess and I are back together,' said Adam.

'I can see that, mate.' Will gave Jess a hard stare. 'Jess?'

Jess squeezed Adam's hand. 'We *are* back together and we've something else to tell you both, but it can wait.'

Will shared a glance with Gaby. 'OK. Now ... our news. The thing is that we – me and Gaby – have a plan. I don't want to ruin your day and we want to discuss it with you and Mum first, but ... I'd like to leave the farm. Not forever, just a year or so. Gaby was willing to stay on, but you know I've wanted to see what's beyond the farm for a long time. I didn't do it when Dad left, but if I don't try now, I never will. I can see this might come as a shock after what's happened and we haven't told Mum our plans yet but ...'

Jess ran up and hugged him. 'Oh for goodness' sake, stop wittering. I know you've always wanted to spread your wings.'

'And you don't hate me for taking him away?' said Gaby anxiously.

Jess had to smile at this fresh turn of events. So now she had another hurdle to get over: running the farm without Will for the near future but somehow, she wasn't as daunted as she might have been. She'd have Adam by her side and that was all that mattered. 'As long as you bring him back from time to time, no. Why don't you tell me more about it?'

'You're staying here, then?' said Will to Adam.

'Yes. That's the plan. Jess is moving into the cottage as soon as we can find somewhere for Keri and Emmy to rent. They're going to stay over the summer and see how they like life on the isles.' Adam's voice was brighter. Even with the shadow of a potential illness hovering, he already sounded more hopeful about his immediate future and Jess dared to believe that was because he had her to support and love him.

Will blew out a breath. 'Wow. This is a turnaround.' He frowned but turned to Jess. 'I feel bad about leaving you with the farm to run.'

'We won't go if you feel you can't manage,' Gaby added. 'I promise. We've discussed it.'

'Adam could help run it,' said Jess.

Will gasped. 'Adam?'

Jess broke into a grin. 'Yes. I think he'd be great.'

'And I am looking for a job, after all,' said Adam with a wry smile and a squeeze of Jess's hand.

Will frowned. 'Mate, I appreciate the sentiment but with respect you know bugger all about flower farming.'

Adam put his arm around Jess who was revelling in Will's incredulous face. 'I can learn,' he said. 'With Jess to teach me and crack the whip.'

'You can be sure of that!' Jess said in delight.

'It's what I want. What we both want, whatever happens afterwards,' he said, stealing a glance at Jess, whose arm tightened around his back. 'So you guys go and do what you want to. You only have one life.'

'True ...' Will looked at Adam. 'Is everything all right, mate?'

'Yeah ... Shall we go and see the *Athene*?' said Adam, which Jess knew was code for 'let's have a proper talk'.

Will hesitated, then nodded. 'I think we'd better. Is this something I need to hear with a large pint in my hand?'

Adam slapped him on the back. 'I think we'll both do that later.'

EPILOGUE

Early July

With Adam's arm around her back, Jess's heart lifted when she saw the farm gate ahead of them. It was late in the afternoon and they'd caught the ferry from St Mary's after arriving on the lunchtime flight. The airport and the harbour had been very busy, the ferry packed with visitors now that holiday season was in full swing. The air was warm and a gentle breeze blew from the west, rippling the shallow sea like a silken ribbon. As they walked home, carrying their bags, the heathland and hedgerows around them were thick with wildflowers.

There were a few people around when they pushed open the gate. The chug of a quad bike, the cry of gulls and bleating of goats blended with the distant drone of a small plane overhead. It was a quiet time of year for the farm with Will, Gaby and many of the seasonal workers gone and only the permanent staff manning the phones, doing the admin, looking after the chalets and essential farm work.

They stopped by the top field and leaned on the fence,

taking in the farm and the rest of the isles dreaming amid a silver sea under a hazy sun.

Adam gazed out over the fence. 'Do you think I've done the right thing?' he said. 'People think we only went for a break in Cornwall ...'

'That's all they need to know.' Jess rested her head on his shoulder and he tightened his arm around her. They had been for a break, but they'd also been to see a genetic counsellor in Truro and discussed Adam's options.

'It helped a lot to talk through what having a predictive test would mean,' he said. 'And I've realised that I don't want to know and that it's not cowardly *not* to want to know. I'd rather live with the fifty per cent risk of not having it, than the certainty of knowing I have.'

'I told you I'd stand by you, whatever you did – or didn't.'

'Talking to the counsellor helped me understand that the fears I had – still have – and that the way I reacted was understandable, even though I still regret every second of hurt I caused you.'

She laid her head on his shoulder. 'That's behind us now.'

'I've also realised that I want to get on with my life, whatever it brings. Even if I do have the gene, it might be years or decades before the condition affects me, so it's more important than ever to make the most of every minute. Who knows, maybe there will be some new treatment on the horizon by then too. I feel I've already wasted so much time and I don't want to waste any more.'

'Good plan.' She smiled, but Adam still looked downcast. It had been an emotional trip even if it had given him some peace of mind in other respects.

He cleared his throat. 'Do you think,' he said quietly, 'that you'd ever think about marrying me?'

Jess couldn't speak for what seemed like an age and when she did, she sounded strange to herself. 'Definitely.'

'What? Think about marrying me or actually do it?'

She gasped in exasperation. 'Actually, do it.'

Adam's smile was so wide, she thought it might crack his face. After what they'd been through, this moment was so sweet, she could hardly bear the happiness. No matter what the future held, it didn't matter, because she and Adam were a thousand times stronger together than they were apart.

When they stopped, Jess giggled as she spotted Len watching them with a disgusted expression on his face.

'Shall we tell our parents first or Will and Gaby?' said Jess.

'Will and Gaby,' said Adam.

'Now?'

'Like I said, there's not a moment to lose.'

Adam pulled out his phone and opened up WhatsApp. 'Smile!' he said, taking a selfie of the two of them, grinning like maniacs. He typed a caption: 'The future Mr and Mrs Pengelly'.

'I don't know if they'll get it. It might be the middle of the night in Adelaide,' he said.

Half a minute later, during another kiss, Adam's phone buzzed. There was a picture of Gaby and Will hand in hand in a beautiful garden, both with floral garlands around their necks. Will was wearing a Hawaiian shirt and shorts. Gaby had a white floaty maxi dress with exotic camellia in her hair and a posy in her hand. The message read: 'Congratulations!

But we beat you to it. Lots of love, The new Mr and Mrs Godrevy.'

Jess squealed in delight. 'Oh my God? They haven't, have they? Mum will kill him! What about her hat? What about the reception? She always wanted Erlicheers and Daymarks at our weddings. I've heard her talking to my auntie about it!'

A new message came through showing Will and Gaby holding up a glass with the words, 'PS We're coming home for a party next month. We'll phone Mum and tell her tonight. We are SO happy for you two. Xxx'

'Those two. What are they like?' said Jess, still wondering what her mum's reaction would be when she heard about the 'secret' wedding. For her own part, she was thrilled. She'd spoken to him and seen him on Skype while they'd been travelling, and could see he was happier than he'd ever been. She couldn't have wished for more for her brother.

'They're full of surprises ...' said Adam. 'Uh-uh. I think Len's after you.'

Len was heading straight for them, scowl on his face.

'Oh dear. It seems as if our "holiday" is over. He's on the warpath, judging by his face.'

'He always looks like that,' said Adam and Jess laughed.

Len caught them before they'd reached the packing sheds. 'Bloody good job you're back. Now look, I've got a problem with a wholesale order for September. It could be the making of us, but not if we can't handle it ...'

Jess interrupted the flow. 'Hold on a second, Len. Can this wait until we've had a chance to dump our bags in the house and say hello to Mum?'

Len huffed.

Adam glanced at Jess. 'And actually, Len,' he said, swelling with pride, 'I've just asked Jess to marry me.'

Len stared at Adam and then at Jess. 'Right. Congratulations. I hope you'll both be very happy,' he said. 'Now, about this order ...'

Leaving their bags in the middle of the yard, with Len muttering ahead of them, Jess and Adam followed him. Life on the farm never stopped and she wouldn't have it any other way. In the fields ahead of them, the bare earth showed not a hint of the green shoots that would peep out in a couple of months' time. Yet, Jess knew the flowers were there, only waiting for the right moment to push their way through and burst into life.

Acknowledgements

When I first decided to write a book about a flower farm, I knew it could make a wonderful setting for a romantic novel but it also needed a *lot* of research. Both have proved true! So first and foremost, I have to thank the Scilly flower farmers who helped me with this novel. My apologies for anything I've got wrong – either accidentally or on purpose.

I'll never forget my afternoon at Churchtown Farm on St Martin's, the home of Scilly Flowers – www.scillyflowers.co.uk – where owner, Zoe Julian, took time out of a busy schedule to show me around her family's beautiful flower fields.

Special thanks to Juliet May, Jess Vian and Drew of Juliet's Garden and Seaways Flower Farm – www.julietsgarden restaurant.co.uk – for answering my questions on narcissi production. During my visit, Jess also told me about the work of the Blue Box Flower Company – www.scentednarcissi.co.uk – which was very helpful.

I would never have even thought of writing this series without my friend, Hilary Ely, who inspired my love of Scilly. Thanks to reader, Carol Hill, and her husband for their advice on water pumps and to Kirsteen Mosson who won my contest to name the Godrevys' boat, *Kerensa*. For the brainstorming sessions in the pub, I'm indebted to my author friends, Liz Hanbury and Nell Dixon. Thanks also to my bookseller friend, Janice Hume, for her support and for the line about an ice cream, I owe Julie Shackman a large drink.

Writing a story may be a solitary process, but getting a book onto shelves and e-readers needs a talented and energetic team. I have a fabulous group of professionals behind me, including Rachel Faulkner-Willcocks, who is a brilliant editor and advocate for my work. Ditto the incredible Team Avon: Helen Huthwaite, Sabah Khan, Elon Woodman-Worrell, Elke Desanghere and Jade Craddock who help to make my stories sparkle and bring them to as wide an audience as possible. Huge thanks too, to the many bloggers who read and review my books and tell readers about them.

I can hardly believe that this is my eighteenth published novel and for each one, my agent Broo Doherty has championed my work and been a great friend too.

Finally, my family are officially The Best Ever. John, Mum and Dad, Charles, Charlotte and James. ILY xx

Return to the little Cornish Isles for Christmas, where the festive season brings mistletoe, surprises and more than a sprinkle of romance ...

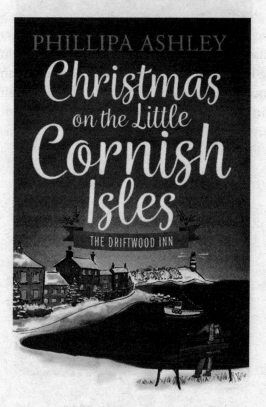

Available now!

And there's more to come from the little
Cornish Isles this Summer ...

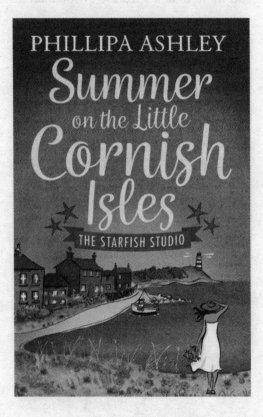

Ebook coming July 2018 ...